NOW OR NEVER

NOW OR
NEVER

Elizabeth Adler

Thorndike Press • **Chivers Press**
Thorndike, Maine USA **Bath, England**

This Large Print edition is published by Thorndike Press, USA and by Chivers Press, England.

Published in 1997 in the U.S. by arrangement with Delacorte Press, an imprint of Dell Publishing, a division of Bantam Doubleday Dell Publishing Group.

Published in 1997 in the U.K. by arrangement with Hodder and Stoughton Ltd.

U.S.   Hardcover   0-7862-1056-7 (Basic Series Edition)
U.K.   Hardcover   0-7451-5434-4 (Windsor Large Print)

The text of this Large Print edition is unabridged.
Other aspects of the book may vary from the original edition.

Set in 16 pt. Plantin by Minnie B. Raven.

Printed in the United States on permanent paper.

British Library Cataloguing in Publication Data available

Library of Congress Cataloging in Publication Data

Adler, Elizabeth (Elizabeth A.)
    Now or never / Elizabeth Adler.
    p. cm.
    ISBN 0-7862-1056-7 (lg. print : hc)
    1. Large type books.   I. Title.
[PR6051.D56N69   1997b]
823'.914—dc21   97-5021

If it be now, 'tis not to come; if it be not to come, it will be now; if it be not now, yet it will come: the readiness is all.

Shakespeare, *Hamlet*

1

The night was cool, dark and moonless, with a slight breeze that lifted her long brown hair. He watched the girl walk slowly across the college parking lot to her little red Miata convertible. His night-vision binoculars picked up every detail. Even though it was late — well past midnight — and the lot was deserted and filled with shadows, her sneakered feet seemed to drag, as though she were too tired even to care about possible danger.

He loved it. . . . he loved the breathtaking innocence of her as she walked unsuspectingly toward him.

He knew all about her. He had watched her for weeks, planning for this night. He knew where she lived, in the off-campus apartment shared with a couple of other students. He knew the layout of that apartment. He had inspected the chaos of her littered room, had stretched out on her bed, smelling the faint odor of her ripe young body on the tangled sheets. To keep that memory, that signal that triggered the excitement that would culminate tonight, he had snatched a pair of her panties from the pile of laundry on the floor, holding them to his face in an agony of trembling passion that had him on the brink.

Controlling himself, saving the savage pleasure and the pain for later, he had glanced distastefully around the littered student digs: at the brimming ashtrays, the empty Coke cans, the discarded pizza boxes and the clutter of CDs, candles and grungy clothing that covered every surface. He had wondered, disgustedly, how she could live like that. Thrusting the cotton panties into his pocket, he had walked calmly back through the French window, across the patio into the alley, and away.

He knew what time the girl's classes were, that she was pre-med and a class valedictorian at her high school in Baltimore. He knew her name, that she wore Calvin Klein underwear and Gap T-shirts and red Converse hightops. He knew where she bought her coffee and blueberry-muffin-to-go each morning, where she hung out in the evening, and what time she went to bed.

He also knew that she had no steady boyfriend, that she dated rarely, and that she was immersed in studying for the end-of-semester finals. And that was why she was dragging her feet as she walked across the parking lot toward him. She was exhausted.

He was wearing his "uniform": a fine quality black turtleneck sweater of the type worn by skiers; a black ski mask that covered his head and face leaving slits for his eyes; black sweatpants and black sneakers. Crouched low in the

8

back of her Miata, his heartbeat went into overdrive as she stepped closer and the adrenaline surge hit him.

His eyes were riveted to the binoculars as she stepped closer. He could see every detail. The way her breasts moved under her white shirt. The way the black leggings outlined her thighs and clung to her crotch. The look of fatigue on her pretty face as she took a final drag on the Marlboro, then flung it to the ground.

The lit butt glowed red and he frowned with anger at her irresponsibility and untidiness. He saw her glance warily at his gunmetal-gray Volvo station wagon, polished to a dull gleam, parked next to the Miata. From the fleeting expression on her face, he saw her dismiss it as the essence of suburban respectability, the safe automobile of a Boston family man or woman.

Clutching her book bag to her chest, she fiddled with her keys, stuck them into the lock and opened the door. He stopped breathing and crouched even lower. Would she check in the back? If she did, he was ready.

She flung the heavy book bag onto the passenger seat with a groan of relief, then put the key in the ignition and fumbled for another cigarette.

He prided himself that she never knew what hit her. The swift expert chop to the carotid artery temporarily cut off the blood to her

9

brain. The pack of Marlboros slipped from her hand as she slumped forward, unconscious, smacking her forehead on the steering wheel.

He pulled her back by her long brown hair, scowling as he saw the already purpling bruise. He liked his girls pristine, unmarked. He slid from the back of the Miata, silently cursing its smallness. He opened her door and hefted her from the driver's seat. For a few seconds he just held her, reveling at her helplessness in his arms, marveling at the feather-lightness of her, at her softness, at the mingled feminine odors of her perfume and lipstick. Then he bundled her onto the floor of the Volvo, quickly taped her mouth, then her wrists and covered her with a dark plaid rug.

The cigarette butt was still glowing faintly in the night. He walked across, stamped it out, then picked it up and flung it in the nearby trash can.

Slamming the rear door, he climbed into the driver's seat and locked the car doors. He pulled off the black ski mask, knotted a discreet paisley silk scarf over his black turtleneck and shrugged on an expensive but comfortably well-worn tweed jacket. Running his hands quickly through his hair, he glanced once more over his shoulder as he started the car and made for the exit. All was quiet. Heaving a pleased sigh, he pushed the CD play button, filling the car with a delicate Bach cantata as he swung left out of the exit.

The drive was quite long — over an hour — but pleasant. He followed the music's complicated geometric patterns expertly in his head, nodding to the rhythms, smiling as he thought of *his girl* "sleeping" in the back, waiting for him. Pulling the Calvin panties from his pocket, he held them to his face, breathing in the scent of her, titillating himself with the promise of pleasures to come.

He drove through Gloucester, then Rockport, a little further north up the coast, slowing as he passed through the deserted main street of a small town. A half mile farther on, he turned the car down a lane leading to the beach and parked in the lee of a small wooden jetty.

He glanced quickly at the three or four small boats, listening to the smooth surge of the ocean on the shore and the slap-slap of the waves against the hulls. Only the stars and a faint phosphorescence hovering over the ocean gave a glimmer of light.

He took off his jacket and the scarf, climbed out of the car and opened the rear passenger door. He glanced at the illuminated dial of his watch. It was two thirty.

She was lying exactly as he had left her, eyes closed, her pretty face pale under her long fling of dark hair. Such soft hair, he thought, running its shining strands through his fingers. Such beautiful, *hateful* long hair.

He dragged her roughly from the car and hefted her in his arms again. He put his hand

11

to her face, ran a finger across her smooth young skin. She moaned and her eyelids fluttered. *Suddenly she was looking at him.*

Her eyes were blue, but the dilated pupils had turned them almost black and she was having trouble focusing. Cursing himself for not putting on the ski mask, he hastily covered her face with the rug and hauled her down onto the beach.

He set her down by the flaking wooden jetty and chopped her neck again with his hand. Her head sagged; she was unconscious. He untaped her hands and then hit her, again and again, beating her in a fury of punches, her head, her face, her breasts. He paused in his work, his breath coming quickly. Then with trembling fingers he unfastened the buttons of her shirt.

He sat back on his heels, staring at her. Her breasts were small, two perfect pink-nippled spheres splotched with ugly red and blue welts where he had beaten her. With an anguished cry he flung himself on her, biting and sucking her breasts with manic ferocity.

After a while he sat up. He took out a small, immaculately clean knife, unsheathed it, and put the plastic cover back in his pocket. He ran the blade across his finger with a satisfied sigh. Then he jerked her head up and began systematically to hack off her long brown hair. It took him about three or four minutes and he enjoyed every second of it. Sometimes he thought this was the best part. He looked at her, lying half naked with her raggedly shorn head, helpless before him, and he laughed. It was a sound of pure pleasure.

He dragged off her black leggings, hurriedly now — he could hardly wait, the urge was building inside him. He pulled down her panties, identical to the pair he had stolen from her room, and stared at the tangled dark bush of hair, quivering as he anticipated how she would feel. He wore nothing under his own black sweatpants, and he was on top of her in a minute, thrusting himself into her, cursing the tightness of her, glorying in the scent of her: hating her.

He thrust himself into her again and again. It was almost too much to bear; the sheer quivering scream of it was inside him as he halted for a split second.

The thin knife was ready in his hand. He turned her hands palm up, then with swift efficiency he slit first her right wrist, and then her left. The rich blood gushed forth, pulsing with his terrifying climax.

He sat back, still shuddering. There was no other sensation in the world to equal it. This perfect moment of power.

His head jerked around as he heard a noise. Someone was on the beach. He could see the glint of a flashlight, hear men's voices. He leaped from her.

The fisherman walking along the beach

13

swung his flashlight upward at the sound. For a split second the man's face was caught in its beam, staring fixedly like a deer caught in headlights.

Then he turned and ran. He flung open the car door, tossing the bloody knife onto the floor as he turned on the ignition. With the lights off, he swung the car around and gunned it down the lane.

"Funny thing, Frank, that guy just speeding outta here," Jess Douglas said to his friend.

"Like a bat outta hell," Frank Mitchell marveled. "Must've been some heavy pettin' goin' on tonight."

Their guffaws echoed over the slur of the waves as they hefted their fishing tackle, heading for the jetty and their boat.

The beam of Jess's flashlight shortened as it struck the girl's spread-eagled, naked body, illuminating, like a black and white horror movie, the dark patches on the sand around her hands and the blood still leaking from her wrists.

"Dear God," Frank said shakily. "Oh, my dear lord, will you just look at that."

Jess dropped his fishing tackle and put his fingers to her neck, felt the flutter of her pulse. "She's still alive," he muttered. "The bastard slit her wrists. Give me your bandanna, Frank — quick, quick."

Frank ripped the red-spotted cotton scarf from his neck and handed it to him.

"Thank the lord for Eagle Scouts," Jess muttered, fashioning a clumsy tourniquet on her left wrist, instructing Frank to bear down on the pressure point on the girl's vein — for all he was worth.

"Jesus God," he said, wiping the sweat of fear and horror from his brow. "No wonder the bastard was outta here like that. He just about killed her. We gotta get help, Frank. You hold on to that girl's arm for dear life while I run to the pay phone down the beach."

"What if he comes back?" Frank peered uneasily into the blackness.

"You scared?" Jess demanded, clambering to his feet.

"You bet your goddamn I am," Frank muttered.

"Me too." Jess was already lumbering away down the beach. "Get the bastard good if he comes back, Frank. Remember, it'll be you or him. Just keep your finger on that pressure point is all I ask.

"Until help comes."

2

The dog, a large silver and white malamute with astonishingly pale blue eyes, slithered from under the bed. It sat alert, ears pricked, tongue lolling, staring intently at the flickering green digital display on the clock radio: 4:57 — 4:58 — 4:59 — 5:00.

Its paw shot out, zapping the snooze button on the first ring.

Boston Homicide Detective Harry Jordan rolled over onto his back, eyes still tightly shut. The dog watched him, waiting expectantly for his next move. When nothing happened, it leaped onto the bed. It lay down with its head on Harry's chest, its eyes fixed on his face.

Ten minutes later the alarm went off again. This time the dog let it ring.

Harry's dark gray eyes snapped open and stared straight into the malamute's pale blue ones.

The dog's tail wagged slowly, but it did not move its head from his chest.

Harry groaned. In his dreams the eyes he had been gazing into did not belong to a malamute. "Okay, I'm up," he said, ruffling the dog's thick neck fur.

Swinging his legs from the bed, he stood up and stretched luxuriously. Then he padded across the polished-wood floorboards to the window to inspect the pewter dawn.

Harry Jordan looked great naked. He was forty years old, six foot two and a lean one hundred and eighty pounds of solid muscle, despite a steady diet of junk food at Ruby's diner, around the corner from the precinct. He had unruly dark hair, level gray eyes, and usually a day-old stubble.

His colleagues called him the Prof because of his Harvard law degree, but they were more impressed by his football record at Michigan State, where his record-breaking 105-yard touchdown was still spoken of with awe. What they didn't know, because he had kept it to himself, and besides he no longer found it important, was that Harry had inherited a great deal of money.

His grandfather had left him a trust fund that he finally came into at the age of thirty, plus the beautiful old brownstone in Boston's Beacon Hill. Harry thought he might have enjoyed the money more when he was twenty instead of thirty-five, but he guessed his grandfather was right and if he'd gotten his hands on it earlier, it would be gone by now, spent on fast cars, fast women and finding himself. As it was, he had had to "find himself" the hard way.

He had never forgotten the words of his

father when he almost flunked out that first year of law school.

"Why the hell don't you get your brains back from your prick and put them to use," he'd snapped angrily. "Zip up your pants, Harry. Give me back the keys to the Porsche. Get your ass into that seat in the lecture room, and get yourself to work."

In the end Harry had straightened out. He'd graduated from law school and gone to work for the family firm, until he could stomach it no longer. Then he'd quit and become a rookie in the Boston Police Department.

When asked why, he gave the same answer both to his father and to the recruiting officer: "Lawyers don't deal in justice anymore. They just deal in legal conundrums, getting guilty men freed on technicalities and pocketing huge fees. At least this way I'll have the satisfaction of catching the criminals."

And he did. Harry was a good cop. He had worked his way up from the patrol car via the rescue services, the fraud squad, the drug and vice squads, to senior detective. He had been married once, when he was twenty-eight and she was twenty, but she hadn't liked the change from attorney's wife to cop's wife. He had been devastated when she left him. He had held her in his arms and kissed her, but it was too late. For her, the feeling had gone.

He converted the Beacon Hill house into apartments and rented out the three top floors.

18

His own apartment was on the garden floor, and when he moved in, he'd bought himself a pup. The malamute. He looked like a wolf and was the closest to a wild creature he could get. He called him Squeeze and the dog went everywhere with him.

Harry paced through the hallway and opened the back door leading into a good-sized walled yard. With a joyful growl the dog shot past him. Squeeze stood for a moment or two sniffing the fresh morning air, then began his usual perambulation around the lavishly untidy pollen-laden garden.

Harry sneezed loudly as he padded to the bathroom. "Got to get that grass taken care of," he promised himself as he did every morning. His only problem was time, or rather the lack of it. Still, he liked his garden, and he liked his bathroom too.

It was huge, square and old-fashioned, with the original black-and-white-tiled floor, a fireplace with a cast-iron grate, a mahogany-paneled tub big enough for a giant, and a Victorian water closet with a blue-flowered bowl and a pull chain. The old marble washstand was big enough for a man to splash around in and it made up for the lack of counter space to put his stuff. He liked it that way.

From the bathroom he walked back through the hall. A Nautilus machine stood incongruously next to the ebony grand piano in what had once been the elegant drawing room of a

19

rich nineteenth-century Boston lady. The Nautilus was his next chore, but first he needed a cup of coffee.

There was nothing old-fashioned about Harry's kitchen — it was all black granite and brushed steel, but these days he never seemed to find the time to cook or entertain. The coffee machine was the only piece of kitchen equipment that ever got a workout. Now it gurgled and coughed, and the red digital timer blinked, announcing it was brewed. Harry thought impatiently that his life was ruled by digital timers; even his watch had one.

He filled a plain white mug with coffee, spooned in two sugars and was on his way to the Nautilus when the phone rang.

His eyebrows lifted resignedly as he answered it. At 5:10 A.M. it could only mean trouble.

"What happened, Prof? Squeeze miss the alarm button this morning?"

Harry took a sip of the hot coffee. It was Carlo Rossetti, his partner on the force and his buddy. "He didn't go for the extra five minutes. I guess he just wanted up and out."

"Sorry to call so early, but I knew you'd want to know right away. There's been another one, a young woman raped and stabbed. Only this one didn't die. At least not yet. She's in Mass General. It's pretty much touch and go."

Harry glanced quickly at the digital watch

that had irritated him only a few moments ago. "I'll meet you there. Tell the chief we're on our way. Is she conscious? Has she said anything yet?"

"Not that I know of. I just got here myself. The night shift was having a slow one when the call came in at about three A.M. A couple of fishermen found her on the beach near Rockport. The emergency rescue squad helicoptered her down from there. The duty officer was McMahan. He and Gavel are over there now, but this is our baby, Harry. I knew you'd want in on it."

Harry remembered the brutally mutilated young bodies of the two previous victims. "I'll be there in ten," he said grimly.

There was no time for a shower or even to brush his teeth. He flung cold water on his face, rinsed his mouth with Listerine, threw on jeans, a denim shirt and an old black leather bomber jacket, and whistled for the dog. In three minutes flat he was out the door.

Harry still hadn't gotten over his passion for fast cars. The souped-up 1969 E-type Jaguar in British racing green was parked in his usual spot across the road. The dog hunkered down on the beautiful tan coach-hide-leather backseat, and a minute later they were speeding out of Louisburg Square to the hospital.

3

Massachusetts General was a massive lime-stone block set back from a busy avenue. Traffic rattled around it, and the morning air vibrated with the perpetual wail of sirens from ambulances and emergency rescue-squad fire engines and the clatter of rotor blades as helicopters landed and took off from the roof.

Harry swung into a parking spot in the reserved zone. He left the back windows open a crack for the dog, hurled himself through the doors of Emergency and collided with a white-coated doctor.

"My, my, you're in a hurry this morning, detective," the doctor said mildly, adjusting his horn-rimmed eyeglasses.

Still running, Harry threw an apologetic glance over his shoulder. "Sorry, doc. Oh, hi — it's you, Dr. Blake. Excuse me, I'm in a hell of a rush."

The doctor shook his head, smiling. "Never saw you when you weren't," he called. "Anything I can do to help?"

Harry waved his hand dismissively as he sped round the corner. "Not your department, doc. At least, not yet." His face grew grim as he thought of the implications of what he had just said. Dr. Blake was head of pathology at the hospital and a medical examiner for the Boston PD.

The Nursing Sister at the desk knew Harry too. "First floor, trauma ward, last on the right," she said, when he paused in front of her. "They've given her fifteen pints of blood. She's comatose and critical. And no, I don't know if she's going to make it."

Harry's bleak eyes met her. "Jesus," he whispered.

The sister crossed herself quickly. "Believe me, she needs Him."

Skirting the crowd waiting for the elevator, Harry took the stairs two at a time. He paused at the top. He took a deep breath and ran his hands through his uncombed hair. He closed his eyes for a moment, steadying himself.

The smell of hospital corridors still got to him. The only time he had ever been an inmate was when he was five years old and had had his tonsils and adenoids removed. They had fed him a steady diet of ice cream for a week. He couldn't remember being traumatized by it, but the childhood fears still stuck.

He swung through the fire door and it whooshed silently shut behind him.

Rossetti was leaning up against the wall, arms folded, one leg crossed lazily over the other. His glossy black hair was slicked flat, his white shirt was immaculate and his black trousers had a fresh crease in them. He was

23

filing his nails and whistling *"Nessun dorma"* through his perfect teeth. He looked like the early version of John Travolta ready for a night on the town instead of a Boston homicide detective on duty at 5:25 A.M.

Despite the tough circumstances, Harry grinned. Carlo Rossetti was thirty-two years old, long jawed, dark-eyed, and a serious ladies' man. He had probably come direct from the previous evening's rendezvous but he looked as though he had stepped straight from his good Italian mama's house: clean, well-fed, and ready for action.

"She's not gonna make it," Rossetti said flatly.

Harry looked startled. "How d'you know?"

"I've seen her. Seen that look before, that otherworldly thing." He shrugged. "Take a look for yourself."

A uniformed cop stood guard outside the door. He saluted and said good morning, standing aside to let Harry in.

Harry took in the scene at a glance: the nurse hovering over the machinery, the monitors flickering in the corner, and the young woman lying motionless on the narrow bed with IVs pumping fluid into her arms. Her bandaged wrists were propped stiffly out in front of her on top of the sheet. And her young face was pale as death beneath the halo of shorn hair.

The nurse glanced at him. "She's in shock.

Maybe she'll come out of it," she said softly.

Harry wanted to believe her and not Rossetti. "Any chance she might wake up and be able to talk to us?"

"If she does wake up, the last thing she'll want to do is talk to *you*."

"We need her. She's our only hope of catching the killer. She might have seen his face. Maybe she even knows him."

The nurse sighed. She had heard of the mutilation of the other young victims. "He didn't cut off the nipples this time."

Harry stared at the young woman with the tubes in her arms, at her severed wrists and bloodless face. The memory would stay with him forever; or at least until he had done his job and the killer was caught. He turned and walked out the door.

Rossetti had finished filing his nails. He was sipping black coffee from a paper cup. He held a second one in his other hand and offered it to Harry.

"So? What d'you think?"

"I think we had better start praying."

They sipped the coffee silently.

"What's with the fishermen?" Harry asked finally.

Rossetti shrugged. "Local police took a statement, faxed it through to the boss. They said they didn't see nothin' that meant anything, just heard a car taking off in the dark. Then they saw the body — excuse me, *the victim.* A few minutes earlier, and they would have caught him in the act. Unlucky for her."

"Do we know her name?"

"They're working on it. She had no identification on her, no purse, no keys. Nothin'."

Harry nodded; there were thousands of young women in Boston, but both the other victims had been students and the odds were that this one was too. It would make the search easier. He expected that they would know her identity within hours.

He drained his coffee cup and looked around for the machine. "I'm gonna get some more coffee, hang around here for a while just in case we — *she* gets lucky. Why don't you check in at the precinct? Let them know where I am, and see how they're doing on her identity and whatever else is going down."

"Will do." Rossetti unfurled himself from the wall. He looked Harry in the eye. "Don't take it personal, Harry. You're just the cop doing his job." He slapped him affectionately on the shoulder as he strode off down the gleaming, antiseptic-smelling corridor. "Never would have taken you for the emotional type. You should save it for the women. They love all that over-the-top stuff. *Madison County* and Clint Eastwood and all that."

Harry smiled. "And how would you know, Romeo?"

"Casanova, y'mean — too old for Romeo." His laughter echoed through the death-stalked corridor as he walked briskly away.

Harry paced the corridor for an hour. He went downstairs and ate a bacon and egg sandwich in the cafeteria. Then he came back and paced some more. At noon he stepped out and walked Squeeze around the corner, where he bought a ham and Swiss on rye from Au Bon Pain. He shared it with the dog and gave him a bowl of water, then returned him to the car.

The dog settled down on the backseat again, his head on his paws, his pale blue eyes gazing reproachfully up at Harry.

"It's a cop's life, Squeeze," Harry said as he slammed the door. "I warned you when you took me on, this is what it would be like."

They were the same words he had said to his wife ten years ago, but they hadn't saved his marriage.

The uniformed cop guarding the door had changed. "Afternoon, sir," he said, saluting. "Officer Rafferty. I'll be on duty until eight P.M., sir. And Dr. Waxman is in with the victim now."

The doctor was standing at the foot of the bed studying her charts. He glanced around as Harry entered.

"How're you doin', Harry?" He smiled. They were old acquaintances, veterans of a decade of trauma victims.

"Pretty good. What about her?"

"She regained consciousness briefly, about ten minutes ago." He sighed regretfully. "At this point I'd be inclined to say it's a triumph of spirit over matter. She's stabilized, for the moment." He shrugged. "Anything could happen."

Harry stared at her, willing her to wake up again. He ran his hands through his still-uncombed hair. "If she comes round, will she be able to talk?"

"Your guess is as good as mine, though I'm not sure I'd advise trying it."

Their eyes met. "It may be our only chance to get him," Harry said quietly. "She might know him. If she talks, she might save others."

"We'll see." Dr. Waxman slipped his charts back into the slot at the foot of the bed. "I'm needed down in Emergency. Are you going to keep vigil?"

Harry nodded.

"See you later, then."

Harry took a seat on the straight-back chair beside the bed. He looked at the girl, then glanced uncomfortably away. He felt like a voyeur, watching her sleeping. Only hers wasn't real sleep. It might be a death watch.

He stared at the ceiling, then at the jagged peaks and valleys that were her vital signs, blipping on the monitors in the corner. He was a good cop, a tough cop, but this helpless young woman had gotten to him.

There was a knock on the door and Rossetti poked his head in. "Thought I'd find you in here." He took a folded sheet of paper from his inside pocket. "Her name's Summer Young. She's twenty-one years old and a senior at Boston U. Her home address is in Baltimore. Her roommates missed her — they got worried when they spotted her old Miata in the library parking lot. The doors were unlocked. The key was in the ignition, and her book bag was on the seat. They called the police."

Harry nodded. The scenario was exactly as he'd expected.

"The parents are on their way," Rossetti added quietly. "Be here in a couple of hours."

They stared silently at each other. They both hoped for her sake that it would be sooner.

"Latchwell's waiting outside," Rossetti added. "Just in case."

Harry's head shot up. Latchwell was the photo-fit expert. He could put a face together from the vaguest description. Sometimes he seemed to conjure it from thin air, honing it down, refining and redefining it: *thinner lips — no, his mouth turned down sort of like this; bushy eyebrows — no, less bushy . . . black eyes . . . well, maybe not black, dark though, and kind of shadowy . . ."* Latchwell had helped catch many a criminal with his uncanny expertise.

Rossetti glanced uneasily at the girl. "I guess I'll get back to the squad room. Gotta talk to those fishermen."

Harry nodded. He wanted her parents to

get here; he wanted them to gather their girl up in their arms, tell her it would be all right, that she would be fine, that she would get over this. But he didn't believe it.

A few minutes later, when she opened her eyes and looked straight at him, he was shocked.

"Hi," he said softly. "I'm Detective Harry Jordan. You've been hurt, but you're safe now. Your mom and dad are on their way. You'll be okay."

Her mouth twisted as she tried to form a word. *"Bastard,"* she whispered.

He nodded. "Tell me, Summer, do you know him?"

She attempted to shake her head, flinching as pain rippled through her body. Her lips formed a silent no.

Harry hated himself for pushing her, but he had to do it. "Did you see him? Can you remember?"

She frowned, struggling. "Soft," she whispered. "Hands."

The nurse pushed the beeper, signaling Dr. Waxman. Placing a finger on the pulse point at the girl's throat, she frowned. "Enough," she whispered.

Harry nodded — he knew he couldn't take it any further now. He looked at Summer one last time. She seemed to be making a great effort to speak and he leaned over her to catch her whispered words.

"Eyes," she said in a voice like a sigh, "dark . . . staring . . ."

He waited, but her eyelids drooped and she lay still again. As he watched, a tear slid suddenly down her pale cheek. "Brave girl," he whispered. "Brave Summer. You're going to be all right."

Dr. Waxman came in as he was going out. "That's enough, detective," he said tersely. "The parents are being helicoptered in now. It's their daughter, their turn."

Harry nodded. "Let me know if anything happens. I'll be back at the precinct."

Latchwell was exchanging views on the Celtics versus the Knicks with Officer Rafferty. He glanced eagerly at Harry as he opened the door. "Ready for me?"

Harry shrugged. "All we've got is dark staring eyes."

"Well, it's a start."

"That may be all we get. Thanks, Latchwell. Sorry for wasting your time."

"All in a day's work." Latchwell shouldered his equipment and strode off.

Harry's cell phone rang. It was Rossetti. And it was bad news. The fishermen had been no help. Their memories were just a blur, more concerned with the girl than with the man.

Harry told the officer on duty he could reach him at the precinct, then headed back to the car.

Squeeze heard him coming. He stuck his nose through the window, his feet scrabbling on the tan coach-hide seats. Harry snapped on the leash and took him for a long walk.

The dog sniffed the street corner and the lampposts, yipping excitedly, but for once Harry didn't notice. Two young women were dead, another was in critical condition, and he was no closer to finding the killer than he had been a year ago.

He turned back to the car, dropped Squeeze at home, fed him and took off again for the precinct. It was going to be a long night.

Five hours later, the call came through. Summer Young had died without regaining consciousness.

4

Detective Rossetti drove his five-year-old BMW too fast down the dark street near the waterfront. Tires screeching, he swung into the empty lot that served as parking for the Moonlightin' Club. He checked the time: it was one thirty A.M.

Flinging open the car door, he headed for the club. Lights spilled from the windows, and as he stepped inside, he was hit by a wall of sound.

Rap blasted from enormous speakers, bouncing back from the walls, hitting the rafters and hurling down again. The young black guy manning the snack bar grinned hello as he walked by, and others high-fived him cheerfully. He grabbed a cup of coffee and walked through to the gym. It was jammed, even this late.

The Moonlightin' Club had been donated anonymously to the city in an effort to get kids off the streets and off crack, and Rossetti and Harry were two of the many cops who gave their free time to help run it. The club had four rules: No discrimination. No drugs. No weapons. No gangs. Whatever the kids were up to in their own world, they were neutral

33

when they came to the Moonlightin' Club and its gym.

The rules had been broken many times but the club still staggered along. Sometimes Rossetti thought they were winning the battle — like tonight, when fifty or so young men were working out or playing basketball instead of shooting up or shooting each other. The basketball team even had a couple of possible rising stars — they were hot and they were good, and the desire to win had overtaken the temptations of the streets. Every little bit helped.

He spotted Harry leaning moodily against the wall, watching the players racing up and down the court. His thick dark hair was tousled from running his hands through it, a habit Rossetti knew his partner had when he was agitated. His clothes looked as though he had slept in them, and his lean face was shadowed with stubble and exhaustion.

Rossetti guessed he had been at his desk, hashing and rehashing every detail of the three murders. He knew it was anger that kept Harry there, and he'd bet it was only pure trembling adrenaline rage that kept him on his feet now. He'd also bet he was no further along than he had been six hours ago, when Summer Young had died.

He sauntered up behind him. "Somehow I guessed I'd find you here."

Harry turned. Rossetti had the usual paper

cup of coffee clutched in his hand like a permanent fixture. His sharp Italian linen jacket, dark pants and fresh white shirt were immaculate and Harry suddenly remembered he hadn't even showered that day, let alone changed clothes. He was still wearing the same jeans and shirt he had flung on at five o'clock that morning.

"I feel disgusting," he said, scowling.

Rossetti grinned. "You look disgusting, Prof. But the dog looks just fine. How y'doin', Squeeze? Got any secrets to tell me about your master? We need a line on him, boy. You know, the truth about his private life? What's he do when he's not working? Women, booze — that kinda stuff?"

Harry laughed. "When am I *not* working, Rossetti? Tell me that."

"Rarely. And that may be your problem, Prof. Now look at me. I quit my shift at eight thirty, had a drink with the guys. A hot date at nine thirty, a good meal, a little lovin' — it makes a difference to a guy's life. So? What did *you* do?" He held up a warning hand. "No, don't tell me. You had a beer and a burger at Ruby's. Then you went back and tried to unravel the serial killer's psyche all by yourself. Waste of time, Prof, waste of time. You need a little fun in your life to sharpen you up. And then a good night's sleep."

Harry sighed regretfully. "You're right, of course. And I didn't solve the murders. But I can't get this one out of my head. Her last words were to *me*. 'Bastard,' she said."

He straightened up, shook his head to clear it. "Ah, what the hell, Rossetti. Forget about sleep. How about you and I hit Salsa Annie's? I'll buy you a bourbon and let you tell me the story of your life, while we raise our blood pressure with a little music."

He held out his palm and Rossetti slapped down on it. It was Harry's favorite club and Rossetti figured his partner could work off his anger with a little hot dancing. "Done," he said, heading for the door. "All this pure physical exercise stuff at two in the morning is too much for me anyhow."

The second dawn Harry had witnessed in twenty-four hours was breaking when they swung their way out of Annie's a couple of hours later. Humming to the music in his head, Harry salsaed across the street to the parking lot.

"Just like Gloria Estefan," Rossetti said, grinning, as he lit a cigarette.

"Thanks for the compliment. And for your company. Good night, Rossetti."

" 'Night, Prof." Rossetti got into his BMW, turned on the ignition, and combed his hair in the rearview mirror. He could see Harry reflected there. He was sitting in the Jag with the dog next to him, holding the steering wheel and staring into space. He watched him for a couple of minutes; then Harry climbed out of the car again.

"Rossetti!" he yelled. "Hey, Rossetti!"

He stuck his head out of the window. "Yeah?"

"Get your ass over here, man. We're off to Rockport."

Rossetti yawned loudly. "Rockport, Massachusetts?"

"No, you jerk. Rockport, Illinois. Where d'you think, Rockport? Just get your smart Italian butt over here. We're going back to talk to those fishermen again. And while I'm driving, you can get on the radio and tell them to get Latchwell up there right away. Those guys *saw* him, Rossetti. They're the only ones, apart from the dead, who did. They've *got* to remember something about him, about his car. It's up to us to jog their memories."

5

Mallory Malone read the brief newspaper report on the rape and murder of Summer Young in the limo on the way to Kennedy airport, about the same time that Harry and Rossetti were on their way to interview the fishermen who had found her.

She read it again, carefully, noting that the police were linking the killing to the deaths of two other young women in Massachusetts in the past eighteen months.

She tore out the report, folded it and placed it in her green leather Filofax, already crammed with notes and cards, names, addresses, telephone numbers and other important information. Then she stuffed it in her sand-colored Bottega Veneta bag.

Besides her passport and tickets, her itinerary and traveler's checks, the bag was also stuffed with the papers she meant to read on the Concorde flight to London. Plus two pairs of narrow gold-rimmed eyeglasses, two identical pairs of sunglasses, several packs of pocket-sized Kleenex and a jumbled bag of cosmetics and lotions.

There was also a Mont Blanc rollerball pen, a couple of unmatched earrings, a few ticket stubs from the last trip and odd bits of foreign currency. On top was a black cashmere sweater that would do double duty in an emergency, day or evening, as well as a change of underclothes.

She had learned from hard experience to be prepared for any eventuality — the time her baggage had not turned up in Rome for the three days of a long holiday weekend, and every store in the city had been firmly closed.

Mal smiled as she thought of the old saying: You could tell exactly what a woman was like from the contents of her handbag. A stranger would probably assume she was a nervous traveler, a pessimist expecting the worst to happen, sloppy and untidy with a chaotic home life. The sort of woman whose car was littered with a week's debris: old coffee containers and take-out cartons, and an assortment of clothes intended for the cleaners — whenever she found the time to get them there.

In fact, nothing could be further from the truth.

She was thirty-seven years old, tall and slender, with the short blond hairdo of a network anchorwoman, impeccably dressed in a simple but expensive beige suit. There was no run in the pantyhose that sheathed her long legs, and her sand-colored suede pumps were pristine and unscuffed. Her makeup was minimal but perfectly applied; the mocha lipstick outlining her full soft-lipped mouth, the brown liner adding a faint emphasis to her large sapphire blue eyes, and the faint, haunting scent of Nocturnes, by Caron, that seemed to enfold her.

Mal Malone was known as "the TV detective." On her prime-time show she followed up violent cases of murder, of fraud in high places, of sex scandals in Washington, and of Mafia drug-running in Miami.

She was famous for taking up the causes of forgotten murder victims, after public outrage had died down and the media had gone on to the next sensational case. With the assistance of the DA, she would delve out every detail, then reenact the crime on TV, jogging the memories of potential witnesses who might just remember something crucial.

The public was riveted by her. She had her finger on the nation's pulse. She knew what was bothering them and she showed them why.

It was debatable whether Mallory Malone was a beauty. Sometimes she looked breathtaking; at others she looked downright plain. It all depended on her mood.

When she was up and hot on a case, waves of energy lit up her face with a thousand watts of candlepower, giving her skin a golden glow and turning her eyes luminescent with concern. And at television award shows and dinners, she was ravishing in her trademark plain evening dresses in her favorite muted colors, the low necklines showing off her pretty shoulders and breasts.

On other days, less frequent now, Mal Malone, the famous TV personality, seemed to disappear into the background. She could walk down Fifth Avenue and not a head would turn in recognition. The golden hair would be slicked back, lacking life and luster. The expensive jacket would somehow look as though it had come from the bargain sale racks. And the glow of vitality, the curiosity, the intelligence that had propelled her into the spotlight would be dimmed like a TV screen fading into a pinpoint of light before being extinguished altogether.

Nobody but Mal understood the phenomenon, and she chose not to explain it to anyone. She was a woman who kept her own secrets, but it was an image that haunted her.

Most days, however, Mallory Malone was on top of the world. This morning, she was on her way to London to interview a voluptuous young American actress who had just become engaged to a man four times her age: a billionaire with a not-too-perfect past and a hunger for more future than was left to him.

Mal had charmed the happy couple into appearing on her show, knowing that the actress was eager for publicity. She was flattered to be interviewed, though Mal had warned her that she would be asking some "impertinent" questions of a personal nature.

"Oh, I know what you mean," the young actress had cried, delighted. "Like, am I marrying him for his billions? Well, I can answer that right now, Mal. *Truthfully.* I'm a woman in love. It's as simple as that. And if you knew him, you'd understand why."

Actually, Mal was not about to ask anything so obvious. Instead, she intended to ask what the rest of the world was asking: Does the lovely twenty-three-year-old have sex with this unpleasant man in his eighties? And if so, what is it like? And if he were not a billionaire, would she even contemplate having sex with him, let alone living out the rest of his days with him?

Mal intended to interview the billionaire separately, have him take her on a tour of his enormous country estate and his palatial London house. She would ask him about his private jet, the suites he kept at the grand hotels around the world, the yacht berthed in Monte Carlo, and the Swiss hideaway where he lived most of the year.

She would draw him out about his achievements, and he would tell her about them because he was a very ruthless old man who really cared for nobody but himself. And then she would ask him, so very gently, about his first wife. The girl from the poor London suburb who had worked at his side in those early years, when they were running a working-

42

men's café in London's East End, before they created their restaurant and hotel empire.

"What happened to that young woman?" she would ask, though of course she already knew. And after his lies and smooth coverup, she intended to confront him with the facts: that as his empire and his wealth had grown, he had no longer considered his wife a suitable consort for a king of business. That his desertion of her and the cruel divorce had left her destitute. And she would ask him about the "accident" at his country home when his ex-wife had gone to beg the business monarch for financial help, a few crumbs from his brimming plate.

The same accident that had left her brain-damaged and in a state mental institution for over thirty years. Alone, with never a visitor, nor a luxury to ease her pain.

"About that accident," Mallory Malone would say, smiling. "It seems there were two witnesses to your wife's "fall' down that magnificent Jacobean oak staircase. How is it they have never come forward to tell what they saw?"

She imagined how his face would redden as he blustered his arrogant way around this. And she would smile and say, "Well, here they are now. Ready and willing to testify that you paid them good money *not* to say what they saw. *That you pushed her down the stairs.* Now they've changed their minds."

And then we shall see what Little Miss Mercenary has to say about how *darling* her billionaire was, she thought grimly. How *virile* and *charming* and *generous*. And how *lovable*.

Odds were, they deserved each other. He had bought the actress on the commodity market, not to line his coffers but to enhance his image. And she had sold her youth and undoubted beauty for the temporary fame and the power of being a rich man's wife — as well as for the millions she hoped to reap in the divorce court after a couple of years. Unless, of course, he died conveniently before that and left it all to her. Mal doubted that he would.

She stared out the limo's window at the snarled traffic edging slowly up the expressway, thinking of the report about the rape and murder of Summer Young. The student was almost the same age as the young actress. She too had had all her life in front of her. Until some bastard had put a stop to it.

It was a pretty name: Summer Young. Mal wondered what she had been like, about her ambitions, her family and friends. Perhaps she had been a loner, dedicated to her studies, determined to make her own way in the world. She shivered, thinking about the horror of what had happened to her.

Lifting the telephone receiver, she dialed her office.

"Beth Hardy here," her assistant answered promptly on the first ring.

"Beth, it's me. I'm on my way to JFK. Did you catch the report on the rape and murder of the young student at BU?"

"I sure did. That's my own alma mater, remember? My God, Mal, what's the world coming to? If only she had called for a student escort! But I know that parking lot — it's only five minutes away from the library. She probably didn't think it was worth it, that there was no danger. Poor kid."

"The police are linking it to two similar incidents in the past eighteen months. Have someone dig out the facts for me, Beth, would you? See what we can get on it."

"Is this going to be a feature, then?"

Mal stared moodily in front of her. The outlying areas of the airport were coming into sight. "Maybe. It's a thought. Let's find out if there's a story lurking under the surface that the police are keeping to themselves. A serial killer on the loose? That kind of thing." She frowned as the phone crackled with static. "I have to go now, Beth. Talk to you from London."

"Bon voyage," Beth called. "Give a good interview."

Ten minutes later, Mallory Malone was being VIP'd straight through to the Concorde lounge, where she boarded the flight immediately.

Fifteen minutes later she was airborne. Refusing a glass of champagne and orange juice, she sipped a cup of tea. The man sitting beside her seemed eager to talk, but she ignored him.

Thrusting Summer Young from her mind, she took out her papers and went over the questions she would ask in the interview.

The flight was almost over before she knew it. She went to the bathroom, flicked powder over her nice but slightly bumpy nose, slicked the MAC mocha lipstick over her mouth and brushed her short blond hair. Out of consideration for her fellow passengers, she did not spray Nocturnes onto her pulse points or into the soft hollow between her breasts.

She stared at herself in the mirror, feeling the aircraft move beneath her feet. Here she was, plain little Mary Mallory Malone, a nobody from a small town in Oregon, flying faster than sound and about to meet one of the richest villains in the world. She smiled. Sometimes she didn't believe herself.

A short while later she was wafted through immigration and into a waiting Rolls, on her way to London and the luxurious Lanesborough Hotel, where she would have a large suite, complete with her own butler.

"Oh, Mary Mallory," she said to herself, awed. "You've come a long way from those all-night buses and the rusting turquoise Chevy with the chrome fins."

6

"Gotta give you A for effort, Prof," Rossetti said six hours later, on their way back to Boston. They were at a roadside café eating either breakfast or lunch — he wasn't sure which, because by now he had lost track of time.

"Thanks. It's not great, but at least we got the framework of a likeness from them." Harry stared at the photo-fit picture of the killer. Caucasian, narrow face, big mouth with thin lips, broad forehead, a shock of dark hair. And those staring eyes that had burned into his victim's memory.

It had taken four hours of intense work to delve from the minds of the two shocked fishermen the vague memory of a man they had glimpsed only for a couple of seconds. At first they had insisted they didn't recall a thing: it had been too dark, too quick, and he had been gone almost before they registered he was there. But then Harry had gone to work on them, leading them back into the moment before they saw the girl, those vital seconds when their brains had taken an instant flash photo of the killer.

He had told them what the victim had said about the man's eyes, and they had choked up when he said they were the last words she spoke. They were decent guys, eager to help. Then Latchwell had gone to work, and now they had a probable description.

"'Medium height and build,'" Harry read again, "'thin-faced, clean-shaven. Prominent eyes with heavy brows. Thick dark hair, the bushy kind that stands on end. Wearing dark clothing. Driving a small dark-colored truck or a wagon.'"

He said, "It'll be front page in the *Herald* and the *Globe*, and in the morning tabloids, and maybe the nationals."

Rossetti shrugged — he didn't expect much from the publicity. "We'll see what it trawls in besides the nuts looking to get in on the act and for a moment of glory. And the little old ladies who are sure he was hiding in their closet last night."

He slurped his coffee noisily, and Harry glared at him. "You should quit drinking that stuff. Your stomach must be lined with caffeine."

"Think how ugly I'd look if Doc Blake took his forensic scalpel to me."

"He'd be afraid to cut you open. There's coffee in your veins, not blood." Harry's eyes met his. "He's doing the autopsy on Summer Young at six."

"You going?"

Harry nodded.

"Count me out, man. I can't take that cutting-open business, weighing the hearts and livers, and all that horror stuff. Tell me, Prof, what makes a guy become a forensic expert, anyway?"

"It's a science. Without doctors like Blake, we might never know what really happened. He's a detective, only his detecting is done after death."

Rossetti shivered. "Yeah, well, I'll stick with the living, thanks."

Harry laughed. "Not if you keep on drinking that coffee."

"So? And speaking of health, when did you last have a real meal? And I don't mean at Ruby's."

Harry thought about it. "Three weeks ago. At Marais, in the company of a delightful woman — unknown to you, so I won't bother telling you her name — whom I was supposed to call back." He shrugged regretfully.

Rossetti stared curiously at him. "A good-looking guy like you, Prof. With your education and that fancy apartment. Women must be fallin' over themselves to get into your bed."

Harry laughed again. He stood up and slapped him on the back. "Thanks for the compliment. But a person needs time to build a relationship. I called, she called back — we had a drink, an evening here, an hour or two there. It's just not enough."

He called for the check, laid the money on

the table and added a five-dollar tip. He had a soft spot for waitresses — they worked hard for their money, and he knew most of it came from tips.

The young woman smiled appreciatively at him as she scooped it up. "Thanks a lot," she called. "You have a good day now."

Rossetti turned and gave her a wink and she laughed.

"See that," he said to Harry. "One encouraging word and you'd have had yourself a date."

Harry sighed exaggeratedly. "Rossetti, Rossetti, you're the self-confessed Casanova, not me. It was you she was smiling at. Besides, she probably has a husband and three kids."

"Since when was that a problem?" Rossetti looked smug.

Harry laughed. "Shame on you, a good Italian Catholic boy. If only your mama could hear you. And your priest."

"Believe me, he hears it all. Including how I feel about rapists and killers and how I want to rip the balls off them."

Squeeze was tied to the post outside the café next to an almost-empty dish of Alpo. Harry unhitched the leash. "Meet you back at the car," he said to Rossetti.

"Sorry about this, boy," he muttered as the dog tugged him down the road. "But it's been a tough couple of days. I'll make up for it with a good long run later."

Squeeze wagged his tail, sniffed the grass, and did his duty. Harry guessed that whatever went down it was all right with Squeeze.

In the car, driving back to Boston, he thought about the woman he had taken out to dinner three weeks ago. She was attractive, charming, cultured and very self-assured. She came from a good Boston family and her parents knew his.

"It's a put-up job between them," she had said when she called and left a message on his machine. "I've been away, working in Paris for a couple of years, and my parents think I'm out of the social swing. And your mother seems to have given up all hope. This may be our last chance as far as they're concerned, so why don't we make them happy? Won't you please have dinner with me, one evening next week?"

He had been charmed when he played back the message, and charmed by her. She was tall and slender with a good body, and she wore her long dark hair pulled back, Spanish style, in a knot at the nape of her creamy neck. Her brown eyes sparkled and so did her wit. Dinner had been fun, and so had the drink a couple of nights later at her place. But he had pulled the eight-to-four shift and had to run. He had seen the regret in her eyes and heard it in his own voice.

His mother had called the other night to say that the woman was seeing an old friend from college and they seemed made for each other.

Harry shrugged. Such was the life of a busy cop — especially a dedicated one.

He glanced at the clock on the glossy burled-walnut dashboard of the Jag. If he put his foot down, he might have time to take a shower and change before he went back to the hospital for the autopsy.

7

A few days later, at seven thirty in the morning, Harry was in the squad room, his hands clasped behind his head, his feet propped on the desk, his eyes closed. He was thinking about Summer Young.

He and Rossetti had just emerged from a grueling meeting with the irate police chief. He had said the mayor was getting restless, he had to answer to the public. Was there a serial killer on the loose in his city? If so, what were the police doing about it?

"What does he *think* we're doing? Sitting on our butts? Just letting the guy get away with it?" Rossetti demanded indignantly.

Harry sympathized. They were both feeling the pressure. "We're doing everything we can," he had told the chief. "We're doing our best to catch the bastard." He would never forget that "bastard" was what Summer had called her killer just before she died.

"Yeah." The chief was upset. "Well, Harry, your best is just gonna have to get better. And fast. The mayor wants this killer caught. Boston is famous for its colleges and he needs their image kept clean. He doesn't want college girls raped and slashed and dead. Besides, he has a girl of his own at Northeastern. He has a personal concern, you might say. He wants action, Harry. Now."

Harry swung his legs off the desk and switched on his PC, summoning up his list of evidence.

The local crime-scene officers had done a thorough job. They had found kneeprints in the sand where the killer had crouched over his victim. From them they had been able to deduce he was a short, stocky man, possibly five foot seven or eight.

They had also found traces of skid marks where the killer had gunned the car in his escape, but the area was too sandy to leave much impression. The crime lab was analyzing the minute particles of rubber that had been scraped from the road, but they didn't hold out much hope for matching tires from them. As for the parking lot near the college, it too had shown a dusty scuffle of unidentifiable tire marks.

But Summer's car told a whole other story. They knew that the killer had hidden in the back of the Miata. He had taken her by surprise with a karate-type blow, evidenced, the police surgeon told them, by the purple bruises on her neck over the carotid artery and on her forehead, where she had fallen forward and struck her head on the steering wheel.

Forensics was leaving no stone unturned. The whole basis of forensic science was that a criminal *always* leaves something of himself at the scene of the crime. And that he *always* takes something from there, on his clothing or on his body: minute particles of skin or dust, a thread, a hair, a flake of paint. Forensics looked for evidence in impossible places.

They had hoped to raise a footprint in the Miata, using an electronic mat. They placed a sheet of foil between two sheets of black acetate and ran a weak electrical current through. The electricity would attract the dust particles to the surface in the shape of a footprint, if there was one. They were unlucky — there was no print — but they collected the dust anyway and took it away to be analyzed.

They had also found a tiny black fiber on the backseat of the Miata, and a couple of hairs that didn't match the victim's had been removed from her clothing. The crime lab was running tests and Harry expected to hear the results soon. Of course the tests would prove nothing by themselves but Harry had learned to respect such evidence. Forensics was the modern-day equivalent of Sherlock Holmes. If the butler did it, they could confirm it.

They were also testing the saliva taken from the bite marks on her breasts, and a forensic odontologist was reconstructing the killer's teeth and dental work from the bite marks.

But the most vital piece of evidence was the semen found on the victim. When the results of the DNA tests came through, it could link the killing to the two other murders. DNA evidence was as damning as any fingerprint. It was what would put this killer behind bars for life.

Meanwhile, a week had gone by since Harry and Latchwell had gotten the photo-fit. The local TV stations had shown it on every news program and all the newspapers had front-paged it, morning and evening. Calls had flowed in, from the usual cranks as well as from the genuinely concerned who thought they might have seen the killer. Every possible lead had been followed. And — nothing.

Harry was beginning to doubt the accuracy of the picture. Maybe he had pushed those fishermen too hard, put ideas in their heads.

Harry thought about what Summer had said before she died. *Staring dark eyes . . . soft hands.* She was the only one who really knew what the killer looked like.

Even Doc Blake, after the autopsy, had seemed skeptical. "Are you sure this is a true likeness?" he had asked. "How can you be certain? Only the girl could have told you, and unfortunately she didn't live long enough."

Dr. Blake was right, he thought, swinging his legs down from the desk and running his hands wearily through his dark hair. Either the photo-fit was not a good likeness, or the killer was not a local man. The case needed more public awareness if they were to keep him from striking again — it needed more nationwide publicity.

"What we really need," he said to Rossetti, "is Mallory Malone."

Rossetti raised his dark eyebrows. He stared at his partner as though he'd gone crazy. "Yeah. Sure we need her. She'd make us look like a couple of dumb cops on network TV, while she batted her baby blues and told the nation that if we were smart and did our job properly, we would have caught this killer first time out. In other words, buddy, you and I would take the rap publicly for three murders. The media would latch on to us like piranhas in a feeding frenzy." He shrugged. "Think again, Prof. That's my advice."

"But what if she displays the photo-fit on her show? Maybe she'd snag the one person who knows who this guy is. In California, perhaps. Or Florida or Texas or Montana. Jesus, Rossetti, we need help, and we need it now. Before the trail goes cold."

"What trail?" Rossetti glared at him. "Why go looking for trouble? Aren't we in deep enough already? Don't we have the chief on our backs, to say nothin' of the mayor and the college presidents . . . hell, all of Massachusetts. So why not Mallory Malone as well? Might as well make a party of it."

His dark eyes met Harry's angrily for a minute, then he shrugged, defeated. "Ah, what the fuck, of course you're right. What's a guy's career worth anyhow if he can't finish the job he set out to do. Call Malone if you have to, but leave me out of it. I'm off to Ruby's to punish myself with eggs and a short stack, and their 'special' ungenuine maple syrup. You comin'?"

Harry grinned. "I'll let you kill yourself with Ruby's kindness on your own. I'll settle for another cup of that black death they call coffee around here."

Harry shouldered through the crush to the coffee machine at the end of the hallway. It smelled of sweat and cigarettes and stale pizza, and even this early in the morning the squad room was buzzing. The graveyard shift had been busy: a domestic dispute had ended in a stabbing — not fatal yet, but odds were it would end up that way; a drug-related shooting and a drive-by. The holding cells were crowded with drunks and domestic-violence and public-nuisance cases, and weary cops were typing up case sheets and answering the constantly ringing phones. Not a bad haul for an eight-hour shift. For the umpteenth time Harry wondered why man never learned that when it comes to violence, nobody wins.

From years of practice, he shut out the racket and sat at his desk contemplating Mallory Malone.

On television she was a hunter. Twice she had uncovered information that led to photo-fit pictures. Twice she had displayed those photo-fits on her program and the suspected criminals had been captured.

Malone made it her business to know everything about the people she was investigating and her research team seemed endowed with second sight. She had contacts in high places and was adept at uncovering even the best-kept family secrets. People joked nervously that your slate had better be as clean as the day you were born if Malone came after you. Even the cops said she was a toughie. They said she sank her teeth into her victims like a rottweiler and she didn't let go.

And the only reason she got away with it was because she looked like an angel.

Her blue eyes always had an innocent and slightly surprised expression, as though she couldn't quite believe what she was doing. In her Donna Karan suits, she looked like corn-fed Middle America hitting the big time, and she had an ingenuous, sunshiny quality that concealed a steely shaft of ambition.

The public might love her, but her relationship with the cops was definitely love-hate. They appreciated it when she helped them get the killers and the crack dealers and the drug runners, but they hated the fact that she made it look as though she were doing their job better than they did it themselves.

Harry shrugged — he was between a rock and a hard place. He picked up the phone and dialed the number of Malmar Productions.

"This is Homicide Detective Harry Jordan of the Boston PD," he told the woman who answered. "I'd like to speak with Ms. Malone."

"One moment, sir. I'll put you through to her assistant."

After a few minutes of surprisingly gentle piano music on hold, another voice said, "Beth Hardy here. How can I help you, Detective Jordan?"

"I have a case I'd like to discuss with Ms. Malone. The murder a couple weeks ago of a young college student."

"Oh, the girl from BU?"

"Then you read about it?"

"I did and I felt especially bad about it. BU's my own college. I'm not much older than she was. I couldn't help thinking, there but for the grace of God goes little old me. Poor kid."

"That's why we could use Ms. Malone's help."

Beth sighed regretfully. "Sorry, Detective Jordan, but your timing's off. She just got back from London yesterday, and for once she's taking a break. Anyhow, the programs are all set for the next six weeks." She hesitated, remembering Mal's telephone call about the case. By now, the research team had probably dug out the information she had requested.

"Tell you what," she added. "I'll give her a call. Maybe she'll be interested, maybe she won't."

Harry frowned. Rossetti had been right. He already felt like a fool for calling, and Malone was just an arrogant TV celebrity. "Thanks a lot, Ms. Hardy," he said skeptically. "I won't wait for her call."

Beth's laugh was mocking. "The chip on your shoulder's showing, detective. No promises, but I'll see what I can do."

8

Mal did not pick up her phone when Beth called. Instead, she lay on an overstuffed sofa in the sitting room of her exclusive Fifth Avenue apartment, staring blankly at the puffy gray clouds building up over Central Park.

She had hyped herself up for the London interview, working on sheer nerves and adrenaline. The billionaire had proven tougher than she expected. But she had set the cat among the pigeons all right, and when the program aired later tonight, it would cause a sensation.

The best thing was, there was nothing the vicious old bastard could do about it. She had cleared every point, every single detail with legal before she had left. He had threatened to sue, but he would not. How could he, when it was the truth. What happened next was up to the police and to his fiancée, though it looked as though she was sticking by him.

Mal shook her head, bewildered. It just went to show the power of that kind of money. Absolutely all that was in the woman's head was that she had caught a Mr. Rich, and not that when he got tired of her, she might easily be the next to "fall" down those stairs. Because this old man was not about to part with one cent. He would take it to his grave or else leave it all to build a monument to himself — an arts center, or a museum with his name on it — so that when he was gone, he would still be spoken of every day. He intended to live after death if anybody could.

Mal yawned wearily; even the Concorde could not eliminate time zones and jet lag completely. She wished now she had taken time to see something of London but, except for her own production crew, she didn't really know anyone there. Of course she'd had plenty of invitations — to dinner, to openings, to charity affairs — the English social season. But that sort of thing was no fun. In fact, it was hard work — just a roomful of strangers who only wanted to be seen with her because she was a celebrity. She would have been the entertainment of the evening. She would have had to smile and be polite, sparkle, and make conversation. She had declined them all.

Only later, after a solitary room-service dinner in her lavish flower-filled hotel suite, had she wondered wistfully if she had done the right thing. After all, there might have been one person out there whose eyes would have connected meaningfully with hers. There might have been one man who recognized *who* she was, not *what* she was. He might have been someone who could make her laugh, someone she could have fun with.

The clouds covered the sun, and she wrapped her soft cream robe more closely around her, tucking her bare feet underneath her on the rose-patterned chintz sofa.

Visitors were always surprised by Mal's apartment. They expected it to be decorated the way she dressed: cool, simple, and mono-chromatic. Instead, they got an old-fashioned country house, complete with family pictures and a terrace garden.

Mal's home was filled with English antiques and comfortable sofas covered in artfully faded floral fabrics. The tables were crammed with silver-framed photographs. There were rare old books on her shelves as well as current biographies and best sellers and crime fiction, and perfectly lit paintings of ancestors and horses and dogs on her pale, expensive silk-covered walls. There were watercolors of villas in Tuscany and soft English landscapes, and art books piled on the massive oak coffee table in front of the French limestone fireplace. Even on a sultry evening like this, a fire glowed in the grate, its heat combated by air condi-tioning, simply because she loved the way it looked.

And she liked flowers around her too, great bouquets of garden flowers: spiky blue del-phinium and fragrant white stock, snapdrag-ons and huge daisies, and fat, fragrant, tumbling pink roses that were duplicated in a painting by a great seventeenth-century Dutch artist that hung on her wall. But the evocative scent of lilacs was her favorite, and when they were in their short, sweet season, she wanted nothing else.

Few people knew it, but in the privacy of her home, more was better for the publicly cool, spare, and uncluttered Mallory Malone.

Hauling herself from the comfortable depths of the sofa, she walked out onto her terrace. Twin stone fountains splashed musically as she inspected her plants, rooting her manicured fingers in the earth, pulling out an errant clump of chickweed, dead-heading the azaleas, picking a tiny branch of rosemary and crushing the leaves for their scent.

She sat on the carved wooden bench overlooking Manhattan's towers. "If I closed my eyes," she said aloud, shutting them tightly, holding the rosemary to her nose, "I might be in Provence. I might be listening to cicadas and birdsong and the wind in the olive trees, instead of traffic and the telephone ringing."

She opened her eyes and looked around uneasily. She wasn't used to leisure time. Now that she had it, she wasn't sure what to do with it.

Standing up, she paced the terrace again. She picked off another dead flower head, frowning up at the lowering clouds as the first large drops of rain plopped down. Lightning flashed and thunder rumbled. Within seconds it was a downpour. Wrapping her robe around her, she fled back indoors.

The phone was ringing again. She ran to the study to answer it, stopping as the answering machine clicked on. She reminded herself that a break was what she needed. That meant no phone calls.

She hesitated, glancing at the machine. There was no harm in seeing who had called, just to make sure they hadn't all forgotten her.

She listened to twelve messages and was bored by the time she got to Beth Hardy's at number thirteen.

"Sorry to interrupt your peace and quiet," Beth said, "but there's a touch of urgency to this one. Remember the BU student? The one who was raped and murdered? You asked me to get the research team onto it in case you got interested? Well, a Detective Harry Jordan called from Boston this morning. He wants you on the case. I told him your schedule was fully booked and you were on vacation. He seemed pretty pissed off that you weren't available, but I thought you would want to know anyway. Meanwhile, I hope you're having fun, or at least a rest. Oh, by the way, I have his office number, and his home number too. Unlisted. Pretty fancy for a cop, huh? Just thought I'd pass that on to you. Here they are, just in case," she added again, with a laugh.

Mal sank into the rose-patterned chair in front of the desk. She hadn't forgotten the young girl who had been so brutally raped and killed.

"Summer Young," she said out loud. It was such a magical name, she knew the parents must have loved their daughter very much. She pulled her bare feet up onto the chair and clasped her arms around her knees, staring into space, thinking. Then she picked up the phone and called Detective Jordan.

His office number rang ten times before his machine answered.

"No wonder you need help, detective," she said irately into the phone. "I almost didn't wait to leave a message, the darn machine took so long. Do me a favor and try for only three rings in future. It saves my time and my temper. You know where to reach me. Oh, by the way, it's Mallory Malone."

Irritated by him already, she slammed down the receiver and stalked into the kitchen. She filled the kettle, drumming her fingers impatiently on the polished limestone countertop while she waited for it to boil. She put a Wild Berry Zinger teabag into a pink-flowered mug and poured the boiling water over it, stirring until it was brewed red enough. Then she grabbed a slab of no-fat lemon pound cake and marched back into the sitting room.

She ate the cake in two minutes flat. "*You* made me do that, Detective Harry Jordan," she said out loud, guiltily assessing the calories. And then she laughed. "Darn it, what I

really need is a good dinner. I can't even remember the last time I ate when it wasn't on
the run. Or else on my own. And what fun is
that?"

Bored, she picked up the phone from the
coffee table and dialed Jordan's home number.

Harry was just walking in the door. He was
wearing gray shorts, a sweat-wet gray T-shirt,
and scuffed sneakers, and he was wheeling a
twelve-speed Nishiki mountain bike and carrying a helmet. Squeeze got to the phone before he did, but the snooze-button trick was
the extent of his technical abilities. He just
barked joyfully at it.

"Out of the way, dog. This is man stuff."
Harry hurled himself into the chair and
grabbed the receiver.

"Yeah, Jordan here," he said, still panting.

"And Mallory Malone here, Detective Jordan."

"Mallory Malone?" He was astonished. She
was the last person he expected to hear from.

"I hope the panting doesn't mean I've
caught you doing something you shouldn't,"
she added spikily.

Harry's eyebrows shot up. "Ms. Malone, I
hope you will never catch me doing something I shouldn't. But then again, we may have
different views on what I should and should
not do."

"I'm sure you're right." Her voice was crisp,
even tart.

He grinned, enjoying her. "Thanks for calling me back. Just out of interest, how did you get my home number?"

"Never underestimate the power of a good research team."

"In other words, it's not what you know, it's who you know."

"Possibly. Meanwhile, why don't you tell me about your problem?"

"More specifically, three problems, Ms. Malone. Three murders, all young college women in New England. The pattern is the same. They were abducted in a parking lot or quiet street at night and driven to a lonely place. Their hair was cut off. They were raped, then their wrists were slit, neatly and cleanly, as though with a surgical knife. They were left to die in pools of their own blood. The first in a derelict country farmhouse; the second, at a deserted boathouse on the river; and this last one on a remote beach. In the first two cases the women had been reported missing but their bodies were found only by chance several weeks later.

"The latest victim, Summer Young, had been studying late at the college library. She walked to the parking lot to pick up her car. She was abducted and driven to a lonely beach. But the beach wasn't as lonely as the murderer expected.

"The attacker took off, but a pair of fishermen caught a brief glimpse of his face in the beam of their flashlight. From their quick impression of him, we managed to put together a photo-fit."

She said, surprised, "You have a picture of him?"

"That's right, ma'am."

"It's Ms. Malone," she retorted, and he could hear the irritation in her voice. "I hate that word *ma'am*," she added. "It makes me feel about a hundred years old."

He said teasingly, "No one would ever believe you were a day over thirty-five, Ms. Malone."

"Thanks a lot, detective." Her voice was edged with ice. "I assume your own looks are standing up to the pressure of time and the pull of gravity. Meanwhile, let's get back to Summer Young. I've been in London for the past week. I didn't realize you had a photo-fit. I want to see it and talk more about the case. I'll need to know all the facts you have. No holding back."

"Then you're interested in helping us?" Harry wasn't joking around anymore.

"I'm interested in helping innocent victims and preventing more killings, detective. Not in helping the police do their job."

Harry took that on the chin. "Yes, ma'am. *Ms. Malone.* Since our objectives are the same, I'm sure we can work together. Amicably."

"Are you free tomorrow evening?"

"I can be. Just tell me the time and the place, and I'll be there."

"I'll come to Boston," she said, surprising him.

"There's no need for that. I'll come to you."

He might not have spoken for all the interest she displayed. "I'll take the seven o'clock shuttle from La Guardia. Is there a restaurant where we could meet?"

"Sure. Around the corner from the precinct house. Ruby's, on Miller."

"I'll be there at eight thirty, detective."

"I'll look forward to meeting you, Ms. Malone."

The phone clicked and the line went dead. "Like hell I will," Harry muttered, running his hands through his thick dark hair.

Squeeze cocked his head to one side, tongue lolling, eyes alert. "They were right, Squeeze." He ruffled his silver fur affectionately. "Ms. Malone *ma'am* is a toughie."

9

Rain bounced from the slick sidewalk as Harry hurried around the corner to Ruby's. It plastered his dark hair against his skull, dripping inside the collar of his old black leather bomber jacket.

The dog trotted at his heels, shooting wary glances at the flashing sky, skittering nervously at the quick rumble of thunder. Harry hoped Mallory Malone would make it through the thunderstorms that had plagued the area all day, but he wouldn't blame her if she canceled. It was a bitch of a night.

The bell on Ruby's glass-paneled door jangled as he pushed inside. The small café was jammed, every booth and Formica-topped table taken. There were a couple of cops and some regular locals he recognized, plus a few strays. The plate-glass windows above the red-checkered curtains were steamed, shutting out the miserable night; and the smell of hot coffee and fried food and chicken gravy hovered permanently over the room, like smog over L.A. A couple of matronly waitresses in red and white aprons and wilting caps maneuvered laden trays skillfully between the scarred red vinyl banquettes, and blue cigarette smoke wreathed to the nicotine-yellow ceiling.

Squeeze shook himself, scattering a waterfall of raindrops over Harry's fraying Levi's, then sat on his haunches, sniffing the air eagerly.

Grabbing a paper napkin, Harry mopped the water from his face and the inside of his collar, then tried to catch the waitress's eye.

"Hey, Doris," he called as she hurried back behind the counter. "How long for a booth?"

She shrugged. "Ten, fifteen maybe."

He grabbed her arm. "I need a guarantee on that, sweetheart." He smiled at her. She was plump and fiftyish and harassed, and he had known her since she was plump and forty and had time to flirt. Time had taken its toll, but they were still good friends.

"You bringing a hot date to Ruby's tonight, cheapskate?" she asked, raising a painted eyebrow.

"It's business, Doris. Just business. But it's a woman and I don't want to keep her waiting."

She grinned. "I always did like a guy with manners. I'll make sure you have the booth in the far corner, even if I have to kick those guys outta there." She sniffed, glancing at the wet dog. "Smells like a farmyard in here," she added as she walked away.

She returned a couple of minutes later carrying a dish of meat. Squeeze did an eager little dance on his hind legs.

"Every dog deserves steak once in a while,"

she said, setting the dish down in the corner. "Even a smelly hound like you."

"You spoil him, Doris. Besides, he just had his dinner. He's going to get fat."

"Yeah. I always liked fat men and fat dogs. And that leaves you out, detective. All muscle and no squeeze." Laughing at her own joke, she shouldered her tray and marched determinedly toward the corner booth.

"Hey, you guys," Harry heard her say loudly, "you gonna sit here all night or what? There's paying customers waiting for this table."

He laughed, and then his cellular phone beeped. Turning away from the noisy room, he pressed it to his ear. "Jordan."

"Detective, where the hell is this Ruby's?" Mallory Malone sounded irate. "The limo driver has never heard of it."

He grinned. "Everybody who's anybody in Boston knows exactly where Ruby's is, Ms. Malone. Put him on the phone, I'll give him directions."

She did not laugh or even say good-bye, or see you in a little while, or anything remotely sociable. Instead the driver came on the line and Harry gave him the directions. By the time he'd finished, Doris had the guys in the booth counting out their money while she stood, arms folded, watching them. Two minutes later they were shouldering past him to the door and Doris was clearing the table.

Harry hated to think of what might have happened if he had kept Ms. "Star" Malone waiting. He edged into the booth, his back to the wall so he could see her come in. Squeeze slid under the table out of the way — and his big head sank onto his paws as he prepared for a snooze.

Harry went over what he knew about Mallory Malone. Surprisingly, for such a public personality, it wasn't much. Just that she was originally from Oregon and had attended Washington State University where she had majored in journalism. After a few jobs in small-town radio and TV, she had become a weather girl on a Seattle station. From there she had been picked up by a network and groomed as a newscaster; then she became a morning anchorwoman, and now she had her own successful show.

There had been one marriage, to a rich Wall Street broker. But that hadn't lasted long. Her hours were different from his and he said she was consumed by her work.

"Mallory has dedicated her life to TV," he had told the press bitterly. "I hope it keeps her warm in bed at night." There were no children.

As he watched, the door swung open and Mallory Malone stepped inside. She glanced around, her eyebrows raised, as though she were wondering if she could possibly be in the right place.

Harry slid quickly from the booth and loped toward her. "Ms. Malone."

Her head swung around and their eyes met. He hadn't realized from TV that hers were such a deep blue, nor that her lashes were so long. When she lowered them and looked down at his outstretched hand, she looked unexpectedly shy. She was smartly dressed in a gray cashmere sweater and skirt with a red jacket, and her golden hair was beaded with glittering raindrops. She looked as out of place in Ruby's as a tropical flower in Alaska. And she had cold hands.

As she shook Harry's hand, Mal thought uncomfortably that she was overdressed in her cashmere, while Jordan looked scruffily at home in his faded jeans and the beat-up jacket. He was younger than she had expected and, damn it, he was attractive. His rain-wet dark hair was plastered to his narrow skull, his gray eyes were penetrating as they looked into hers, and his firm mouth looked sexy. He had at least a day-old black stubble and looked way too sure of himself. Disconcerted, she removed her hand.

"Detective Jordan," she said coldly. "It took my driver half an hour to find this place."

"I'm sorry, though it's really not that hard."

Antagonism crackled between them. She glanced disparagingly at the counter with its mirrored display of pies and chocolate cake; at the steamy little kitchen and the cracked red vinyl banquettes and the waitresses slinging hash and fried eggs and burgers and cholesterol.

She raised a superior eyebrow. "Slumming, Detective Jordan?"

Harry gritted his teeth. What the hell did she expect, Le Cirque? "I'm sorry it's not up to your standards, ma'am. But it *is* close to the precinct house, and I *am* on duty." He shrugged, "Besides, cops can't be choosers, with what they earn. All the guys eat here."

Her blue eyes narrowed. "Most cops, Jordan. But not *rich* cops."

Harry knew he was in trouble. She hated Ruby's, she hated cops, and she hated rich cops even more. He wondered how she knew — then he guessed it was the same way she had known his unlisted home number. She made it her business to know exactly who she was interviewing, whether it was on TV or not.

Heads turned in recognition as he led her to the table at the back, but she seemed unaware that there were other people in the place. As she slid into the booth opposite him, her foot encountered the soft bulk of the dog. Startled, she peeked underneath, then a sudden smile lit up her face.

Harry stared at her, dazzled. It was as though somebody had switched her on.

"Say hello to the lady, Squeeze," he instructed, and the dog, true to his name, squeezed out from between their knees. He sat next to Mallory, then raised his right paw politely.

"Oh, *cute*." She threw Harry a for-God's-sake glance. But she took the paw and patted the dog, murmuring sweet nothings to it.

"Back, Squeeze," he commanded, and the dog slunk obediently under the table again. He rested his head on Harry's shabby suede Paraboots, waiting for him to make his next move.

Her eyes met Harry's across the cigarette-scarred Formica table. "Isn't Squeeze an odd name for a dog? Shouldn't he be called Rover or Fido or something?"

"He's called Squeeze because he can squeeze out of any place. As he proved when he was just a pup. You name it, he squeezed out of it. Under the backyard fence, out of a car window, out of my bedroom at night. I thought about calling him Houdini, but then I thought, nah, too fancy. Squeeze is better."

She nodded, agreeing with him, and her chrysanthemum crop of blond hair, sequined with raindrops, fluttered like petals across her smooth brow.

Harry dragged his eyes from her and passed her a grease-spotted plastic menu. "What'll you have? I can recommend the ham steak and home fries."

She threw a quick glance at the heaping plates being passed over the counter. "A beer will do just fine."

Beer did not seem her style; he would have thought she would go for coffee — black no sugar — but he guessed shrewdly that she knew when to play at being one of the guys.

He signaled Doris and ordered two beers. Doris's jaw dropped when she saw his companion. "Two beers?" she demanded, astonished. "Ya should be buyin' this lady champagne. Cheapskate."

Mal laughed as Doris winked at her. "Us women gotta stick together," Doris said, heading to the counter. She was back in a flash with the beers and her order pad.

"Could ya just put your autograph on here, Mal?" she asked, thrilled. "Otherwise my kids are not gonna believe it when I tell 'em who was in Ruby's tonight. Aw hell," she added resignedly, as Mal signed her name with practiced ease, "they're not gonna believe me, anyways. They'll think I just made it up."

"But you and I will know you didn't." Mal smiled up at her.

"Yeah. And that's what counts. Thanks, Mal, I appreciate it. And while you're at it, don't let this hunk give ya the run-around. I always tell him he's all muscle and no brains."

There was laughter lurking in Mal's blue eyes as she took a sip of her Bud Light. Then she slipped off her red jacket and looked squarely at Harry.

"Okay, Jordan," she said, suddenly all business, "you're on."

"I feel like I'm auditioning for the show," he said uneasily.

"You may be. So get on with it."

He told her the facts about the murders and that there had been no connection between the three young women — they had not come from the same towns or even from the same states. They had not known each other. They had not lived near each other. They had not attended the same colleges.

"These were not random killings," he said. "This guy is precise. He's an organized killer. He knew exactly what he was doing. I think he knew where his victims lived and their daily routine, what times their classes were, and when they were likely to be alone."

Mal's eyes widened, and a little shiver ran down her spine. "You mean he *stalked* them?"

"I believe he did."

"That's terrible," she said soberly. "A maniac on the loose around all these college kids. He can just take his pick. Don't you have any line on him at all?"

"Forensics is working on scene-of-crime evidence — fibers, hairs, semen. We'll have the DNA in a couple of weeks, and I'm certain it will link him to the two previous attacks. And the students are aware of the danger now. They've been warned not to wander around campus after dark. The schools have escort services to walk young women back to their dorms. It'll help for a while."

"You think he'll strike again?"

"I'm certain of it. The FBI's Behavioral Science Unit has a psychological profile. They say we're looking for a guy with a deep psychosis against women. Cutting off their hair is symbolic — he's divesting them of their femininity. Rape proves his power over them, and the slitting of the wrists probably brings him to a climax he can never otherwise reach. For him, it's probably the ultimate moment of power. The women are helpless, they feel pain — they are dying while he lives."

Her horrified eyes met his. "Oh, my God."

He nodded grimly. "So now you see why we have to catch him before he strikes again. From his pattern I'd guess he'll take his time — perhaps a couple of months. He'll survey the scene, pick out his victim, trail her, maybe even break into her house, get the feel of her, the scent of her. Like an animal stalking its prey. He's methodical. That's why he's been so successful."

"Why do men do these things?"

Harry shrugged. "Studies show that all murderers of this type come from dysfunctional homes — drug abuse, alcohol, criminal activities, you name it. There's often mental illness in the family, and they probably suffered serious emotional and physical abuse in childhood. Usually the mothers dominated them, demeaned them, systematically emasculated them. In turn, they become sexually dysfunctional adults, unable to sustain a mature, consensual relationship with another adult."

"You think this is what happened to our killer?"

"I wish I knew." Harry ran his hands wearily through his still-wet hair. It stuck up spikily, and Mal thought interestedly that he looked as though he'd just stepped out of the shower.

"The public always thinks a murderer looks like a monster," he said. "But the fact is, mostly he looks like any guy on the street. The FBI profile says our killer probably lives a 'normal' life. Meaning he is a man with a deep psychosis able to put up a facade of normality. He lives alone, in a house rather than an apartment because he needs privacy for his comings and goings. He's of neat appearance and orderly in his daily life. He holds down a decent job, white collar rather than blue. He might even be from a higher social level. He carries out his job well, has no friends, and is obsessively tidy."

"So we're not looking for a freak or a down-and-out vagrant roaming the streets. We're looking for a regular guy, a man his neighbors and co-workers think quite normal. No different from you or any other man in Boston."

"A needle in a haystack," he agreed.

"It's lucky you managed to get the photofit."

Harry slipped the picture from the manila

envelope. "One other thing. The last victim, Summer Young. Before she died, she managed to tell us two details. That he had dark staring eyes. And smooth hands."

"So he's definitely not a manual worker."

"It's unlikely."

"Did she say anything else?"

"Yeah. She called him a bastard. Those were her dying words."

Shaken, Mal looked away from him. She took a sip of the beer.

She studied the picture for a long minute, and Harry studied her. He liked the way her eyelashes curled, sweetly, at the tips.

"This is taken from the description of the two fishermen?" she asked at long last.

"Yes. They caught him in their flashlight for a second before he took off. But a police artist enhanced the eyes to match Summer's memory of him."

Mal's voice was colder than the beer. "I'm afraid it's not much to go on, Detective Jordan. It's not accurate. And it's certainly not enough to base a national TV program on. I'm sorry, but I can't help you."

Picking up her jacket and purse, she slid out of the banquette.

Harry stared at her, stunned. One minute she had been ready to get out there on TV and save other young women from a terrible fate. The next she had slammed the door in his face.

"Wait just a minute." His voice was harsh. Under the table Squeeze raised his head and growled softly.

Harry leaped to his feet. She turned away, but he grabbed her shoulder. "What happened?"

"What do you mean?" He let go of her and she thrust her arms hurriedly into her jacket, avoiding his eyes.

"One minute you're hot for the story. The next you're not. I'd like to know why."

She shrugged. "I let you tell your story, detective. I listened. I made a decision. That's the way I do things. Rejection is not sweet, Harry Jordan, I understand that."

She picked up her purse, still avoiding his eyes. "Nothing personal, of course." Then she strode past the cracked red vinyl booths, out of the diner, and into the waiting limo.

10

Mal stared determinedly out the rain-streaked windows at the passing scenery, willing herself not to think about it. On the flight back to La Guardia, she read four long articles in the latest *Vanity Fair*, though if you had asked her later, she would have been unable to tell you a thing about them.

The sight of her own front door had never been so welcome. She closed it behind her and leaned against it, her heart thudding as though she had just run five blocks.

Her housekeeper had left the lamps lit and she glanced gratefully around her peaceful home. Kicking off her shoes, she padded through the hallway to her bedroom.

The crisp cotton sheets were already turned down and the enormous French antique bed was puffy with pillows and covered with a soft cashmere throw. She could hardly wait to crawl into it.

She unhooked her gray skirt and stepped out of it, then tugged the sweater over her head and flung it onto the pale-carpeted floor. Her pantyhose and underwear followed in a little trail as she walked to the rose-marble bathroom.

She found a match and lit the lilac-scented candles amid the ferns and greenery surrounding the tub, then turned on the faucets. Leaning on the cool marble sink, she peered at herself in the mirror. She was shocked to find she looked so normal. She still looked like Mallory Malone, star investigative reporter with her own successful prime-time show.

She climbed into the tub and lay back in the soothing warmth of the water, her eyes closed, waiting for the familiar scent of lilacs to transport her back to a memory she still treasured, to the one moment of perfect happiness she could remember. But tonight the magic wasn't working.

She climbed wearily from the tub and wrapped a fluffy white towel around her. She looked in the mirror again.

Her own eyes stared back at her, dark with panic. She had forgotten to take off her makeup. Quickly, she went through the familiar nightly ritual: cleanser, toner, moisturizer, a little cream under the eyes. She was on automatic pilot.

She brushed her hair, then walked naked to the enormous closet. Still chilled, she put on a gray sweatshirt and a pair of white socks. She turned and stared at herself in the full-length mirror. It was as though the light had gone out inside her. And she was Miss Nobody again.

Her head drooped as she trailed desolately

from the bedroom into the kitchen. She put water in the kettle and waited, motionless, for it to come to a boil. She fixed her favorite wild berry tea, but this time she did not even think about the lemon pound cake.

Carrying the mug carefully, she walked back to the bedroom and placed it on the silver tray on the night table, then climbed into bed. She sank thankfully back into the comfort of the white pillows, switched on the TV set, and pressed the mute button.

Headline News flickered silently onto the screen. She sipped the tea and swallowed two Advil for her lurking headache, watching the world events listlessly.

After a while she turned out the lights. Shivering, she curled up in a fetal position, waiting for sleep to come and blot out her memories.

The comfortable bed seemed to be dragging her down, the soft pillows were stifling her, she was free-falling into a bottomless dark pit. . . .

With a terrified cry she shot upright. She flung off the covers and slid from the bed, shaking. Her throat was dry and little tremors rippled through her body. "Oh, God," she whispered, "oh, God, no."

She had not had the nightmare for a long time — she had thought it had finally gone, buried with all the rest of the bad things in the secret place in her mind, where she had banished it. But it was still there. *It was still there.*

Quickly, she turned on the bedside lamp, then the overhead lights, the bathroom lights and the closet. She ran through all the rooms, switching on every light, turning up every dimmer until the apartment blazed like a department store window at Christmas. She stared around, still trembling. There was no place for a ghost to hide now. She was in control again.

She went back to the bedroom and took a suitcase from the closet. Hurriedly, she began to fill it. Just simple things — workout stuff, sweatshirts, sneakers.

When she had finished, she looked at the bedside clock. It was two thirty. She would fax the spa in Tucson and tell them to expect her. That left three and a half hours to kill before she could call the airlines for a reservation on the earliest flight out. Three and a half hours before she could run away from Harry Jordan — and from her past.

At the same time, two thirty A.M., Harry was in the gym at the Moonlightin' Club. He had played a lengthy game of basketball and then worked out for forty-five minutes. He gave one final heave on the 160-pound overhead lift of the Nautilus machine, held it, then lowered it smoothly back into place. Sweat trickled down his neck into his tangled dark chest hair.

Watching him, Rossetti sighed. "I left a soft bed and a warm woman to come here and find you, Prof. What's with you? You have dinner with Mallory Malone, and you don't take calls anymore? You too good for us regular cops now, or what?"

Harry toweled off the sweat. "I had a lot on my mind."

"Me too, remember? You were putting my career on the line tonight with Ms. Malone. You don't show up, you don't call —"

Harry strode past him, heading for the showers. Rossetti followed.

Harry stripped, turned on the shower, and stood under the spray, his head tilted back and his eyes closed.

"What kind of excuse is that?" Rossetti complained. "You've got a lot on your mind. And I don't, is that it? I thought it was the two of us — the two Musketeers — searching for a killer. I guess it's the three Musketeers, now that Malone's in charge."

Harry shook the water from his eyes and looked at the irate detective. "Wrong," he said. "Mallory Malone declined to help us."

Rossetti's long jaw dropped. "She did?"

"She did." Harry stepped from the shower and dried off. "She said there wasn't enough information to build a TV program on. And that the photo-fit wasn't accurate."

"And how the hell would she know?"

Harry shrugged. He pulled on a pair of dark

blue boxers and stepped into his Levi's. "Maybe she's got second sight, I don't know. All I know is, she was hot to help and then she wasn't."

Rossetti glared suspiciously at him. "You come on to her or what?"

Harry laughed as he tucked in his shirt. "No, I did not make a pass at her. She is Ms. Frosty Freeze personified. Most of the time."

"What about the rest of the time?"

Harry buttoned his shirt, thinking about it. "The rest of the time she was kind of sparky but nice," he said finally.

"*Nice?*"

"Yeah, you know, a nice girl. Woman," he corrected himself, though now that he thought about it, there was something girlish under her career-woman facade. Perhaps it was the eyelashes. "She liked Squeeze."

Rossetti grinned. "The way to a guy's heart — it works every time. 'Love me, love my dog.' "

"It didn't quite get that far, Rossetti. Meanwhile, she pissed me off so bad, I had to come here and work it off. Otherwise I might have ended up punching someone."

"Frustration, huh?"

Harry flung a weary arm across Rossetti's elegantly tailored shoulders as they walked back through the gym to the lobby. The club was buzzing with people coming and going and the café area in the lobby was crowded.

They grabbed some coffee, said hellos and good-byes, and pushed through the heavy swing doors. They stood on the steps sipping their coffee, staring into the rainy night.

"You got it in one, Rossetti," Harry said.

The windshield wipers blinked away the heavy rain as he drove the Jag back through the quiet city to Louisburg Square. It was three A.M. and he was exhausted, but he knew he wouldn't sleep.

Squeeze recognized the familiar sound of the Jag's engine and the solid slam of its door. He was waiting in the front hall, tail wagging, eyes alert.

Harry slipped on the leash and stepped out again into the rain.

"This is a quickie, old fella," he muttered, head down, avoiding the puddles. "Sorry about tonight, but I needed to be alone."

He grinned at himself — apologizing to the dog as though to a neglected wife. "Aw, what the hell, Squeeze, what I need is a drink. And what you need is a bone." Hauling on the leash, he dragged the reluctant dog back up the street and in out of the rain.

He strode into the kitchen, fed the dog the bone, and took a fresh bottle of Jim Beam from the cupboard. Pouring himself a slug, he added ice, then wandered into the sitting room and turned on the lamps, dimming them to a faint glow. He put Neil Young's *Harvest Moon*

on the CD player and settled back in his favorite old leather chair that was as beat up as
his favorite old leather jacket.

Sipping the bourbon, he savored it slowly
on his tongue, then put his head back and let
the music fill his head. The track was "Unborn
Legend." It was a song that always reminded
him of his ex-wife, Jilly. But more than that,
it described the way he'd felt about her when
he'd met her. And even though he told himself it was over, passé, gone, that what he'd
thought it was had really never been, the song
still brought the ache back to the bruise in his
heart.

Squeeze dropped the bone onto the magnificent eighteenth-century silk Bokhara rug at
Harry's feet, then settled down, chewing contentedly. The rug had belonged to his grandmother. "Ah, what the hell. It's only a rug,"
Harry said resignedly. "It's meant to be used.
Before it became an antique, probably half a
dozen babies peed on it, and maybe a few cats
threw up on it as well."

He switched his thoughts to Mal Malone.
He ran his meeting with her like a reel of film
in his head, from the beginning, when she had
given him that first challenging look. He re-ran
her intelligent interest in the case and her horror when he'd told her what the killer had
done. He re-ran the image of her looking at
the photo-fit.

There had been no flicker of expression as

she looked at the face of the killer. No distaste, no horror — not even interest, for God's sake.

And that was what was wrong. Mallory Malone had been interested at first, all right. He had seen it. Then when she had looked at the picture her face had become immobile. But her eyes, as she handed it back to him, had not. There had been a hint of something there. It wasn't recognition, or even fear.

For a fleeting instant, Mallory Malone had looked *haunted.*

He sipped the bourbon thoughtfully. He thought Ms. Malone was hiding something and he wondered what. Could it be the pattern of the killings? Or the identity of the young victims? There was definitely something. She had done a good job of disguising her reaction — but then, she was an actress, or at least a woman with a public face. He thought she was everything he liked least: spiky, tough, a hard-bitten career woman all the way.

Then he remembered the smile that had lit up her face when she'd seen Squeeze. He remembered the raindrops glittering like sequins in her hair and the unexpected blueness of her eyes. Perhaps he had got her wrong after all.

He heaved a weary sigh. "Ms. Malone is a woman with secrets," he told the dog. "She knows more than she's telling. And I intend to find out exactly what that is."

Squeeze lifted his head and looked at him. He wagged his tail and returned to the bone.

" 'Love me, love my dog,' " Harry repeated, smiling. Glancing at his watch, he decided to call her in the morning. Which was only a couple of hours away by now.

11

The man drove the gunmetal-gray Volvo carefully around the corner. He was late getting home this evening. He didn't like that, but it couldn't be helped. There had been a problem.

The treelined street was pleasant, with large well-kept houses set back on velvet-green lawns. Expensive automobiles were parked in the driveways, and gardeners toiled for seasonal perfection, replacing dying spring bulbs with fresh early summer flowers.

His home was at the very end opposite a vacant lot, hidden from its neighbor by a thick bushy screen of leylandia. Leylandia wasn't as beautiful a shrub as he would have liked, but it had the advantage of being dense and fast-growing, and that had taken precedence over beauty. The rest of his garden, though, was a showplace, his pride and joy.

He swung the Volvo up the driveway and pulled into the garage. He switched off the engine and pressed the remote, waiting until the garage door was fully closed before he got out of the car. Taking a red box-file from the seat, he slammed the door and locked it.

The locks on the back door of the house were expensive and complicated. There were two of them: a Chubb deadbolt and a Yale mortise lock. He took out the keys, unlocked each one, stepped inside, then turned and re-locked them. He pushed two enormous bolts into place, one into the floor, the other into the wall.

As he walked through the tidy white-tiled laundry room into the kitchen, he glanced sharply around, his dark eyes taking in every detail. It was exactly as he had left it.

He strode into the hall and examined the front door, which had the same arrangement of locks and bolts. They were firmly in place.

Satisfied with his security arrangements, he went to the wood-paneled study and placed the box-file on the desk. He walked away — then, irritated, turned back and realigned the pile of books waiting for his attention. He straightened the pens in the pewter containers, putting the red ones together, then the blue and then the black. He couldn't work unless everything was neat and precisely arranged. "Ship-shape," his father, a navy man, used to call it.

At least "a navy man" was what he grandiosely told people his father had been, and it was partly the truth. But even as a young lieutenant, his father's drinking had been a problem. There were "incidents": barroom brawls, fights in foreign ports, drunkenness on duty. He was warned. Then he had gone too far — he'd beaten up a woman, a prostitute in San Diego, and almost killed her. His father had been dishonorably discharged.

He was six years old at the time. His mother had told him the sorry story later, though of course she'd never let on to their neighbors. She kept it a family secret. Meanwhile, her husband staggered from job to job as a traveling salesman, eternally on the road and eternally in the saloon.

It wasn't the only family secret.

The boy had been sleeping in his mother's bed since he was out of diapers. He had always hated it — she was a big woman with large floppy breasts that she still offered to him to suckle every night, even after he was weaned and no longer wanted her milk. And then shamefully, she kept offering them to him all the time he was growing up.

"Go on, do it," she would urge him, thrusting her giant brown nipple into his reluctant mouth. "Relieve me of the burden of all this milk. It's all your fault anyway — you caused me to swell up like this And it's your fault your father no longer wants me."

The musky female scent of her would envelop him as he felt her fumbling under her nightdress. She moaned and trembled.

"What are you doing," he'd demanded, terrified, taking his mouth from her, but she simply forced his head back again.

"Do it, just do it," she ordered. And when he pulled away, she smacked him viciously

97

across the face. "Do as I say, or I'll have the hide off you," she hissed, shuddering with excitement when he obeyed. And then she had put her hands on him too.

But he didn't want to think about that.

His bedroom was as immaculate as the rest of his house: a plain beige carpet, a plain wooden headboard, and glass-topped wooden night tables. The bed was a single — the very idea of sleeping next to someone nauseated him. This room was his alone.

He removed his tweed jacket and hung it neatly in the closet. He took off his gray flannel pants and hung them up too. He removed his shirt and his jockey shorts and tossed them into the laundry basket. Then he took a long shower.

Afterward, he dried off and inspected himself, naked, in the mirror. He was short and stocky, with big shoulders from early years of weight training. Unlike the thick hair on his head, which was toned to a blackish-brown at a downtown Boston salon every month, his chest hair was gray. And when he needed a shave, so was the stubble on his chin. When he had first started graying at the age of twenty-six, he had thought it looked quite attractive. *Distinguished* was the word he had used about himself. But he had soon been forced to the conclusion that premature grayness meant premature aging. He had been coloring it ever since.

He looked nothing like the photo-fit. He smiled at the irony of it. Except for the eyes, of course — but then, he always wore contacts when he was "hunting."

Picking up his heavy-rimmed glasses, he put them on, then brushed his hair, parting it precisely on the left. Naturally, when he had pulled off the ski mask, his thick coarse hair had stood on end, which was how it looked in the photo-fit. Not smooth and sleek the way he always wore it, glossy with just a touch of old-fashioned pomade.

The rest of the picture had been meaningless except for the broad strokes: the narrow face, the heavy brows. But the mouth was all wrong, and so was the jaw. He laughed out loud, just thinking about it. And about how much cleverer he was than the cops. They would never catch him — not in a million years.

Hunting was the word he preferred to *stalking,* which was what the police called it. He was a huntsman seeking a worthy prey. It took him a while because he was picky, and besides he enjoyed the search. He knew exactly what he was looking for. Then came the "chase," and the perverse excitement in the fact that the woman was unaware that he knew her almost as intimately as she knew herself. And that was the time he struck. The perfect moment.

He pulled on a pair of black cotton sweatpants and a white polo shirt and sneakers, then strolled back down the hall. He stopped outside the locked door. He stared consideringly at it for a long time, but he would not go in there tonight. There was no need.

Back downstairs in the kitchen he opened the refrigerator. He had already eaten dinner at a small bistro in town, one of several he enjoyed. They had come to know him because he was a regular, and they never minded that he was always alone rather than a couple, which would have meant more money in their cash register. He always drank one glass of red wine, always ordered mashed potatoes, and always overtipped, guaranteeing himself good service on his next visit.

He inspected the refrigerator's contents. There was a large bottle of Smirnoff, a couple of bottles of soda and three lemons. And a small narrow steel knife in a plastic case.

He took out the Smirnoff and poured himself a tumblerful. He cut a slice of lemon and put it in the vodka. Taking a sip, he walked back into his study and sat down at the desk.

Taking a framed photograph from the top drawer, he set it in front of him. The glass was shattered, but it was still possible to see the woman's face: fleshy, stern, unsmiling. He lifted his glass in a toast.

He said, "To the mother. Who made all this possible." Then he drank the vodka in one go.

Unclipping the fastener on the box-file, he

took out the papers. They were press reports on the rape and killing of Summer Young. He read each one avidly, spending a long time on those that gave details of the discovery, smiling again at the useless photo-fit.

Later, he took half a dozen Polaroids from a locked drawer and spread them out on the desk. Then he returned to the kitchen and refilled his glass.

Back at the desk, he stared at the photographs. They were all of young women. He glanced quickly up at the mother's picture, feeling her eyes on him. He reached up and slammed it facedown onto the desk, cursing as a shard of glass cut into his thumb. Sweeping the mother's image into the drawer, he put his bloody thumb into his mouth and sucked on it.

The Polaroids had been taken from the car and the girls were unaware they were being photographed. In some, they were walking toward him along the street; in others, they were walking away.

He sat for a long time, picking them up, studying the details of each one, comparing them. Finally he took a red marker and made an *X* on the girl of his choice.

He put the papers and the Polaroids back into the drawer and locked it. Then he put the file away, next to two others, in the wooden cabinet in the corner. *Along with the files of those who had gone before.*

Whistling, he got a pair of pruning shears from the garage and walked out into his back garden. It was as immaculate as the house: every plant was neatly in its space, everything was weeded and cared for. He bent over his roses, snipping a stem here and there.

He was just like any other suburban man on a fine early May evening. Except for the locked room in his house. And the slight bulk of Summer Young's underpants in his pocket. Every now and then he stopped what he was doing and slid his hand in there. Just to touch them, remembering. For the moment, it was enough.

12

Malmar Productions' Madison Avenue offices were awake and bustling with activity at eight thirty the following Monday morning, when Mal breezed in wearing black biker's shorts, a black baseball cap and a white sweatshirt with a Tucson logo on the front.

Beth Hardy was on the phone. She swung her chair around and looked Mal up and down, her eyebrows raised. "What happened to you? You look radiant!"

Mal laughed. "Twelve hundred calories a day. A four-mile walk at six every morning. Abs, buns, and thighs workout at nine. Funky aerobics at cleven. A little yoga stretching at noon" -- she paused and struck an athletic pose — "and you too can look like this."

Beth sighed regretfully. She was petite and rounded, with long dark hair and an ample bosom. "Not even starvation and twelve-mile hikes would change these boobs," she said gloomily. "The hell with them. All I want is to look good in clothes."

"Most women want to look good *out* of their clothes."

"Yeah, well not this one. I'd settle for being a *Vogue* waif."

Mal laughed. "Your husband would miss you if you changed."

Beth rolled her expressive brown eyes. "Husbands." Then she laughed too. "I guess you get what God gives you, and you just have to make the most of it."

"Meanwhile you look great. I love the suit."

Beth was wearing a cream fitted jacket and skirt that enhanced her curves. "Calvin. Bloomie's sale last year. It's our anniversary. Rob's taking me out on the town — dinner, champagne, all that romantic stuff." She laughed again, and Mal could see how happy she was.

"How many years is it now?"

"Seven and counting. We got married right out of college. I guess we're going for the record."

"Lucky you," Mal said quietly, meaning it.

"I've called a staff meeting at nine," Beth said. "But I'll get my stuff together and bring you up to date on Tuesday's program first. Then if you have any problems with it, we can hash them out at the meeting. As you know, the next six weeks are set. We can go through them, and research can update you on their progress."

"Okay." Mal turned and headed toward her own office.

"Oh, by the way — Detective Harry Jordan called. Several times. He didn't seem to believe me when I told him you'd gone away. I guess he didn't think you're entitled to a vacation. I told him you'd be back today. I also had Research find out his life story — the report's on your computer."

Mal paused, her hand on her office door. "Did he say what he wanted?"

"Yeah. Your home phone number." Beth looked curiously at her. "So? Are you going to tell me what happened at that meeting in Boston?"

Mal shrugged and turned away. "A wild-goose chase. That's all it was. Detective Jordan didn't have his act together."

Beth nodded speculatively. "Then this is a personal matter? Just between you and the detective, huh?"

Mal popped her head back around the door. "Of course not," she said indignantly. "I have absolutely nothing to say to the man."

Her office was large and light, with floor-to-ceiling windows that gave a bird's-eye view of the traffic surging down Madison. The Italian steel and rosewood desk was empty of papers, though that would change when her staff arrived for the production meeting at nine. Chairs were arranged around the oval rose-wood conference table at one end of the room, and juice and coffee and a platter of low-fat brownies waited on the steel console.

She sat at the desk, took off the baseball cap and ran her fingers through her hair, thinking about Harry Jordan. She had behaved stupidly. He must have thought it odd, her walking out on him like that. She poured herself a glass of juice. Jordan had caught her off-guard, that was all.

As the staff straggled in for the meeting, she resolved to put the whole incident and Harry Jordan out of her mind. After all, she would never see him again.

Her day was a busy one. At the meeting she went over the script for tomorrow's show, plotting out the sequences and making several changes. She added a follow-up to the previous week's program about the billionaire, which had received sensational press. They had new film of his grand country house and the infamous Jacobean staircase, plus paparazzi stills of the old boy jumping naked from his yacht into the blue Mediterranean in the company of three naked young women.

Mal grinned at Beth's comment on the stills: "It's a good thing he has money, because the rest of his attributes wouldn't get him anywhere."

After the meeting Mal changed into a pale gray pantsuit for lunch with the network president at The Four Seasons, where they discussed her future plans. "If it's working for you, it's surely working for us," he told her, thrilled with the ratings, especially for last week's program.

From there she went to the studio for another production meeting that took longer than she expected, after which she went to the gym to work out for an hour.

It was six o'clock by the time she returned, and except for Beth the office was deserted.

Beth finished applying her lipstick and perfume. She smoothed down her skirt, smiling at Mal. "How do I look?"

"Great. In fact, you look lovely. Rob is a lucky man."

"I tell him that every morning when he wakes up."

"And does he tell you that every night before he goes to sleep?"

"Among other things." She winked, laughing. "Well, I'm out of here. Anything you need before I go?"

Mal shook her head, but she looked wistful.

Beth hesitated. "What are your plans?"

"I just got back. I guess I'll have an early night, catch up on some sleep."

Their heads swung around in unison as the telephone rang. Mal glared at it. "Go," she told Beth. "You're out of here, remember?"

"I never could resist a ringing phone. I mean, it might be really important; vital; life or death." She picked it up. "Malmar Productions."

"Hi, Beth," Harry Jordan said.

Her eyebrows climbed into her hair, and she mouthed "Harry Jordan" to Mal, who shook her head.

"No," she mouthed back.

"An A for persistence, detective," Beth said, smiling.

"Thanks for the grade, but what I'd really like is to speak to Ms. Malone."

"Hm, well, she's — she's busy." She looked at Mal, who was nodding encouragingly. "I guess," she added, sounding doubtful.

Mal could hear his laugh booming over the phone. "I'm glad she's back. Tell her I missed her."

"He says he missed you," Beth said, covering the mouthpiece with her hand.

Mal rolled her eyes and heaved a sigh.

"You might also tell her that I'm downstairs in the lobby, and I'd surely like to see her."

Mal shook her head again. *"Why not?"* Beth whispered, but Mal ran her finger across her throat, frowning.

"Sorry, detective, she's just too tired. First day back at work and all that."

"I'll wait," he said firmly as Beth hung up.

She looked inquiringly at Mal. "So why not? I mean, the guy's only doing his job. What would it take just to give him the time of day, let him explain his case? Anyhow, he has a great voice. Sexy, I'd say."

Mal flung herself into the chair and propped her feet on the desk. She glared at Beth. "He's old, decrepit, and ugly. And you're going to be late," she said firmly. "Go on — don't keep your man waiting."

Beth sighed. She thought that, for a top TV

personality, Mal looked awfully lonely.

She swung round as the elevator pinged and a man stepped out. Her eyes widened as she took him in. He was tall and lean with dark hair and a day-old stubble. He was wearing a funky black leather jacket and beat-up Levi's that looked as though he had slept in them, and there was an air of confidence about him. He was very definitely appealing.

"Detective Jordan," she guessed.

"Beth Hardy. Glad to meet you. At last."

He held out his hand, and she shook it. "How did you get in here?"

He smiled at her, and she stared back at him, dazzled. "A detective's badge can get you in almost anywhere, Ms. Hardy."

Mal's voice was icy. "I'm surprised you didn't bring the dog along."

Harry gave her a cool look, noticing her long legs, tanned from the Arizona sun, the baseball cap, and the sneakers. She looked pretty good — casual and un-made-up.

"Squeeze isn't too good about flying. And I don't think New York City is his style."

"And what makes you think it's your style, detective?"

Beth glanced interestedly from one to the other. "I'm gone," she murmured, picking up her purse. "Nice meeting you, detective." Behind his back, she raised her eyebrows and made an approving face at Mal. "To die for," she mouthed.

She was still laughing as she waited for the elevator.

Mal didn't ask Harry to sit down, and he leaned lazily against the wall, his hands in his pockets, looking at her.

"You're just too pushy for a rich detective," she said frostily. "You should know when to take no for an answer. Especially from a lady."

"I don't give up easily, Ms. Malone," he said with a smile in his voice. "Actually, I came to invite you out to dinner. A personal invitation. Nothing to do with my work."

She threw him a skeptical glance. "My blue eyes get to you, huh?"

"That — and you like my dog."

Mal laughed. "You mean you're offering me a repeat at Ruby's?"

His eyes met hers — they were deep set and a beautiful pewter-gray. She could see every little dark fleck in them. She lowered her lashes, cutting him off.

"I know a little French place in the Village. I think it would suit Madame. Please, won't you join me?"

Maybe it was the *please* that suddenly made her say yes. Or his beautiful gray eyes. Or maybe because she felt lonely and he made her laugh. But she set a condition: "No business."

"I promise." He crossed his heart and looked sincere, and she laughed as she agreed to meet him at Bistro Arlette at eight thirty.

13

Remembering Harry's old leather jacket, Mal dressed down in simple black pants and a sweater.

She knew she had made a mistake as soon as she entered Arlette's. It was small and very chic, with tall arched windows and spare decor and interesting paintings on the walls. And Harry Jordan had dressed up.

He was waiting for her at the small bar, looking like a cross between Harrison Ford and John Kennedy in what she could have sworn was an Armani blazer, taupe linen pants, and a soft white shirt. He was even wearing a tie.

"I'm glad you came," he said, looking as though he meant it. "I was afraid you'd change your mind."

"Obviously we're not on the same wavelength," she said, irritated at being caught on the wrong foot. "Had I known, I would have dressed."

He sighed exaggeratedly. "I thought you would know Arlette's. It's the new in place."

"Sure. Like Ruby's."

He smiled teasingly at her as they were escorted to a table near the window. "Maybe next time we'll get it right. Sartorially speaking."

"Next time?" She took a seat and looked questioningly at him. "Aren't we getting a little ahead of ourselves?"

"I'm a great believer in advance planning."

Mal laughed, relenting. His eyes had a mischievous twinkle in them, and a smile lurked at the corner of his mouth.

Sitting opposite her, Harry thought she was the most attractive woman he'd ever seen — even though her nose had a definite bump in the middle, and her deep blue eyes were too wide set, and maybe her jaw was a little too round. But her mouth was generous, full-lipped, and vulnerable-looking, and she had a sort of a golden glow about her. He liked her cool energy and the intelligence in her eyes. And her sharpness. In fact, he liked the whole package. Even her ears, and he was particular about ears. Hers were beautiful. Small and set flat against her perfectly shaped head.

It was a pity she was being so cagy with him on the photo-fit. Otherwise he might enjoy himself.

He called the waiter and ordered champagne without consulting her. She raised her eyebrows in surprise. "If you hate it, I'll order something else," he said. "I just wanted you to try this. It's a small label I discovered in France, and it happens to be one of the best."

"What if I prefer a martini?"

"Then you'll have one."

"I see. You're a man who likes to take charge."

He put his elbows on the table, rested his chin on his fists. He leaned closer and looked into her eyes. "Only when I feel certain it's what the other person would like."

Mal matched him, propping her chin in her hands. Their eyes locked. She noticed his had darker rings around the pewter-gray. She thought he was attractive. It was a pity he was so cocky. Besides, she was sure he was still pursuing the photo-fit. She wanted nothing to do with it. Otherwise she might have fancied him.

She said challengingly, "So tell me, detective, why did you really ask me out?"

"I thought this would be a good opportunity for us to get to know each other."

She smiled a sly little Cheshire cat smile. "Better watch out. I might know more about you than you think. However, since you're such a take-charge guy, why don't you just order for both of us?"

His eyebrows rose in surprise. "That's very trusting."

"*Trust* is not a word that exists in my vocabulary."

He gave her a skeptical sideways look, but she just smiled. He signaled the waiter, gave him the order, then turned back to her.

" 'Detective' is a bit formal for two people

sharing a culinary experience," he said. "And besides, I'd hate anyone to think I was on official business. Why don't you call me Harry?"

The waiter poured the champagne, and she took a sip. She looked approvingly at him. "You certainly know your wines."

"Among other things," he agreed.

"Hmm, not exactly modest either, detective."

"Not about things I'm sure of. And it's Harry. Remember?"

She tilted her head, considering. "I'm not sure I can get used to calling you Harry. But then, I won't have to, since this will be our one and only *shared culinary experience,* as you so elegantly put it."

"I hate to think this might be our last meeting, as well as our first, Ms. Malone."

" 'Ms. Malone'?"

He raised an eyebrow. "Would you prefer 'ma'am'?"

She laughed. "I didn't know teasing came in the detective manifesto."

"It doesn't, but you haven't yet asked me to call you Mallory. Ms. Malone, ma'am."

She raised her glass in a toast. "Here's to you, Harald Peascott Jordan the Third. Scion of a wealthy upper-class family of eminent lawyers." Her blue eyes danced with mocking laughter as she looked at him. "Son of one of the greatest trial lawyers of his era. An expert

in courtroom interrogation, known for his ability to find a legal loophole that would get his
client off. Even though he and everybody else
knew his client was guilty as hell. *And* for his
brilliance at effecting plea bargains for those
he couldn't expect to get away with it."

Harry groaned. "Let's not drag out all the
family secrets."

She smiled wickedly at him. "But you,
Harry the Third, skipped the family tradition.
You went to Michigan State and became a
football great. An academic All-American
with a straight-A average. A star pick for the
pro-football recruits that year — an offer you
didn't accept." Her eyes met his curiously.
"Why, Harry? What happened?"

He shrugged and sipped his wine. "You
mean you don't know?"

"Even I cannot know a man's inner
thoughts, his personal reasoning. But I can
make an educated guess. Your father?"

Harry nodded. "He was getting older. He
was already in his forties when he married. By
the time I was at college, he was in his sixties.
He wanted to be sure things continued exactly
the same way they always had, even after he
was gone. So he did what he knew how to do
best: he plea-bargained with me.

" 'I'm getting old, Harry,' he said to me,
tugging at my heartstrings and my guilt. 'At
my age, you never know how much time there
is left. And remember, we have your mother

to think of — the continuity of her life — after I'm gone. I need to know the firm will be in your hands, safe in the family and not taken over by grave-robbers.' "

Harry smiled. "He meant his partners. He always thought they were waiting to step into his shoes, and I guess he was right. Anyhow, he told me to go to law school first. Then we'd see about the football.

" 'Don't think I'm not proud of you, son,' he said to me. 'What father wouldn't be proud to see his son score that winning touchdown against Notre Dame? Why, I cheered fit to bust along with the rest. But facts are facts, and I'm just not getting any younger. Face up to your responsibilities, Harry. Think of your mother.' "

"So you were a good boy and went to Harvard Law — and almost flunked out the first year. Probably in an effort to get back at your father."

He said, astonished, "Has a man no privacy, Malone?"

"Of course," she replied demurely. "But not when it's a matter of public record. You spent more time dating sophomores at Brown than you did at law school. You cracked up your Porsche twice, you frequented too many bars, and your grades were nonexistent. You were suspended."

Harry threw his hands up in despair. "This isn't exactly what a guy wants on a first date

116

— a rundown of all his youthful mistakes. Are you deliberately trying to undermine me?"

There was more than just curiosity in her eyes now. There was warmth and sympathy, just the way there was in her TV interviews, when her subjects suddenly got the feeling she really cared and spilled their guts to her.

"It's all right, Harry. You can tell me," she said gently. "I promise it's just between you and me."

He went along with her. "I wanted to go back, but it was too late — I'd burned my bridges. In the world of football, I was yesterday's news. There was already a new crop, younger, keener, fitter. *Better* than me. My father said nobody was sorrier than he was, but family came first and he was never a man to shirk responsibility. And he didn't expect his son to either."

Harry laughed as he told Mal exactly what his father had said about zipping up his pants.

"So you went back to law school?"

"I knew he was right. Opportunity knocks but once in the short sweet life of a professional athlete. It's now or never. When it comes, you grasp it, or suddenly a year or two has gone by and you're already too old, passed over in favor of the new crop. I graduated from law school and went to work for my father."

The waiter arrived. Mal's eyes grew round with pleasure as she looked at the plates of

117

salmon tartare served on top of tiny crisp potato cakes. Harry thought she looked like a little girl with a birthday cake.

"Taste it," he encouraged. "See if it's as good as it looks."

"Mmm." She rolled her eyes happily, her mouth full. "Better."

"I'm relieved to see you're human after all. I was beginning to think the Mal Malone we see on television was the real you."

"Perhaps she is." She wasn't about to explain herself to Detective Harry Jordan. She picked up on her theme again. "You lasted two years working for your father. And then you quit and became a cop. Why?"

Her bright blue eyes felt as though they were drilling into the back of his head, seeking out the truth from him. But behind the soft voice and appealing manner, he was aware that her mind was clear and razor-sharp; he guessed it was that combination that had made her such a success.

"Since you know so much, I assume you already know the reason."

After a pause she said, "What about your wife? Did you love her?"

"Jesus, Malone." He glared at her, shocked. "Of course I loved her. And if you want to know, it hurt like hell when she left. And why, may I ask, do you want to know?"

"Just checking that rich cops have feelings too."

118

"Like you, Malone?" he said coldly.

She grinned. "*Touché,* detective. Tell me about the Moonlightin' Club."

He had to laugh. He said admiringly, "How the hell did you find out about that? It's supposed to be a secret." Harry had bought and donated the gym anonymously — only a few of his superiors knew about it.

"It's my job to know things about people. I know you're in the process of fitting out a second gym in another area, this time with a swimming pool. And that you and some of the other cops give generously of your free time to help out." She looked seriously at him. "You did a wonderful thing, Harry. A lot of men wouldn't have considered spending that kind of money to help street kids."

He shrugged. "Other men don't see them on the streets every night the way I do. Somebody's got to help and I figured since I didn't earn the money, why not put some of it back where it came from?"

"Very noble," she said, meaning it.

"Oh sure, Saint Harry. I feel as though I'm on your show," he added, exasperated. "I think it's time we talked about you." He took her hand and turned it over, studying the lines. "Or do I have to read your palm?"

Mal eyed him uneasily — she was good at interviews, but not so good at giving answers. "There's nothing to tell. Just the usual format — small-town girl goes to college, gets job in

119

small-town TV station, becomes a weather girl, and is taken up by a network." She shrugged. "The rest is history."

"Hey, hey, hey." Harry held up his hand. "Slow down a minute. *What* small town? How about your family? Brothers and sisters? Boyfriends? Your marriage — and I demand equal time on this one. Come on, Malone, this is no fair exchange."

Mal's eyes met his briefly. In that second they had the same haunted look they'd had in Ruby's when she'd given him back the photo-fit picture.

"Forget it," she said. "That's all there is. I'm the least interesting woman on the planet."

Suddenly she looked different — lost and forlorn. Harry shook his head. He just didn't get it.

Then she tilted her chin and gave him that dazzling smile that lit up her face. "Just joking, Harry. Just joking."

The waiter removed their plates and they sat silently for a moment, looking at each other.

"So why the full psychological breakdown on me?" he asked. "I'm not likely to be on your show, though I can't figure out why. But I'm warning you, I'm still working on it."

She ran her fingers up and down the stem of her glass, then said softly, "Perhaps I was interested in what made a man like you tick.

What your motives might really be for asking me to dinner."

"And what about your motives for accepting my invitation?"

Tension crackled between them as their eyes locked. "I just wondered what you were really like," she said, looking innocent.

Harry ran his hand thoughtfully across the stubble that was already darkening his jaw. "Am I to understand it was just an *abstract* thought? Or are you thinking of getting to know me better, Malone?"

She gave him that cool little smile again. "Just joking, detective. I couldn't resist."

He sighed regretfully. "I was hoping it was sexual harassment."

He watched, amazed, as she tucked into her dinner. She looked as though she lived on fresh air and rosy apples, not real food. He said, "You eat as though you haven't had a square meal in a long time."

"I haven't. I've been on twelve hundred calories a day for the past week. And when I was a kid, I never had good food. Sometimes no food at all. I guess that's the reason I enjoy it now."

Finally she had revealed something about herself — a small chink in her protective armor. He said, "You surprise me. I imagined you came from the sort of nice home we all dream about. You know, with Mom in the kitchen cooking up great meals, Dad mowing the lawn or shooting baskets with his sons, taking his family fishing. You making cheerleader and homecoming queen, and all the guys competing to take you to the prom."

"It's a nice image." She sat back in her chair, her arms folded defensively over her chest. "Unfortunately, we are not all born with silver spoons in our mouths, like you, Harry Jordan."

"True, but neither one is anything to be ashamed of."

She gave a skeptical laugh. "And how would you know? You probably didn't even know what the wrong side of the tracks looked like until you became a cop."

"Is that where you lived then? On the wrong side of town?"

"I was discussing the matter in the abstract. It's my job to know how the other half lives."

"Mine too."

She glanced reflectively at him. "So what does a guy like you usually do on his nights off?"

"You know me through and through. Why don't you tell me?"

"You hit the night life — those little hole-in-the-wall salsa clubs you seem to like. You're a hot dancer, you're a wine connoisseur. You enjoy good food in charming little restaurants like Arlette's, and women find you attractive."

"We're back to that again."

She leveled that cool innocent look at him

122

one more time. "Funny how it keeps cropping up. Look, Detective Harry, I hate to break the spell between us, but I have to do the Cinderella act. I'm taping a show first thing in the morning, and I need to get some sleep."

"Pity. I thought I was just getting to know you."

"Is *that* what you thought?" She threw him a mocking glance over her shoulder as she headed for the ladies' room.

He shook his head, watching her weave gracefully through the tables. It was not what he thought. In fact he thought he didn't know much more about her now than he had when he came in here.

"You don't have to take me home," she said later, outside the restaurant, waiting for a cab.

"I always see a woman to her front door."

"Things have changed since your mother's day, detective. Women are independent now. They take cabs all by themselves."

He threw her an irritated glance. "You can say what you like, I was brought up to have good manners."

"Oh? A mama's boy?"

"Like the killer. Remember?"

"You promised no business," she reminded him soberly.

"I'm a man who keeps his promises."

The cab arrived. He held the door for her, then climbed in next to her. She didn't protest. She gave the driver the address, then sat quietly looking out the window. She wondered what it would be like, to be loved by a man like Harry Jordan. A man with old-fashioned good manners, a man who kept his promises. A man whose hard thigh she was much too aware of next to hers.

Harry could smell her perfume, soft and grassy. His eyes followed the antique moonstone pendant she wore to where it lay in between the soft curves of her breasts. He cleared his throat, breaking the silence. "Thank you for a delightful evening, Ms. Malone."

She gave him a long look. "It was a pleasure, Detective Jordan."

"Back to formality again," he shook his head sadly. "But then, you never did ask me to call you Mallory."

"I didn't, did I." Her blue eyes were guileless.

The cab pulled up at the curb and Harry got out and held the door for her. "You'll have to get used to my manners if we're ever going to do this again," he said.

She gave him that skeptical look but made no reply as they walked up the steps to her building.

"No nightcap, I guess?" he said regretfully. "You're taping that show early tomorrow."

"Right."

"So this is good night, then?"

"Good night, Detective Jordan."

124

Harry stood with his arms folded, watching her walk into the foyer. She stopped, hesitated for a moment, then turned and came back toward him.

"Tell me something, Harry. The time I called you on the phone — Exactly *why* were you panting?"

He ran a hand through his hair, smiling. "Truth or dare?"

"Truth."

"Pity. I had all kinds of good answers for the dare. The truth is, I had just been for a bike ride. I take the dog along. It's a good way to get us both some exercise."

Mal threw back her head, laughing. "I just wondered. Good night again, Harry." She walked back up the steps.

"You know what, Malone?" he called after her.

She turned. "What now?"

"If you could think of one word to describe me, what would it be?"

She frowned. "What is this? A test?"

"Unh-unh, it's truth or dare. Remember, you started it."

She thought for a minute. "Cocky," she said. "Yes, *cocky*. That describes you exactly."

"Okay. Now you're supposed to ask me."

She put her hands on her hips, looking disbelievingly at him. "Okay, so I'm asking."

"An enigma," Harry said. "That's exactly what you are, Malone. An *enigma*."

Mal thought for a moment. "I take that as a compliment, Harry," she said, walking back into the lobby. "Good night, and this time I mean it."

She raised her hand in farewell, not looking back.

14

Mal was at the studio at seven the next morning. They weren't taping until ten, but she always got there early, along with the production crew, to make sure everything was exactly the way she wanted it.

"Even though we've gone over it a hundred times," Beth complained. "After three years, Mal, surely you can trust us to get it right."

"I just need to be sure, that's all," Mal insisted.

"Okay. It's no skin off my nose if you want to get up early. How about a cup of coffee and a doughnut?"

Mal looked scandalized. "Caffeine and sugar? After last week I'm so pure, just the sight of it might make me swoon." She eyed Beth's cup longingly. "Well, perhaps just half a cup." Beth grinned. "Of decaf," Mal added guiltily.

"And just one bite?" Beth waved the jelly doughnut under her nose.

Mal closed her eyes against the tempting sight. "Get thee behind me, Satan," she said, waving it away.

She scanned the script while she sipped the coffee. Then she checked the activity in the studio. Everything was on schedule, so she wandered down to makeup.

"Here I am, ready for my other face," she said to Helen Ross, who had worked with her ever since that first nervous show three years ago.

Helen put her head to one side, studying Mal's unmade-up features. "You always say that, but you know, you don't look that much different with the makeup. Just a little more defined for the cameras, that's all."

"It makes me feel better, thinking I look like someone else." Mal flopped into the chair and regarded herself in the mirror. "It's the other woman they see on their screens, not the real me."

Helen shook her head, not understanding. She began smoothing toner, then moisturizer onto Mal's clear skin.

"Helen?"

She glanced inquiringly at Mal in the mirror.

"Do you think I'm a control freak?"

Helen laughed. "I don't. But I know those who do."

Mal scowled. "I suppose I am," she admitted reluctantly. "But it's my show. And if I didn't keep on top of it, it wouldn't be number one."

"I guess so," Helen agreed mildly.

She finished the makeup in friendly silence, and Mal reread the script while Helen blow-dried her hair. But for once she couldn't concentrate.

She wondered for the fourth, or was it the fifth time that morning, what Harry Jordan was doing. She imagined him riding his bike, pounding those strong thighs she had felt next to hers last night, the big silver-gray wolf-dog running alongside. Or she saw him in Ruby's, oblivious to the smoke and the racket as he demolished a plate of eggs and home fries with never a thought for his waistline. Not that he had anything to worry about, she thought, remembering the way he had looked in his Levi's.

But Harry had taken the day off yesterday to be with her, so most likely he was back at work today. She imagined him in the squad room, wearing his old leather jacket, his hair attractively rumpled, joking with the guys.

Then she told herself abruptly that she was being ridiculous. She had no idea what his life was like. All she really knew about him were the few facts research had gleaned on his background. She didn't know the real Harry Jordan. She didn't know whether he had loved his father, even though he had wrecked his football career. She didn't know about his wife and how they had met and how much he had cared about her. She didn't know about his job, except that he was good at it — a dedicated man who gave his time and tenacity to solving homicides, like Summer Young's.

She turned the page of the script, forcing herself to concentrate. She had no business thinking about Harry Jordan, she told herself. Anyhow, she had a show to do. That was the most important thing.

At the end of the long day, she went to a Chinese restaurant around the corner from the studio with the production crew, where she drank jasmine tea and laughed a lot as they discussed the show, letting out the tension.

It was nine o'clock when she got home. As soon as she opened the front door, the scent of lilacs surrounded her.

She closed her eyes, thinking she must be dreaming. When she opened them again, there was a big crystal vase on the console in the hall, full of fragrant white lilacs as well as a dozen or so tight creamy roses and lilies. She reached out and touched them, entranced.

The card lay on the table, but she knew they were from Harry Jordan. With an apprehensive little shiver, she wondered how he had known about lilacs. Then she told herself he must have called Beth and asked what her favorite flowers were.

There was also a small parcel. Kicking off her shoes, Mal padded into the living room and flung herself into the big chair. She smiled as she read his note.

"Enigma," it said. "A person of puzzling or contradictory character. Perplexing, mysteri-

ous. From the Greek *ainigma,* from *ainissesthai* — to speak in riddles. (*Random House Dictionary*)"

"Very clever, Harry," she said, amused.

She looked at the parcel. The wrapping paper had scarlet Santas and Happy Christmas in gold, with a red bow stuck clumsily in the center. She guessed it was all the wrapping he had on hand. Still, she ripped it open as eagerly as a child on Christmas morning.

It was a CD. *The Enigma Variations* by Edward Elgar. Smiling, she went over to the machine and put it on.

She sat cross-legged on the floor, gazing into the flames as the romantic music filled the room. The scent of lilacs permeated the house and the logs crackled comfortingly in the grate. Somehow, because of Harry Jordan, tonight she felt less lonely.

It hadn't always been that way. Once upon a time she had been Mary Mallory Malone, the invisible girl at Golden Junior High. And the loneliest girl in the world.

Mary Mallory had not been born in Golden. She and her mother had gone there when she was twelve, after her father had walked out on them. She had never seen him again, but to this day she could remember how he looked: tall and wiry, with a tattoo of a mermaid on one sinewy arm and a deep scar cutting across his left cheekbone. He would flex the muscles

131

in his arm so it looked as though the mermaid's breasts were jiggling, then laugh uproariously, glancing slyly at Mary Mallory and her mother, knowing he was embarrassing them.

He was a sailor, of sorts. He worked as a stoker on the merchant ships that sailed from Seattle to Asia, but all he ever saw of the vast oceans he crossed regularly was in the brief respites from the sweltering heat in the boiler rooms, when he would go on deck for a smoke, staring with narrow, wary brown eyes at the heaving expanse of water. Then he would disappear quickly below again, to his bunk to sleep or back to shoveling coal into the giant furnaces.

It was different when he hit port. Mary Mallory knew, because she'd heard him telling her mother about it through the thin walls that separated their bedrooms. *Torturing her* with graphic accounts of his exploits would be a more accurate description.

Mary Mallory would cover her ears and bury her head under the covers, so as not to hear about the women he'd bought in Macao and Taipei and Honolulu. But her mother was forced to listen as he told her exactly why she could not compare to his roving sexual conquests.

"You know what they do," he would say in his hoarse, menacing, cigarette-scarred voice. "They grip you with their muscles. Yeah, these." He thrust his hand into her cruelly, and she muffled her terrified cries with the sheets, so as not to frighten her young daughter in the next room.

"You're useless," he snarled at her as he pounded futilely into her, blaming her for his own inadequacies. "You're nothing, you hear me? *Nothing.* Nothing but a crazy woman."

And then would come the sound of his hand striking her soft flesh. Mary Mallory heard it and her mother's high wail of pain, even though she stuck her hands over her ears.

"Oh, God, oh, God, please don't let him hurt her," she would pray, jolting upright in bed. "Don't let him hit her. Stop him, stop him."

Sometimes her prayer would be answered. She would hear the bed squeak as her father swung himself to his feet, and the rustling of his clothes and the clink of the metal buckle on his belt as he fastened it; the thump of his boots on the floor and the squeak of the bedsprings as he sat down to put them on.

Then a long silence when she knew he was standing there, looking at her mother. Mary Mallory crossed her fingers; she crossed her arms and her legs and squeezed her eyes tightly shut. "Don't hit her again," she prayed. "Just don't."

Sometimes he did, sometimes he didn't. Afterward, she would hear the clump of his boots on the stairs, and the front door would slam so hard, it seemed to rock the flimsy little frame house on its foundations.

Mary Mallory froze, straining her ears. Only when the car's engine started up did she sag with relief, sure they would not see him again that night.

She stared at the wall, hearing her mother's muffled sobs, sharing her despair, not knowing what to do about it. She couldn't go to her. She couldn't throw her arms around her and comfort her. Things were not like that in their household.

No one ever spoke about their feelings and Mary Mallory had come to the conclusion that you weren't meant to have them. In fact, no one spoke much at all in her house, except to say things like "pass the salt."

Her mother seemed locked in her own private misery. She drifted around the tiny house in a faded pink cotton wrapper, like a woman in a dream. She would sit at the kitchen table for hours over a cup of coffee, staring vaguely in front of her, smoking cigarette after cigarette.

Mary Mallory would leave her there in the morning when she went off to school, and often she would still be there in the afternoon, when she got back. Still at the table, still with the coffee cup, still the cigarette.

"Mom," she suggested tentatively, when her father was away on one of his long voyages and things were easier, "Why don't we go to the movies? They say there's a good one playing at the Rialto."

Her mother's dull eyes shifted onto her for a second. Her brows lifted as though she were surprised to see her there. "You go. There's money in my purse."

So she went to the movies alone, losing herself in the Technicolor glamour of the latest Hollywood musical, drinking in the music and the laughter and the wonderful dresses until she was practically living life up there onscreen with them. Only when the credits rolled and the lights came up did she return to the awful reality of being Mary Mallory Malone.

She saw everything that came to the Rialto, sometimes twice or even three times, sneaking in the side door on Saturday afternoons when she had no money, which was almost always, living vicariously and storing the images in her head so she could dream about them later in bed. Until she was twelve years old, she believed life really was like in the movies. It was just her own life that was different.

Except she had a problem with the love stories. She didn't believe people really looked at each other like that, with their hearts in their eyes, that they hugged and kissed and said I love you. She knew her own parents did not love her and she wondered if it was because she was ugly. She was a mousy child, thin, with limp fair hair and myopic blue eyes hidden behind ugly, thick-lensed plastic glasses.

In her whole life she could not remember either of them ever putting their arms around her, hugging her, kissing her. They never called her by affectionate pet names, never made her feel special.

When she was eleven, her father didn't come home at the end of a voyage. A year passed, and suddenly one morning Mary Mallory came downstairs to find her mother sitting at the kitchen table, smoking as usual. Only this time she was clutching a letter. She held it nearsightedly to her blue eyes, scanning it over and over, her brows raised in perplexed surprise.

"Mary Mallory," she said in a strange new voice, "it says here that we have defaulted on our mortgage payments. It says here" — she put a trembling finger on the line — "that we have ignored all their previous letters and that unless we vacate the premises by Saturday morning, the bailiffs will be sent to evict us."

She lifted her eyes and looked astonished at her pale, bespectacled daughter standing by the door. It was as if she had suddenly seen the light at the end of the tunnel, the happy ending she had always been searching for. Galvanized out of her lethargy, she got briskly to her feet.

"You've got to help me," she said, glancing wildly around the scabby little kitchen. "We need to pack. Dishes and stuff, and clothes." She thought for a minute. "You know what

136

this means, don't you?" Her usually dull eyes were alive with triumph. "We'll never have to see your father again."

It was sad that it had taken the repossession of her home to free her mother from the tyranny of her sadistic husband, but Mary Mallory didn't think of that then. All she felt was relief. And after that, worry.

"But what shall we live on, Mom?" she asked, scared.

"I'll get a job," her mother said airily, opening a drawer and flinging a battered collection of dimestore cutlery into a plastic bag. "As a clerk in the supermarket, or a waitress maybe. Somethin', anyhow."

Mary Mallory didn't think so, but she knew they couldn't stay where they were. So she found a cardboard box and obediently filled it with their cheap dishes, stacking them neatly.

She stopped and looked uncertainly at her mother. She was humming tunelessly, and it occurred to Mary Mallory that she had never seen her mother excited before. She had just one question: "Mom, where shall we go?"

Her mother paused, thinking about it. "You know what? I've always wanted to live by the ocean." She laughed, an alien sound that rippled through the sour old house like the fresh sea breeze she was dreaming about. "Yes, that's where we'll go," she said exultantly. "To the seaside."

It was the only moment in her life that Mary Mallory caught a glimpse of the pretty girl her mother had once been. Before she married, and before the black depression had claimed her.

Her spirits rose to match her mother's. She could almost believe that happiness lay ahead, there at the seaside, where the rainbow ended. And she laughed too, as she flung pots and pans into another cardboard box with a great clanging of metal.

"We're off to the ocean!" she yelled, delighted. Closing her eyes, she breathed deeply as though she could already smell the salty spray and feel the tug of the wind in her hair, as though she could already taste their happy new life.

A couple of hours later, they had piled their few remaining worldly goods into the ancient turquoise Chevy with the chrome fins. Mary Mallory's mother got behind the wheel and Mary Mallory reminded her that they had better fill up with gas since they were going on a long journey.

At the gas station her mother counted out the money carefully, then winked at her and went into the little store and bought her a Coke and a Snickers bar.

"Lunch," she said cryptically, lighting a cigarette from a fresh pack of Marlboros as they drove off down the road.

It wasn't until they were passing the place

that Mary Mallory even remembered.

"Mom, what about school?" she asked, suddenly brought back to sober reality.

"There'll be a new school," her mother said, not bothering even to give it a glance.

"But shouldn't we tell them or something?"

"Unh-unh." She shook her head. "No need. Believe me, they won't even notice you're not there."

Mary Mallory looked back at the ugly red-brick school she had attended for the past four years. She had no friends there; even the teachers had ignored her.

She knew she was different from the other children at school. She had seen their parents when they came to the meetings or the play at Christmastime. They were nice, ordinary smiling people who laughed and talked to each other and joked with their children and the teachers. The sort of people who linked arms or held hands as they walked across the schoolyard, leaning affectionately into each other, their heads together as they talked. Nobody ever *talked* at Mary Mallory's house.

Her mother and father never came to the school, not once the whole time she was there. And the teachers never asked her about them. They just looked knowingly at each other when they saw Mary Mallory alone at a concert or on sports day.

The other children didn't ignore her — they just never seemed to notice her, that's all.

Mary Mallory was like the runt of the litter, kept outside the pack to live or die as best she could.

She knew her mother was right — no one would even miss her. She hoped things would be different at her new school at the seaside.

They drove through pleasant countryside, and Mary Mallory gazed out at the black and white cows, and at chickens clucking in the barnyards, and once even a herd, or was it a flock, of pink piglets trotting along on delicate little hooves in wake of their enormous lumbering mother-sow.

She ate the Snickers bar in tiny little bites, making it last for a couple of hours, but by the time they hit the coast road, darkness was falling and she was starving.

"I'm hungry, Mom," she said. "What are we going to do about dinner?"

Her mother glanced at the dashboard clock, "Goodness, is it that time already?" she said, surprised. She swung the wheel suddenly to the left, and the car skidded across the highway in front of a logging truck, into a gravel parking lot.

The sixteen-wheeler loaded with fresh-cut logs screeched to a halt behind them. "God-damn women drivers!" the truck driver yelled, wiping his sweating brow. "You don't learn to signal, lady, you'll end up dead."

Mary Mallory bit her lip anxiously, but her mother seemed not to have heard. "Sorry,"

Mary Mallory mouthed to the driver, but he shook his head and glared menacingly at them.

"Come on," her mother said, getting out of the car and heading for the brightly lit café.

She hurried after her. "Mom, don't you think we'd better lock the car?"

"Lock it? But why?" She glanced back helplessly. Mary Mallory took the keys and ran back and locked the doors.

The truckstop café was fluorescent-bright, smoky, and crowded. It smelled of bacon and burgers and coffee. Music boomed from the jukebox in the corner, competing with the roar of conversation and the sizzling and clattering coming from the short-order kitchen.

Ignoring the other customers, her mother strode to the head of the line. She turned to look at Mary Mallory, who was hanging back nervously.

"A burger okay with you?" she called. Without waiting for an answer, she ordered two burgers and two root-beer floats.

She picked up her tray and, oblivious to the scathing comments of the irate truckers, stalked to a table near the window. Mary Mallory slunk after her, head down, hoping no one would tell them off for pushing into the line like that.

She sat silently opposite her mother, eating her burger. She couldn't remember the last time they had done this together, and her spirits rose. She began to believe there really was a new life awaiting them at the seaside. Her mother seemed so different — strong and purposeful, as though in ridding herself of her husband, she was leaving behind the terrible past and that other sad, frightened woman. Mary Mallory knew she would get a job. They would have a proper home and friends, and they would be happy.

Back in the car, she fell asleep. She didn't move until her mother nudged her and said, "Wake up, Mary Mallory. I've found the seaside."

They were high up on a cliff. In back of them stood a forest of trees, so tall they seemed to touch the clear night sky. And before them lay the ocean, eerily dark except for the clear silver path laid across it by the full moon.

Mary Mallory rolled down her window and poked her head out, breathing the cold fresh air. She stuck out her tongue, tasting the salt on the wind. The ocean surged restlessly, murmuring, groaning, hissing when it struck the rocks below, like some gigantic prehistoric beast.

"It's the seaside all right, Mom," she said.

Her mother yawned. "I guess we may as well spend the rest of the night here," she said, sliding down in her seat and closing her eyes.

Mary Mallory glanced over her shoulder. The back of the car was piled with boxes and plastic bags and her mother's scattered clothes. There was no room there for her to stretch out. She rolled up the window and slid down in her seat like her mother, shuffling until she arranged herself in a bearable position.

She smelled the salty ocean in her dreams that night, and when she awoke, the sun was dappling the trembling ocean with flecks of gold. And her mother was fast asleep with her head on Mary Mallory's shoulder.

It was the closest she could remember ever having been to her mother. She sat completely still, afraid of losing the contact, feeling the warmth of her mother's soft cheek against her arm. She watched the colors of the sea change as clouds filled the sky, turning the innocent blue-green to carbon gray. A couple of squirrels scuttled past the car as the first drops of rain splattered onto the roof. The rain became a downpour, and the sea turned into a raging, roaring ocean, hurling itself at the cliff.

"Goodness, it's raining," her mother said, sitting up and rubbing her eyes. "We'd better get going, Mary Mallory. I need to make a pit stop."

They bumped back down the slippery lane, through the forest onto the highway. The wipers swished uselessly back and forth in the deluge as her mother pointed the turquoise Chevy south, peering over the hood into the gloom.

The rain was still bouncing down as they pulled into a gas station half an hour later.

They emptied a couple of plastic bags and tied them over their hair to keep it dry, then ran to the rest room, giggling like a pair of silly schoolgirls. They washed their hands and faces but had no toothbrushes, so they got a pack of spearmint gum from the machine instead, and then they were on their way again.

"Darn," her mother said as they turned onto the highway. "I meant to get gas."

Mary Mallory checked the gauge — they still had half a tank. She stared out of the window at the cascading waves of water thrown up by the passing logging trucks, barreling down the highway as though they owned it.

"Mom, I'm hungry," she said an hour later, over the pop music blasting on the radio.

"You're hungry? Again?" Her mother threw her a disbelieving glance as she lit another cigarette. "Seems to me you're always hungry these days." Then she grinned. "It must be the sea air."

Mary Mallory, who had breathed nothing but secondhand cigarette smoke for the past hour, thought a breath of sea air wouldn't be a bad thing. She rolled down her window, but all that came in was a blast of icy wind and a torrent of water.

"Close the darned window, Mary Mallory, or I'll catch my death," her mother exclaimed, shivering.

Mary Mallory rolled up the window again

and reached into the back for a fuzzy blue mohair sweater. "Here," she said, offering it to her mother. She didn't seem to notice, but she placed it round her shoulders anyway.

They just kept on driving and driving through the pouring rain — for hours, it seemed to her. Then the engine began to cough and splutter. Her mother frowned and shoved her foot harder on the gas pedal. Mary Mallory looked at her, alarmed.

Her mother edged the big old car to the side of the road as the engine gave a final cough, then died. She stretched her arms over her head, easing the ache of the long ride out of her spine. "Well, I guess this is it," she yawned. "We're out of gas. It's the end of the line, Mary Mallory. Here we are, and here we stay."

Mary Mallory rolled down her window. She poked her head out and read the sign immediately in front of them.

It said, YOU ARE NOW ENTERING GOLDEN, OREGON, POP. 906.

15

Harry had put in a long hard day, and it wasn't over yet. He had other cases on his workload besides Summer Young, and he had one more visit to make — to the Mass General — before he could go home, pour himself a bourbon, take a long shower, put on some music, and think about Mallory Malone's possible reaction to his enigmatic note.

He had deliberately not put his name on the card and he suddenly thought it would be pretty funny if she had no idea who the flowers were from. "Nah," he told himself with a reminiscent grin, "of course she'll know. Malone is one smart woman." He had been going to say "cookie" but caught himself in time. Ms. Malone *ma'am* would not appreciate being termed a "cookie."

He eased the Jag into a spot between a red Ford Explorer and a gunmetal Volvo station wagon, automatically noting their license numbers as he did so. It was the cop's built-in reaction from his days in the patrol car, always with an eye open for stolen vehicles or wanted criminals on the run. Storing the numbers in his head, he walked across the lot to the Emergency entrance.

A couple of hours ago, he had been called to the scene of what at first had looked like a hit-and-run but on closer investigation was more like a gang killing. Except that the victim did not seem too ready to expire. Without a body, a homicide cop was out of a job, but Harry was checking anyway, to make sure the situation hadn't changed.

The waiting room smelled of disinfectant and blood, and as usual it was fraught with tension. The wounded and the sick waited their turns patiently. Babies were screaming, distraught parents were pacing, and silent relatives were waiting in white-faced vigils to hear the news — bad or good — about their loved ones.

"Evening, Suzie," he said to the young nurse at the desk. "Keeping you busy tonight?"

"Don't they always?" Suzie Walker gave him a special smile that told him she wouldn't mind if he asked for her phone number, but she had seen Harry a dozen times at the hospital and he never had. "I guess you've come to see the hit-and-run victim. He's been moved into a ward — third floor on the left. And by the way, Detective Rossetti beat you to it."

"Story of my life." Harry grinned, taking the steps two at a time just to prove to himself he wasn't really tired. Then he loped down the hallway to where Rossetti was loitering, coffee cup in hand.

"How's he doing?" Harry asked, heading for the coffee machine.

Rossetti took a final bite of his tuna on rye. "Pretty good," he mumbled, his mouth full, "for a guy with two broken legs and a fractured skull. He went right over the top of the vehicle. Smacked his head good. Lucky for him, he didn't break his neck. Unlucky for us, because he claims he can't remember much about it. Just the color of the van — white."

Harry walked back, carrying his coffee. "No point in hanging around, then."

"Gaylord and Franz are in charge now." Rossetti drained his cup and heaved a sigh of weariness. "Tomorrow is another day, Prof. I don't know about you, but I'm beat. I'm gonna have an early night." He glanced uncertainly at his watch. "Well, maybe ten is a bit *too* early."

"Only if you're sleeping alone, Rossetti. And if I'm to believe you, that never happens."

Rossetti refilled his cup and they ambled back down the corridor, sipping their coffee.

Harry said thoughtfully, "We're not having much luck recently, vehiclewise. A black truck or van in the Summer Young case, and a white van in the hit-and-run. Think the fates are against us, Rossetti? Or are we too stupid to find the clues staring us in the face?"

"What clues?" Rossetti looked gloomy. "All we know is that the butler didn't do it."

"Oh, we've got plenty of clues, Sherlock.

Forensics says the fibers found in Summer's car were cashmere. Black cashmere."

Rossetti gave a low amazed whistle. "Seems our man has expensive taste in sweaters. Maybe he knows a good discount outlet. Or else he's got money. You got the guys checking the stores?"

Harry nodded. "And checking the manufacturers and importers. The crime lab says the fiber is not the cheaper kind of cashmere. It's the long-staple good stuff, from the belly of the best goats, possibly Mongolian. The manufacturer is probably European, most likely Scottish. That'll narrow our search to the more expensive stores and boutiques."

"What else?" Rossetti demanded.

"The hairs found on her clothing are Caucasian. And they were dyed. Their true color is gray."

"You think he was deliberately disguising himself? Or he's just an older guy trying to look younger?"

Harry shrugged. "All we know is that he's older than we thought."

They waved to Suzie Walker as they passed the desk, calling good night.

Rossetti looked admiringly back at her. She was young and pretty, with fiery red hair and wide green eyes. He'd been trying to get a date with her for months.

"When're you gonna relent, Suzie, and go out with me?" he called.

"When you grow up, Detective Rossetti," she replied without lifting her eyes from the notes she was reading.

Harry laughed. "Great technique, Rossetti. Works every time, huh?"

"Win some, lose some, Prof. You just gotta bet the numbers, that's all."

They pushed open the door and stood for a minute on the steps looking out across the parking lot, discussing the progress forensics was making.

"One more thing," Harry said. "They found particles of nitrogen in the dust taken from the Miata. Probably a fertilizer, the sort you can buy at a garden store to use on your roses."

Rossetti looked gloomy. "Are we gonna have to check out every gardener/handyman in Boston?"

"Nope." Harry grinned. "In Massachusetts. And the odds still are that he's an ordinary family man who enjoys a bit of gardening on weekends."

"When he's not enjoying killing, you mean."

Harry sighed. "You got it, Rossetti."

The man in the gunmetal Volvo wagon watched them standing on the steps, through his binoculars. He knew who they were. If he could lip-read, he would have known what they were saying, the image was so sharp. He'd bet a hundred they were talking about him, though.

The idea pleased him, and so did the fact

that they had nothing on him. They didn't even know what he looked like, and he had left them no clues. Besides, they were still working on the past, while he was already looking to the future.

He patted the Polaroid camera, waiting on the seat next to him. It was like an old friend — it always came through for him. He knew Suzie Walker's shift finished in fifteen minutes and he glanced anxiously at the two detectives, still talking on the steps. If they didn't leave soon, they would ruin his photo opportunity.

He breathed a sigh of relief when Harry Jordan finally slapped his friend on the shoulder and they yelled cheerful good nights.

Jordan was striding across the parking lot toward him. The Volvo's windows were black-tinted, but he wasn't taking any chances on the sharp-eyed detective noticing him. He slid down onto the floor and pulled the plaid rug over himself.

He lay as still as his victims had, his breathing quiet and even. He had no fear — he knew he was cleverer than the police, he had already proven that many times. The police didn't even know yet exactly *how many*.

He heard the detective's footsteps, then the sound of the Jag being unlocked. Suddenly there was a ferocious barking — a dog was scrabbling at the door of the Volvo. He held his breath nervously.

"Squeeze, what the hell's gotten into you?"

Harry yelled angrily. He grabbed its collar and hauled the dog away, running his hand anxiously over the Volvo's paintwork.

Squeeze lunged forward against the wagon. He stuck his nose in the slightly open window, sniffing and growling.

Harry hesitated. It wasn't like Squeeze to behave so aggressively. He peered into the Volvo's window, but the tint was too dark to see much. He noted that it was locked and wondered about the alarm. He took a look at the license plate — the tax sticker had been renewed recently. There were no dents or scratches. It looked like a perfectly normal well-kept vehicle. It probably belonged to a family with several children and a couple of dogs. That must be it. The dogs would ride in the back where the window was open. Squeeze had caught their scent and didn't like it.

"You crazy mutt." Harry hauled him back. "You could have cost me a new paint job."

Still growling, the dog jumped reluctantly into the back of the Jag.

The door slammed; there was the sound of the engine starting, then the squeal of tires as Jordan drove away.

The man began to laugh, a great rumbling burst of laughter as he thought of Detective Harry Jordan's dog, who knew a killer when he smelled one. He thought Squeeze was a whole lot cleverer than his master.

It was almost time. He sat up, camera at the ready. He was about to make Miss Suzie Walker a star.

In the car on his way home, Harry remembered he hadn't eaten anything since a blueberry muffin at Ruby's at seven that morning. He stopped off and picked up a pepperoni pizza, eating a slice as he drove. The dog was slobbering down his neck, dying for some. He laughed.

"No chance, fella," he said. "I'll put up with the bone on the antique carpet, but you're not gonna slobber greasy pizza over my coach hide."

When he got home, the red light was flashing on the answering machine in the kitchen. He opened a can of Alpo for the dog, took another bite of the pizza, and pressed the play button.

There was just the faint sound of music in the background. He cocked his head to one side, smiling as he recognized the Elgar. Then her voice came on.

"Thanks, Harry," she said softly.

He stared at the machine, waiting for more. But that was it. He rewound the tape and played it back. Then he threw back his head and laughed. Malone knew when to be a woman of few but meaningful words. And there was a definite purr in her voice when she had said *Harry.*

Still smiling, he poured himself a shot of Jim Beam, tossed in a few ice cubes, picked up the box with the pizza, and walked into the living room. He checked the VCR, then rewound the tape.

Hurling himself into his old leather chair, he switched it on. Mallory Malone's face was right there in his living room. That same bright, sunshiny smile that had been specially for him last night now lit up the screen for millions of viewers. Her eyes gleamed like wet sapphires as she spoke movingly of the English billionaire's brain-damaged wife, locked silently away in an institution. And then she showed stills of the old goat cavorting naked with three young beauties.

"This man can forget," she said in her low gentle voice. "But should we? Ask yourselves that question when you lie sleepless in bed tonight, just the way I shall, thinking about her. Ask yourself if there should not be some justice in the world for abused women like her. Ask yourself if this might not have been you."

She looked directly into the camera for a second, then lowered her delicious lashes, her eyes cloudy with unshed tears. In that second she had taken the audience into her world, she had involved them in the cause of the abused wife.

Harry thought she was either a great actress or she really meant it. Then he remembered that brief instant at dinner, when she had looked so lost and forlorn. "The least interesting woman in the world," she had called herself. At that moment, he could have sworn she meant it.

Mallory was more than just an enigma: she was a woman with secrets, and she was holding out on him.

Picking up the phone, he dialed her home number.

"Hello?" she said in a sleepy voice.

He glanced guiltily at his watch. It was eleven thirty. "Ms. Malone?" he said. He heard her sigh.

"Call me Mallory."

"Mallory." He enjoyed saying her name.

"Yes, Harry?"

"I didn't realize it was so late. I'm sorry," he said, smiling and not sorry at all.

"It's not late. I just went to bed early." She shuffled upright against the pillows.

"I got your message."

"You did?"

He thought she sounded breathless. "It wasn't very long."

"I thought it said it all." She was smiling, enjoying him despite herself.

"Succinct," Harry said.

"That's me."

He could hear the smile in her voice. "What does it feel like to be an enigma?"

"Oh, enigmatic, I guess." Then she laughed.

"The flowers were beautiful. How did you know lilacs were my favorite?"

"I didn't, but I'm glad they are. I just thought they suited you. Fresh and fragrant, like spring."

"You're getting poetic, detective."

"It's Harry. Remember? Did you ever think you might drive a man to poetry?"

"Or to music. I like the Elgar."

"It's romantic, over-the-top."

"And so, I suspect, are you, Harry Jordan."

He grinned, imagining her lying in bed. "How about giving me a chance to show you how romantic I am? I could wangle a night off tomorrow."

She hesitated. He could almost hear her thinking it over. "I'd like that, Harry. Only dinner's on me this time. My place at eight?"

"Eight it is. Mallory," he added. "And thank you for the invitation."

"I think I'm looking forward to it," she said cautiously.

"Me too."

"Then I guess this is good night."

"I guess it is. After all, I'm in Boston and you're in New York."

"Not much we can do about it, is there, detective," she said, laughing. Then: "See you tomorrow, *Harry*," and she hung up.

Harry was still smiling as he put down the phone. He forgot that he was supposed to be finding out what she knew about the man on the photo-fit. He felt like a young guy taking out the prom queen.

He whistled for the dog, clipped on his leash, and took him for a long walk. He wondered what Mallory Malone wore to bed.

Mal lay back on the pillows, thinking worriedly that she really should not have succumbed to Harry Jordan's charm. He was a threat to her — he could ruin her carefully constructed life. But she couldn't resist him. And it was just this once. She would have to be on her guard, that's all. Then she turned on her stomach and buried her face in the pillow. She was asleep within minutes.

16

Harry was happiest in comfortable well-worn jeans, but for her he put on his one and only good jacket and pants, a white linen shirt, and a bright silk tie he'd picked up on sale somewhere. As he tied it in the mirror, he thought with a grin that this was twice he had dressed up for Ms. Malone. He hoped she appreciated his sacrifice.

He had taken a room at the Mark Hotel on Madison and planned on catching the early-morning shuttle back to Boston. He felt like a kid playing hooky. As if to remind himself that he was not here solely on pleasure, he picked up the manila envelope containing the photofit of the killer, folded it, and put it in his pocket.

The concierge called from downstairs to say that his flowers were waiting. He took one last glance in the mirror, straightened the tie, ran his hands through his too-neatly combed hair, and headed out.

The florist had done a terrific job, filling an enormous wicker basket with parma violets. Clutching it gingerly, he edged into a taxi.

"You goin' to a funeral, bud?" the driver asked sourly.

"I hope not," he said, "but flowers sure smell better than this cab."

At the apartment building he gave the doorman his name. "The penthouse floor, sir," the doorman told him. "Ms. Malone is expecting you."

In the elevator on the way up, Harry checked his digital watch. He was right on time. He smiled, anticipating what she would look like, what she would say, being alone with her.

Carrying the enormous basket of violets, he stepped from the elevator into a marble foyer. There were expensive antique Venetian mirrors on the walls, soft-hued French rugs on the floor, and an attractive woman in a red silk dress was smiling at him. It wasn't Mallory.

He said uncertainly, "I think I'm in the wrong place."

The woman had long black hair, laughing dark eyes and a sexy smile. She looked him slowly up and down, then shook her head. "Oh, I do hope not." Then she laughed. "Who are you looking for?"

"Mallory Malone."

She stepped closer to him, inspecting the violets. He could smell her perfume over the scent of the flowers, spicy and strong. "Then I'm glad to say you are in the right place." She gave him another sexy little smile, then led him to the door.

"Mal," she called loudly over the babble of conversation. "The delivery man is here. Come and look at him."

Mal appeared in the doorway. She was wearing a tight black lace sheath lined with gold satin. The scalloped lace at the low neckline clung to her breasts as though it belonged there, and the short skirt and high-heeled black suede sandals made her legs look impossibly long and slender.

"Oh, it's you, Harry," she said, putting her fingers to her mouth to hide her laughter at the sight of him clutching his big basket of flowers, and at Lara's introduction of him as the delivery man.

The room was crowded with people, and waiters were busy passing canapés and drinks. Harry's eyes met hers.

"You didn't mention a party," he said, surprised.

She lifted one tanned slender shoulder in a careless shrug. "We just heard the ratings for last week's show were the highest yet. I decided to throw a party to celebrate."

The woman in red watched them interestedly. "You mean you're not the delivery man?"

Harry handed the basket to Mal. "These are for you."

She buried her nose in them. "They're heaven, gorgeous, like woods in springtime." She smiled up at him, genuinely pleased. "And so many of them, Harry, you must have plundered all the florists in Manhattan. Thank you."

For some silly reason he melted when she smiled at him like that. She looked as though he had given her the world on a plate instead of a bunch of violets. Still, he was disappointed about the party, though he supposed he had no right to be. He had no claims on Mallory Malone, and she had none on him.

"Come on, Harry," the woman in red said gaily, linking her arm in his. "You look like a party animal to me, and personally I'll settle for just the animal. I'm Lara Havers." He could feel her warm body next to his as she stepped closer. "And exactly who *are* you?" she asked, half laughing.

"This is Homicide Detective Harry Jordan of the Boston Police Department," Mal introduced him coolly.

"A cop? But how exciting. Tell me, Harry" — Lara drew him into the buzzing room — "are you here on business? Or purely pleasure?"

Mal stood by the door holding the basket of violets, watching them jealously. She felt that sudden clutch at her heart that she used to feel as a child when she had been the one not invited to the party, or asked to sleep over, or chosen for the team. For a minute she felt like Mary Mallory again, the loner and the loneliest.

161

She shrugged it off. This was *her* party, *her* home, *her* guests. It was *her* success that had brought all these people together. What did she care if Harry went off with Lara Havers, anyway? He meant nothing to her — just a flirtation that's all.

Then why had she woken up this morning with Harry on her mind? Why had she hurried to inspect her closet, filled to overflowing with beautiful clothes, and decided she didn't have a thing to wear? Why had she rushed out to Dean & Deluca and picked up all those goodies to cook for him tonight? She had even called the wine merchant and had him locate the champagne Harry liked.

And why had she also dashed into Barney's, first thing, and dithered like a teenager over whether to buy the sexy black lace or the demure cream satin shirt and black leather pants? She had been determined not to be caught on the wrong foot — sartorially — this time, so she had bought both.

And then she had told herself that she was crazy. There were a dozen men she could go out with tonight. She didn't need Harry Jordan or his serial killer, and somehow she just knew he intended to bring up that subject again.

She had been quite relieved when the ratings had come in and the producer had suggested a party to celebrate. "Let's have it at my place," she had cried enthusiastically. "You're all invited, every one of you."

Beth had called the caterers, and she had called her friends, and before she knew it, she was stashing the Dean & Deluca goodies in the refrigerator and changing into the little black lace, and there was a party going on.

She watched Harry from across the room. He was surrounded by attentive women, Beth and Lara among them. Harry was telling them a story and they were laughing and flirting with him. He looked as though he was having a great time.

She walked to her bedroom and put the basket of violets on the table under the window. She sank into a chair, looking at them. They weren't just a nice bunch of flowers — they were a sensitive and thoughtful gift chosen specially for her. She decided Harry really was sweet after all, under that tough cop exterior. She got up, smoothed her skirt, took a deep breath, and walked back to her party.

It was eleven o'clock when people finally began to leave and she still had not had a chance to say one word to Harry. He had been the star of the evening, entertaining her guests with stories of murder and mayhem. He'd taught Lara and Beth and her other friends how to dance to Gloria Estefan's "*Si Señor,*" and he had promised to show them the perfect exercise for abs. He had discussed basketball with the guys and talked about the Moonlightin' Club and how well it was doing, and that maybe they would build an ice-hockey rink and get up a team. He was everybody's friend, and she was the busy hostess.

Mal watched mockingly as every woman there kissed Harry good-bye, and she laughed when Lara whispered, "Isn't he the sexiest cop you ever saw outside of TV? And so much more available, darling. You won't mind if I call him, will you? I mean, he said it was just a business thing between you two."

"Go right ahead," Mal said airily. "There's absolutely nothing between us."

Lara shook her head, amazed. "You must be out of your mind, darling. But lucky me, then."

Mal said good night to the director and his wife, and the producer, and then to Beth and Rob.

"Oh, wait just a minute," she said, running into her bedroom. She came back seconds later with a parcel. "Anniversary present," she said, handing it over. "Sorry, I forgot. The London trip erased all my memories."

As Mal waved good-bye, she was aware of Harry's eyes on her. She turned and looked at him. He was standing by the fireplace, his hands in his pockets, leaning casually against the mantel. His hair was rumpled, and his beard was growing in. He looked like a man who wanted to take off his jacket.

"What does a guy have to do to get some food around here?" he asked with a grin.

She shrugged. "There was food. Good food, and plenty of it."

"Tidbits," he said, still looking at her. "Remember me? I'm the guy who was asked to dinner."

"If you hadn't been so busy teaching my friends to dance, you might have noticed the fine food from the top caterers that most of the other people were eating."

"I only taught the *women* to dance. And dinner doesn't count unless you sit at a table to eat it. Preferably opposite the person who invited you."

"What makes you think I invited you to dinner anyway?" she said, amused. "I never mentioned the word *dinner*. Or has your perfect cop's memory let you down tonight?"

"Sure," he said casually. "The way yours let you down over the photo-fit. Exactly what was it about that picture, Malone? Did you recognize him or what?"

She shrugged impatiently. "Don't be silly. Of course I didn't recognize him. Why should I?"

"Well, for one thing, it's your job to recognize killers. You've met plenty of criminals. I thought it might be someone you'd met in passing. Or maybe it's your brother?"

"Are you out of your mind?"

"Okay, so it's not your brother. Then who the hell is it, Malone?"

"How the hell do I know?"

They faced each other, glaring silently.

"Are we having a fight?" he asked her with a grin.

"That only happens to people who know each other well, and let me remind you, detective, that we do not."

"I thought that was why you invited me tonight. So we could get to know each other better."

She laughed. "If it weren't for the violets, I might think you just wanted to ask me about the killer."

"They were a small gift that I thought the beautiful woman I was going to have dinner with would like."

"You really think I'm beautiful?"

"Half of America thinks you're beautiful."

"And that means the other half doesn't." She bit her lip, wishing she hadn't said that; she had let her guard down in front of him.

He stared, astonished at her. "What does it matter to you what they think? You know what you look like. You're great at what you do, a big success. Can you really be that insecure, Malone?"

She shrugged, avoiding his eyes. "I was just joking."

He watched her puzzled. "No, you weren't," he said gently. "You want to tell me about it?"

"There's nothing to tell."

"Yes, there is." He cupped her chin in his hand, forcing her to look at him. "You can tell me, Mal," he said. "I promise I can keep a secret."

"Oh, Harry," she said, laughing, "you sound just like me."

"Sometimes *you* don't sound like you. And that's the puzzle." He ran his fingers along the nape of her neck, up through her soft hair.

Mal could feel the pads of his fingers against her scalp and the warmth emanating from them. A tiny frisson of pleasure ran down her spine, and she leaned into him. He held her gently, massaging her neck until she drooped with sensual pleasure.

"Feel good?" he whispered.

"Mmmm. You're in the wrong career, detective. Your true vocation is as a masseur." She was melting and she knew it.

She tilted her face up to him. Their eyes locked in a long deep look. His lips brushed hers softly, and she sighed. Then she pulled her wits together and stepped away from him.

She hitched up the bodice of her lace dress, smoothed her hair. "I know that at heart you're just an old-fashioned guy and not out to take advantage of me," she said, throwing him a flirtatious glance under her lashes, as she headed for the kitchen.

Harry followed her. He took off his jacket, then stood, arms folded, propped against the kitchen door. "True," he said. "Only thing is — and I don't know if anyone else has ever told you this."

She looked expectantly at him.

"Your lips are as velvety as the violet petals."

"Hmm. Is that so, detective?" She took the bottle of champagne out of the refrigerator and held it up. "Your favorite. I didn't forget."

He nodded, impressed. "So you didn't." He took the bottle from her, opened it without spilling a drop, and poured the champagne into two thin crystal glasses.

"Here's to a jolly evening, Detective Harry," she said, back to her old mocking self.

"You mean it's not over yet?"

She laughed. "I can't send you home hungry. There's food in that refrigerator too."

He pulled open the door and inspected the contents. "Looks like you were planning a dinner party."

"I was, until I chickened out."

He took out the boned quail. "You were going to cook these? For me?"

"Yup. And the stuffed zucchini flowers. And the couscous with scallions and spinach and lemon."

He raised his eyes to the heavens. "She can cook too," he said in an awed voice.

"How about a sandwich? It's quicker. Mayo or mustard?" She held up the jars.

"Both."

He watched as she fixed the sandwiches and put them on bright blue and yellow plates.

"Matisse would have painted them just like that," he said admiringly. "Still life of two turkey sandwiches in Manhattan."

"Don't forget the bottle of champagne." She snatched up the glasses and led the way back into the living room. She put the champagne on the coffee table, kicked off her sandals, then sat on the rug in front of the fire and pushed the CD button. Elgar's *Enigma Variations* wafted through the room.

She glanced at Harry, sitting opposite her. "I'm wondering how a man who can compare a turkey sandwich to a Matisse painting ended up as a detective."

"You already know how. We went over it on our last date, remember?"

"Our last *date?*"

"What else would you call it?"

She took a bite of her sandwich, thinking about it. "A meeting. That's what it was."

"Maybe for you."

"And 'velvet violet petals.' That's not cop talk."

"How do you expect a cop to talk?"

"Oh, you know. Hard, tough, down to earth. Black and white, and no nuances."

"I'm known for my nuances."

She laughed. "I see you're enjoying the sandwich."

"I missed Ruby's tonight. Still, everything considered — the luxurious surroundings, the high quality of the sandwich, the yellow and blue Matisse plates, the velvet lips — I'd rather be here."

He didn't say "with you," but she knew he meant it. Pleased, she sat back on her heels, sipping her wine, watching as he finished the sandwich.

He glanced around the room. "It looks as though you've lived here forever. The ancestral home, forebears on the walls, family photos in silver frames."

He picked up a photograph from the side table and inspected it. It was a picture of a couple. The man was tall and good-looking in a burly outdoors way, and his arm was draped around the shoulders of a petite, preppy-looking blonde with a big smile. It had been taken on the wooden deck of a substantial home overlooking a lake, and they looked happy and comfortable with each other.

"Your parents?" he guessed.

She lifted a shoulder. "Do I look like them?"

He studied the photograph. "I think so."

"That's why I chose them."

His head shot up. "You *chose* them?"

"Of course I did. In a junk shop. I chose all the people you see here, in the photos and paintings. When I was reinventing my past."

Harry put the silver-framed photograph down carefully. "You want to tell me about this, Malone?"

"No. You know what I mean."

Her mouth was suddenly tight, and she had that bruised look.

"I don't think I really do know what you

mean." He walked over to her and took her hand. "But I think you need to tell somebody about it. Why not me?"

She shrugged. "Oh, I don't know. It's a commonplace enough story. It's just that I've tried so hard to put it all behind me. To become someone else." He frowned, puzzled, and she said, "The truth is, I didn't really exist until I invented myself." And then suddenly she was telling him about her childhood — about her brutal father and depressive mother, and about them running away to the seaside, and Golden.

"A bitch of a little town," Mary's mother had called it when they first arrived there with all their worldly belongings piled into the ancient turquoise Chevy with the chrome fins. And she was right.

Golden's gray weather-scarred wooden buildings clung with ferocious tenacity to the windswept shore. There was a Kiwanis Lodge and an Elks; a Veterans War Memorial and the Midway Supermart; a diner masquerading as the Lido Café; and old folks growing older. It was a cheap little place that flirted briefly with the stray summer visitors, struggling under faded, festive buntings to look prosperous and inviting. But these visitors who stopped to look never stayed. They drove quickly on, searching for livelier, gayer venues.

Golden's residents had all been born there,

and their fathers and grandfathers before them and they quickly labeled the Malones trash and locked them out of their clannish little society.

Mal had no words to describe the terrible loneliness of those years. The sheer bleak aloneness of it, stretching endlessly behind her, infinitely in front of her. The only person close to her was her mother, but only because they lived together, not because her mother cared; she cared about nothing. Sometimes, lying in the orange vinyl sofa, trying to sleep, Mary Mallory would be overcome with terror, because she knew if she died that night nobody on God's earth would care. She was truly no one.

Mal could still see the drafty old trailer, smell the sea and rotting garbage and the sour odor of poverty. In that instant, she was there again — living it, breathing it, *hating it.*

The trailer was meant to be a summer rental. It was small and worse than shabby — it was ugly. Everything in it was worn and gray, except for the vinyl sofa, and even that had faded from red to a dull blood-orange. Her mother occupied the one bedroom at the rear, with a small window that refused to open even on the hottest days, though Mary Mallory had done her best with the screw-driver, prying and hammering to no avail. So when it was hot, her mother simply sat in the living room with the door wide open and the

TV set on all night, while Mary Mallory gave up hope of getting any sleep.

Her mother was addicted to TV. She watched everything, all the late-late shows, though Mary Mallory swore she never heard a word they said. It simply passed in front of her eyes — people, places, events — while smoke wreathed endlessly up to the ceiling as she lit cigarette after cigarette. Mary Mallory doubted her mother lived vicariously through TV, the way she herself did through movies; it was just there to remind her she was alive. She never even switched channels. Whatever was on the channel when she turned it on, that was what she watched.

Mary Mallory would try to coax her to bed. "Come on, Mom," she said, placing herself in front of the set. "It's awful late, and I've got to get some sleep." Her mother glanced vaguely up at her and lit another cigarette.

"I'm watching TV," she said mildly. But looking into her mother's desolate blue eyes, Mary Mallory knew she had her own sound-track running in her head.

Her mother never did get a job. They were living on welfare, and it was Mary Mallory's duty to go the welfare office every Monday after school and pick up food stamps.

"You again," Miss Aurora Peterson said, looking down her long nose at Mallory and adjusting the string of small cultured pearls at her scrawny but respectable throat and

173

reached for the Malone file. Even though Mary Mallory was certain she knew the details of their poverty by heart, the supervisor still made a great show of flicking through the papers, glancing up every now and again, and saying, "Hmm . . . hmm . . . I see."

Mary Mallory often thought it was a great pity that the welfare office was not staffed by the same people who needed the help, because they surely would have been nicer and had more genuinely charitable feelings in their hearts for unfortunates like herself.

But Miss Aurora Peterson lived in a nice white-painted house, shaded by old oak trees, on the right side of Golden's tracks — the very same house she had been born in and that had been left to her by her father. She wore pale blue twinsets and had her hair permed three times a year at Jody's beauty salon, where they also painted her nails a safe clover pink. She drove an almost-new white Buick, took her two-week vacations at the same resort in the mountains each year, and attended St. John's Presbyterian Church in Golden every Sunday, even though she had no love in her heart for anyone — and Mary Mallory suspected that that included Jesus — but it gave her an opportunity to wear her latest hat.

Mary Mallory stared down at the scarred linoleum floor and the shabby shoes of the other people standing in line while Miss Peterson examined her file as intently as if she were cracking a mysterious code. After five minutes or so, the woman glanced up and said wearily, "Oh, you Malones. When is your wretched mother ever going to get herself a job instead of letting us taxpayers take care of you?"

She took out a big rubber stamp and banged it down on the page, then finally counted out the food stamps and pushed them through the little opening at the bottom of the glass window that separated her from the roughness and uncouth manners of those who had fallen on hard times. And not once did she even glance at Mary Mallory.

Her cheeks burning with embarrassment, Mary Mallory walked to the Supermart at the other end of town. She grabbed a cart and walked quickly up and down the aisles, picking up cornflakes, milk, margarine, Velveeta cheese, bologna, and sliced Wonder Bread. She picked up a can of beans, and half a pound of the cheapest hamburger meat, and whatever instant coffee was on special. She went to the produce section and bought two baking potatoes and, for a treat, two green apples. Then she went and stood in line at the checkout and prepared herself for the second humiliation of the day.

Her cheeks flamed again with the shame of it as the manager counted her food stamps. She was always terrified that she had spent too much and would have to put things back.

Clutching her brown paper bag, she walked down the street to the little gas station, where the owner let her buy cigarettes for her mother even though she was underage. It was the one act of kindness in her day, though he was doing it because he never let a sale pass him by, not because he took pity on her. Still, it saved a lot of trouble because after that first optimistic year, her mother had practically stopped going out of the house at all, and without her cigarettes Mary Mallory was sure she would have gone really mad.

The only time her mother left the house was when the very blackest of depressions came over her. Then, when she came home from school her mother would be gone. She would find her mother on the cliffs, staring out to sea, or walking slowly along the beach, oblivious to the storms and the rain and the giant pounding waves roaring in with the sound of an express train, making the earth tremble beneath her feet.

Eventually, she would return home. She would dry her rain-soaked hair and fix a cup of coffee and turn on the TV. It was as though the violent storm had soothed whatever it was that tortured her.

Once, on her way home from the market, Mary Mallory passed girls from school. They were wearing smart new sweaters and riding metallic-red bikes, and their mouths were bright pink with a kissy-looking new lipstick color. They didn't seem to notice her, though, or if they did, they avoided looking at her. They were busy chatting with one another about boys as they cycled aloofly by in a heavy cloud of perfume, just purchased at Bartlett's Drugstore on Main.

Mary Mallory shifted the grocery bag to the other arm. She adjusted her owlish plastic eyeglasses and peered enviously after them. She was blind as a bat, and the lenses were so thick, they looked like the bottoms of Coke bottles. She felt hidden behind them, and that the girls couldn't really see her, or else why wouldn't they have said hello at least. But then, no one ever said hello.

She remembered her first terrible day at school. The secretary had escorted her into the homeroom and pushed her out in front of the class. Thirty pairs of eyes had bored into her, taking in her washed-out dress that was too short, her worn sneakers, and her ugly glasses. With the well-honed instinct of the pack, they knew instantly that she was an outsider — "a weirdo" and "ugly," the girls whispered to each other behind their hands, giggling.

"Say hello to Mary Mallory," the teacher ordered, glancing impatiently at her, still standing forlornly in front of the class.

"Hello, Mary Mallory," they chorused, then collapsed into giggles.

Mary Mallory muttered a quick hi, then

hurried to the desk the teacher had pointed out.

She was dreading recess, but she needn't have because no one spoke to her anyway. No one offered to show her around or be her friend. No one even bothered to stare at her or make fun of her. For all the seventh grade of Golden Junior High cared, she might have been invisible.

It was the silence that got to her. At home her mother rarely spoke, she was always lost in her own world. And at school, apart from occasional questions from the teacher, no one even greeted her. She had always been shy, but now she became inhibited. She told herself it was because she was ugly, because she was poor, because her mother was a "crazy woman," because she had to line up in front of patronizing Miss Aurora Peterson and then hand over her humiliating stamps in the Golden Supermart. Because her clothes were cheap and purchased from the secondhand store; because she could never buy *Glamour* magazine and a soda and try out all the new lipsticks and perfumes at Bartlett's. Because she was no one. Nothing. The invisible girl of Golden Junior High.

She took home the groceries and put them away in the cupboard. She gave her mother the cigarettes and saw a hint of pleasure in her vacant eyes. "Thanks, Mary Mallory," she said in a voice that cracked from disuse. And that was all she said for the rest of the night.

Mary Mallory put on a sweater and walked along the cliffs, staring at the heaving green ocean, remembering how thrilled she had been that she was coming to live at the seaside, in Golden pop. 906. She'd bet they hadn't even changed it to pop. 908 now that she and her mom lived there. They weren't real citizens like Miss Aurora Peterson; they were just trash living on decent taxpayers' good money, that's what.

Down below on the beach, she saw a couple of boys running with a dog. They were having such simple fun, hurling pebbles into the sea while the dog chased them, that she longed to join in. She felt like screaming, "I'm here, can't you see me? Inside of me is a real person who wants to be like you. I want to laugh and have fun and be friends."

She wondered what they would say if she did, but she couldn't do it anyway. Her shyness was like a crippling disease. She was on the outside and always would be.

Except in her dreams. When her mother finally went to bed, she lay awake dreaming of security. She dreamed of having a white-painted house like Miss Aurora Peterson's, filled with solid pieces of oak furniture. She dreamed she was driving a white Cadillac convertible with the top down and the wind in her wavy blond hair, instead of the old turquoise Chevy and her straight mousy locks.

She dreamed there was chicken on their table for Sunday dinner and fresh-baked apple pie, and of her mother in a new hat and herself in pink lipstick, attending church, stopping afterward to chat with their neighbors, maybe getting an ice cream soda at the drugstore later.

As she grew older, her dreams grew bigger. She dreamed of success. She knew there were other places, other worlds, where people did not live the way she did, or even Miss Aurora Peterson, and she fantasized that one day she would be part of that world. Then she would buy her mother a new home overlooking the ocean, any place she wanted — anywhere except in Golden. She would buy her pretty clothes, diamond earrings, make her smile again the way she had that one time when she had realized she would never have to see her sadistic husband again. Mary Mallory wanted to make all her mother's dreams come true. And her own.

But the next morning, when she woke, she was still the girl who didn't exist.

Mal dragged her thoughts back from her painful childhood. She lifted her head and looked at Harry. She saw the sympathy in his nice gray eyes. "I've never told that to anyone before," she said sadly. "I was too terrified to go to a psychiatrist. I just couldn't verbalize it, admit it. I was afraid if I did, I would revert back to being Mary Mallory again, and everything I've fought for, everything I've become, would disappear."

Harry reached out and took her hands. They were cold, and her lovely face looked pinched and pale. He turned her hands palm up and kissed them. "You were brave, Mal. You won," he said admiringly. "However did you do it?"

She shrugged. "The usual. I was clever, a hard worker. I studied, got a scholarship to college. That's all my life consisted of for years — study and hard work." She sighed, remembering the long, hard, poverty-stricken years. "Then I graduated, and — well, you know the rest."

She scrambled to her feet, tugging down her pretty lace skirt, hitching the straps onto her shoulders, suddenly afraid she had embarrassed him. "I'll bet you're sorry you asked," she said, managing a smile.

He shook his head. "Oh no, I'm not."

She was so aware of him standing next to her, she felt she was drinking the air he breathed. "Don't go, Harry," she said suddenly, resting her head against his arm. "I'm afraid."

He pulled her to him, smoothed back her hair. He thought she looked shattered, as though she had just relived her long ordeal. He said reassuringly, "There's nothing to be afraid of. It's all over, gone. That's what the past is. Sometimes we're sorry we lost it. And sometimes we just thank God we don't have to live through it again. Believe me, I know."

She looked at him, big-eyed, wondering what he meant. Then he said, "But I shouldn't stay, Mal. It's the wrong moment, wrong timing."

She clung to his hand — she couldn't bear to let him go. "I know. It's just that I'm afraid to be alone."

He traced the contours of her face with his finger. "There's nothing to be afraid of, Mary Mallory, I promise you."

She looked away. Suddenly, a fat crystal tear rolled down her cheek.

He caught her to him, shocked: The steely wonder woman of television was crying. He held her close, told her everything would be all right, that of course he would stay. He stroked her hair, wiped her tears, gave her his handkerchief to blow her nose.

She smiled shakily at him. Her eyes were swollen, and her nose red. He guessed he shouldn't have, but anyhow, he kissed her. Her mouth opened under his and he lingered. He had been right the first time — her lips were like velvet.

He held her away from him, smiled at her. "I guess I'll sleep on the sofa."

"There's a guest room, but I don't think the bed is made up."

"Just give me a pillow and a blanket and I'll be in dreamland before you know it."

He let go of her hand. She hesitated for a moment, then went to her room.

He followed her. "Mmm, cozy," he said, looking around. "When I'm alone in my own little bed, I can think about you alone in your big one."

She tossed the pillow at him, and he caught it deftly. "Don't let your imagination run away with you, Jordan."

"It may be tough, but I'll try not to." He grasped the pillow to his chest instead of her. "Sleep well, Mary Mallory Malone. And promise me, no bad dreams."

"I promise." She crossed her heart with her finger, the way she used to when she was a kid.

"Good night, then." He dropped a quick kiss on the tip of her nose.

"Good night, Harry."

As the door closed behind her, he wondered why there was that little purr in her voice again when she said his name. But later, tossing and turning and wide awake, he wondered why he still had the sneaking feeling that she had not told him everything. That she still had secrets she wasn't yet prepared to let go of.

Mal sat up with a jolt. She looked at the clock: five A.M. She closed her eyes, listening. There it was again — the sound of water running. She smiled, leaning back against the pillows, clutching the sheet under her chin. The detective was an early riser.

She swung her legs over the edge of the bed, slipped on a short pink cotton robe, and padded barefoot to the kitchen. She stood in the doorway watching him. He was wearing dark blue boxers and nothing else; his body looked lean and hard, his hair was standing on end in cute little spikes, and he was attempting to make coffee in her machine.

"You hair looks as though you've slept in it," she said.

He turned and looked at her. "Sorry, I didn't think to bring a comb. Nor a toothbrush."

"I can provide both."

"Such efficiency at five in the morning. I didn't mean to wake you."

"That's okay. I wouldn't have missed the sight of you in those shorts for anything."

She grinned. The past was behind her, and she felt like Mal Malone again. Better than that, she felt happy, confident. She took the coffee from him and scooped it into the filter. "I'd have bought bagels, had I known."

"I would have bought them, if I'd known."

They looked at each other and laughed. He linked his arms lightly around her waist. "Would this be an appropriate moment, Ms. Malone, ma'am, to ask for a date? A real date this time. No fooling."

She leaned back, a finger to her lips, considering. "I think we know each other well enough now. Why not?"

"My place or yours?"

"Yours this time. It's my turn to find out how the other half lives."

"It will be my pleasure to show you, Ms. Malone, ma'am," he said. "Unfortunately, first I have to consult my work schedule."

"Me too."

"Then I'll call you later today."

The coffee machine burped and gurgled. She swung from his arms and took out mugs and milk and sugar.

"Only skim, I'm afraid," she said, pouring coffee.

"I take it black."

Her eyes connected with his. "I learn new things about you all the time."

"True." He moved closer, took the mug from her. She could smell his freshly showered skin, see the hair curling on his throat and chest. He was definitely dangerous.

"Your stubble is showing." She turned away, poured milk into her coffee.

Harry ran a hand ruefully across his dark bristled chin. "A dead giveaway," he said. "Whatever will the doorman think?"

She laughed. "He can think whatever he likes."

"Then you're not afraid he'll sell his story to the *Enquirer*?"

"I'm a modern woman." She shrugged. "I'm not supposed to be celibate."

185

He tasted the coffee. "I have to get my things from the hotel and catch the six o'clock shuttle from La Guardia."

"Then you'd better get a move on."

"True." He lingered, sipping the coffee. "Mal, thanks for trusting me last night."

She nodded. "You'll miss that flight," she said, not wanting to remember how much of her private self she had given away to him.

He went back to his room and dressed quickly. She was waiting for him when he emerged.

"I feel like the other man," he said, "sneaking out into the dawn."

"Except, thank goodness, there's no husband."

"I'm glad. I like my women free and clear of all encumbrances."

"Just in case you get serious," she teased.

"Just in case." He put his arms around her.

She could feel the hardness of his body against hers, and that faint masculine scent was in her nostrils. She leaned against him, wishing he didn't have to catch the plane. Then he kissed her.

The same long, gentle kiss as last night.

He let go of her and walked to the private elevator. She said jealously, "Lara Havers is going to call you."

"Too bad my number's unlisted." She was smiling as the elevator doors slid open. "I'll call you," he said.

The smile was still on her face as the doors slid shut and he disappeared from her sight. She went back to her bedroom to prepare for the busy day ahead, glancing at the basket of violets on the table under the window. Next to it was a creased-looking manila envelope that she had not seen before. Puzzled, she opened it. She stared into the dark menacing eyes of the serial killer in the photo-fit.

"Oh, Harry," she whispered, shocked. "You did it after all. You lousy, cheap-trick bastard."

17

Thunderstorms and a torrential downpour with severe winds delayed Harry's flight back to Boston — the TV news said it was a tropical storm. He mooched around the departure lounge at La Guardia, sipping the free coffee and thinking about Mal Malone. She was still an enigma, though now he understood her better. What he still did not understand, because she had avoided it, was about the photo-fit.

He wondered what she would do when she found the picture of the killer. He hoped it would trigger her memory. Or if not, that she would at least come clean and tell him what it was about the man's image that affected her so deeply.

For the first time ever, he was late for his shift. He didn't even have time to get home and see Squeeze, who had been left in the tender loving care of Myra, the dog-walker. Myra was a sixties person with a comfortable figure, untended coppery hair flowing past her waist, long skirts, Birkenstocks, and love beads. She looked like a human version of the red setter down the street that she walked every day.

"You sure chose your moment to be late," Rossetti said when Harry finally walked in. "The chief called a meeting at eight. He was pissed off beyond belief when you didn't show up. And I got the full brunt of his rage. 'How can I expect you guys to catch a moving violation, never mind a killer' was about the gist of it."

Harry grinned. The chief knew his record. Sure there were unsolved crimes on it, but his score was good, and the chief knew he was a dedicated cop and a hard worker. And that he never let go of a murder case: he worried at it like Squeeze unearthing a bone in the backyard — carefully, systematically, layer by layer. He wasn't about to let Summer Young's killer remain free. Not if he could help it.

"Have a nice vacation, Prof?" Rossetti tilted his chair back. He folded his arms, grinning at him, one bushy dark eyebrow raised in a question.

"You may have perfect teeth, Rossetti, but your mind's in a rut. A night off hardly constitutes a vacation."

"In your world it does. She must be pretty special for you to skip town."

Harry met his brown eyes squarely. "Yeah, she's special."

"Do we know her name?" The chair teetered back and forth as Rossetti rocked it, still grinning.

"You don't. I do."

"And that's the way it stays, huh?"

"Yup." Harry sorted quickly through the mass of paperwork on his desk.

"It wouldn't be Malone, by any small chance?" Rossetti pushed the chair too far. There was a loud crash, and Harry turned to look at him lying on the floor. He laughed as Rossetti sat up, rubbing his elbows.

"They don't make chairs the way they did when I was a kid," Rossetti grumbled.

"They don't make detectives that way, either. They broke the mold with you, Rossetti. Instead of fishing for information about my private life, why don't you bring me up to date on the situation with the chief."

Rossetti did just that, efficiently. Then all hell broke loose as a call came in about a shooting at a 7-Eleven. They were out of there in seconds, with no time even to think about Ms. Malone.

Uniformed cops were cordoning off the forecourt of the 7-Eleven store when the homicide squad screeched to a halt, sirens wailing. A police helicopter hovered overhead as Harry and Rossetti leaped from the car and surveyed the scene.

The emergency ambulance pulled in right behind, and the paramedics ran past them, carrying their equipment. Behind them came reporters from the *Herald* and the local television news crews, who were filming within minutes. Rossetti went to talk to the cops in the patrol car who had been first on the scene, while Harry made his way through the crowd to the entrance.

"Detective Jordan!" It was the reporter from the TV station. "How many victims are there, detective? And what do you know about the killer?"

He held up his hand. "Give me a break, will you, Lucia?" He was walking away from her. "I'll tell you what happened as soon as I know myself."

The sound man swooped on Lucia with his boom mike, and she turned to the camera. "News just breaking of a shooting at a local convenience store," she began, competently taking over. "We are not yet sure how many victims, but word is there may be more than one. And no news yet on the perpetrator, though we expect more on that soon. What we do know is that it was a robbery and several shots were fired. We'll keep you up to date on the story as it breaks."

Inside the store Harry stared down at the victims. One was only too obviously dead — the top of his head was blown away. The paramedics were bending over the other, a young black guy, inserting IVs into his arm. There was not much blood — just several neat round holes in his chest — but when they picked him up to wrap him in shock-foil, there was a pool of blood under his back. He was unconscious as they shifted him gently onto a gurney.

"The other guy's all yours, Prof," the paramedic said as they rushed the younger man into the ambulance.

Rossetti came in. He stood next to Harry, looking at the dead man. He said, "Prof, do you ever think you chose the wrong profession? You should have stuck with the law. Nice and clean and simple. It pays better too."

Then the medical examiner arrived, and then forensics, and the all-too-familiar routine that followed a homicide began.

Outside in the forecourt the police were questioning two eyewitnesses who had seen the killer running from the shop. They said he was toting a gun and had jumped into a waiting car and taken off. The injured young man worked at the store; the older man who had died must have been a customer.

"For him, it was just the wrong time, wrong place," Harry said bitterly as the medical examiner concluded his examination. Forensics drew a chalk outline around the victim. Then the remains were placed in a body bag and zipped up. Harry thought sadly that there was nothing left when a person was murdered, not even the normal dignity of death.

"It was an assault weapon of some sort," the ME said briskly. "Probably an Uzi. Forensics will tell you exactly which model."

The cops had a description of the escape vehicle — a white utility van. Harry's ears pricked up, and he questioned the two eyewitnesses closely. One, a middle-aged woman, said she had been on her way into the store when the man had come running out.

She was pale and breathing heavily, but she managed to give them a good description. "It coulda been me," she repeated over and over. "Two minutes earlier, it coulda been me."

The other witness was a homeless guy who hung around convenience stores searching garbage cans for soft drink cans to trade for a few cents deposit, maybe make enough to buy a cheap bottle of liquor to ease his woes. But it was early, he hadn't yet made enough for the day's booze, so he was coherent about what he saw.

"A white Ford utility," he said firmly. "Old and beat-up lookin'. Kinda rusty. A car like that shouldn't be on the road, detective. No sir, you should get that scum off the streets."

"You're right, buddy." Harry slipped him a couple of dollars when no one was looking. He wished he could have gotten him off the streets, never mind the rusty van.

An all-points was put out on the utility, but Harry knew it would have been stolen, and anyway the shooter would have dumped it as soon as he could. He'd bet his boots it was a drug-related killing. And that it was linked to the other killing a couple of weeks ago — the supposed hit-and-run. He would go to the Moonlightin' Club that night and ask around a little. Not that the kids were informers, but if their own were being slaughtered, someone might be willing to pass on what they knew.

Forensics got on with their job, and he and Rossetti took off for the precinct.

A second call came over the radio as they were heading back: a homicide in an old warehouse on Atlantic Avenue. An Asian man decapitated. Harry figured it was drugs again — it almost always was.

"Drugs, sex, and money," Rossetti agreed. "Pick any one, and you've got your motive."

It turned out to be a long, hard, gruesome day, the kind that left memories like sores in the mind, if not in the soul, the way Summer Young's death had.

Harry's only break came much later, back at the precinct, when a call came through with the results of the DNA tests on the semen found on Summer Young. It was a match with that found on the two other victims. They were definitely looking for a serial killer. He thought triumphantly of the photo-fit. He was certain the national networks would cooperate now and broadcast it. And that meant he was off the hook with Ms. Malone.

By evening, the thunderstorms had spread to New England, rattling the city, lighting it up like a Fourth of July fireworks display. Until the power went out downtown, that is. As well as in some of the suburbs, causing multiple pileups as vehicles hydroplaned and trucks jackknifed on the expressway. The emergency room at Mass General was chaotic, with victims rushed from the ambulances, lined up on steel gurneys for a doctor's attention.

Suzie Walker worked steadily alongside the other nurses, helping stabilize the patients, doing whatever was needed, while the doctors rapidly assessed the extent of their injuries and listed the priority cases for emergency surgery.

It was all hands on deck — the chief gynecologist was helping out, as well as Dr. Waxman. Even Dr. Blake, who had been on his way home and hadn't had time to put on a white coat, was working alongside the others.

"Wouldn't you think they'd have the sense to drive slowly," he muttered, carefully cleaning a long gash across a woman's forehead. "God, it's so senseless, people killing themselves on wet highways." He inspected the patient and the wound critically. Her eyes were open, rolled up into her head with just the whites showing. She was breathing slowly and with a terrible rasping sound.

"Fractured skull," he said with a sigh, "and a bad one. Get her to the scanner," he said to the male attendant, "fast as you can. I'll alert the surgeon."

He turned to the next gurney, where a small boy, maybe six years old, lay watching him with dark shocked eyes. "Mommy," the boy whispered, his eyes following the gurney being wheeled away.

Dr. Blake shook his head. The odds were,

the kid would not have a mother by morning.

"It's all right, baby," Suzie said soothingly. "The doctor's taking care of your mommy. And now he wants to make sure you're okay. All you have to do is tell him where it hurts."

Dr. Blake sighed again as he got down to business. Scenes like this only reinforced his decision to specialize in forensic pathology. His patients were a fait accompli by the time he saw them. Their children already knew their mothers were dead; all he had to do was tell them *how* she died.

Rossetti pushed his way through the door and surveyed the scene. It was like a war zone. A forty-car pileup, an eighteen-wheeler overturned on top of two automobiles, and innumerable single-car accidents, with people crushed by falling trees or skidding into walls.

"You'd think some folks never saw rain before," he marveled to the fraught nurse at the desk. "This makes my task look piddling. I'm talking about the shooting at the 7-Eleven."

She punched the computer, checking her records. "Trauma ward, the usual."

"Is he gonna make it?"

She checked again. "They removed three bullets from his chest. Two others passed through him. No, detective, I wouldn't bet on him making it."

Rossetti shook his head soberly. The man who had been shot was African American, only twenty-five years old, with a wife and a young son. Bitterness surged through his heart as he remembered his own big, vital Italian family. His father ran a small pizza parlor in the North End. Fast-food and takeout establishments were the hardest hit in robbery and violence, and he didn't like it one little bit. It hit him too close to home.

He walked through the waiting room to the stairs at the end of the hall. There were no seats left as frantic relatives flocked in search of their loved ones. Their faces were white and strained, big-eyed with fear.

Suzie Walker was walking toward him. There was blood on her white overall and she looked exhausted. She nodded to him, unsmiling, as they passed. There was no banter tonight. As she opened a door, he glimpsed a child on a gurney and Dr. Blake in civvies, tending to him.

"It's one of those nights," he thought gloomily. "Just one of those awful fuckin' nights that happen in a city every few years."

When he came downstairs again half an hour later, the waiting area had miraculously cleared and calm had descended once more.

"A lull before the storm?" he asked the duty nurse.

"I hope that's the end of it," she said. "Some of our staff have been on duty since this morning."

Rossetti glanced at the clock on the wall. It

was after midnight. "Good luck," he said as he left. But luck had already run out for the victim at the 7-Eleven, and it was his job to tell the young wife that she was now a widow. He did not look forward to it.

Harry had just got home when Rossetti called with the news. It was what he had expected. He wished he had a stronger word to use than *bastard* for the shooter. And he was glad it wasn't him who had to break the bad news to the widow tonight.

He dropped his overnight bag on the hall floor, then took the excited Squeeze for a splashy walk around the block, not caring that he left muddy footprints all through the hall when they got back. He felt glad to be alive.

He thought regretfully, it was too late to call Mal, and decided to do it first thing in the morning. He imagined her asleep in the luxurious antique French bed. There was a smile on his face as he stripped, took a long shower, and put on a pair of sweatpants and a white T-shirt that said "Fuzz-Buster" in red on the front. He peered hopefully into his refrigerator. There was a carton of milk with an expired sell-by date, a box of three-day-old pizza, and a couple of cans of Heineken.

He warmed up a slice of pizza in the microwave, opened a can of beer, and carried it all into the living room. He broke off a piece with pepperoni and gave it to the dog. It was like giving Tic-Tacs to an elephant — it disappeared as though it never existed.

He set the beer can on a side table and switched on the TV. *Headline News* was full of the storm front — a hurricane they called it now — and the numerous accidents and fatalities it had caused along the eastern seaboard. He hoped, worriedly, that Mallory had not been caught in it. His eyes drooped and he leaned back in the comfortable old chair. He was asleep within minutes.

Squeeze sat at his feet. He cocked his head to one side, waiting. When Harry didn't move, he turned his attention to the pizza on the side table. The can of beer toppled to the floor as he grabbed it, dribbling crumbs, melted cheese, and beer onto the carpet.

He checked Harry again. He was fast asleep. With a satisfied sigh he dropped down next to him, rested his head on Harry's bare feet, and closed his eyes. It had been a long day.

The gray Volvo was parked at the end of the street, half hidden under the sweeping branches of a red maple.

He parked here most nights now, waiting for her. He needed to track her movements as precisely as an air traffic controller tracks incoming flights. He needed to know her daily routine and her work schedule, when she would be working nights, and when she was likely to be alone.

She was different from his other girls in that

she had a busy social life as well as working. He would have preferred a student — they were younger and easier prey. But it was too risky. There were too many alerts out, and the college girls were on their guard.

Of course, he already knew she lived alone in a small one-story cottage. That was necessary for her to qualify. It was too dangerous to have to climb into second-floor windows or get in and out of a busy apartment building. There were always too many people around, and you never knew who might notice. Even though he had the kind of ordinary prosperous look that seemed to blend in with the everyday background of life, he had to be careful.

He had been there tonight, in the emergency room along with the hundreds of others. He looked no different from them, just another anxious face in the crowd. He had seen Suzie Walker there, tense-faced and hurried like everyone else. It had been easy to slip behind her desk when she was called away. He already knew that she usually kept her purse in the cupboard underneath, and he'd had her keys out of there in seconds.

He laughed to himself, thinking about it. He could have had a career as a cat burglar, stealing rich women's jewels — he was that good. Wait a minute, though — didn't they used to be called "second-story men" in the old days? Like Cary Grant in *To Catch a Thief?* He wouldn't have been any good after all — he had no head for heights, and it was too risky. He might get caught. He smiled again at the very idea; he was invincible by now. He knew it.

Pulling a tissue from the box of Kleenex in the console, he wiped the mist from the side window. He couldn't turn on the demister, because he would have to run the engine and draw attention to himself. He opened the window a crack instead, letting in a blast of cold wet air.

Headlights flickered through the rain, and he quickly picked up the night-vision binoculars. It was the electric-blue Neon.

Suzie Walker turned the car into the concrete parking area that had once been the garden of the little clapboard cottage. She sighed with relief as she switched off the engine. It was one o'clock in the morning, and she had been on duty since noon. She didn't grumble — nursing was the profession she had chosen, and it was her job to be available in emergencies. But she was exhausted, dead on her feet. All she wanted to do was fall into bed.

She climbed from the car, slammed the door, and locked it. She fiddled in her purse for her housekeys. She never kept them on the same ring with the car keys because there were just too many, and they were too bulky. She had a front door key, a back door key, a locker key at the gym, and a key for her safety deposit box, where she kept her only possession of value — a gold watch given to her by her parents on her twenty-first birthday.

Usually, the keys were easy to locate in the dark because of their bulk, but tonight she was having trouble. She frowned, peering into the recesses of the black leather bag, sweeping her fingers along the bottom. They were not there.

She glanced nervously over her shoulder. Not a soul was in sight. Apart from the sound of the rain bouncing off the sidewalk, there was silence. She checked the neighboring houses, but no lights were on. She hesitated, uncertain what to do, wondering where she could have lost the keys. The wind rattled the branches of the big old maple down the block, startling her. Fear pricked her spine. She glanced quickly over her shoulder, and, re-membering the recent murder, her skin crawled. You never knew who was out there, watching, waiting.

Her fingers trembled as she unlocked the car door and climbed quickly back inside. She pressed the central lock and began to breathe again. She wished she had listened to her father when he had said she should get a cell phone in case of emergency. She switched on the engine, backed out of the parking stand, and spun out into the slick wet street. Driving too fast, she shot down the road, past the parked cars and away.

He watched her go, smiling. Then he put down his binoculars and slipped on his raincoat. Of course he could have taken her then. She was there for the picking, ripe as a plum in summer. Except that wasn't his way. He needed to know more about her first in order to enjoy her properly.

That was what the public never understood about him, he thought as he walked quickly through the rain and turned in at her gate. It wasn't just the final act that was the pleasure. It was the buildup to it, the careful preparations, his cleverness at gaining access to the girl's home, his peek into her life, into her personal things, into her cheap feminine soul.

He smiled with pleasure as he put her key into the lock and walked into her house. He stood in the dark, listening. There was no sound. He took a mini-flashlight from his pocket and shone it cautiously around. A cat's eyes beamed redly back at him for a second. Then there was a faint scuttling sound, and it was gone.

He unbuttoned his raincoat and put on the thin rubber gloves, perfectly at ease. He would take his time, do a thorough job. Tomorrow, first thing, he would have a copy made of the keys. Then he would go back to the hospital and drop them in the parking lot in the spot where she had parked tonight. Someone would find them and hand them in. She would think she had dropped them carelessly. And he would be free to come and go in her house as he pleased. Until he decided her time was up, of course.

18

That same morning, after Harry had left for Boston — and left her the photo-fit — Mallory had gone to the gym and burned off as much of her anger as she could, fighting for those wholesome, calming endorphins that were supposed to flood your body and your head with a sense of well-being — if you worked hard enough at it. It didn't work. When she set out to walk to the office, she was still fizzing with rage and disappointment.

The aroma of roasting coffee slowed her footsteps. She hesitated. Then with a what-the-hell shrug of her shoulders, she stepped into the steamy little deli and ordered lox and cream cheese on a toasted sesame bagel and a large coffee. Then she waited, drumming her fingers impatiently on the counter, thinking how stupid she had been to trust Harry with her most personal memories, her deepest fears.

When the bagel came, she devoured it without a scrap of guilt, then continued on her way, blaming Harry for her indulgence with every step.

Her mood fluctuated between anger and sadness all day. Of the two, she preferred the anger. At least it was positive, though it was hard on her staff, who took the brunt of it.

"It's not you," she kept apologizing. "It's just one of those days."

"Morning after the night before," Beth said, wagging a knowing finger at her. Mal was wearing a dark-green sweater and skirt and black high-heeled boots. She looked good; if you discounted the shadows under her eyes and the tense body language. "So what time did he go home?"

"Who?" Mal asked too innocently, and Beth laughed.

"That may be your worst performance yet. But okay, if you don't want to tell me, you don't have to. I can wait." She shuffled the papers on her desk into a tidy pile. "But this can't, sweetheart. We've got some work to do, and I have to ask you to get your mind off whatever happened — or didn't happen — last night, and switch over to Tuesday's taping. You ready now?"

Mal nodded, but she said enviously, "You're so lucky with Rob. You're so well suited, so nice to each other."

"Hah! You haven't seen us going at each other. Like over who promised to pick up supper on the way home, when neither of us has done it, and we're both tired after a long day, and there's nothing in the house to eat, and I'm too exhausted to drag myself out and order something in a mediocre restaurant and then wait until it comes and finally not enjoy it when it does. *That's* when a marriage can go on the rocks. Believe me."

Despite herself, Mal laughed. "I think I'm glad I haven't seen you."

"You should be. It's not a pretty sight." Beth looked at her curiously, then patted her hand. "Sure you don't want to tell me about it?"

Mal shook her head.

"I know Harry was still there when we left," Beth persisted. "And Rob and I were almost the last to go."

"He stayed over," Mal admitted.

"Wow." Beth's eyes widened. "Was it that bad?"

"Of course not. Nothing happened. I just didn't want to be alone. And no, it wasn't bad. He brought me violets."

"I saw them. Enough to stock a shop."

"He's not a man who thinks small."

"That's good. So what was the bad part?"

Mal shrugged. "He's not interested in *me*, Beth. He's interested in what I can do for him. So when he calls today, would you please tell him that I'm out, or I'm too busy to come to the phone, or some excuse like that?"

"Oh, come on, Mal, give him the benefit of the doubt. I mean, any man who buys you a whole basket of violets can't be all bad."

"How about if he leaves the picture of the serial killer next to the violets — for me to find after he's gone?"

"He did that? Poor devil." Beth shook her head sympathetically. "He's really on the outs. But what a waste of a lovely man."

Mal glared at her. "Oh, for God's sake, he teaches you to salsa, and you're a pushover, just like Lara and the others."

Beth stood up and gathered her papers. "For a woman who never wants to see the guy again, it seems to me you're shouting about it too much. And isn't that a touch of green I see in your eyes?" She slammed the door behind her as she left.

Nerves snapping, Mal got through her day. At six she put on her lipstick and her jacket and walked through to the outer office. Beth had not mentioned Harry again.

Mal stopped at her desk. "Any messages before I go?" she said too casually.

"He didn't call, if that's what you mean."

"That's good," she said, not meaning it.

"He's still getting to you, isn't he?" Beth said shrewdly. "Maybe you'd better take his call, after all."

"*What* call? I can't even trust him to do that!"

Beth stared curiously at her. "Seems to me it's yourself you can't trust. What's the matter, Mal? Seriously, what's up?"

Mal swung her little black purse nervously by the strap. "It was so — so good last night, you know, friendly, nice. And then after he's gone, I find the photo-fit. He didn't mention he was bringing it, he didn't say he was coming over to discuss it again. He just left it there for me to find. Afterward."

"So what's wrong with discussing the photo-fit, anyway? I mean, this was a terrible murder, and if it turns out that there is a serial killer on the loose, maybe you *should* try to help him."

"But the photo-fit is no good."

Beth frowned, puzzled. "Tell me, Mal," she said, "how do you know the photo-fit is no good?"

"I — oh, I don't *know*." Mal subsided into a chair. She put her elbows on the desk, hiding her head in her arms. "I don't know if the photo-fit is accurate, of course I don't," she repeated. "It — well, there was something about it that upset me. The expression in his eyes. It was too creepy, sinister." She shuddered. "I don't know if I'm ready to take on a serial killer, Beth."

"I can understand that. But why on earth don't you just tell Harry? I'm sure he'll understand too."

Mal doubted it. "Harry Jordan is a cop first and a man second. I believe the only thing on his mind is catching the killer."

Mal thought Harry would call her that evening, so she made a point of being out. She had a date with some friends — a newscaster, his wife, and their new baby.

She brought flowers and a huge cuddly toy tiger and hovered over the baby. He was adorable, with a tuft of black hair and shoe-button dark eyes, and he lay quietly in his bassinet by the table while they ate. They quaffed a good bottle of wine, talking of their hard times on the climb up the TV ladder to fame and fortune.

"Sometimes, though," Josh said thoughtfully, "I think that those early years were the fun times."

"Only in retrospect," Jane reminded him. "Sure we had fun, but isn't it better when you've finally made it? I mean, you should know, Mal. You're the big success."

"It was no fun on the way up," Mal said vehemently. "In fact, it was hell." Then she laughed, embarrassed. "You know how it is when you're a woman — discrimination, harassment."

"I'm just glad I have all this instead," Jane said, yawning from lack of sleep and the demands of her new way of life. "Everything's a learning process, but I can tell you, Mal, this one is best of all."

Later, when she left, Mal took the memory of the evening with her. It was a soundbite of reality in her unreal world. A woman as a mother, a baby to care for, the animal warmth of the relationship between the couple. Their apartment, once done up in cool minimalist chic, had evolved into a proper home, as solid as any in suburbia. Compared with theirs, her own busy life seemed empty. She envied them their happiness and their child.

Back home again she checked her messages. There was E-mail — all business — but no friendly red blink on the answering machine. Harry hadn't even called.

The photo-fit was still on the table where she had thrown it. She picked it up and studied his face again. Then, shuddering, she ripped it to tiny pieces and threw them into the fire. Black smoke curled from the paper, finishing forever something that had never begun.

She took a shower, put on a T-shirt and a pair of pink boxers, and brushed her hair and creamed her face. The TV news flickered in the background, detailing the daily horrors, but she wasn't listening.

Then the newscaster said, "The City of Boston is on the lookout for a serial killer today, after the DNA samples found in the bodies of three young women victims were proven to match."

A photograph of a pretty young woman took the place of the newsreader.

"The latest victim, Summer Young, was twenty-one years old, class valedictorian at her local Philadelphia high school, and premed at Boston University. Like Mary Jane Latimer and Rachel Kleinfeld, she was abducted and raped. She was left for dead on a lonely beach.

"The Boston PD have issued a photo-fit of

the suspected killer. They ask that if you know this man, or have seen him, please contact them at the number appearing now on your screen. All calls will be treated with utmost confidentiality."

Suddenly the screen was filled with the photo-fit, while the newscaster gave details of his estimated height and build and the vehicle he was driving.

"The face of the suspected murderer of Summer Young, Mary Jane Latimer, and Rachel Kleinfeld," he concluded. "Again, anyone who can help trace him, call the Boston PD immediately."

Mal realized now why Detective Harry Jordan hadn't called her. He had gotten the killer's picture on national TV. He didn't need her anymore.

19

At seven the next morning, Harry wheeled the mountain bike back through Louisburg Square. Squeeze trotted, panting, at his heels. They had taken the eight-mile Greenbelt Bikeway from Boston Common, ending at the Franklin Park Zoo. He would have liked to have gone on longer, but as usual there was no time.

He left the bike in the hall, got a bowl of water for the dog, who drank it noisily, then grabbed the phone and called Mal. He couldn't wait to tell her about the networks picking up on the case. He frowned, disappointed, as the machine answered.

"I called," he said quickly. "Catch you later."

Then he leaped into the shower, ran an electric razor over the stubble, dressed quickly, and whistled for Squeeze. He was walking out of the door when he remembered. He strode back to the bathroom, ran a comb quickly through his hair, and was on his way out again in seconds.

Ruby's was still full of last night's nicotine as well as the beginning of today's quota. He took a seat at the counter and ordered coffee, two eggs over easy, ham steak, and home fries with a toasted bagel, wondering exactly how much secondary cigarette smoke he inhaled daily with his breakfast. And with the odd snack during the day and the occasional after-hours beer, and sometimes at supper as well. Then he told himself it was irrelevant because he wasn't about to give up Ruby's. He didn't remember eating yesterday, and he was starving.

Doris wasn't on duty this morning, so the dog went without his tasty treat. He squeezed into the narrow spot between the stool and the counter and settled down to wait.

Harry gulped down the coffee, asked for a refill, then walked to the pay phone near the entrance. He called Mal's number again, and again he got the machine.

He smiled; she always sounded as though she were hoping someone would call — *please leave me a message, even just a little one.* She was terribly insecure, though you would never know it to look at her. It was her own well-kept secret that she had shared with him and no one else.

"It's seven thirty, earlybird," he said. "I guess I missed you. Hope you survived the mini-hurricane yesterday. I'll catch you at the office later."

As he devoured the eggs and home fries, he thought that if she would only share the rest of her secrets with him, she might be a happier woman, and he would certainly be a happier man.

He called several times that day and left messages. He couldn't get her at the office — they said she was out. And no, she could not be reached. He called her in the evening and got the machine again.

"Listen," he said, exasperated, "you're so damned elusive, I'm running out of coins for the pay phones. I wanted to ask you about that date. You remember, the one we were supposed to have?

"I know this may sound a bit sudden, but it's my mother's birthday on Friday, and she's having a party. Of course I have to go, and I was wondering whether you might like to come with me. It's a bit soon to spring the whole family on you, but you've already met my dog, so you may as well meet the rest, and then you'll really know everything about me.

"I thought maybe afterward I'd take you to a little club I know, and one or two other places. Then the next day we could take a drive out to Vermont. I have a cabin there, in the mountains. We could get in a little hiking, spend the night. No strings. Honest," he added with a grin. "Call me, Ms. Malone, ma'am, if you would. *Please.* I'll be home after nine this evening. With a bit of luck.

"Oh, by the way, did you catch the photo-fit on the networks? The bastard is a serial killer after all."

Harry got more news from the crime lab that day. The sweater was a Scottish label, Pringle, that had been sold at Neiman-Marcus in Boston. It was a single-ply black cashmere turtleneck and had cost $365. The sweaters had sold well and had never been reduced and placed in a sale. Unfortunately the store had not stocked them for a couple of years, and they had no record of who might have purchased it.

"Our man is definitely well-heeled, Rossetti," Harry said that night over a beer at the Sevens pub on Charles Street. In fact, Harry was the one drinking the beer. Rossetti had ordered a vodka martini — shaken, not stirred, and with an onion, not an olive.

Harry threw him a sideways glance. "You think you're James Bond tonight, Rossetti, or what?"

"You're behind the times, Prof. Martinis are what the smart set are drinking these days. Women like 'em, y'know. They think they're glamorous."

"Whatever happened to the glass of white wine?"

Rossetti laughed. "That's what I mean. You're behind the times. You haven't even caught up to margaritas yet. What are you gonna offer Malone if she ever takes you up on that date?"

"Champagne," he said. "It suits us both." He wondered if she had called him back, and whether they were destined to miss each other's calls and never actually speak to each other again. He had meant to go home and get an early night, but Rossetti wanted him to meet his new girlfriend.

"My new woman," Rossetti corrected him. "And here she is now." He adjusted the knot in his yellow silk tie, smoothing back his hair with both hands.

The woman threading her way to the bar was petite, dark-haired, very young, and very pretty. Rossetti grabbed her possessively by the hand, deposited a kiss on her mouth, then slid his arm around her shoulders, drawing her forward.

"Vanessa," he said proudly, "I'd like you to meet my buddy on the force. His name's Harry and he usually comes with a sidekick by the name of Squeeze, except they don't allow dogs in here. And anyhow, Squeeze is too good for this joint."

She laughed at him. "What about me, then?"

"You're too good for almost every place except heaven," he said, looking admiringly into her eyes.

"Good to meet you, Harry," she said, offering her hand. "It's a pity about Squeeze."

Harry thought she was nice as well as pretty. "It's a dog's life, all right," he said, taking her hand and holding it to his lips.

Rossetti gave an astonished whistle. "Hey,

hey, I'm the Latin lover, remember? Okay, Vanessa. What'll you have?"

"Perrier with lime, please."

Rossetti raised an eyebrow, glancing questioningly at the martini.

She said, "Just think how it would look for a cop to be caught purchasing liquor for an underage female."

He clapped his hand to his forehead. "I forgot! No, I didn't. I never knew. How long have we been seeing each other?"

"Two weeks."

"And how old are you — exactly?"

"Twenty-one next month."

"Great," he said, relieved. "We'll have a party. And you can invite Harry. He could use a little social life."

She measured Harry in a glance. "I think Harry is perfectly capable of finding his own social life. But if there's a party, he's welcome to come."

Harry downed his beer. "Thanks for the vote of confidence, Vanessa. I'll leave you two to work out the party details. It was nice meeting you."

He said good night, then walked back down the street to where the Jag was parked. Squeeze poked his nose hopefully out of the window, and he took him for a quick walk around the block. He spotted the gunmetal Volvo again and instantly recognized the license number from the hospital parking lot.

Boston really was a small town, he thought, noting the name of the restaurant it was parked in front of. You tripped over someone you knew around every corner.

He stopped off at Au Bon Pain and bought a turkey and Swiss on sourdough, remembering the sandwich Mal had fixed for him the other night. Then he drove quickly home and checked the answering machine. It was blinking, and he pushed the play button impatiently.

He smiled when he heard her voice.

"Thank you for the invitation, detective," she said in a tone as brittle as frost on a windowpane. "Unfortunately, I'm planning on being extremely busy this weekend. Just one thing — the photo-fit you left at my place? Was it meant to get you on my show? I suppose the question is irrelevant now, since you have already succeeded in covering every network. Nice work, detective. Just shows it pays to cover all bases."

He groaned out loud. "Aw, Harry, now look what you've done." He replayed it just to make sure he'd heard right. It sounded even more final than it had the first time.

He stalked gloomily into the kitchen and poured Jim Beam liberally. Chucking in some ice cubes, he paced the floor, taking a slug every now and again, asking himself how he was going to get out of this one.

"What the hell is wrong with her, anyhow,

Squeeze?" he demanded. The dog looked back at him, his pale-blue eyes anxious.

"She's crazy," Harry said, stalking the perimeter of the kitchen again. "Out of her head. First I ask for her help, and she turns me down, no explanation. Then I ask her for a date, and she acts like I'm an impertinent upstart for even mentioning that I'd like to see her."

Blazing with anger, he picked up the phone and dialed her home number.

"Hello?" Mal said.

After getting the answering machine for two days, he was stunned into silence.

"Hello?" she said again.

"What the hell do you mean by leaving a message like that?" Harry yelled. " 'Unfortunately you are planning on being extremely busy this weekend.' What does that mean, Miss Star Malone, ma'am? That you're pissed off at me for leaving the photo-fit with you? Then why don't you just say so?"

"I'm saying so," she yelled back. "Now I'm saying so!"

"Why don't you tell me what it is about the goddamn picture? Just get it off your chest."

She clenched the phone tighter and said through gritted teeth, "It's nothing. And anyhow, it's nothing to do with you."

He paced the floor, phone clamped to his ear. "So all this fuss is about nothing, huh? Well, I've about had it with your *nothings*

Malone. I asked you for a date, and you accepted. I called — a bit late I admit, because circumstances were against me. But I called. And I invited you for the weekend. Now are you going to come or not?"

Mal was hunched in her favorite chair in front of the fire. She looked at the place at the other side of the coffee table where Harry had sat just the other night, and she remembered how good it had been.

"Yes," she said quietly.

"Yes . . . what?" Harry ran his hand through his hair, scowling. He didn't understand whether she was accepting his invitation or not.

"Yes, please, Harry."

He held the phone away, he stared at it, then at Squeeze. He couldn't believe what he was hearing. He said astonished, I was right, she is crazy. Then he said to her, "You mean it? You'll really come, Friday?"

"I would like to come, Harry," she said in a small voice. "I know you must think I'm crazy, but there was something about that picture and it being a serial killer. I just couldn't do it. You don't need me for that now, anyway."

"Was that what you thought? That I was using you?"

"Weren't you?"

"Maybe it started out that way. But not afterward. Not now."

"I believe you," Mal said. And she told her-self this time she really did.

Harry stopped prowling. He sank into the chair, and Squeeze subsided thankfully onto the floor next to him. There was a smile in his voice again. "Malone, why do we always fight?"

"It's you. You just seem to rub me the wrong way."

"Funny, I thought it was you."

Mal leaned back in her overstuffed rose-patterned chair, feeling the tension in the back of her neck beginning to relent. "Do you think we'll fight this weekend?"

"Not if I can help it. Do you approve of the itinerary?"

She thought for a minute. "Party, night-clubs, a cabin in the mountains? It may be the most adventurous weekend I've had in a long time." She curled her bare legs under her, snuggling further into the chair.

"Well, let's not make too much of it. My mother's parties are black-tie stuff — all the old die-hard New Englanders — stiff as they come. And the nightclubs are not exactly high-style — more like local hangouts. And the cabin in the mountains is just that — a log cabin. So bring your warm pajamas and your hiking boots."

"I'll remember to do that."

Harry hesitated, uncertain how to phrase it. He didn't want her to think she was committed to anything just because they were going to be together for the weekend. There was still that unknown element to her that he didn't yet understand, and he didn't want to scare her away.

"When I said 'no strings,' Mal, I meant it. This is a just-friends weekend."

"Okay," she agreed, but he could tell she was laughing. "By the way, what time is the party?"

"Eight, for an eight-thirty dinner. And as my mother told me, that means *prompt* eight o'clock, *prompt* eight thirty. She's a stickler for punctuality."

"A woman after my own heart."

"Mine too, I guess, though not for the punctuality."

"I'll be at the Ritz-Carlton," she said. "I'll meet you in the bar. Just tell me what time."

Any stray thoughts that she might want to share his bed quickly disappeared, and he said with a tinge of regret, "At seven, then."

"Harry."

Her voice had that purr in it again, and he grinned. "Yeah, Malone?"

"I can't wait."

Mal put down the phone, smiling. She felt as though a weight had been lifted from her shoulders. It wasn't what she had intended. In fact, she had meant very definitely not to answer the telephone. But somehow her hand had just reached out and done it. It had had nothing to do with her at all. And she had gotten it all off her chest in a good shouting match.

She laughed, remembering. She was a woman known for her control, but Harry Jordan had a knack for making her lose it. She really couldn't wait to see what the weekend held.

20

Miffy Jordan was not your average-looking woman and certainly not your usual mother figure. She was tall with good long legs and an elegant body that had barely changed its shape since she was a trim, athletic twenty-one year old and had married Harry's father. She kept it effortlessly in shape doing the things she had always done as a way of life: sailing, playing tennis, going for long walks, and gardening.

"I'm a low-maintenance kind of woman," she told her friends briskly when they inquired jealously how she managed it. "My mother was just the same, and my grandmother. It's in the Peascott genes."

The Peascott genes went back a lot of generations to the original settlers of Boston, although it wasn't something she ever boasted about. It was simply a fact. But when Miffy looked in the mirror in the morning, she always thanked God for the good Peascott bones.

She was about to turn sixty-five years old, yet she had no need of a face-lift. She had been sailing since she was a child -- her own father had taught her — and those lines around her eyes from squinting into the sun and the wind were her personal reminders of a happy life. And her cheekbones still supported their light burden of smooth flesh very nicely, thank you.

She had thick smooth hair that had once been blond and that had naturally, with the years, turned into the kind of muted platinum that women pay smart hairdressers a fortune to achieve. It was cut to just below her ears, and she wore it swept off her face in a smart bob.

She dressed neatly and conservatively in what she called respectable clothing, bought from the expensive stores and boutiques whose staff knew her well and understood exactly what suited her. Her everyday jewelry was a single strand of huge creamy pearls with matching earrings, a diamond wedding band, and the gold Cartier tank watch that her husband had given her thirty years ago.

In fact, Miffy Jordan looked as preppy as they came, but the truth was, she was as unconventional as her son. She traveled the world alone, trekking in the Himalayas; driving a four-ton truck through the Sahara and getting hopelessly lost; racing Ferraris in Monte Carlo; spending a month in a Buddhist retreat in Vietnam; and paddling the length of the Amazon from Brazil to Colombia. She had narrowly escaped death en route from poisoned darts, as well as from a bomb meant for a member of a drug cartel in Bogotá.

"I'm not the velvet-hairband type. I can't while away my days playing bridge and sipping iced tea," she told Harry when he had suggested she cool it — after all she wasn't getting any younger. "I'm not meant to die in my bed. Peascotts never do."

Remembering her family history of whaling captains and explorers and seafarers, as well as bankers and pillars of society, Harry guessed she was right. "Whatever makes you happy," he told her. "Just, for God's sake, be careful."

Her gray eyes, exactly like his, raked him scathingly; "Give me credit, Harry, please. I've gotten to this age without too much trouble, and I'm more likely to be run down on a Boston street than in the Sahara."

Nevertheless, she was sixty-five, and her contemporaries had long been surrounded by daughters-in-law and babies. She wanted Harry to marry again and give her grandchildren.

She had liked Harry's first wife, even though she was not exactly the girl she would have chosen for him. But Harry was an independent cuss — always had been, always would be. It was a nice surprise, therefore, when he called and told her he was bringing a date to her birthday party.

"Do I know her?" she asked, still thinking hopefully of her friend's charming daughter whom Harry had taken out a few times before his job got in the way, as usual.

"Perhaps you do, though not intimately" was his cryptic reply, which immediately set her to thinking of everyone she knew's daughters. So as she prepared for her birthday party, she anticipated more than just blowing out the candles, seeing old friends all together again under her roof, and opening her presents.

The party was to be held at her weekend house, an hour's drive out of town. It was a sprawling old place — a Jordan home, not a Peascott — and it brought back memories of her husband. It was the greatest pity, she thought as she did every year at this time, that Harald could not be there with her to celebrate, but they had both known when they married — he was in his forties and she just twenty-one — that they would not see out their old age together. Still, it had been worth it for the love and satisfaction their marriage had brought her. Harald would be there, in spirit, to wish her happy birthday, she knew it.

The white clapboard heart of the house had been a farm in the early eighteen hundreds. Dormers and wings and extra bits had been added haphazardly over the decades until it was a hodgepodge of oddly-shaped rooms, with strange staircases that sometimes led to nowhere more than a landing with a window and a view; as well as a generous supply of comfortable bedrooms and well-appointed bathrooms.

It straddled a small hill whose sloping pastures were dotted with horses and a flock of Jacob sheep. The long wooden "sunset" porch overlooked a rushing little stream where visiting children liked to sit, with a miniature rod and line, hoping to catch brown-speckled trout.

Of all her houses — and she had three, including the old Peascott mansion on Boston's Mount Vernon Street and a seaside villa on Cape Cod — Jordan's Farm was her favorite.

An enormous tent lined with yellow taffeta had been erected on the back lawn. The round tables had matching pale yellow cloths, trailed with dark green ivy and full-blown cream roses. There were Georgian silver candlesticks on the tables and plain but elegant sterling flatware, and Lenox crystal next to the Henredon plates, even though she had been warned by the caterers that some would surely get broken.

"Let them," she said, as carelessly as her son had of his antique rug when the dog chewed a bone on it. "They're only plates. All they're meant for is to give us pleasure. Just see that you have extra staff to wash whatever is left by hand, that's all I ask."

Her top-notch team of caterers, butlers, and waiters were busy in the kitchen and in the tent. The vintage champagne was on ice in the old wooden milking pails. Every room in the house was filled with her weekend guests, and more were en route in the buses she had chartered to transport them.

A string quartet from Boston's Berklee School of Music was rehearsing in the center hall, the canapés were arranged on silver trays, and a band, which would play the nostalgic tunes Miffy was so fond of, was set up for dancing later. It promised to be a great evening, and she could hardly wait.

All she had to do now was to put on the sea-green Valentino that she had picked up in Rome a couple of months ago on her way back from Turkey. And then to wait and see exactly whom Harry was going to surprise her with.

Harry was in the Ritz bar at precisely ten minutes before seven. He settled in a corner table where he could see the door, remembering when he had done this at Ruby's and Mal had stepped in out of the rain looking like a tropical flower in a bunch of weeds. He straightened his black bow tie and ran his hands through his hair. It was still wet from the shower, and he wondered vaguely whether he had combed it. At least he had remembered to shave.

Thinking of Rossetti, he summoned the bartender and ordered two vodka martinis, but with olives — not the onions his buddy preferred — and he didn't add the shaken-not-stirred bit either.

The waiter set the martinis on the table along with a dish of pretzels and nuts. When Harry glanced up, Mal was standing in the doorway, looking at him.

She was wearing a long taupe-colored slip dress in some sheer material, swirled with the tiniest golden beads and cut to a very low V in front. It clung to the right bits of her as though it had been designed specially to show off her graceful body. What there was of the dress was held up by two barely visible straps. Harry figured they must have sold it by the ounce.

He loped across the room and took her hand, then gave her a courtly little bow. "You look sensational," he said, dazzled. "Whatever do you wear under something like that?"

She gave him a smiling sideways glance as they walked to the table. "Don't even ask."

The back of the dress was cut even lower than the front, and as she walked, it slithered smoothly over her beautiful butt like cream over peaches. Harry took a deep, amazed breath, running his hands through his hair as they sat down.

She looked severely at him. "You shouldn't do that. Now it looks as though you forgot to comb it." Then she laughed. "Come to think of it, I've yet to see you with your hair combed." She eyed him up and down, considering. He looked handsome and totally at ease in a well-cut dinner jacket. In fact, he looked like a man in a Ralph Lauren ad — the kind who made women's hearts beat a little faster. "I thought you'd been born wearing Levi's and black leather. I'm glad to see I was wrong."

"Classy, huh?" He fingered his satin lapels, grinning confidently. "By the way, I ordered drinks."

She eyed the two martinis with raised eyebrows and he said, "I've been informed by a reliable source that martinis are the drink of the moment. And that women consider them glamorous."

She tasted the drink cautiously. "I've never had a martini before."

"I never even got as far as margaritas."

Their eyes met, and they laughed. "Wouldn't you rather have a beer?" she said.

He shook his head. "This is definitely a champagne occasion, and as Doris noticed the first night we met, at Ruby's, you are definitely a champagne woman. I just ordered the martinis to impress you with how au courant I am in the fashionable world of drinking and dating."

"Is this really a date?"

"If it isn't, I don't know what is."

"Then I intend to enjoy myself."

"Okay. So do I." He took her hand, and they smiled happily at each other. "We've been together five minutes and not one cross word."

"Must be some kind of record."

He nodded. "Are you going to drink that thing?"

She shook her head. "I'm saving myself for the good stuff."

"Very wise." He signaled the barman for the check. "We'd better get going."

She looked surprised. "I thought you said eight o'clock."

"I forgot to tell you it's out of town. Mom always throws her birthday bash at the farm."

She glanced at her dress, dismayed, imagining a country barbecue. "I'm not dressed for a farm."

"Don't worry, they'll lend you some overalls and gumboots when you get there."

He paid the bill and swept her out of the bar and through the foyer.

She stopped at the front desk and picked up a gold-wrapped parcel. "Birthday present," she explained, when he looked questioningly at her.

He groaned. "I knew I forgot something."

An enormous white stretch limo was waiting at the curb. Mal laughed. "Nice going, detective," she said. "I feel like a Hollywood starlet."

"Detectives and starlets never drink and drive. And let me assure you that the last time I did this was on prom night. With Jessica

Brotherton in strapless shocking-pink taffeta that shocked the hell out of me — I'd never seen so much bare skin. We necked all the way home, and she let me put my hand inside her dress."

He grinned at her, and she said crisply, "Don't bet on lightning striking twice, detective."

He clasped his hands to his heart, gazing to heaven. "Oh, Malone, you don't know how those words wound me."

She gave him a scathing look. "Now I know you're crazy."

"Me? I thought it was you."

She looked around for the dog. "What, no Squeeze?"

"He's not good at parties. He's staying with Myra tonight." She raised her eyebrows. "Myra's the other woman in my life."

"I should have known there'd be another woman," she said resignedly as the limo edged its way out of the city.

Harry took a bottle of his favorite champagne from the ice bucket and poured her a glass. "Welcome to Jordan's Farm, Mal Malone," he said softly. And he meant it.

It was a magnificent night: balmy, cloudless, a full moon. The string quartet was playing Haydn, and white-jacketed waiters were crisscrossing the wide flower-filled porch serving canapés and champagne. Guests milled on the lawns and lingered by the stream. Miffy Jordan drifted elegantly around, greeting the new arrivals with little shrieks of delight, kissing everyone soundly.

"None of this air-kissing rubbish," she said, handing them a Kleenex from the box she carried. "You just have to wipe off the lipstick, or else live with it like a badge of honor given you by your hostess."

The long white limousine looked out of place as it rolled up the lane behind the chartered bus. "Now I really feel like a starlet," Mal said, glancing uncomfortably at the sedate black Mercedes and Saabs parked in the yard.

"Old guard New Englanders don't belong to the if-you've-got-it-flaunt-it category," he explained. "Except for my mother. Wait, you'll see what I mean."

Miffy was in the hall asking the classical musicians if they could play "Smoke Gets in Your Eyes." "It's my favorite song," she explained as they stared blankly at her.

Mal thought she looked exactly like the Hollywood version of a well-brought-up rich woman of a certain age: flawlessly dressed in Valentino couture, every perfect natural platinum hair in place, cheekbones to die for, and a tight elegant body.

Harry gave her a big hug, then took Mal's hand and introduced them. "Mom, this is —"

"Mallory Malone," she said, astonished. "Well, I never. What a pleasant surprise. And so much lovelier even than on television. Welcome, my dear, welcome to Jordan's Farm."

She gave Mal a lipsticky kiss, then handed her a Kleenex. "I don't care what they claim, nothing is kissproof," she said, taking Mal by the arm and leading her into the throng. "Now, I want you to meet my guests, all family and old friends." She glanced shrewdly at Mal. "You needn't worry, I shan't let them pester you with questions."

"Besides, Mom's the star of this particular show," Harry said. "She doesn't need you stealing her thunder."

"Is that a gift, dear?" Miffy said, ignoring him. "How kind of you. I expect Harry forgot again. He always does. Harry, put it on the table with the rest. I'll open them later."

"After midnight." Harry remembered the annual routine from his childhood days. His mother had been born at midnight, and she claimed both days as her anniversary. The candles were blown out on the stroke of twelve, and the presents were opened after that.

Miffy had her arm around Mal as she introduced her to her friends. She turned and looked over her shoulder at Harry, beaming and nodding approvingly. He groaned — he only hoped his mother wasn't going to read more into this than there was, because at the moment, there wasn't much. Besides, he had promised Mal no strings, and he meant to keep his promise.

21

At about the same time that Miffy Jordan's birthday guests were sitting down to dinner, the man parked the gunmetal Volvo on the shabby little street in South Boston where Suzie Walker lived, in the turn-of-the-century cottage that, like so many others, had become a rental unit.

The upstairs portion of the house had been vacant for several months, which was quite a relief to Suzie, because when she worked nights, she needed her sleep and the previous tenant had been a student who liked to play Whitney Houston singing "I Will Always Love You" at full blast, any hour of the day or night.

She relished the peace and quiet. Besides, it meant she could give a party — and play her own choice of music as loudly as she liked — without having to consider the upstairs tenant or, worse, invite him.

She was working the night shift this week, and she had spent a pleasant afternoon having her hair styled and doing a bit of shopping, finding a couple of bargains at the Gap and a terrific little silk dress that she could have sworn was Anne Klein II in Filene's Basement. Her sister, Terry, was having a party next week, and it would be exactly right.

She puttered about the cottage, hanging her purchases neatly in the closet, tidying up. She preferred living alone in a cheaper area to living with a couple of roommates in cramped quarters nearer the hospital, sharing a bathroom and getting on each other's nerves.

The night was warm and she opened all the windows to let in whatever breeze there might be. She fixed herself a cup of herbal tea and took two Tylenols for the headache that had been bothering her all day, then heated the packaged low-fat-chicken-with-pasta she had picked up in the supermarket. She ate it standing at the kitchen counter, rereading a letter from her sister that said she was getting engaged to the young man she had known since high school, and that the wedding would be in July and would she be the bridesmaid.

Suzie wondered if bridesmaids could wear black — at least it would be useful afterwards.

After she had eaten, she called her mother, as she did every Friday at this time unless work prevented it. They always had a nice chat about the weekly events and this time about Terry's wedding.

"You will be able to come to the party next week, Suzie?" her mother asked hopefully.

"I wouldn't miss it. I even bought a new dress," she promised. "In fact, I'm seeing Terry tomorrow, but I'll call now and tell her."

Terry wasn't home, so she left a message on

her machine saying she would call back later. Then she hurried into the bathroom to shower. She hadn't noticed how the time was flying, and now she would have to rush or she would be late.

The bathroom was at the side of the house, right in his line of vision. He had the binoculars trained on the window the instant the light came on. The glass was frosted, but tonight she had opened it a crack because it was so warm, and given him an unexpected treat.

A stream of obscenities spat from his mouth as he caught a fleeting glimpse of her stripping off her clothes. She stood there in her bra and panties, glanced doubtfully at the window, then stepped across and closed it firmly.

"Cunt," he muttered, "bitch, whore, cunt . . ." The words tumbled over each other in a vicious litany of hate.

Suzie dressed quickly in her white uniform, then picked up her purse and checked for her keys, thankful they had been returned to her.

The headache was still pressing behind her eyes and she thought it was a good thing she had the weekend off. It had been a hectic few days at the hospital, and she had put in long hours — she could use the break. She planned on spending a lot of it in bed, just catching up on sleep, as well as doing some studying because she had exams very soon. She had arranged to see Terry later in the afternoon, and they would talk about weddings and dresses. And then Sunday she had a date with a young intern from Beth Israel Hospital, but he'd probably be exhausted — interns always were — so it would be another early night.

She checked her appearance in the mirror before she left: smoothing her skirt, straightening her collar, tucking back her hair. Noting the shadows under her eyes, she thought longingly of sleeping in the following day. She smiled at her reflection and told herself encouragingly, "This time tomorrow you will look like a different woman, Suzie Walker."

She had gotten as far as the door before she remembered that she had not closed the windows, and she rushed around hastily latching them. She checked the back door while she was at it and pushed the bolt into place. Then she walked outside and locked the front door, testing it to make sure it was secure.

Her neighbor, Alec Klosowski, who worked at a bar on Newbury Street, was leaving for work at the same time. He called hello and waved. "You can never be too sure," he said, locking his own door firmly. "There's too many crazies around to be careless about locks."

Suzie looked doubtfully at him. "I lost my keys the other day. I dropped them in the parking lot. They were found and handed in, but I wonder who had them that night."

He looked seriously at her. "You should get

the locks changed, Suzie. You never know."

"I guess so."

They waved good-bye, and she got into her little Neon and dumped her bag on the seat next to her. She edged the car out, thinking worriedly about what Alec had said. But she told herself that whoever had found the keys didn't know they belonged to her, and besides it was so expensive to get locks changed. On her nurse's salary she just about made it through the month — there was never anything left over for extras.

Anyhow, it was the least of her problems. She rubbed her eyes wearily as she drove off down the street. Right now she still had the headache, and she had exams coming up next month and a bridesmaid's dress to worry about.

He watched her go, her face and her flame-red hair a quick blur as she drove too fast down the street, late as usual. He shook his head, deriding her tardiness. He was never late for anything. His daily schedule was timed as precisely as if he'd worked out every blink of it with a metronome. He could tell you exactly where he might be at any given time on any day or night. Except on nights like this, of course. These were his special nights. Other people went to the movies, he preferred reality.

He glanced at his expensive steel and gold watch. The dial had little red and blue enameled flags instead of numbers. It was the sort of trophy a rich yachtsman owned. Although he was not a sailing man, he liked to give the impression of being an outdoors, sporty person. Whenever he was asked what he was doing on a weekend, he would say casually, "Oh, I guess a little sailing out at the Cape, if the wind's good. Maybe some kayaking, we'll see."

It was all a lie, of course. The only times he went to Cape Cod were when he was hunting — selecting future media stars. He figured they should thank him for giving them a moment of glory in their otherwise mundane lives.

It was still too early for action — lights were on in other houses, and the odd person was hurrying down the street. Safe behind his dark-tinted windows, he took the silver flask of good brandy from his pocket and poured some into the little cup. He settled down to wait, sipping it thoughtfully, anticipating the pleasure to come.

22

At the party, the last time Harry had seen Mal his uncle, Jack Jordan, had had his arm around her waist and was whispering in her ear. And Mal had been laughing. That was half an hour ago.

Jack Jordan was a notorious ladies' man, with four marriages and a string of mistresses to prove it. He still had an eye for a pretty woman plus he was tall, silver-haired, and handsome with a little mustache, and he still had a great line in flattery, which seemed to get him everywhere.

"The old boy's gone off with my date," Harry complained to Miffy.

They were in the tent, checking that the arrangements were as perfect as she expected.

"Don't worry, Harry. He'll have to return her for dinner. She's sitting here, next to you." She plucked Jack's place card and deftly switched it to a nearby table. "And now Jack is sitting next to old Biddy Belmont, who is even older than he is and deaf to boot. He'll have to repeat every word he says twice. That'll take the fizz out of his champagne."

They laughed, and he gave her a hug. "Anyone ever tell you you're a pretty special woman?" he demanded, his arm still around her.

"Your father, the day he asked me to marry him. Come to think of it, I don't remember him ever mentioning it again after I said yes. I'm sure there's a moral in that, somewhere," she added vaguely.

The butler pounded on a brass gong, announcing that dinner was about to be served and guests thronged into the gorgeous tent, assailed by the scent of roses and good food.

"There you are," Harry said as Mal appeared, her arm threaded through Uncle Jack's.

The old boy raised a wicked eyebrow. "I was seeing that Mallory had a good time, Harry. Couldn't let her loose in this lusty mob of Peascotts and Jordans, could I?" He patted Mal's hand possessively, and she beamed up at him. "I hope I'm sitting next to you, my dear."

"No, you're not," Harry said firmly. "You're sitting next to Biddy Belmont."

Jack groaned, "Your mother's punishing me again."

"She expects every man to do his duty. It's her party, after all."

"See you later, Jack," Mal called after him, as he made his way to the neighboring table with a deep sigh of regret.

"I'm jealous," Harry said, looking at her.

She laughed. "He looks like a central casting version of a benevolent rich uncle."

"And I can assure you, he's played that role with quite a succession of young 'nieces.' "

"More power to him. He's adorable."

"Remember me? The guy you came in with?"

"My date, I believe."

"Same fella." They took their seats at the table, and he leaned across and whispered in her ear, "Besides, I missed you."

She slid him a sideways glance, and he saw laughter in her eyes. "Never thought I'd hear you admit that, detective."

"I'm human."

She looked mockingly at him, then turned to her neighbor on her right. And then the caviar was served, three different kinds over lightly scrambled eggs, and the celebration dinner was under way.

Mal knew she was enjoying herself because she didn't even think about it. She never asked herself, as she so often had at parties, "Is this really fun? What am I doing here?"

She had never been to a grand family party like this one, where everyone had known everyone else all their lives. They had seen one another through births, marriages, and deaths and shown up loyally for the funerals as well as the celebrations. They probably never even thought twice about it. In their circle it was just what you did — that was the way life was. But she would have traded all her success just to have belonged to it from birth.

She glanced at Harry, who was listening with interest to a discussion on the merits of retrievers versus pointers as gun dogs. He turned and met her eyes, then gave her an encouraging smile. "You okay?" he murmured in her ear.

"Couldn't be better."

He glanced at his inexpensive but practical digital watch. "The dancing should be starting soon. If you had a dance card like in the old days, I'd write my name in every one."

"Even the waltzes?"

"You think I don't know how to waltz?"

"It's not exactly a required credit for a homicide cop."

"Ah, but remember I was a legal man before that. And before that, I was an obnoxious little prep-school boy whose mother sent him to dance classes, so he could escort young ladies to cotillions."

She shook her head, marveling. "Is there no end to your achievements?"

"It just goes on and on," he agreed immodestly, as the music started up.

His mother took to the floor first, circling in the arms of her brother to the strains of Jerome Kern's "Smoke Gets in Your Eyes," while everyone applauded.

"It was their song," Harry told Mal as he

246

took her hand and led her to the floor. "Hers and Dad's. She always dances this one first, for him."

How lovely, Mal thought a touch enviously. And then she was in Harry's arms, his hand was pressing firmly into the small of her back, and the other was holding her fingers, curled lightly in his. They danced silently. Her eyes were half-closed, and there was a dreamy look on her face.

"You dance well," he whispered.

She looked at him. "I promise you I didn't learn at prep school."

"Where did you?"

"I took lessons. Later. I took lessons in everything."

He said astonished. "Lessons in how to live?"

She nodded. "No one taught me the rules when I was a kid, the social niceties. I might have been brought up with wolves in the forest for all I understood."

He held her closer — her hair tickled his nose, and he thought it was like spun golden silk. Her skin had the faint elusive scent of flowers and did wild things to his nerve endings. The tune ended, but he held on to her hand. "Care to take a stroll around the garden with me, Malone?" She nodded, and they walked hand-in-hand from the tent.

Miffy and Uncle Jack watched them go. "What do you think of her?" she asked.

"Fine young woman. Top class. You can always tell."

"Stay away from her, you wicked old man," she warned. "I have high hopes for her, if Harry can tear himself away from the job for more than half a minute."

"He'll be a fool if he doesn't," Jack said. "A darned fool, I'd say," he added admiringly.

Harry led Mal through the gardens his mother cultivated with such loving care. The trees were strung with little white lights, and pretty Chinese paper lanterns dotted the banks of the stream. As they wandered through the rose garden, Mal checked every name on the tags, even though the roses were still just buds.

"Old-fashioned roses are my favorite," she said. "I grow some myself, on my terrace, but the wind and the pollution wreak havoc with them."

"You must tell my mother. She'll be thrilled to know you're a gardener too. Among your other talents."

The sound of the band playing "Moon River" drifted on the warm breeze. He stared at her. She was still looking at the roses, and he had a sudden overwhelming urge to take her in his arms. "Maybe it's the romantic lighting, or maybe the music, but I was wondering whether 'no strings' included a kiss? Just between old friends, of course."

She took a step closer. "Technically, we're

not old friends. And a verbal contract is binding."

"You obviously haven't read the small print." He slid his hands around her waist, pulling her gently to him. "Tell me, have I kissed you before?"

Her eyes linked with his, and she felt that interesting little catch in her heart. "I believe so. A friendly kiss, naturally. Before the verbal contract and 'no strings' clause."

"I think I've met my legal equal," Harry murmured, bending his face to hers.

She slid her arms around his neck, wanting to be held closer, feeling the warmth of his hands on her naked back.

They heard voices over the music, coming closer, and stepped hastily apart as a group of guests wandered by. "There's no privacy in the countryside," Harry whispered, disgruntled. "Anyhow, this contract would never hold up in court."

"Why not?" She could see he was smiling.

"Because I'm my father's son, and I'd plea-bargain with you and make a deal."

"What kind of deal?"

"Extra kisses on demand."

She threw back her head and laughed, but he stopped her mouth with a lingering kiss that sent little silken quivers through her belly. It was just as well she was protected by the "no strings" clause, she thought, because she liked it a lot when Harry kissed her like that. But more people were coming. He took her hand, and they walked back to the house.

"I grew up in this house," he said as they strolled through the beamed living room to the pine-paneled library. Mal looked around with interest. The shelves bulged with an ancient collection of classics and best sellers. Parchment-shaded lamps cast a pleasant glow, and comfortable sofas covered in plain yellow linen flanked the fireplace, where an enormous bouquet of garden flowers bloomed instead of a fire. A painting of a horse, a big bay mare, hung over the mantel, and other paintings, mostly of horses and dogs, were interspersed between the shelves of books.

Mal thought, with an envious catch at her heart, that it was the real version of the fantasy world she had created in her penthouse.

"The large painting is of Horse," Harry said, "my father's favorite. And the one of the retriever is Dog."

She held up a protesting hand. "Wait a minute. *Horse? Dog?*"

He shrugged. "He said he didn't have time to be thinking about names, and when he called, they came anyway. I'm just surprised I didn't end up named Boy. Though come to think of it, he did tend to call me Son a lot. He grinned at her. "And you thought you had problems."

"I would have settled for Girl if it meant

being brought up here," she replied wistfully. "Did you hate him?"

"Of course I didn't hate him." He looked astonished at the very idea. "He was my father — he was who he was. He might not have had time to think up names for his animals, but he cared about them all right. And he cared about me."

"Then you loved him? Even though he cost you your football career," she added.

"Come on, Malone," he said, amused. "I'm not on your show." He picked up a photograph in a silver frame. "This is him," he said, handing it to her. "The genuine article."

Miffy appeared suddenly in the doorway. "Oh, Harry, you're showing Mallory the house. How nice." She drifted, smiling, toward them. "Harry spent his boyhood here, you know. And I spent my honeymoon here. Never wanted to go anywhere else then. Now I'm older, I'm making up for lost time. I can't get around to all those distant countries fast enough."

She noticed Mal was holding the photograph. "Ah, that's Harald. My one and only true love. I miss him like billyo," she added regretfully.

Mal looked questioningly at Harry. " 'Like billyo' — an antique English expression often used by my mother, which we take to mean 'like crazy,' " he explained.

"They should write a song," Miffy said

thoughtfully. " 'I'm Billyo Over You.' "

Mal laughed and looked at the picture. She could see where Harry came from all right.

Miffy read her mind. "No chance Harry was adopted, is there?" She laughed. "His father always said he was a true chip off the old block." She picked up other photographs from the collection massed on the tables and sideboards, explaining who they were and how they were related. "It's all quite complex because the Peascotts go back so many years and have so many branches. And the Jordans are almost as bad.

"What about your family, my dear?" she asked, putting the beautifully framed photographs back in their places. "Not as big as ours, I hope. Just think of —" She stopped herself in time as she caught Harry's warning eye. She was getting ahead of herself again — she had been going to say, Think of the size of the wedding party.

She laughed merrily. "Forgive me — Harry always says I ramble on. And after all, you two hardly know each other yet, do you?"

Mal threw an amused glance over her shoulder at Harry, as Miffy linked her arm and drew her out onto the porch. He shrugged and pulled a pained face as though he didn't know what his mother meant, though of course he did. He thought he'd better get Mal out of there before Miffy really put her foot in it.

"Almost time for the cake, Mom," he called.

She glanced at the beautiful diamond evening watch she was wearing; another long ago birthday gift from her husband. "So it is, so it is. Oh, what fun."

Harry marveled at her enthusiasm as she darted off to make sure her cake would appear on time in the tent. "She goes through the same performance every year. And every year I swear she enjoys it more."

"She's wonderful," Mal said. "So . . . vital." She thought that Miffy Jordan was everything her own mother had not been.

Everyone seemed to know the midnight routine and was heading in the same direction. They crowded around as the lights were dimmed. The butler struck the gong loudly twelve times; it reverberated until their ears hurt, and then the cake was wheeled in. It was yellow, of course, and topped with yellow roses. The band played and they all sang "Happy Birthday" as Miffy blew out her candle and cut the first slice of cake.

"As you all know, this first slice is for Harald, up there in Heaven. May you enjoy it the best way you can, darling. And of course, the second slice is for my dear son, Harry."

She continued cutting her cake and listing names, adding anecdotes and endearments.

Watching her, Mal felt like the little girl at the movies again. She was in a magical place where everyone wore beautiful dresses and lovely jewels; life was wonderful, and everybody lived happily ever after. Only this time it was real, and they had let her be a part of it.

23

At midnight the lights were out in all the houses on Suzie Walker's street. He got out of the Volvo, stretching with relief. It was later than he expected, but he wasn't worried about that. Suzie was on the night shift. He knew he had plenty of time.

Keeping to the shadows, he walked quickly down the street. He was not wearing his uniform — that was for the special event. Instead, he had put on dark pants and a black shirt so if by chance he encountered someone, he would look like any ordinary passerby.

He slipped across the road and into the tiny forecourt where she usually parked her car, then glanced quickly over his shoulder. No one was in sight. He turned the key in the lock and stepped inside, closing the door silently after him. The thrill of the illicit, of the unknown, hit him in a rush of exhilaration.

He stood in the dark hallway, waiting, feeling the dense silence. He was breathing heavily, his pulse raised several notches by the excitement of his own daring, his own cleverness.

He took the miniflashlight from his pocket and flicked it on. This time he heard rather than saw the cat as it scuttled away in panic. He smiled — he liked animals. He used to experiment with them as a boy. He'd cut them up just to hear them scream and see what was inside them, and his mother would laugh and tell him he should be a surgeon.

He stepped into the kitchen, keeping the beam low as he pulled down the window-shade. He did not turn on the light, in case someone noticed it had not been on earlier, when Suzie left for the hospital. He took a pair of thin rubber gloves from his pocket and slipped them on, then shone his flashlight around, frowning as he saw the half-eaten supermarket meal abandoned on the counter and the pile of dishes in the sink. She had a dishwasher — why the hell didn't she use it?

He saw the letter, written on pale pink notepaper decorated with pastel flower garlands, and read it interestedly. So Suzie was to be a bridesmaid. Smiling at his own power over her, he wondered if she would make it to the ceremony. He knew the answer was in his hands.

The minuscule living room was on the other side of the kitchen, separated by the counter. He looked around it quickly, then crossed the narrow hallway into her bedroom.

He stood in the doorway, breathing deeply, like a dog seeking the scent of her.

Each woman was different; each had her own particular odor. Summer Young had been perfume and lipstick and cigarettes, but Suzie was sharper, clean, faintly hospital-antiseptic, overlaid with the rainforest scent of her bath oil. She smelled exactly like the person she was — a nurse and an outdoors woman who liked to walk in the woods on her weekends off. But under it they were all the same. They all had that vile, musky female scent. Like his mother.

Her bed was unmade — they always were. He thought there was probably not a single woman in the United States under the age of twenty-five who ever made her bed in the morning. He sat on the edge of it, running his hand over the dark-green sheet printed with a flashy gold pattern. At least her sheets were clean, even if they did look like a whore's.

He wandered around the bedroom, picking up her things and inspecting them: the medical textbook on her bedside table, the holiday photograph of her parents holding hands and smiling at the camera. Her sister — the one who was about to be married, he guessed. She looked like Suzie, only with dark hair and maybe not as pretty. A red-haired boy, probably her younger brother.

He opened the dresser drawers, fingering the underwear flung in any-old-how. Her taste ran to lacy thongs and push-up bras. He liked that. Strings of glass beads and pearls dangled from the mirror over the dresser, and a box decorated with a pair of entwined blue and pink bunnies held a tired-looking collection of inexpensive earrings.

He stepped into the closet, rifling through the garments hanging on the rail, sniffing them, rubbing them against his face. Her shoes were flung untidily into a corner, even though there was a plastic grid to hold them. Still, he liked the contrast between the nurse's comfortable rubber-soled white flats and her spiky patent leather stilettos. He picked up the black patent shoe, caressing its heel as he walked through into the bathroom.

This was his treasure trove, the place he liked best. Her personal things, the face creams and the makeup, were piled in dusty Lucite trays on the cracked tiled countertop, and a fresh bar of antibacterial soap perched on a grooved wooden holder that probably contained more germs than the soap could ever counteract.

He opened drawers and cupboards, fingering her tampons and pads. A damp green towel hung over the shower rail. He pushed it to one side and inspected the tub. The thin beam of the flashlight showed a single dark-copper pubic hair curled near the drain. He picked it up and held it between thumb and forefinger, examining it. Then he took a tissue from the box on the counter, wrapped it carefully, and put it in his pocket.

He looked around for the laundry basket. It was under the window. The black cat was sitting on top of it, watching him. This time it did not move.

Getting used to me, he told himself smiling. Anyhow, he had no need to disturb it. When Suzie undressed for her shower, she had thrown her discarded underthings on the floor. They were still there.

He pulled off the gloves and, trembling with pleasure, picked up the black lace thong and matching bra. He turned them over and over in his hands. He looked at the label: Victoria's Secret. He held them to his face, inhaling the terrible female scent of her. And he groaned out loud.

The cat took off, its claws skittering on the tiled floor as it ran past him. He didn't even notice.

Still clutching the thong to his face, he walked quickly into her room and sank down on the bed. He lay back and unzipped his pants, pressing the black lace underwear to his crotch. He groaned again, lost in a solitary sexual frenzy, writhing, moaning. *But what he really wanted to do was scream.*

It was no good of course. It never was. The only time he could ever reach that ultimate tearing climax was when he killed them. Tremors shook his body violently, as if he were suffering a fit. He was out of control again, caught up in the past. Thinking of his terrible mother who, even after all these years, still dominated him.

He was a boy again, trapped in her bed, she was hitting him with her shoe because he wouldn't touch her. The spike heel zapped painfully into his bruised flesh, into his genitals, as she whispered the horrors she would inflict on him if he ever told. . . .

Suzie drove slowly back down the street. She parked the Neon, thankful to be home again. She got out and stood for a moment, breathing in the warm night air. It seemed to swim around her in a haze, counterpointed with flashes of light as the migraine hammered her brain. She clutched her hands to her head, praying for it to stop. The head nurse had given her some pills and told her to go home and get some rest; he said she was no good in the state she was in. She knew he was right and that it would only get worse before it got better. That was how it always was.

Sighing, she put her key in the lock and opened her door. At least she hadn't lost her keys tonight, she thought gratefully. She switched on the hall light, and the cat came running. It had been a stray and their relationship was friendly but cool: as long as she remembered to feed it and let it sleep on her bed, it was okay. She was surprised when it rubbed around her ankles, miaowing.

"You've picked the wrong night to look for affection," she told it wearily.

She walked into the kitchen, blinking with pain as she switched on the overhead light, then went to the window to pull down the shade. She stopped in surprise. It was already down. She remembered running back into the house to close the windows, but she didn't recall pulling the shade down. She shook her head in bewilderment as she turned away.

The cat jumped onto the counter, watching as she took a bottle of water from the refrigerator, poured some into a glass, and swallowed the pills. She pressed her hands down on the counter, letting her head droop forward. She felt terrible.

She wasn't supposed to come back. He sat on the edge of the bed, listening. Panic rose like bile in his throat as he thought of her out there, of her coming into the bedroom. He had never encountered this situation before; it wasn't in his plan of action. It didn't happen to him.

He could hear her moving around in the kitchen. A shaft of light shone from the hall through the crack in the bedroom door. He glanced at the window, but there was a screen on the outside. He hurried into the bathroom — the window was too small. He was trapped.

He heard her in the hall. He went quickly back into the bedroom and stepped into the closet. His heart thudded, his pulse raced, and sweat trickled down his back. It was the sweat of fear. He had never been confronted by any of his girls. His plans were always flawless. He was always the one in control.

He slid his hand into his pocket, took out the small knife, and removed the plastic case. Then he stood perfectly still behind the closet door, the knife ready in his hand. Waiting.

24

Mal and Harry were in the stretch limo on their way back to Boston. He was holding her hand and singing along with Santana, complete with expressive Latin shakes of the shoulders and hips.

There was a smile on Mal's face as she watched him — he was certainly full of surprises. "Is this a preview of what I can expect at Salsa Annie's?"

"Unh-unh. This is peanuts, chickenfeed, *nada*. Just you wait 'til I get you on that dance floor. Which, by the way, is about the size of the table where you ate dinner. It's hip-to-hip out there, Malone. You're gonna love it."

"I wonder."

"It's more fun than a lonely bed at the Ritz-Carlton."

"How would you know?"

He thought about it. "You're right. I don't. I've never slept at the Ritz — alone or with anyone else."

"Now that you've relieved my mind on that score, could we turn that down just a touch."

He grinned at her. "You want something smoochier? 'Moon River' again?"

She laughed; he was so silly, she could have

hugged him. "I'm not sure that Salsa Annie's is a good trade for Jordan's Farm. I hated to leave."

"I had to practically drag you out of there. Fallen for it, have you?"

"It was a wonderful party."

"Want to make a date for her sixty-sixth?" When she laughed, he said, "By the way, Mom meant it when she said she loved the present. And she meant what else she said too."

Mal had given his mother a beautiful dark-blue suede photograph album. Miffy had thanked her with a kiss and said, "My dear, I shall save it for my grandchildren's pictures. When I'm lucky enough to have any, that is." And she had looked meaningfully at the two of them.

"I tried to head her off," Harry apologized, "but she's single-minded on the subject. Mothers get that way."

"Not mine."

He gripped her hand tighter, but this time he did not ask any questions. He wasn't about to spoil the mood.

They were driving through town. When they got to the street with Annie's, he told the limo driver to let them out at the corner.

"I'd never live it down," he explained when she looked questioningly at him. "The tough homicide cop arriving at a funky hole-in-the-wall club in a limo."

"Just like a movie starlet," she added with

a smirk, and he laughed.

A battered steel door, painted a flaking chili-red, was set flat into the wall of an old warehouse. A few guys lounged outside, smoking. Some gave Harry a friendly high-five as he walked by, but a couple of others slid quickly away into the shadows. Harry's eyes followed them, but tonight he was definitely off-duty. And besides he was enjoying himself too much to worry about small-time drug dealers. He would leave them to the guys working the graveyard shift.

When he opened the door, a wall of sound hit them. He took a deep breath, eyes closed, absorbing it. "Great, isn't it," he said in Mal's ear. She just looked at him, eyebrows raised in amazement.

The band numbered at least a dozen, with electric bass and guitar, plus horns, flutes, fiddles, and a piano player revving them on with a terrific underlay of rhythmic Latino melody. A long-legged Cuban girl in a tiny green satin skirt that just about covered her busy hips, and an even briefer satin top, belted out the song in Spanish, dancing up a storm as the trumpets counterpointed the rhythm. The whole place vibrated with vitality. Harry put his arm around her and drew her onto the floor.

"But I don't know how to do this," she protested.

"Just hold on to me, Malone and I'll show

you," he said, sweeping her to him.

Rossetti watched from the balcony at the far end. "Will ya just look at that, Vanessa," he said. "If it isn't the Prof — and with a date. Jeez," he added, stunned. "The Prof's wearing a tux. And she looks like an ad for Armani." They hung over the rail, staring. "And I'll be darned if the date isn't Ms. Mallory Malone," he added, grinning. "The Prof sure knows how to keep a secret. We've caught our workaholic, too-busy-to-date Jordan red-handed."

"Just like you were Sherlock Holmes and he was Moriarty," Vanessa added, grinning.

Rossetti glared exasperatedly at her. "Did you ever hear the old saying about being too smart for your own good?" He grabbed her hand and hurried her down the stairs.

"Where are we going?" she gasped, clutching the metal banister, trying to keep up with him in her high heels.

"We're gonna say hello to the detective and his friend." He pulled her onto the dance floor, edging closer to Harry.

Harry was smiling into Mal's eyes, holding her at arm's length. "Like this," he said, demonstrating. She bit her lip, concentrating as she tried to follow him.

"I think you need Latin blood for this," she muttered, throwing her head back and abandoning herself to the music.

"You're lookin' good, Malone," Harry yelled over the wall of sound. "Only thing is,

266

you're supposed to be doing that in close proximity to me."

"Uh-oh, there goes our contract again." She was in his arms, gripped confidently close to him. She could feel his hard body against hers. "Does this get any better?" she murmured, nestling closer.

"It could do." He liked the way she fitted against him, the movement of her hips under that slinky slide of gossamer. In fact, he liked her a whole lot. . . .

"What d'ya say, Prof? Enjoying yourself tonight?"

Harry groaned. He lifted his head from where it had been grooved against Mal's and looked into her eyes. "Detective Rossetti," he said exasperatedly.

"He thinks he's Sherlock Holmes," Vanessa added.

"Hi, Vanessa." Harry turned reluctantly, his arm still around Mal's waist.

"We interrupt somethin'?" Rossetti glanced innocently at the two of them. They looked hot and happy, and her hair was mussed.

"Mallory Malone, meet Detective Carlo Rossetti. And this is Vanessa, who will be twenty-one in a few weeks' time."

"You're invited to the party," Vanessa said. Then: "Oh wow, you're *that* Mallory Malone. Hey, you're great."

Mal smiled. "Thanks. It's nice to meet you."

"Good to meet you too." Rossetti shook her hand. "You guys absconded from the Ritz tonight or what?" he asked, eyeing their smart getup.

Mal laughed. "We left the limo at the corner. We didn't want to look like movie starlets."

"No chance of that," Rossetti said gallantly. "You're a bona fide star. Of course, I can't say the same for the Prof."

"Why does he call you the Prof?" Mal asked Harry.

"The Harvard law thing," Rossetti told her. "You get it?" She nodded, laughing.

"If you must know, Rossetti, we've just come from my mother's birthday fiesta," Harry said.

"You took her home to meet your mom already? Nice going, Prof."

Harry groaned. He clutched Mal to him, hiding her. "Good night, detective."

"Good night, Prof." Rossetti was laughing as he swept Vanessa into the dance.

"See you at my party," Vanessa called over her shoulder.

"Come on," Harry said to Mal, leading her to the door.

"Where are we going?"

"On to the next event. You haven't forgotten our itinerary, have you?"

They walked back to the limo, and Harry gave the driver the address.

"Another club?" Mal took a compact out of

her tiny gold bag and powdered her nose.

"Wait and see." He watched, fascinated, as she applied her lipstick. Her mouth looked red and juicy. It seemed to be sending him a little message: *Lick me.* . . . With a sigh of regret, he contented himself with holding her hand until the limo dropped them off, ten minutes later, outside a more discreet-looking club on Brookline.

"You know how to play billiards?" Harry asked as he pushed open the door.

"A little."

He grinned. "This is really your night for learning, isn't it. Come on, I'll show you."

Inside it was furnished like a classy English library. There was a bar and pool tables with shaded lights slung low over them, and like Annie's, it was crowded.

They knew Harry there. He got a table and chalked up her cue. "Okay, now watch," he said, demonstrating how to hold the cue, how to slide it between her fingers, how to measure up the ball.

"Okay."

He placed the cue ball and the red and told her where to stand. "Go for it," he said, stepping back, watching her.

Mal leaned over the table and took careful aim. The gossamer dress slid up over her beautiful butt as she moved. Harry shifted his eyes regretfully away from temptation.

The red glanced off the white and rolled

gently into the side pocket. She looked up at him and winked. "S'easy, Prof."

He sighed. "In my mother's day you would have let the gentleman win. Made him feel good, soothe his masculine ego."

She grinned. "I'm more the salt-on-wounds type. Set 'em up, Prof."

He looked suspiciously at her. "Why do I get the feeling you've played this game before."

"Probably because I used to work in a place like this. Once upon a time. Many moons ago. Though it didn't look exactly like this," she added, remembering with a shudder the bleak little pool hall with the fluorescent lights and the hollow-eyed men coughing cigarette smoke into their beer.

She lifted one eyebrow and threw him a challenging look. "Bet you fifty I can beat you."

"You're on. I have the feeling I may regret this."

She proved him right, and half an hour later he handed over the fifty.

"I'd tuck it down the front of my dress in true barhall style," she said, "but as you may have noticed, the neckline is too low for that."

"I did notice, and I might add that it was worth the fifty just to see you lean across the table in that dress."

"Sexist pig," she said, linking her arm in his. "What next, Prof?"

"Oh, I think maybe, a nightcap."

The limo dropped them in Louisburg Square. She stared, astonished, at the magnificent old house. "This is where you live?"

"Only on the lower floors. The other apartments are rented out."

He opened the door, and she stepped past him into the hall. The mountain bike was propped against the wall, and his helmet sat on a beautiful eighteenth-century console table. There was a pair of Rollerblades underneath, and a dog's chewbone in the center of the dark green Persian rug.

"It looks like home," she said approvingly, as he showed her into the living room. "Seriously, Harry, it's beautiful. Even with the Nautilus in here, this room still manages to capture the graciousness of another era."

"Thank you, Malone. Just make yourself at home. What can I fix you?"

"Coffee, please."

She peeked curiously into his bedroom. It was minimalist, in bronze tones, with a hard-looking Jacobean four-poster, a couple of night tables, an old chair, a chewed rug, and not much else.

"Squeeze ate the rug when he was a pup," Harry called from the kitchen. "He was sick for a week. Never chewed anything he wasn't meant to again."

The bathroom was like a time warp. "How do you function in here?" she wondered, looking for counter space.

"Very well, thank you." He switched on the coffee machine. "It works for me."

"Mmmm." She wandered into the kitchen. "Would you just look at this?" She marveled at the high-tech steel and granite. "You never told me you could cook."

"I can't — it's all for show. I always meant to learn. One day I'll take that trip to cooking school in Tuscany, see how I'd make out as a chef."

"I can bet you right now. Not good."

She leaned against the granite counter, arms crossed over her chest, looking at him. "I've had a great time tonight, Harry. Thank you."

"It's my pleasure, *ma'am*." He gave a courtly little bow.

"Mal," she corrected him.

"And not a day over thirty-five."

She laughed and pummeled him in the chest. "Oh God, you're the pits, Harry Jordan. I was being serious."

"I know you were." He caught her to him, cupped her face in his hand. They looked searchingly at each other for a long moment.

"What about the verbal contract?" she whispered.

"This is a supplementary clause," he said. And then he kissed her.

It was a tender kiss, trembling as a teenager's. His lips were warm, hers soft, parting as he banded his arms around her.

272

She forgot about breathing — it didn't seem to matter. All she wanted was his mouth on hers. She laced her hands through his thick curling hair, and tilted her head back, feeling his fingers on her skin. She was lost in it, drinking him in.

He took his mouth away, and she gasped for air. "I promise I didn't mean to do that," he said shakily, still holding her.

"Me neither." She thought if he let go of her, she would simply slide to the floor.

"Coffee?"

She nodded, big-eyed, breathless. He helped her onto a stool at the kitchen counter and poured coffee into two plain white mugs. "How about a sandwich?"

She began to laugh, helplessly. "Oh, detective," she groaned, "how did you know it's exactly what I want?"

He grinned back at her. "Extrasensory perception." He took two jars out of the refrigerator. "Mayo or mustard on your turkey?"

"Both," she said, still laughing.

25

Suzie kicked off her shoes as she walked into the bathroom. She brushed her teeth, rinsed her mouth, and washed her face. She held the cold washcloth to her throbbing head; it felt soothing and she decided to fix an ice pack.

She padded slowly back into the kitchen and opened the refrigerator. It was an older model, without an automatic ice-maker, and the ice-cube tray was empty. She sighed — she must have forgotten to fill it last time she used it.

Then she remembered the two-pound bag of frozen peas she had bought a couple of months ago when she had sprained an ankle. It had worked as good as any expensive ice pack because it was flexible. She could wrap it in a pillowcase and put it on her head.

Carrying the bag of frozen peas, she trailed into the bedroom. The pills were making her feel even woozier — the head nurse had told her they would make her sleepy. "You'll probably sleep most of the day," he had said. Suzie had felt relieved because, sleeping, she wouldn't have these flashing lights in front of her eyes, and hopefully the crushing pain would go away.

But if she were sleeping, she would miss her

meeting with her sister. She glanced doubt-fully at the clock. It was very late, but she knew Terry would still be out on the town with her fiancé. So she decided to call and leave a mes-sage on her machine.

She put down the frozen peas and began unbuttoning her nurse's white overall.

The cat ran to her. He jumped onto the bed, then crouched, gazing at her, tail swishing.

"What's the matter, Quentin?" she asked, surprised. "Settle down, why don't you."

She stepped out of the overall and took off her bra, then sank onto the bed, rotating her neck slowly, trying to ease the pain. Wearily, she picked up the phone and dialed Terry's number, waiting patiently for the answering machine to pick up.

He stepped from the closet. Her back was toward him. He tiptoed closer.

"Hi, Terry, it's me," she said when the ma-chine picked up. "I'm not feeling too great — it's this migraine thing again. They gave me some pills at the hospital. They'll make me sleep, so I don't think I'll be able to make it tomorrow. . . . Well, it's today really. . . ."

The cat stiffened, staring balefully over her shoulder. It arched its back, hissing, its eyes glinting like red coals in the lamplight.

"Quentin, what's gotten into you?" Suzie turned to see what he was staring at. Cats go spooked at nothing sometimes. . . .

"Oh, my God," she said in a strangled

whisper. "Oh, my God, oh, my God." She clutched the telephone receiver to her heart, anguished. "What are you doing here?" she said. "What —"

He swept the phone to the floor and grabbed her. With a terrified cry she slid down through his arms and out. She was running. He hurled himself after her, took her in a tackle, grabbed her leg, brought her crashing down.

Suzie screamed. She screamed and screamed. . . .

He was sitting on the floor. He grabbed her thick curling red hair in his fist and dragged her viciously toward him until her head rested in his crotch. She lay helplessly on her back between his legs. Her face was drained of color, her eyes dark with shock.

He wrapped her hair around his hand, twisting it tighter, and she moaned with pain. Suddenly, she began to scream again, a high-pitched wailing sound.

He held the tip of the knife against her throat. "Scream, and I'll kill you," he whispered.

She stopped screaming and lay still. He shuddered with relief. He was in control again.

Next door, Alec Klosowski was returning from his job as a barman. He had just put his key in the lock when he heard a noise. He swung around, listening. He could have sworn it was a scream — and that it came from next door.

He noticed, surprised, that Suzie's car was back. He had assumed she was working the night shift. A light was on in the kitchen too. He guessed she had come home early and that the noise had been a cat yowling. There were plenty of strays around here, and they often made a racket at night. Suzie had even adopted one of them, though she said it still acted like a stray.

He unlocked his door and let himself in. It had been a long night.

The two-pound package of peas chilled Suzie's spine where she had fallen on top of it. She shifted slightly. He nicked the knife across her throat, and she felt blood trickle down her breasts.

She stared up at him, too terrified to speak. He was mad, she could see it in his eyes. She knew she had to do something, but she dared not scream. Tremors ran through her body, and she understood she was in shock. She was fading into unconsciousness — this was her last chance. She slid her right hand under her body. Arching her back slightly, she clutched the bag of peas.

His eyes were closed; he was thinking of what he was about to do, enjoying as he always did this ultimate moment of power. Even though it was not happening exactly the way he had planned, Suzie Walker was his.

Suzie grasped the frozen peas, her only weapon. If she could distract him even for just

277

a moment, she could run out into the street and shout for help. Surely then someone would come and save her.

It was now or never. Heaving herself up, she flung the frozen peas into his face. The bag split from the force of the blow, and the peas rattled onto the floor.

He let out a roar, and his hands went automatically to his eyes. She was on her feet, crunching over the peas. The front door had never seemed so far away. . . .

She heard him cry out. She had three more steps to go. . . . Oh, God, she couldn't get the latch to open. . . .

He grabbed her from behind, and dragged her head back. Suzie's eyes were black with horror as she gazed back at the face of her killer. "Don't," she begged. "Please don't."

And then he raised his arm and brought the knife swiftly down across her throat.

A gurgling scream erupted from her. He let go of her hurriedly as the blood spurted. Still making that terrible bubbling, retching noise, she staggered toward the bedroom. She reached the door, clutched at it. Her bloody hands left a red trail down it as she sank to her knees. He watched for a minute, then he went and stood over her.

Suzie could no longer lift her head. She knelt on the floor, staring dully at his shoes. She was drowning in her own blood, and she was never going to come up again. She slithered in slow motion down and down and down. Her head came to rest on his black Gucci loafers.

He stared coldly at her. She was finally quiet. But she had seen him. He had to be sure.

He grabbed a handful of her hair, lifted her head, and slit the carotid artery. Just to make sure.

He let her drop back to the floor and stood there, breathing heavily. She was naked except for her underpants, but he had no sexual feeling toward her. It was not the way he did things; this was different.

He glanced down at himself; and saw her blood on his shirt, on his pants, on his shoes. *Her blood was all over him.*

Panic set him trembling violently. Suddenly he was like a man in the final stages of malaria, sweating and shaking. *It was all her fault. She shouldn't have come home when she wasn't meant to. It would have been so precise, so clean, so satisfying later, if only she had kept to her usual pattern of behavior. He had had it all planned.*

Crazy with rage, he dropped to his knees and began hacking at her. He slashed her over and over again. Tears ran down his face, *"Whore,"* he sobbed, *"vile filthy bitch. . . ."*

It was over in a minute. He controlled himself and stood up. He stepped back from her, contemplating his handiwork. Then he looked at his bloody hands. He was still wearing the thin rubber gloves. He had been clever after all.

He walked into the bathroom and rinsed the blood from the gloves. He patted them dry, blotted her blood from his clothes with the damp towel, cleaned the knife, and put it in his pocket.

He turned off the bathroom light, then the lamp in the bedroom. He took one last look at Suzie lying in the doorway. Then he stepped over her body, walked into the kitchen, and turned out the light. He peered anxiously through the window into the street. It was empty. The frozen peas crunched under his feet as he went to the front door.

The terrified cat ran from its hiding place under the hall table. He stumbled over it, cursing as it fled into the darkness. The small knife slipped from his pocket and fell, unnoticed, to the floor as he eased open the front door.

He closed it softly behind him, hearing the latch click shut. He looked left and right, then hurried across the street into the shadow of the parked cars.

Alex Klosowski was just opening his bedroom window when he saw him. He smiled — so that was why Suzie was home early, he thought as he climbed, yawning, into bed. He heard the engine start up and then the car pass his house. But by that time, he was almost asleep.

"I missed Squeeze tonight," Mal said, snuggling further down in the tan coach-hide bucket seat as Harry drove down an almost-empty Charles Street back to the Ritz.

He shook his head, disbelieving. "Malone, you hardly know him."

"I hardly know you too."

"You surely know me better than I know you."

She glanced warily at him. "We're not back to that again, are we?"

He shrugged. "Why not?"

"Okay, I promise to tell you all about myself this weekend. Not that it makes fascinating listening, but I guess there's not much else to do in the mountains."

"It's a good place to purge your soul." She was silent, and he added, "I'll let you take Squeeze for a long walk in return for your confidences."

"Thanks."

"Here we are, Cinderella." He pulled up in front of the hotel. She had insisted she must get back to the Ritz before dawn, saying she couldn't just walk into a hotel at breakfast time wearing last night's evening dress and makeup. Even though it was all innocent.

She smiled at him, then leaned across and kissed him on the mouth. "I'll see you tomorrow. *Today.*"

"Seven o'clock," he said. "Bright and early."

"Hardly worth going to sleep."

"Certainly not alone — and at the Ritz."

She was laughing as she walked, with that tantalizing little cream-over-peaches movement, away from him and into the hotel. He would carry the memory into his dreams.

The man forced himself to drive the Volvo slowly. He couldn't afford to get stopped by the police, not in the state he was in.

The journey home seemed to take forever. He didn't even hear the classical music he usually enjoyed while driving back from his killings, sated and happy. It had never been like this before — out of control. It was all he could do to concentrate on driving. He knew that if he got stopped, he was sunk.

He breathed a sigh of relief when he finally turned into his own street and then into his own driveway. The garage doors swung shut behind him. He cut the engine and leaned limply over the steering wheel. He was shaking.

He climbed out of the car, hurried to the door, and unlocked his battery of locks and bolts with numb hands. Finally he was inside. He leaned against the wall for a minute, gasping for air like a man having a heart attack. And then he stumbled upstairs to the locked room.

He wore the special key on a long silver chain around his neck, tucked into his shirt, where no one would ever see it. When he fumbled for it, his fingers encountered the soft, pungent stickiness of Suzie's blood. He groaned, pounding frantically on the door with his fists.

"Let me in. Please, let me in. . . ."

He began to cry.

He ripped off his bloody shirt, then knelt in front of the lock and fitted the key shakily into it. Finally the door swung open. Moans ripped from his throat as he struggled to his feet. Then he stepped inside the room and slammed the door behind him.

26

Harry thought life was pretty good. It was the next morning, and he was driving his Jeep. Squeeze was in the back, and Mallory Malone was in the passenger seat — where, he thought, she looked as though she belonged.

She was fast asleep. Every now and then he stole a glance at her, marveling at the long eyelashes curving along her cheeks, missing the mocking sidelong glances she gave him every now and then to keep him on his toes.

Squeeze had his head out of the window, sniffing up the fresh piney smells, as they wound up the side of the mountain. Harry took a side road through the woods, bouncing over the potholes. They drove past a small inn on the edge of a placid brown lake, famous for its trout fishing, then through a minivillage, with a red barn that was also the general store, selling everything from milk and bread to hammers and nails, and kerosene for lamps, plus gas from a solitary pump out front. A few houses were huddled together like cows in a field, painted white, with black gingerbread trim over the Victorian gables and wide front porches. A couple of dogs lazed outside and one ran after the Jeep, barking halfheartedly at Squeeze who put his paws on the backseat, eager to get out after him.

"Where are we?" Mallory slithered upright, looking around.

"We're here," he announced, taking the slope up to the cabin in a final fast sweep. He swung into the graveled driveway, stepped on the brakes, and spun her around. "Only way to get her up here," he said casually as Mal gasped, clinging to her seat. "It's hell trying to back down that slope."

"It must have taken a lot of practice to perfect that maneuver." She glared at him. "I thought my end had come."

He grinned as he opened the door for her. "That's only the beginning. Madame." He bowed, holding out his hand.

Ignoring him, she jumped out. "Oh," she said, and then "Oh" again, smiling.

"Do I take those as words of approval?"

"Oh, definitely."

The log cabin was perched at the top of a steep incline. It was square, rugged, and compact, built of cedar, with soaring windows and a peaked overhanging roof, meant to shoulder a hefty burden of snow. There was a broad porch all the way around it, and a wide chimney built of local rock. Flowers grew in mossy baskets on the porch, and the tall double doors looked thick enough to keep out an invading army.

Mal sighed enviously. "What other real-estate surprises do you Jordans have in store for me? A castle in Spain? A villa in Tuscany?"

"This is it, I'm afraid. Besides, I think you need to be at least a marquis to qualify for a castle. All we Jordans can run to is plain mister."

"And detective," she reminded him.

"Let's forget the detective, just for this weekend."

Squeeze whined, and she said, "Oh, poor darling, we forgot him."

Harry opened the car door, and the dog gamboled around their feet in an ecstasy of excitement.

"I can see I'm not the only one who loves it here," she said.

Harry laughed as the dog chased off into the woods. "I think he feels closer to his wolf ancestors here. He's back to being a wild creature."

He took out the bags and carried them up to the house. Mal followed with the picnic basket she'd had the chef at the Ritz prepare. He unlocked the door, and she stepped inside another of the Jordan set-pieces of perfection.

The curved cedar logs had faded to a mellow hue, and the wide-planked floors gleamed under colorful rag rugs. There were Navaho wall hangings, and Frederic Remington bronzes of horses and riders on the massive side tables. A Norman Rockwell of a New England family was propped on the solid six-inch thick slab of cedar that formed the mantel. The wall-sized fireplace was built of rock and was wide enough to roast an ox, if you were so inclined, and the huge sofas arranged in front of it were deep enough to get lost in.

"Oh," Mal said again. "Oh, Harry."

He ran his hand over the stubble on his chin, looking amused. "For a reporter, you are surely a woman of few words."

"I thought that said it all. But if you want it in writing, *it's bliss*. Harry, do you realize a woman could marry you just for your real estate? Each place you take me, I never want to leave." She plumped down in a corner of the toast-colored sofa, beaming at him.

"I'll bear that in mind, Malone. Come on, I'll show you the rest."

They walked to the soaring wall of windows at the back, where Mal gasped with delight. The side of the mountain fell away in a sheer drop, and through a lacy vista of greenery, she could see mountain peaks and a distant lake. Harry opened the glass doors, and they went onto the deck, leaning on the porch rail, drinking in the silence and the beauty. High in a tree a bird warbled a riff; the wind rippled through the leaves, and small creatures rustled through the undergrowth. Even the sunshine seemed tangible, bathing them in warmth and adding a golden sheen to the view.

"I've run out of superlatives," she said, weakly.

"Every time I come here, I ask myself what I'm doing on the city streets, hunting down killers," Harry said. "I see firsthand the hell man inflicts on man. Close up and in Technicolor. And then there's all this." He swept his arm across the view. "It's kind of a renewal, coming here."

" 'It restoreth my soul,' " she quoted, looking at him.

"Whoever wrote that psalm got it right. Though some I've brought here would not agree with that sentiment."

She knew who he must mean. "Your wife?"

He nodded. "Jilly hated it. Once was enough for her. She said it was just the kind of place she had been running away from all her life." He made a wry face. "She was twenty-one at the time."

"And a nice, well-brought-up young debutante whom you had escorted to cotillions, and who led you on by letting you put your hand down her dress on the way home from the prom."

"Is that what you really think?"

She shrugged. "Who else would you marry?"

He was leaning on the porch rail, staring at the view, but she had the feeling he wasn't seeing it.

"Jilly was nineteen when I met her," he said quietly. "She was a waitress, working at a roadhouse outside of town. Country Cousins, it was called.

"She was from a small town in Alabama, and she had this soft southern accent that turned my bones to jelly, just listening to her. She had long blond hair and eyes the color of whiskey, and when she walked across the room, every guy in the place watched her. She was wild and reckless. She drove an old Harley, and I'd wait around until she got off work, just to see her take off down the highway, blond hair flying.

"When I asked her out, she turned me down flat. 'Go home to your pa, sonny,' she told me, with all the superior wisdom of a mature woman of the world talking to an ignorant student. Not even the Porsche could entice her to go out with me. 'There's guys with Ferraris come in here. So tell me, why do I need you?' she said to me.

"I kept after her for months, but she wasn't having any of it. She said we were just not on the same wavelength.

"I knew she was doing drugs. I even knew the guy who supplied them." He looked at Mal. "You have to understand — Jilly looked like the role model for Miss Health and Purity. The tall blond all-American girl. I hated the drugs, and I hated him even more for getting her them.

"Then I asked her to come to my graduation, at Harvard. I was astonished when she agreed. 'What do they wear at these fancy graduations?' she asked, and I could see for once she was nervous. 'Whatever,' I said. 'Just keep it simple.'

"She showed up in a sweater set and pearls and a knee-length plaid skirt, with her hair tied back with a ribbon. I thought she looked wonderful, like a girl from the fifties instead of the usual black leather spaced-out hog-rider.

"My graduation changed her life. She sat there next to my mother and father, conducting herself like a lady, saying all the right things in that slow southern drawl and just eating it up.

"We had the celebration dinner at Lock-Obers, where she insisted I tell her the story of why the painting of the reclining nude, over the bar, was draped in black whenever Harvard lost to Yale. She was suddenly fascinated by all the tradition that came with college and money.

" 'This is it, Harry,' she said to me later. 'I'm quitting waitressing, I'm quitting doing drugs, and I'm quitting the Harley. I'm gonna be a lady.'

"And she did. It was effortless — the right haircut, the right clothes, the right manners. She was charm itself by the time we got married. And then I went and pulled the upper-class image right out from under her.

" 'I married a lawyer, not a cop' was exactly what she said to me when she told me she was leaving. We had been married two years, but the last year had been lonely for her. She already had someone else waiting in the wings."

Harry dragged his eyes back from the view, but Mal could tell it was his past he was still seeing. He shrugged. "That was that. I had offered her what she wanted and then taken it away. She liked the social life and the parties and the lunches and the clothes. She has it all now, in Greenwich, Connecticut. She has two children and devotes a great deal of her time to charity affairs."

Mal could see he was wounded from the expression in his eyes. She said gently, "I'm sorry, Harry."

"Don't be. I'm over it. I can even wish her well now. We speak occasionally. She's a nice ordinary woman." He gave a wry grin. "She wanted a lawyer, and I wanted a Harley rider with her long blond hair blowing in the wind. I've had a soft spot for waitresses ever since."

He slid his arm along her shoulders, drawing her nearer. "I told you this was a good place to purge your soul."

He kept his arm around her shoulders as they walked up the wide staircase. The old pine treads were broad and shallow and creaked noisily. He flung open the big arched door at the top and said, "It's all yours."

She took in the beamed cathedral ceiling and the wall of windows overlooking the same magnificent view. And the simple pine bed, puffy with feather quilts, and the polished floors scattered with silky old rugs. The huge armoire must have been hewn by a master craftsman on the spot, because there was no way it could ever have been carried in there. A couple of comfortable old chairs, covered in red-and-white-checked wool were arranged in front of the stone hearth, and a faded chaise longue had been placed in front of the window to catch the spectacular view. Rosy-shaded lamps were meant to cast a warm glow on cold winter nights, and the shelves were stocked with an eclectic selection of books for the insomniacs.

"I almost wish it were snowing." Mal heaved a contented sigh. "We could throw a log on the fire and light the lamps and . . ."

"And?" He raised a hopeful eyebrow.

"And eat our picnic," she finished firmly. "I don't know about you, but I'm starving."

They walked back downstairs and into the big square kitchen. It was unexpectedly old-fashioned, with tiled countertops, simple pine cupboards, and an ancient steel restaurant stove that took up half a wall. There was a stone fireplace in the corner, and a rugged old pine table that had been scrubbed clean for so many years it was bleached white. A dozen mismatched chairs were arranged around it.

"The cabin always used to be crowded when Dad was alive," Harry said. "And my grandfather before him. It was always full of aunts and uncles, cousins, grandparents, friends. And dogs, of course. This old stove has yielded up many a simple banquet. When I was a little kid, I used to hide under the table when I was supposed to be in bed and they were eating dinner. Of course they knew I was there, but they let me pretend I was putting one over on them. The wine flowed, and the anecdotes and reminiscences, the stories of the fish they'd caught, or the quality of the day's skiing, depending on the season.

"I liked it best when the snow was falling against the windows and the fire roared in the grate, and there was the smell of the rich stew my mother cooked up, and the fresh-baked bread that was Dad's specialty. His relaxation, he called it. He would stand there punishing the hell out of the dough with his fists, kneading it. Mom always said he was imagining it was his clients he was beating up."

There was a reminiscent smile of pure pleasure on Harry's face that Mal envied. She envied him those kind of memories, because all she had were blank spaces where there should have been family, friends, warmth, and relationships.

Harry rubbed his hand across the fast-growing stubble on his chin, smiling. "They knew how to enjoy themselves in those days. Very little man-made entertainment was allowed up here — no TV, no radio, though my mother was permitted her old record player. It's still there on a shelf next to the fireplace in the living room, along with her collection of long-playing vinyl records — including 'Smoke Gets in Your Eyes.' And then there was the old upright piano that everyone took a turn at, even me, though none of us was very good at it. We would play board games, or poker, on the afternoons when it was too snowy to venture out, and charades after dinner. Then someone would tinkle a tune on the piano, or maybe Mom would put on a record while they sipped a bedtime glass of brandy, with the dogs stretched out in front of the fire."

He said, "I can still see them all, in the glow of the lamplight, exactly as they were, though so many of them are just ghosts now. Happy ghosts, I like to think. Sometimes when I'm here alone, I imagine I can feel them around me. It's a comfortable feeling, easy, like being with old friends."

Mal was staring at him, as eager as a child listening to a fairy story. He shrugged and said, "Now you know why I love the place. It's the continuity of it, the memories. The kind of memories I'd like to hand down to my own children."

He went to the counter and opened the picnic basket. "I thought you were starving." He was back in a teasing mode again, but Mal was still thinking about the glowing picture he had painted of an unknown world. She was greedy for his life, not for the food.

Harry scooped Purina Chow Mix into Squeeze's metal bowl, and the dog came bounding in from under the deck, where he'd been sniffing out potential rabbits.

Mal arranged the picnic out on the deck, while Harry got plates and cutlery.

He eyed the lavish banquet of roast chicken, with new potatoes in dill vinaigrette dressing and fresh asparagus spears, amazed. There was a wedge of French Vignotte cheese, a loaf of crusty bread, and fresh pears poached in red wine. "I was thinking along the lines of a Matisse sandwich," he said, amazed.

Mal groaned. "I bring you food for the gods, and you want a sandwich."

"Just fooling. In fact, this picnic calls for a good red wine."

He made to go into the house to get some, but she called him back. "Water's good. I need a clear head for the hike you're taking me on afterward."

"Afterward? I might just need a rest."

She laughed. "Listen, Harry Jordan, I bought the proper hiking gear specially for the occasion, and I intend to use it."

The dog's pale blue eyes were fixed longingly on the food. Harry threw him a piece of chicken. "A dog's got to get his strength up for this marathon hike you're taking him on," he said.

She smiled, chewing contentedly on a spear of asparagus, sipping icy mountain water, and drinking in the view. Happiness was like money, she thought; when you didn't have it, you didn't really know what it meant, and when you did, you didn't even think about it. It was just there.

They dawdled over their picnic, then sounding very official, Harry said, "Okay, you have five minutes to change, then we're off. Before the weather turns."

She gave him an oh-come-on look, checking the cloudless sky as she ran up the stairs.

"By the way," she said when she got to the top, "where do *you* sleep?"

He gave her a cheeky grin. "I thought you'd never ask. I'll show you when we get back. Don't worry. There are enough bedrooms here for you and Squeeze and me to each have our own space, plus a fair number of others should anyone drop in. Not that it's likely, Malone."

"Mallory," she corrected him over her shoulder, as she walked into the wonderful room that she was being allowed to pretend was hers just for one perfect night.

She changed quickly into sturdy hiking shorts that had what seemed an excessive number of pockets, a white polo shirt, thick gray socks, and stiff heavy-soled boots that took ages to lace. She put on fresh lipstick and her baseball cap and clomped back down the stairs.

He was watching her, arms folded, Squeeze

by his side. He was wearing baggy coral-colored sailing shorts, a faded rugby shirt, a beat-up pair of boots, and a Canucks cap. There was not a hint of a smirk on his face as he looked at her, but she knew it was lurking there somewhere.

"I have a feeling I've got it wrong again. Sartorially speaking," she said uncertainly.

"Let's just say it's a touch serious for the occasion."

They had told her it was the correct gear at the store. She frowned, looking him up and down, and said sarcastically, "I suppose I should have chosen something in pink, like you."

"I shall take that blow like a man, Malone. Though for your information this particular shade is known as Nantucket pink. Everyone wears it on the island — sailing, dining —"

"Hiking?"

"I may be unique in wearing it for that activity. And now that that's settled, how about we get going?"

Squeeze recognized the words and leaped to the door in a series of wild gambols and yips. Mal paused at the top of the steps to watch him tear joyfully around, barking madly, wild with freedom. She thought with a smile that she knew just how he felt.

27

Harry took an upward trail through the woods. Squeeze led the way, circling back every few minutes to check that they were still with him. The bracken at the side of the trail smelled moist and green, and high above them birds fluttered from their nests, urgently trilling the alarm.

After half an hour Mal was panting for breath, but Harry was marching steadily on. She was determined not to give up.

By the time they reached a grassy plateau, another half hour later, her boots were gripping her swollen toes like a vise, her heavy shorts were rubbing her thighs, and she was sweating. She flung herself thankfully onto the grass, too winded even to speak.

"Enjoyed that, huh?" Harry said.

She glared up at him. "Sadist," she gasped.

He hunkered down next to her, running his fingers over the red weals where the thick canvas shorts had rubbed her thighs. "What have you got on under there?" he asked.

"This is entirely the wrong moment for that kind of talk, detective."

"Give me credit, Malone. I'm not making a pass at you. I asked what you're wearing underneath because you can't wear these ridiculous shorts on the way back down. Unless you enjoy having your skin flayed from your bones."

"Oh," she said, disgruntled. "Okay. I'm wearing boxers."

He nodded. "Then take off the shorts. But whatever you do, don't take off your boots. You'll never get them back on again. Here, wait a minute — let me." He knelt in front of her and loosened the laces. The circulation started to flow again, and she breathed a sigh of relief.

He turned his back while she removed the shorts. "Okay, I'm decent," she said in a small embarrassed voice.

He looked at her, then laughed. "Well, what do you know. *Pink.*"

"Stop it, Harry Jordan, just stop it," she said furiously. "My underwear has nothing to do with you."

"Right now it does, Malone. It's your pink butt I'll be following all the way back home." He relented and took her hand to help her up. "Hold on to me," he said, "it can get a bit slippery."

Halfway back down the trail, she noticed that the sky had clouded over. Within minutes its color turned from dove gray to steel, then to graphite. The rain hit the canopy of leaves above them like rifle shots, pelting down in huge fat drops, then quickly turned into a sheet of water.

She lagged behind. Harry marched ahead, unperturbed by the sudden deluge, and beyond him Squeeze's tail waved like a flag. She trudged on, determined not to complain. Her clothes stuck to her like wet laundry, her feet hurt, and the trail had turned into mud. She slipped and fell, then got up quickly, gritting her teeth. "You are not going to whine," she muttered to herself. "You are definitely not going to say why the hell did you bring me on this ridiculous hike. You are most definitely *not* going to cry."

"Just look at that, will you." Harry stopped suddenly, and she barged into him. He grabbed her to keep her from falling and whispered, "Look. Up in the tree."

A family of raccoons were perched in the branches. They stared solemnly down at them, their round eyes ringed in black and white like cartoon characters — a mother, a father, and two babies. It was one of the most entrancing things Mal had ever seen. Somehow the silver sheet of rain made it even more magical.

Harry noticed the megawatt smile light up her face. She had abandoned her baseball cap, and her wet hair was plastered to her skull. Her shirt and pink boxer shorts clung affectionately to her body, spattered with mud. She must have fallen because her knees were skinned, though she had not complained.

"Let's go," he said.

"How much further?" Mal hated herself for

saying that — it had just sort of slipped out.

He glanced over his shoulder at her, one dark eyebrow raised. "You quittin' on me?"

"No, I am not."

"Good. I'd hate to have to carry you."

She glared murderously at his back, then plodded after him, putting one foot after the other, her eyes fixed on the muddy ground. After what seemed a long, wet, painful time, he called over his shoulder, "Home at last."

They were at the bottom of the steep incline leading up to the cabin. She stared at the slope. It looked like Mount Everest. Her thighs felt like rubber, her shins hurt, and her feet were twice their normal size. She gulped, wondering how she was going to make it.

"Not thinking of giving up now, are you, Malone?"

He was standing next to her. Her lip trembled, but she wasn't going to be beaten. "I'll do it even if I have to crawl on my hands and knees," she muttered.

He shook his head, marveling at her. "There's no need for such an act of penitence."

"You bastard, Harry Jordan," she cried, limping determinedly toward the slope.

He grabbed hold of her and swung her into his arms. She fought him, but he said, "Come on, Malone. You know you'll never make it." It was true, even though she hated him for saying it.

He carried her into the house, across the hall, all the way up the stairs to her room. He deposited her in a chair, put a match to the logs in the grate, and strode into the bathroom.

The bastard wasn't even winded, Mal thought bitterly. She heard water running, then the scent of lilacs filtered into the room.

The fire was crackling nicely by the time he returned. "Your bath is ready, madame," he said. She hadn't moved a muscle since he had put her in the chair, and his guess was that she couldn't.

Kneeling in front of her, he unlaced her boots, easing them off as gently as he could. She groaned as he pulled off the thick socks. There was a trail of blisters across her pink toes and raw places on her heels where the boots had rubbed. He sighed, then brought a bottle of antiseptic and some gauze from the bathroom.

She was slumped in the chair with her head thrown back and her legs sticking out in front of her, like a broken doll. "This is going to sting a little," he warned. Squatting beside her, he cleaned her grazed knees and wounded feet.

"Ouch," she muttered without opening her eyes, "Ouch, ouch, ouch."

"Okay, the worst is over. Now it's bath time."

She opened her eyes and looked warily at him, but he simply picked her up again and carried her into the bathroom. "I assume you are able to disrobe entirely by yourself?"

"You assume entirely correctly." She glared furiously at him.

He smiled cheerily as he closed the door. "Oh, Malone?" He popped his head back in again and heard her groan. "I had intended to take you to the inn for dinner tonight, but I think we need to take time out for injuries. What do you say I cook up a little supper here at home?"

"You? Cook supper?" She gave a skeptical laugh.

"Wait and see, Malone, before you criticize," he said loftily as he disappeared.

Just lying in the hot bath water in the huge, old, lion-clawed tub was the closest thing to heaven Mal had experienced all day. With the exception of the picnic, perhaps. And the raccoon family peering at her through the rain. And the sight of Squeeze cavorting with the sheer joy of being alive.

She wallowed in the tub like a seal in surf, her aches diminishing as the wonderful warmth seeped back into her veins. The bathwater smelled of lilacs. She noticed a new jar of bath oil on the Victorian washstand. It could not belong to Harry's mother; it simply was not her style. Harry must have bought it specially for her.

He wasn't going to get around her that easily, she thought, amused, not after what he had just put her through.

She climbed from the tub, wrapped herself in an enormous fluffy white towel, then limped into the bedroom. She lingered in front of the fire, drying herself, reveling in the heat. There had been a moment, there in the great outdoors, when she had thought she might never be warm again.

She brushed her hair, rubbed moisturizer into her weather-battered face, and patted soothing lotion onto her wounds. She hesitated for a second, then without stopping to think why, she sprayed herself liberally with Nocturnes.

Then she pulled on a pair of oversized blue flannel men's pajamas, stuffed her blistered feet into white sweatsocks, and rummaged in her bag for a robe. She had forgotten to pack one. Fuming, she tugged a blue sweater over the pajamas.

Then she brushed her damp hair and inspected herself in the mirror. Her face was pink from the bath, her hair was flat, and she had no makeup on. She removed her contact lenses and put on her small gold-rimmed glasses. If Harry Jordan had had any amorous ideas, she thought, he would forget them the moment he clapped eyes on her. She looked a mess.

Good smells were coming from the kitchen as she limped stiffly down the stairs. The lamps were lit, and an enormous log burned crisply in the huge grate. One of Miffy's ancient long-players spun a little scratchily on the record player, but the music was good: Nat King Cole singing "When I Fall in Love." An open bottle of wine, with two plain but beautiful glasses, awaited them on the coffee table in front of the fire.

Mal sank into the sofa nearest the blaze. She put her feet up with a thankful sigh, wondering how long blisters took to heal and whether she would ever be able to get her shoes on again. The rain was still beating against the wall of glass, and the tops of the trees were tossing in the wind.

She snuggled into the depths of the sofa, feeling a sudden glow of well-being. There was something secure about being in a cozy firelit room while a storm raged outside.

"There you are." Harry breezed in, wearing his frayed 501s and a white shirt. A blue-striped butcher's apron was tied around his waist, and a clean white dish towel was slung over his arm, exactly like a French waiter. He poured wine into their glasses, glancing at her, taking in the oversize pajamas, the sweater, the absence of makeup, and the little gold spectacles. "Feeling better?"

"Thank you, yes. But I'm still mad at you for that hike."

A pained expression crossed his face. He gave her a glass of wine and ran a hand through his already tousled hair. "It was those ridiculous new boots that gave you problems. In the right boots you would have been able to walk ten more miles."

"How many miles did I walk?"

He shrugged. "Five. Six, maybe."

"Vertically."

"Oh, come on. The gradient was minor."

"Minor!"

She glared at him, and then he said, reasonably, "You could have called it quits anytime on the way up. How was I supposed to know you were in pain? What are you, a martyr or something?"

She knew he was right and that it was her own stubbornness, plus her ill-fitting expensive new boots, that had been the trouble. "We're fighting again," she said.

Their eyes connected, and that little electric current passed between them.

"This wine's too good to waste in a fight."

She took a sip. "Is the food going to be as good as this?"

"The food!" He ran for the kitchen, and she smiled, relaxing. He was right — this was an evening to savor. The storm outside, the crackling log fire, the lamplight, the sweet music, the good wine. She sighed happily. It was almost worth the torture of the hike.

"Dinner is served." He came back bearing a tray. "I thought we might eat here, in front of the fire. It's a frittata omelette — my only claim to culinary fame."

He put down the tray and cut a wedge from the thick, round, slightly burned omelette. He slid it onto a green plate shaped like a lettuce leaf and set it in front of her.

"A Van Gogh omelette," she said admiringly. He wasn't listening — he was looking at her. "You remember, like the Matisse sandwich," she prompted.

"I was just thinking how very pretty you look tonight. The sweater matches your eyes — sapphire blue. And I like the glasses."

"Now you know the worst. This is the real me." She couldn't take him staring at her like that. Why did he have to look as if he knew more about her than she knew herself?

Harry gave her a skeptical look, but all he said was, "Eat your omelette, Malone, before it gets cold."

She took a bite. "This is delicious. Whatever did you put in there?"

"Asparagus, potatoes, chicken — the picnic, in fact. Plus eggs, a little onion, a touch of garlic."

"You were holding out on me. You *can* cook."

"This is it. Usually it's pizza and the microwave."

She laughed. "With me it's cornflakes. A no-cooking standby from my childhood."

"Tell me more about that childhood."

She took a sip of wine, looking away from him into the flames. "It's a shame to spoil a beautiful evening talking about me."

He shook his head, exasperated. "There you go again. Anyhow, it was in our deal, remember? I tell you my story, you tell me yours. As of now, only one of us has completed that part of the contract."

Mal had edited her life story to such a minimum, she almost believed that was all there was to it. Great painful chunks had been lopped out, discarded with the person who used to be Mary Mallory Malone.

Her cheeks were burning as she tugged off her sweater. She fanned her face, pretending it was the heat of the flames and not his gray eyes that were raising her temperature.

Nat King Cole ground scratchily to a halt. Harry got up and ran his finger along the stack of titles. He chose one, put it on, then turned down the dimmer and came and sat next to her.

The log shifted, sending a pretty shower of sparks up the chimney. Rain beat against the windows, and the mellow strings of Nelson Riddle swooned in back of Sinatra singing softly, "Come fly with me, Come fly, Let's fly away. . . ."

Mal felt as though she were flying, suspended in time and space. There was just this cabin on the side of a mountain miles from anywhere. In fact, it was altogether too dangerously seductive.

He said, "I often come here alone. After a

hard day's hike or a bike ride, I light a fire, open some wine, put on some music . . ."

"Dim the lights."

"Sure I dim the lights. That way I can see the trees outside, and the moon."

"In case you hadn't noticed, there's no moon tonight."

"I was speaking figuratively."

She peered at him over the top of her glasses, wondering about the women he must have brought here. It was too much to expect a man like Harry to have been alone all the time. She felt that little tug of green-eyed jealousy again and told herself sternly it was none of her business. Oh, yeah, she answered herself, mockingly, then why do you want to reach out and touch him? And why can't you take your eyes from his?

Harry couldn't drag his eyes away from her either. Her face was flushed, and her blond hair had dried into a smooth golden helmet. Her blue eyes looked huge behind the strong lenses. He'd bet that without the glasses, she couldn't see more than two feet in front of her.

Hypnotized, Mal unfurled herself from the sofa. She stood just a pace from him, their eyes connected with that live-wire tension again, and a tiny shiver ran down her spine. "Why did we have that 'no strings' contract anyway, Harry?" she asked softly.

"It's like a no-claims policy, I guess." He put

his hands on her shoulders, and she thought her bones would melt under his touch. "We could always add a rider to that clause stating 'with the exception of tonight.' "

He took off her glasses and placed them carefully on the table. She peered nearsightedly at him, her heart pounding somewhere in her throat. Then he reached up and ran his finger across her mouth. The sensuousness of the gesture made her shiver. She closed her eyes as he dropped soft kisses onto her eyelids, then ran the tip of his tongue along her lashes.

"Sweet," he murmured, "so sweet. I wondered how you would taste." He licked the corner of her mouth, kissed the tip of her nose, nuzzled his face into her neck. She sighed softly.

He pulled her closer, and she slid her arms around his neck, tilting back her head, wanting to be held, wanting to be kissed. When his lips skimmed hers delicately, she murmured with pleasure, absorbing the feel of him. Then his mouth closed on hers, parting her lips, drinking her like a thirsty man, and she was lost in the moment, wanting it to go on forever.

When he finally took his mouth from hers, she clung to him, her eyes still shut. Harry looked tenderly at her, then he picked her up and carried her back to the sofa in front of the fire.

"I can walk," she protested dreamily.

"Blisters, remember?"

He set her down on the cushions, smiling. She looked like a teenager in the ridiculous blue flannel pajamas and socks, with her hair all mussed and her cheeks flushed pink. But then she opened her eyes and gave him that enigmatic sapphire look that was half *please* and half *no,* and he knew it was no simple girl he was looking at.

"You nervous, Malone?" he asked, taking her left foot and pulling off the sock.

"Mallory," she corrected him.

He pulled off the other sock. "You didn't answer." He began to massage her foot, gently, rhythmically.

"Of course I'm not nervous." She watched him, big-eyed, not wanting him to stop.

He ran his hand along the smooth length of her calf, massaging the aching muscles. It felt wonderful, and she relaxed into it. "Mmmm, good," she murmured, "that's so good. . . ." She leaned over, looking deep into his eyes. "When are you going to kiss me again?"

"Since you ask . . ." He cupped her face, kissing her lingeringly, then hefted her into his lap and crushed her to him. Minutes slid slowly by as they kissed. She couldn't get close enough to him. She pulled out his shirt, running her fingers over his naked back, feeling the sleek muscles.

His hands were under the blue pajama top, exploring her skin, then, with just the pads of his fingers, he circled her breasts. Mal gasped at the sheer electric shock of it. She leaned back in his arms, surrendering herself to his touch.

Harry's fingers trembled as he unbuttoned the pajama top. He looked at her lying there, golden all over from the Arizona sun. Her round breasts tipped with coral nipples invited his mouth. He inclined his head, ran his tongue over them, tasting her flesh, trailing along the line of her throat, circling her breasts, inching down.

He untied the pajama cord and slid off her pajamas, drinking her in with his eyes. She was all hot silken-fleshed woman: soft, golden, responsive. She shuddered as his fingers traced the taut line of her belly, arching against him as he gripped the soft mound of hair, then ran his finger gently over her sweet center. She cried out in soft throaty little moans, thrusting upward into his hand. He jammed his mouth onto hers, biting, kissing, searching, as she demanded more, reaching for it as his fingers brought her to the brink, and then with a cry that was half groan, half scream, she shuddered over the edge of control. "Oh, Harry, oh, Harry," she moaned.

He gazed down at her, loving her for her abandonment to the moment, as crazy for her as she was for him.

She watched like a woman in a trance as he undressed. Firelight licked at his body, and she gazed longingly at him, wanting to taste him, wanting him to taste her.

She edged over on the deep sofa, making room for him. "Harry," she said in a deep purring voice, "Harry . . ." And then he was lying beside her, his flesh cool against her heat as he devoured her, in a give and take of pleasure that sent ripples of delight through her. Then they slid gently, all of a heap, from the sofa onto the rug.

She sprawled before him, her body sculpted in the fire's glow, her eyes locked with his. Waiting. She was damp, beautiful, softly sensual, and deeply exciting. Desire leaped like a knot of white heat in his belly. He lay over her, holding her, taking her mouth again. Her fingers clutched his hair as he entered her, and she shifted against him, wrapping her legs around him, moving against him. . . .

His need for her was urgent, he was trembling with it, but he wanted her to be his equal, to give her pleasure. "Wait," he murmured, "Mal, wait." He took a deep shuddering breath, holding back, and then she said, "Harry," again in that purring little voice that sent a groan of pleasure from his throat, and he was lost.

She cried out with each stroke, tiny moans that grew deeper. He rested, leaning on his hands, looking at her. She met his eyes — they were drowning in each other, as he slowly took her to the brink again, and then they were both tumbling over the cliff, arching, flesh against hot damp flesh, warm wet lips colliding fiercely. And then they were still.

Mal lay under him, her arms and legs still wrapped around him, floating somewhere in space, not wanting him to leave her. His weight was beautiful, his smooth skin, beaded with sweat, was delicious under her skimming hands, and the rough masculine scent of him was in her nostrils.

"Ohhh, Harry," she murmured.

"Mallory," he growled, and she smiled, coming slowly back to earth again.

"I'm crushing you." He eased himself away from her, and she sighed with regret. Sex was not something she indulged in simply to satisfy a momentary urge. The act meant more to her than mere pleasure; it meant that, for that moment, she felt loved. She wanted to hold on to that moment as long as she could. When his body left hers, she was bereft, alone again.

She sat up and clasped her knees under her chin. Harry looked at her for a long moment, and she tried to read the message in his eyes. Then he bent his head and gently kissed her blistered toes, one by one.

Tears pricked her eyelids. The tough cop was a tender lover, thoughtful and generous.

He picked up her sweater, wrapped it around her shoulders, smoothed back her tangled hair. His hand was shaking, just like hers, as she touched him, wonderingly, running her fingers gently along his jaw, across the stubble that had bristled her tender female parts, and she hadn't even minded, she had been so lost in it.

The Sinatra record was still spinning on the phonograph, long since finished. She put her hand on his chest, feeling his heartbeat thudding like hers, and she smiled.

Harry thought she was like a candle glowing in the dark. He took the glass of wine, held it for her while she drank, then inclined his head to her and licked the wine from her lips.

"I don't need wine," he told her throatily. "I can drink you instead."

She stretched her arms over her head, lithe as a cat, contented — until he cupped her breast again, running his thumb across the nipple, following it with his lips. And it was starting all over again.

The log had burned through, slipping lower in the grate. Only the red glow remained when they finally came to their senses. The record was still spinning without music, and the wine was still undrunk.

Harry eased his arms from under her, and she protested muzzily as he stood up. Her eyes followed him as he walked across the room. She thought he was beautiful. He turned off the record player, then picked up a soft chenille throw from the back of the sofa and a couple of cushions. He lifted her head, arranged the cushions beneath her, and covered her with the throw. Then he lay down beside her again.

"Comfortable?"

"Mmmm." Her eyes were half shut, and a blissful fatigue drew her down. Harry kissed her gently as he put his arms around her, fitting her head snugly into the groove of his shoulder. "Custom made for you, Malone," he said, closing his own eyes.

"Mallory," she corrected him. Then before she knew it, she was asleep.

Squeeze woke them early the next morning, whining at the door to be let out. Harry edged his numb arm from beneath her and got to his feet.

"Don't go," she said in a muffled voice, her head still hidden beneath the blanket.

"The dog," he explained. "I'll be right back."

He let the dog out, then threw another log onto the embers, blasting it with a pair of ancient leather bellows until it sparked into flames again.

He looked at the blanketed mound still lying motionless on the rug. All that was visible were her feet, sticking out at the end, blisters and all. Even her feet were pretty. He pulled on his boxer shorts, then walked barefoot to the kitchen.

"You're so goddamned *busy*, detective."

Her complaint floated after him.

"And you are consistent, Malone," he called from the kitchen.

Mal snuggled back down into the rug, listening to the early morning sounds: birds singing, the dog barking, dishes rattling in the kitchen. Soon the good-morning aroma of fresh-roasted coffee drifted her way, along with Harry's voice singing something in Spanish. She wondered if he was dancing.

"Room service."

She shuffled upright, clutching the chenille throw modestly over her breasts. Her eyes widened. "Mmm, coffee. And *muffins*."

He held out the basket. "Blueberry on your left, jalapeño cornmeal on your right."

"Jalapeño cornmeal?"

He looked apologetic. "My one indulgence, I'm afraid."

"Oh? I thought I noticed a few more 'indulgences' last night."

He lifted an eyebrow. "You noticed?"

She laughed, and he bent and kissed her. "Your hair's a mess," he murmured, tasting her earlobe.

"Mmm, then I must look like you."

He ruffled her hair affectionately. "Eat your muffin, and stop complaining, Malone — *Mallory*."

"You finally got it." She took a bite of the muffin. "Do these taste like heaven or what?"

"Low-fat heaven."

"They're not!" She looked astonished, and he laughed.

"No, they're not. I just said that to make you happier. And while you're eulogizing, how's the coffee?"

"Bliss."

"What more can a woman want?"

"Not much," she agreed, leaning comfortably against him, eating the muffin, still clutching the blanket over her breasts.

"Too late for the blanket," he said, sipping his coffee. "I've seen it all." To his astonishment, she blushed. "Malone, you can't be *shy* with me now," he said. "Remember me? I'm Harry, the guy from last night?"

She nodded, blushing. "My date."

"The guy who brought you to the party," he murmured, bending to kiss the nape of her neck. "The one you let put his hand down the front of your dress."

"We're a little too old for necking in the backseat of the limo, though." She leaned her neck into his hand, and he massaged it gently.

"Oh, Malone," he sighed pleasurably, remembering — "that was not mere necking."

She laughed, then drained her coffee mug, took the last bite of muffin, and put on her glasses. She wrapped the chenille throw around her and got up. "I'm off to take a shower."

He sat on the sofa, looking at her. She looked back, taking in his broad shoulders, his dark curling chest hair, the bluish stubble in dire need of a razor, the sleek muscles in his arms, and the way the flesh clung to his taut rib cage. Just the way she had clung to him last night, flesh on flesh. She felt hot just remembering.

She gave him a happy smile, then walked sedately away. His eyes followed her. Halfway across the room the chenille throw began to slide. She turned, threw him a sexy look over the top of her glasses, and let it slither down her back, tantalizingly slowly, lower. And lower. Trailing it behind her, she sashayed naked across the room, turning to give him one last wicked look.

"Like cream over peaches," Harry marveled, hearing her laughter as she walked unhurriedly up the stairs.

28

When Mal came downstairs again, Harry was sprawled on the sofa. He had obviously just showered because his hair was still wet. He had on his frayed Levi's and a white T-shirt, and he was fast asleep.

She watched him affectionately. He looked like a man born to wear jeans and a T-shirt. And he looked exhausted.

He opened his eyes suddenly and looked directly at her. His gaze was so deep, so intimate, it was as though he had touched her. He took her hand, drew her down beside him, and slid his arm along her shoulder.

"You smell delicious," he murmured, "like all the good things in the world. Fresh-cut grass, or maybe sweet summer hay. A garden after rain. A soft ocean breeze on a tropical island."

"It's Bactine," she said honestly. "On the blisters."

He laughed. "How many men do you know who could mistake Bactine for a soft ocean breeze on a tropical island?"

"Very few. In fact, probably only you, Harry Jordan."

He pulled her to him and kissed her soundly.

"Now you're all lipstick." She ran a finger across his mouth.

He kissed her fingers, then the palm of her hand, then her mouth again, just as the old grandfather clock in the hall struck twelve, right on cue. He had to work that night, she had to catch the shuttle back to New York, and the long drive was still ahead of them.

"Why does this have to end," he murmured, "when I feel it's only just beginning."

"Cinderella again," she whispered regretfully.

He nuzzled her neck. "Did anyone ever tell you you're adorable? When you're on your good behavior, that is."

She sighed. "You couldn't just leave it at adorable? And since you're asking, actually no. No one has ever told me."

He lifted his head and stared at her, astonished. "Only me?"

"Only you."

His eyes softened. He tilted her chin with his finger so she was looking at him. "Poor Mary Mallory Malone," he said softly. "Not even her mother told her."

"Not even my mother," she agreed sadly.

He felt the sudden change in her mood, and he wanted to say don't worry, everything's all right now. But it wasn't. He knew if she didn't talk to someone about what had happened, share her emotions, she would be crippled by her past forever.

"You never did finish telling me about those years in Golden," he said.

She shrugged, suddenly remote. "I lived there. Then I left."

She paced restlessly to the big wall of windows, stood, arms folded, gazing out.

"And your mother? What happened to her, Mal?"

Her back was rigid with tension under the sapphire sweater. "What does it matter to you?"

He strode across the floor to where she was standing. He grabbed her shoulders, but she shrugged him off, took a step away from him.

"You have to tell me," he insisted. "It's the only way it will ever get better."

Mal looked at him through suddenly shuttered eyes, hating him for forcing her to remember, hating the memories that lay like dead dogs in the murky depths of her mind.

"Just who do you think you are anyway, Harry Jordan," she cried, upset.

He looked steadily at her. "A friend."

Her eyes dulled with despair, and her head drooped. She looked lost, grief-stricken, and Harry knew he had catapulted her into the past and that he was looking at the girl she used to be.

Mal could feel little tremors of panic rippling down her spine as she was forced to think about it again. She could remember every detail of that day. She could hear the desolate whine of the wind and the roar of the waves, see it all as perfectly as if it were a rerun on television.

It was Thanksgiving, and she was eighteen years old. The journey from Seattle to Golden had been long and tedious, and the local bus had rattled her bones and her teeth for the last hour. She didn't know whether to be relieved or frightened when it finally bounced over the bumps and potholes into the town parking lot and ground to a halt.

"End of the line," the driver said, removing his peaked cap and wiping his sweaty brow. Without looking at her, he eased his bulk from the undersprung seat and clambered down the steps.

Her eyes, hidden behind thick pale-rimmed spectacles, followed him. Leaning unsteadily into the wind, he walked toward the weathered clapboard shack that served as ticket office, café, and tourist information center. She had lived in Golden for six years. She had ridden Chuck Montgomery's bus a hundred times, and he had never once acknowledged her. It was that kind of town.

"A bitch of a little town," she remembered her mother calling it when they first arrived there, with all their worldly belongings piled into the ancient turquoise Chevy with the chrome fins. It hadn't changed.

Hefting her small black duffel, she climbed down the steps, gasping as the gale-force wind snatched her breath away, wrapping her cheap cotton skirt around her legs and flattening her sweater against her chest.

She glanced anxiously around the parking lot. It was empty — there was just the desolate whine of the wind, and the ever-present boom of the Pacific waves roaring into the silence.

She waited uneasily for a few minutes, but there was still no sign of her mother and the familiar battered Chevy, even though she had written from college to say she would be arriving on the two o'clock bus. She might as well not have bothered. She could never rely on her mother for anything.

"Why couldn't you have been here, Mom? Just this once, when I really need you?" she murmured, tears prickling her eyelids.

There was no point in waiting. Picking up her bag, head down against the punishing wind, she trudged into town.

The trailer park was up a hill, on the wrong side of Golden's tracks. At the top she turned and looked back at the ocean view. The huge waves were racing in, crashing so violently onto the shore, she could feel the earth shudder from their impact, hear their desolate, booming echo and the wind drumming in her ears.

She walked slowly toward their trailer. A

"motor home," her mother had always called it, as though the word elevated them to a higher social status. The window boxes that, in their first optimistic year in Golden, were filled with cheerful scarlet geraniums and purple petunias, had been washed out long ago by the violent storms. They hung, lopsided, dribbling rainwater onto the stained cement. Ruffled net curtains trailed tiredly at the grimy windows, and no welcoming smell of roasting Thanksgiving turkey came from the chimney.

The door was unlocked. She stepped inside and glanced around.

"Mom?" She went into the kitchen.

"Mom?" she called again, dropping her bag. Her letter saying she would be coming home was lying on the table alongside an empty coffee cup.

She strode through the narrow living area to the bedroom in back. Her mother was not there. She checked the bathroom. Nothing.

She hurried back to the kitchen and touched the coffee pot. It was still warm.

Suddenly she knew where her mother had gone: where she always went when the bad moods came on her and depression settled like a black cloud around her shoulders.

Rain spattered in a torrent at the windows. Hastily pulling on her old bright-yellow oilskin poncho, she ran out of the trailer and down the cliff road, battling the wind, until the road turned into a lane leading down to the beach.

She was used to the great winter storms of Oregon, where enormous waves were generated by four thousand miles of traction all the way from Japan. The storm winds would whip them into giant froth-capped monsters, hurling onto the rocks, tearing at the dunes, ripping apart anything in their path.

Wiping the rain from her face, she braced herself against the gale-force wind, shading her eyes with her hands. Then she saw her, a tiny figure standing on the rocks, staring out to sea.

As she watched, her mother took a step forward onto a rock closer to the waves. She paused. Then she took another step. Then another pause. Mary Mallory thought, puzzled, that it looked as though she were playing a childish game of giant steps.

Too late, she realized what her mother was about to do. "Mom, Mom, don't," she screamed.

Another step forward. A great wave was roaring in, building height and power as it came. Her mother raised her eyes to the sky and lifted her arms exultantly over her head as the wave took her. In a second it swept her into its green depths, sucking her down.

Mary Mallory stared numbly at the place where her mother had been. She watched in stunned silence as the great wave came surging back. She could see her mother's slender body, trapped high in its curl, as it took her higher and higher. Ten, twenty, thirty feet, until it seemed to touch the lowering gray clouds. Then the wave curved into a magnificent crest of foam and hurled her mother back onto the rocks.

Mary Mallory screamed as the eddying wave sucked her out again, out and under into the raging gray-green depths.

They never found the body.

Harry stroked Mal's bent head gently. Pity for her wrenched at his heart as he remembered his own idyllic childhood at Jordan's Farm. She glanced up at him, her eyes blurred from unshed tears. He caught something in her expression — hesitation, longing — and then it was gone again.

He held her in his arms, and she huddled into him, like a stray cat seeking warmth and protection. It was as though her mother had died yesterday. The wound was still that raw.

"I always thought she did it because of me," she whispered. "The letter was there on the table, saying I was coming home. I told her I needed her, and she didn't want that. *She didn't need me.*"

He said gently, "It wasn't your fault. There was nothing you could have done to save her." But she just hid her face against his chest. "It's over, Mal. It's the past, and you have to let go."

"I know."

Her voice sounded as bleak as the scene she had just described.

Harry sensed she was keeping something back. He wanted to ask her to tell him all her secrets and finally free herself from the past. But she had gone through enough emotion for one day.

The dog bounded in, bringing the fresh scent of the forest and the wind on his thick silver coat. Squeeze stopped and looked at them, his head on one side. Then he gave a little bark and came over and nuzzled Mal's hand.

She lifted her head and looked at Squeeze. She was still choked up as she said, a touch enviously, "Oh, God, Harry, you are really a man who has everything."

But she was smiling as she caressed the dog's head, and he knew the worst was over. For now.

29

Harry still had Mal on his mind when he showed up for work that night. He had driven her to the airport, escorted her to the check-in, and kissed her discreetly on the cheek as they said good-bye. He was dimly aware of other people's stares; he had almost forgotten that she was a celebrity, her face as well known to most of the people shuffling wearily through the departure gates as their own. After this weekend she was simply Mal to him: a maddening woman who got under his skin and who fought with him all the time; a beautiful woman who made love to him as though she meant it; a woman who seemed inextricably bonded to her mysterious and tragic past.

"Shall I see you next week?" he asked as they walked to the departure gate.

She gave him that wry, cool look. "Think you can put up with me?"

"I might. Just." He grinned at her, then kissed her on the cheek again. He breathed deeply, inhaling her elusive scent. "That's not Bactine," he whispered. "I swear it."

She was laughing as she waved good-bye and strode off to the gate. "Call me," she said.

Then she turned and looked back at him. "Harry."

"Yes, ma'am; Malone. . . . Mal."

"Thanks."

He lifted his arm in salute. And then she was gone.

Why was it, he thought, staring at the empty space where she had been, that he still had the uneasy feeling she had not told him everything?

He dropped the dog back home and left him curled contentedly under the bed, no doubt dreaming of rabbits and squirrels and raccoons. Then he took off for the precinct.

It looked like it was going to be a quiet night. Sundays were often like that — the public seemed to prefer to destroy each other on Fridays and Saturdays, giving him a break on God's day.

It was ten o'clock when the call came through. A woman had telephoned, worried about her sister. They were supposed to meet; a strange interrupted message had been left on her answering machine; and now the machine didn't answer. A squad car had gone to check the house. The sister had a key, and what they had found when they opened the door was not pretty.

"We're on," Harry said to Rossetti, unfurling himself from the chair and heading for the door.

Rossetti grabbed his coffee cup and headed

after him to the car. Harry got behind the wheel, and they took off, sirens wailing, through the quiet streets.

"What a way to end a great weekend," Harry said glumly.

"It was that good, huh?"

"I had fun, Rossetti." The car rounded the corner, then shot the red light, sirens still blasting the peaceful night.

"Vanessa said don't forget the party. She's only gonna be twenty-one once."

"I won't forget."

The street in front of the little clapboard cottage was cordoned off with yellow crime-scene tape. Three squad cars were already parked outside, and an electric-blue Dodge Neon was in the small forecourt. A little knot of curious neighbors hovered nearby, and two burly uniformed men stood guard outside the door.

A young woman was crouched in the back seat of one of the squad cars, weeping. Harry shook his head sadly. He figured her for the sister and knew he would have to question her later. Murder was never a happy event.

He greeted the uniformed officers, asked a few questions, then opened the door and stepped inside. Rossetti followed him.

The smell of blood and two-day-old death hit them like a blow. They shone their flashlights around. Nothing had been touched by the cops — the lights had not even been turned on, in case the killer had left a print on the switch. Something squished as Harry took a step forward, and he shone the flashlight down.

"Peas," Rossetti said, astonished. "Maybe she was caught in the middle of fixing dinner."

A huge pool of congealed blood lay immediately in front of them, mixed with what looked like the peas. And blood was spattered on the walls, on the coat thrown over the small chair, and on the door.

"Jesus," Rossetti muttered, "it's a fuckin' bloodbath."

Harry played the flashlight over the trail of blood that led to the body, slumped in the bedroom doorway. She was on her knees, her face pressed into the bloody carpet, and she was naked except for her underpants. Her long, vibrant red hair shone under the light, and a black cat crouched beside her, his tail twitching as he stared back at them.

"This is not going to be nice, Rossetti," Harry said quietly. "Where the hell is forensics?"

"Right here, detective." The first of the crime team stepped in the door, glanced around, and gave a low amazed whistle and then a sigh. "What can I say," he said with a shrug as the medical examiner shouldered past him. It was Dr. Blake, one of the forensic pathologists employed by the city.

"They had to drag me out for this one, Detective Jordan," Blake said testily.

"Careful where you step," Harry warned. "This is a clean crime scene so far."

"I know, I know," the doctor said. "Goddammit, detective, I've been doing my job for twenty years. I don't need you to tell me my business. And can anyone tell me why the hell people have to get themselves killed on a Sunday night, when a man is enjoying a peaceful nap in front of the evening news?"

"Way of the world, doc," Rossetti said, making way for the photographer and his equipment.

Within minutes he had set up his lights and commenced videotaping the scene and the victim, as well as taking stills.

Dr. Blake crouched next to the body. "Not much mystery about how she died," he said briskly. "Both the jugular and the carotid slashed. Two different cuts. Plus multiple other stab wounds." He made careful notes, pointing out the wounds to the photographer for close-ups.

Harry waited by the door, arms folded, his face expressionless. "When did it happen, doc?"

Blake adjusted his glasses. "What's today? Still Sunday?" He looked at the greenish stains on the flanks of the abdomen, indicating the beginnings of putrefaction. He lifted her wrist; the body was still slightly stiff. "There's still some rigor mortis. I'd say Saturday, early. Around thirty-odd hours ago. I'll know better after I check the vitreous humor at the autopsy."

Harry knew he was talking about the jelly-like fluid in back of the eye, which he would extract with a fine-needled syringe and which, because it was resistant to postmortem changes, would give a more accurate indication of the time of death.

Blake carefully placed plastic bags over the hands and feet to preserve any trace evidence adhering to them. "No rape, though, detective," he commented. "Or at least no immediately visible signs of it. I could be wrong. Again, we'll see at the autopsy."

Dr. Blake looked at the battered, blood-encrusted face, seeing her as a person for the first time, instead of a dead body. He looked at her for a long time. "Do you know who she is?" he asked Harry.

Harry shook his head. "Her sister is outside. She'll identify her."

"It's hard to tell under all that blood, and her so cut up, but she looks kind of familiar." He packed his instruments away in his black bag and got to his feet. "Well, that's my job done. For the moment. She's all yours, gentlemen. See you at the mortuary."

"Thanks for coming out, doc," Harry said.

As Blake edged carefully past him, his foot struck something. He didn't notice, but Harry heard it. He hunkered down, looking at the object on the floor.

"Detective," he said triumphantly to Rossetti, "I think we have our murder weapon."

It was a small knife, maybe seven inches long, with a plastic cover over the narrow blade. There were no visible bloodstains — Harry guessed the killer had cleaned it.

He signaled the photographer to take pictures and measurements. Then someone from the crime lab, wearing protective gloves, picked it up, bagged it carefully, and took it away.

Harry spotted the bloody bag on the floor: "Birds' Eye Frozen Peas," the label said. "2 lbs." Avoiding it and the trail of blood, he edged toward the body in the doorway.

It was as bad a horror scene as he had witnessed in his career. Her bloody hands had left a scrabbled trail down the door, and around where she lay crouched on her knees was a lake of congealed blood. It looked as though her entire blood supply had ended up on the carpet.

Forensics had dusted the light switches, and now they turned on the lights. An ambulance wailed its arrival as he crouched over the body.

There was a gaping hole where her throat had been, and her face had been savagely carved. Her eyes were open, rolled up into her head.

Rossetti was standing over him. "Oh, my

God," he said in a strangled voice. "Oh, my God, Harry, it's Suzie Walker."

Harry's spine crawled, and the hairs prickled the back of his neck. He had never had to deal with a murdered person he'd known, had never known personally someone who was now just a mutilated body instead of a vital, attractive young woman.

Stunned, he got quickly to his feet, staring down at her, filled with violent rage. "Christ," he roared, slamming his clenched fist over and over again into the wall. "*Why?* Why the fuck did he pick on her?" He was rigid with anger at the senselessness of it.

Rossetti stood rooted to the spot. "Excuse me," he said, hurriedly making for the door. He walked to the end of the street, and hidden in the shadow of a large red maple, he vomited.

Harry stood, stone-faced, as the paramedics zipped what was left of Suzie Walker into a body bag, then placed her on a gurney and wheeled her into the ambulance. There was no need for emergency sirens as it took off.

He thrust his burning fists into his pockets. If he'd had the murderer right there before him, he would have killed the bastard. Strangled him with his bare hands. Kicked him like the beast he was. Then he reminded himself soberly that he was a cop. He needed to be dispassionate, detached, an investigator, and that was all. But in his mind he still saw Nurse

Suzie Walker smiling at him with those beautiful green eyes, heard her retort to Rossetti when he asked her for a date.

"Why the hell did it have to be Suzie, Prof?" Rossetti stood beside him. His face looked gray in the harsh overhead light, and there was a bleak look in his eyes. "She was nice," he said somberly. "She was dedicated to her job, she was a good woman."

Now was the time to make the speech about nailing the bastard, about seeing him put away for what he had done to Suzie. Now was the time to say she had deserved better. But Harry could not. He thought bitterly that there would be no comfort in that for her family. And besides, he had said the same thing about Summer Young. With an effort he switched his mind away from the victim and back to the job facing him.

He grasped Rossetti's shoulder comfortingly, then systematically began to search the bedroom.

30

When Harry and Rossetti emerged from Suzie's cottage an hour later, Alec Klosowski was waiting outside for them. He had already told the uniformed cop what he had heard, and now he told Harry.

He was a nice-looking young man with shocked brown eyes and dark hair smoothed back in a ponytail. "It was Friday night," he said, "about eight o'clock, and she was dressed for work. We were both locking our doors. She told me she'd lost her keys the night before. Someone had handed them in, and she wondered who might have had them. I told her to get the locks changed, you couldn't be too careful." He turned his head away. "Oh, God," he said with a catch in his throat, "I didn't expect this, though."

"You couldn't have known, Mr. Klosowski," Harry reassured him gently.

"We both drove off, and I assumed she was working the night shift. She's — she was a nurse, you know, at Mass Gen. I was surprised when I came home and saw her car parked outside again. Then I noticed a light on in the kitchen, and I thought I must have got it wrong, or else she had come home early."

"What time was that, Mr. Klosowski?"

"Oh, around two, I guess. Yes, that would be about right. I'd just finished work you see, at Daniels on Newbury Street. I'd just got the key in the lock when I heard the scream."

He looked numbly at Harry. "At least, I thought at first it was a scream. I listened, but there was nothing else, and I told myself it must be cats yowling. There's a lot of strays, feral cats, around here, and they often sound like that." He hung his head, close to tears. "God, if only it could have been that. Just cats. If only I'd had the sense to realize she was in trouble."

His young face was haggard as he looked back at Harry again. "I feel responsible. If I'd done something, knocked on the door and checked that she was okay, or called the police —"

"I doubt there was anything you could have done," Harry said. "It doesn't pay to think that way. You're helping now by giving us valuable information."

"There's more," Klosowski said. "I saw him."

"Jesus," Rossetti muttered, "an eyewitness."

"I got ready for bed, went to open my window. I saw him walk from her house across the street. He was hurrying, and when he got to the other side, the parked cars blocked my vision. Not that I was looking, really — I just thought, oh, there's the reason Suzie came home early. I smiled, for God's sake."

"Can you describe him?" Harry was praying he could.

"All I can tell you is he was sort of a short guy, stocky. Dark hair, I guess."

"What was he wearing?"

Klosowski looked puzzled. "I didn't notice, but it must have been dark clothing because he sort of blended into the night."

"Did you see him get into a car?"

"No — yes . . . I mean I did, then I heard it drive past."

"What sort of car, Mr. Klosowski?"

"I'm not sure exactly. It was kind of a wagon. You know, maybe like a Jeep Cherokee or perhaps a station wagon. Smallish, a dark color, I couldn't say which."

Harry breathed a sigh of regret. "Mr. Klosowski, would you be willing to come to the precinct and make an official statement about what you saw?"

"You bet."

Harry thought Alec Klosowski would be willing to do anything to absolve himself of the terrible guilt he was feeling. He was a good witness, though, coherent and reliable despite the shock.

"Detective Rossetti will take you there now, sir."

Rossetti looked expectantly at him and said,

"I'm off to the hospital to interview the sister. She's in shock — they took her there. I'll see if she can talk. I understand the parents are with her."

Harry drove through the quiet night streets, replaying the information they had collected on Suzie's killer. They had the weapon, an eyewitness description, a basic description of the vehicle, and the approximate time of the murder. The crime officers who were still going over the cottage would surely come up with further forensic evidence.

This wasn't a planned, premeditated murder. He would bet it was a robbery gone wrong. Suzie had come home unexpectedly and caught him in the act. And he had killed her.

That was his theory, for now, until something proved him wrong. He was always ready for the unexpected; when you were dealing in homicide, nothing was written in stone.

He parked the car outside Emergency and walked up the steps. There was a leaden feeling in his heart as he walked toward the admission desk where he had so often seen Suzie. The two nurses on duty looked at him with shocked eyes.

"It's true then?" one of them asked, "about Suzie?"

He nodded. "I'm sorry."

"She was a great girl," the nurse said, her face beginning to crumple. "Always pleasant, even when we were overworked. And so pretty. . . ."

"And she was a good nurse too," the other one said, her hands gripped into tight fists as she fought back tears. "The shit," she muttered angrily. "The dirty bastard. They are like vermin, these killers. They should be eradicated, the same way we do rats."

Harry thought she was right. "I'm sorry," he said again, then went slowly down the corridor to the booth where the Walker family awaited him.

Terry Walker was lying on top of the bed, fully clothed except for her shoes. She had been sedated; her eyes were open but slightly unfocused. Nevertheless, she managed to raise herself into a sitting position when Harry came in. She looked a bit like Suzie, only with darker hair.

Mrs. Walker was sitting in a chair next to the bed, and he saw instantly that her girls took after her. She had the red hair and green eyes, the pale freckled skin and the angular bone structure that gave them their pixieish look. Tears were cascading down her face, though she made no sound. Her husband was standing next to her, holding her hand tightly. He was tall and rangy, with dark hair, and there was a look of total devastation on his face.

Harry would have given anything not to put them through this, but it was part of his job.

He introduced himself and shook hands with the father, whose own hands were icy cold.

"Mr. and Mrs. Walker, I knew your daughter. I often saw her here at the hospital. I am most deeply sorry, and I am sorry too that I have to inflict these questions on you at such a time. But if we are to catch this — the perpetrator of this crime, there are certain things I need to know from you."

"Dad, tell him about the tape." Terry's voice was shaky. She had closed her eyes again as though she couldn't bear to look at him.

"It's all on the tape." Ed Walker handed the small answering machine over to Harry. He was making a great effort to get the story straight, but his voice trembled, and he seemed to be searching for the right words.

"Suzie . . . she called Terry, left a message on the machine. . . . She broke off in the middle — she just said, 'Oh, my God, oh, my God, what are you doing here?' and then there was just this terrible sound, and then . . . nothing."

Harry could hardly believe what he was hearing. They had the actual crime on tape? He could already see the metaphoric noose tightening around Suzie's killer's neck.

"We were supposed to meet on Saturday," Terry said in a weary voice, her dull eyes looking into his. "And I know she had a date Sunday night with a guy from Beth Israel. His name is Karl Hagen — he's an intern there."

"Had she known him long?"

She shook her head, "I don't know. But I think maybe he did it."

"Do you have any reason for thinking that, Terry?"

She shook her head. "Suzie was too busy to date a lot, but these things are usually about sex, aren't they?"

Harry heard Mrs. Walker gasp and said, "I doubt it, this time. At the moment we're thinking more in terms of an interrupted robbery."

"But what did Suzie have worth stealing?" Ed Walker demanded, anger suddenly exploding from him. "She was just a young woman, a nurse still studying. She had no jewelry, no money. Just a TV and a cheap hi-fi."

"Sometimes when people are looking for money to buy drugs, Mr. Walker, available is all that matters."

Ed Walker stared down at the floor, unable to speak, and Harry touched his shoulder lightly in sympathy. "Thank you, sir," he said quietly. "I won't disturb you anymore. When you're ready to leave, a squad car will be waiting to take you home. We can talk again later."

Harry interviewed the charge nurse next. Like Klosowski, Nurse Jim O'Farrell was blaming himself. "I told her she was no good for work, so she might as well go home," he said in a stunned voice. "I did it. I sent her to her death."

"Accidents and homicide are most often the

result of a chain of events," Harry told him. "Suzie had a migraine and couldn't work. She would have had to go home anyway."

"You think so?"

Harry could tell he wanted to believe it, and he wanted him to as well. "Sure I do. That's usually the way it happens. A victim walks into an unknown situation. It's sad but true."

"But she was a good nurse, a nice girl. Christ, she was hardly old enough to be called a woman — she was too young, too . . . aw, she didn't deserve this."

"No one does," Harry said. He took a statement, then grabbed a cup of coffee and made his way to the morgue.

The air conditioning was blasting noisily as he stepped through the steel doors into the cold, white-tiled autopsy room. Over the din he could hear Dr. Blake humming as he analyzed Suzie Walker's body.

She was lying on a steel autopsy table beneath a strong overhead light. Blake had already cleaned the body and completed his preliminary examination, dictating his notes into a microphone suspended over the table as he went along. Each fingernail had been scraped for particles of skin or fiber that might have been caught in the struggle, and hair samples had been combed and clipped from her pubic hair as well as her head and eyebrows. The body bag, along with her underwear, had been preserved for trace evidence and would be sent to the crime lab.

A photographer was taking still shots and videotaping the proceedings. Blake was proceeding with his examination.

"No hypostasis, indicating that she was not killed when lying on her back and then moved. She probably died in the kneeling position in which she was found," he said briskly into the microphone. Then he hummed some more, as he indicated on a chart the exact locations of the stab wounds and their depth. He took swabs to establish whether there had been a sexual assault and stated that evidence already indicated that there had not.

He glanced up at Harry, still standing by the door. "Come on in, detective," he said mildly. "Might as well make a night of it, now we're all up anyway."

Harry stayed where he was; what had happened to Suzie was obscene enough, and he didn't want to see her defiled by Dr. Blake, even if it was his job.

"You'll know by now who this is," Blake said matter-of-factly. "I didn't really know Nurse Walker myself — not in my department, y'know. But she worked alongside me the other week, when the tropical storm caused all that mayhem on the roads. She was a good nurse, quick-thinking, clever. It's a great pity. Yes, a great pity."

Blake was humming tonelessly again as he picked up the dissecting knife. Harry wished impatiently that he would at least find an identifiable tune. He sounded like a percolator on the bubble.

Blake held the knife over Suzie's body, then made a deep incision from the neck to the pubis, detouring the navel, where the tissue was tougher.

"Hmm," he said, inspecting his handiwork. "Hmm, I see." He removed the organs, slid the stomach away, opened it up with scissors, and proceeded to empty the brownish contents into a large container.

"Not much here," he said to Harry. "She didn't eat much on her last night apparently. Nor did she drink."

Harry had been present at many autopsies, but this was like watching Suzie being killed all over again. Sickened, he turned away. "Let me have the results as soon as you can, doctor," he called, pushing back through the heavy doors. He told himself it was the icy room, but he felt chilled to his bones.

Driving slowly back to the precinct, his mind was still filled with the sights and sounds of the terrible night.

Rossetti was at the computer, he was busy putting the evidence on file.

"What d'you think, Harry?" he asked somberly.

Harry flung himself into an office chair. He

swung it from side to side, staring upward into space.

"I think life's a bitch, Rossetti," he said. And he meant it.

31

Mal couldn't sleep that night. She shuffled her pillows around, seeking a comfortable spot, threw off the blanket, and tossed and turned until she was wrapped like a mummy in the wrinkled sheets. Sighing, she unraveled herself and got up.

Folding her arms over her chest, she went to the window. The night was clear and starry, filled with the pinkish glow from the lights of Manhattan. She thought about Detective Harry working at the precinct, drinking too much coffee, the way he'd told her he always did on the graveyard shift.

The graveyard shift. The words repeated themselves in her head, and she shivered, thinking again about her mother.

She remembered how she felt the day the letter arrived from the college admissions office: dizzy with excitement and sick with fear. The white envelope with Washington State University printed on it lay on the gray plastic kitchen table with the angled metal legs that somehow always smacked you right in the shin when you sat down. She couldn't bear to open it. Her mother was smoking, staring blankly into space. There was a furrow between her brows as though she was suffering, but Mallory knew her pain came from the dark thoughts in her mind.

"It's the letter from the university, Mom," she said.

Her mother's gaze shifted momentarily into focus. "Oh," she said.

"I'm scared to open it, Mom," she persisted. "Why don't you do it for me?" She pushed the envelope across the table with the tips of her fingers. All her hopes were in there. It was life or death. If she got in, she lived — she would work hard, and she would have a future. If she failed, she would work at the Lido Café or the Golden Supermart until she died from monotony and loneliness. She held her breath as her mother reached out and slowly picked up the envelope.

She looked at it, read the name and address, turned it over and over in her thin nervous fingers. She sighed and pushed back her straggling gray-blond hair, took a sip of the cold coffee, and lit another cigarette from a burning stub.

Mary Mallory thought she would just die from the tension. "Open it, Mom," she urged, hardly recognizing her own voice, it was so rough with anxiety.

Her mother stuck the cigarette in the corner of her mouth. Narrowing her faded blue eyes against the smoke, she ran a broken fingernail under the seal. Mary Mallory clasped her hands tightly together on top of the table. She hardly dared look as her mother slowly unfolded the letter.

Her mother ran her eyes over the few lines. Then she refolded the letter and put it back on the table. Her eyes became blank again.

"Mom?" Mary Mallory controlled herself and there was only a tiny wobble in her voice.

Her mother took another puff on the cigarette, waving away the smoke with a thin hand.

"Mom!" she cried, agonized. *"What did it say?"*

Her mother shook her head, startled out of her torpor. "Oh. Oh, it said they have given you a scholarship . . . I think."

Mary Mallory took a great gulp of air and snatched up the letter, opened it, read it. And then she screamed. She leaped to her feet; she kissed the letter and screamed again, jumping up and down, wild with joy, until the flimsy trailer rattled on its cinderblock supports.

"I got in!" she yelled. *"Mom, I got in!"*

Her mother was staring out of the window. "Look, Mary Mallory, it's raining again," she said matter-of-factly.

And then Mary Mallory did something unthinkable. She ran to her mother and she kissed her. On the cheek. Her mother flinched and put a hand to her face, shocked. "Put on your poncho when you go out in the rain," she reminded her.

But Mary Mallory didn't care. Nothing mattered except that she had been accepted. She wouldn't have to die alone in Golden.

Graduation from high school passed in a quick blur. Her name was read out, and she walked, blushing, onto the platform to pick up her diploma, but her mother was not there to see her.

She did not attend the prom. For weeks all the other girls had talked about was their dresses and boys, whether they would receive a corsage, and who they would neck with afterward in lovers' lane on the cliff road, hidden by towering sequoias and madronas and ponderosa pines.

Mary Mallory had kept out of their way. She wished she could plug up her ears so she would not have to listen to their endless chatter, but still it seeped through in the rest rooms where they endlessly fixed their hair, in the schoolyard at recess, in the cafeteria where she ate lunch, her nose in a book, alone as always.

Only one teacher bothered to congratulate her on getting a scholarship.

"You're a hard worker, Mary Mallory," she said approvingly. "With a college education, you'll be able to get a decent job and make something of yourself." She didn't say "instead of ending up like your no-good mother," but Mary Mallory knew that was what she was thinking.

For a long time now, she had been working

evenings and weekends at the Lido Café; chopping onions and clearing dishes and pouring cups of coffee to earn extra money. Now she began to save up for college.

She took an extra job through the summer at Bartlett's Drugstore, stocking shelves and unpacking; anything menial they needed, she did it. She was able to buy herself a couple of sweaters and T-shirts and a pair of jeans, as well as a cheap duffel bag to pack them in. She thought the long summer days would never end, she was so eager to leave and begin living. But she worried about leaving her mother alone.

Finally, her bag was packed, the bus ticket purchased, and the address and phone number of her dorm carefully printed out and stuck on the old refrigerator door. They couldn't afford a telephone, and in case of emergency she told her mother to use a pay phone. She had washed and polished the Chevy — all she had to do now was convince her mother to drive it, so she could pick up the food stamps and buy her own groceries.

"Come on, Mom," she said, taking her arm and levering her from the chair where she was watching television. "We're going out for a drive."

"You go, Mary Mallory." Her mother pushed her arm away, but Mary Mallory was determined. She threw her arm firmly around her shoulders and walked her from the trailer into the hazy late-afternoon sunshine.

"It's a lovely day, Mom. I thought we'd go buy your cigarettes, then maybe pick up something nice for supper at the market. It's a celebration, you know."

Her mother allowed herself to be bundled into the driver's seat, and Mary Mallory put the keys in the ignition. "Remember when you drove here, Mom? All the way from Seattle? All you have to do now is drive to the market and the gas station."

Her mother crouched over the wheel. She put her foot on the gas and they sped off down the hill. Heads turned as they walked together into the Supermart, and Mary Mallory blushed, feeling eyes on them. She knew they made an odd couple: she with her thick bottle-glasses, her thin sticklike limbs, and her old flowered cotton dress from the thrift shop; and her mother with her wild curling hair, her vacant eyes and emaciated face, in a once-white shirt and blue skirt that exposed too much of her skinny legs. They looked *poor*, she thought angrily. They were poor. In fact, people didn't come much poorer than she and her mom. How much further down could you go when you had nothing?

Then she reminded herself that *now* she had something. She was going to have a college education. She felt that same surge of elation she had experienced the day her mother had told her they were going to live at the seaside.

With a college education she would finally be someone.

They paced slowly up and down the aisles while she showed her mother what to buy and what to do with the food stamps at the checkout. Her mother walked through it like a woman in a dream. Mary Mallory only hoped she would remember what to do.

Back home, she barbecued the celebration steaks on the rusted little hibachi outside. She opened a can of baked beans to go with them, and they sat silently across the table from each other. Her mother toyed uninterestedly with the steak. As Mary Mallory looked at her, her heart filled with despair. She had needed to share her small triumph, her pleasure, her excitement with her mother, but it was no good. Even the celebration supper was a failure.

Her mother was sitting on the orange vinyl sofa the next morning, watching the *Today* show when Mary Mallory came to say goodbye.

"I'm going now, Mom," she said wistfully to the thin, pathetic figure hunched in a corner of the sofa. Her mother glanced vaguely at her, then back at the program. She said again, "I'm leaving for college, Mom."

"I know," her mother answered in the same mild tone she used for any news, good or bad. "Have a good time, Mary Mallory." And she lit a cigarette from a butt in the ashtray.

Mary Mallory let her hand rest for a moment on her mother's hair. Tender feelings flowed from her — she wanted so badly to hug her, to kiss her, to know that her mother cared. "Bye, Mom," she said.

Her mother got up and poured herself another cup of coffee. "Good-bye," she said distantly.

The campus was much bigger and more sprawling than Mary Mallory had expected. Nor had she realized she would have to share a room in the dorm with another girl. She knocked nervously on the door, waiting, until someone called, "Come in."

Junie Bennett frowned when the door opened and Mary Mallory stepped inside. "Oh my lord, look what the cat dragged in," she muttered under her breath. "Hi, I'm Junie Bennett," she said out loud. "The bed nearest the window's mine. Yours is over there." She pointed to the one against the wall. "First come first served." She inspected her roommate with critical green eyes.

"I'm Mary Mallory Malone." She held out her hand, smiling hopefully.

"Mary Mallory." Junie raised her eyebrows. "Don't you have a nickname?"

"Oh . . . just Mary." Surprised, she changed her name in an instant.

"I'm going out to meet some friends." Junie snatched up her sweater and her bag. "Just keep your stuff to your own side of the room, please."

Mary gazed wistfully after her. Junie Bennett was everything she would like to be — tall, blond and pretty, with a pert nose, red lipstick, loads of confidence, and a real gold bracelet on her summer-suntanned wrist. She even had a pet name — Junie. Mary bet she had been a cheerleader in high school. And she was so well-dressed — her smart red skirt and white shirt looked expensive and brand new.

Junie was definitely unfriendly. She had her own group, and they did everything together. Mary was not invited. Junie bitched to her friends about having to room with such a geek and ignored her as much as possible.

Looking in the mirror, Mary knew why. She was seventeen in age, but in life experience she was almost zero. She was plain, mousy, and crippled with insecurities, and she was so poor, she couldn't even afford a cup of coffee. So she just stuck her nose in her books and got on with learning, never missing a lecture, never failing to turn in an assignment. The college found her a job in the cafeteria, and after a few weeks she got herself another job in a nearby café, working the dinner shift.

Somehow she got through the terrible lonely weeks. At first she hoped to make friends — she made a point of smiling and saying hello to her classmates. But they all had busy lives and hung out in a crowd that definitely did not include her. There were other outsiders like herself, but she avoided them because she couldn't bear to admit that kind of defeat. Instead, she bolstered up her courage, thought of the future when she would have her degree, and concentrated hard on her studies.

She decided she wanted to be a journalist. Writing words was so much easier than speaking them, and because of her deprived childhood, she had an inexhaustible curiosity about how the other half lived. Besides, journalists didn't have to answer questions — they asked them. She could keep her silence and her privacy.

She crept around campus like a slight gray ghost, keeping to herself, speaking only when she was spoken to, in class or in the cafeteria. But it was never about anything personal.

The first college year passed slowly. At the end of it she had still not made any friends, but she had excellent grades, and with her two jobs she was making ends meet — just. She went back home to work all summer at the Lido Café, only now that she was older, she was promoted to waitressing.

The proprietor, Dolores Power, a plump round-faced woman with hard eyes whose husband was president of the local Chamber of Commerce and the Elks Club, commented that she was surprised at Mary's professionalism.

"I work nights at a café near college," she explained. And that was the only exchange between them, except for issuing instructions and handing over the paycheck on Saturday nights.

Mary couldn't tell if her mother was glad to see her, but she seemed relieved not to have to collect the food stamps and do the shopping for a while. She was even thinner than before, and Mary suspected she wasn't eating. So she spent a lot of her pay on good food, trying to entice her with roast chicken for Sunday dinner with apple pie for dessert, and she bought lots of fresh fruit and granola and whole milk. But her mother only picked at it, and her eyes told her she was tasting it only to pacify her.

It was a relief to get back to the university, and for a while everything continued just as before. Then suddenly it all went wrong.

That was when she went home at Thanksgiving and saw her mother walk into the ocean.

Sighing, Mal stepped away from the window with the glamorous Manhattan view. She had not thought consciously about her mother for years, not since she had left Golden. There had been no memorial service for her; after all, no one had even known her while she was living, so who would come to pay their respects now that she was dead?

There had been no final moment for Mal either — no good-bye scene, no purging of the guilt. She had not even had a time to grieve. Instead, she had been forced to cut her mother out of her mind as finally as her mother had removed herself from life.

It was something she had had to do in order to survive. She was just eighteen years old and alone in the world, a college student, and still the invisible woman. She had no money and no friends because she had never learned the art of making them.

It had been a long hard haul from that non-person to the woman she was now — harder than anyone knew. And that was the reason Mal never allowed herself to think about it. Except when the nightmares happened.

They had come often at first, sneaking un-bidden into her sleep, little black demons of memories, tripping on spike-tipped toes through her subconscious. Then gradually she had left them behind, and they happened only rarely now.

Mal paced through the darkened apartment, her arms clutched over her chest, thinking about Harry. She wasn't afraid tonight — there was no need to rush around switching on lights to keep the black memories at bay. And she knew she could thank Harry for that.

She went out onto the terrace and stood gazing out over the city, feeling the cool breeze on her bare arms and legs, ruffling her hair.

She could picture her mother perfectly, as though she had seen her just yesterday: thin, fragile, her cheeks sucked in as she drew on the eternal cigarette, her hair faded into an indeterminable mixture of gray and sand. She remembered the letter lying on the kitchen table, telling her she was coming home for the weekend.

She remembered the endless journey on three different buses. "It's all right," she had told herself as they lurched through the night, "you'll be home soon."

But there had been no home and no mother and no comfort for her. There had been nothing — except her own determination.

Later, she had gone back to the university and to the jobs at the cafeteria and the downtown café, while living in a bare little room in an old house she rented from another student.

Somehow she completed her courses and was given her degree. Then she got herself a job at a local radio station as a back-room typist, collating accounts. With a little money in her pocket, she smartened up a bit and bought herself a couple of decent-looking work outfits. Then she found a new position at a small local TV station.

Her official title was researcher, but she was really a gofer. She typed letters, delivered mail, answered the phones, and fetched coffee and doughnuts. She was drab, mousy, and unassuming, with no sense of herself because she had still not discovered what that was. But somewhere inside lurked ambition. She dreamed of being a TV news reporter, out on location reporting local events.

Then a new girl was hired, fresh from college, smart as paint, blond hair flowing around her shoulders, her lipstick and eyes sparkling. Within weeks the new girl was on camera doing location shots for the news, on a foggy car pileup, or a bank robbery, or a bridge swept away in a flood.

Mary felt demeaned, less than nothing. She had worked hard, and she had learned. She had hoped so badly that any new girl on camera would be her.

Then she looked in the mirror. She saw her straggling blond hair and her ugly glasses. She saw that she was still drab and mousy, she was still inhibited and shabby, with a shy whispery voice. And she had asked herself, despondently, why anybody would want to look at her, anyway.

Now, sitting on the garden terrace of her beautiful Manhattan penthouse, Mal remembered the awful truth of that moment. She had been faced with the terrible reality that this was who she was and this was the way her life would always be. No one was going to wave a magic wand and change it for her. Her fate was in her own hands.

A sort of rage had swept over her: anger at her parents, who had left her without love and without identity; anger at the pretty, sparkling girl who had got the job she'd wanted; anger at her own helplessness. She was at a cross-roads.

At that moment she had decided to change her life. She would drag herself up from this. By sheer force of will, she would succeed. It was now or never.

She withdrew her small savings from the bank and made herself over. She had her hair cut neatly and tinted a more golden blond, invested in some contact lenses, bought a few simple, unfussy clothes in clear colors. She asked the TV makeup woman what cosmetics to use and how to apply them. She studied the techniques of the interviewers, not just at her local station but on the networks. She watched Barbara Walters and the morning show presenters like a hawk until she knew every expression on their faces, every inflection in their voices, every inch of their craft.

When she was ready, Mal asked the station manager to give her a chance at becoming a reporter. She burned with resentment, even now, remembering the contemptuous way he had looked at her and the smirk on his face, and the you-must-be-joking tone of voice as he turned her down. She gave her notice on the spot, and that week she left the small town for a bigger one.

With her carefully prepared résumé and her new appearance, she got a job at another television station as a production assistant. The pay was better, and she was treated like one of the team. Her co-workers smiled at her and acted friendly, and she reveled in the surprise of it. She smiled back cautiously at first, afraid of being rebuffed when she made a friendly overture, never quite sure of herself. But she was accepted. They assumed she was just like they were. She went out with them after work, for a drink or a meal.

She joined a gym, worked out, got herself into shape. She even began to date, though nothing more serious than dinner or a ball-game or a movie. And she was always cautious, always holding herself back. The "mystery woman," they called her jokingly. But to her astonishment she was enjoying herself.

When the weather girl took a vacation, she got the job temporarily. Now she knew exactly what to do: how to look, how to smile and act vivacious. Now she, too, looked as smart as paint, her blond hair flowing, her blue eyes sparkling, a ready smile on her generous mouth. Brimming with newly found vitality and eagerness, she had learned how to be entertaining.

Then the call came from the network news producer: she had caught his eye. He asked her to come to New York for an interview.

Sitting on her terrace, Mal remembered how giddy with excitement she had been, and how sick with nerves. She had pushed away the old sneaking insecurities, told herself this was who she was now, and who the network wanted. And then she went out and invented Mallory Malone.

She splurged on a little black Donna Karan suit that fitted her svelte body like a glove. She went to a well-known hair stylist at an expensive salon and had her hair cut in that now-famous chrysanthemum bob, then had it lightened until it looked naturally streaked by the sun. A top makeup artist did her face, and when she looked at the result in the mirror, she barely recognized the glamorous young woman looking back at her with surprised blue eyes.

It had cost her every cent she had, and as she set off for the interview and the camera tests, she hoped nervously it would be worth it.

When the cab dropped her outside the studio, she gazed at the imposing building and the guarded doors and the people hurrying in and out on important business. She knew it was all hers for the taking — if she had what it took. Sticking her chin in the air, she walked, tall and purposeful, through the doors. It was now or never. Again.

It was that reinvented Mallory who had married a successful Wall Street broker a couple of years later.

Matt Clements was older, handsome, graying at the temples, and the perfect social animal. She had liked him immediately because he was a sort of father-figure and also a self-made man. Using his own street-smartness and astute financial brain, he had dragged himself from a lowly Brooklyn tenement to where he was today. On top of the world in one of Manhattan's grandest skyscraper tri-plex apartments, loaded with classy antiques and style.

"Money can buy you anything in this city," he told her when he invited her to dinner and she wandered through the rooms, amazed at the sheer, staggering luxury of it all. "Includ-ing style. And don't forget that in a city like New York, style gives you your credentials. Money plus style equals class, and that means you've got it all."

They laughed, and she admired him for his honesty — and she envied him because he brought no baggage from his past. He made no secret of his lowly beginnings. He wasn't proud of them, but they were just a fact.

At that time she was a network newsreader, and the prospect of moving to the morning show at some future date was being dangled under her nose. She was torn between her career and the heady excitement of being with him.

He looked after her, cared about her, made her feel beautiful and wanted. For the first time, with a man, she felt able to let her guard down a little. He understood her ambition and applauded her for it. She never had to explain herself to him.

When he asked her to marry him a month later, she said yes instantly. She told herself it was love, and she did love him in a way. And she was certainly physically attracted to him. But what she really wanted was to be part of his busy life.

That turned out to be the problem. He was a busy man, and she was a busy woman. Something had to break, and it turned out to be their marriage.

"Give it up for me, Mal," he had said.

He was sitting opposite her on a big gold brocade sofa in the smaller of the sitting rooms in their grand apartment. He was in a dark green silk robe, and she was wearing a white terry one. They were both naked underneath, and they had just made love. It had been fine, good; when she was with him, everything was okay. But he was away too often, and without her job, without what she did, she felt that she was nothing.

"You would hate me in two months if I did," she said sadly.

"We could buy a house in the country, have a baby."

She had looked at him, anguished. She told herself she couldn't have a baby. She had never really been a child herself. She was afraid she would not know how to love it — after all, she had no role model. "I don't think I could do that," she said soberly.

"The offer is still open," he said. And then he kissed her and went to get dressed. Half an hour later he left for Zurich. He would not be back for a couple of weeks.

A few months after that, she realized it was not going to work. She needed her career, and he lived for his. She hadn't really minded when he blamed her publicly for the breakup. After all, he had offered her what most women wanted. She was different, that was all.

Mal walked to the edge of the terrace and leaned her elbows along the rail, gazing down at the streets of the tough, glamorous city that had taken her to its heart. She had never looked back since that day. And she had never looked back to the past, until Harry had forced her into it.

There were still things she knew she could never talk about, secrets she could never expose to the light of day. But they were from another time and place, and she had told herself long ago that the only way to survive was to go forward.

Harry had been right, of course. She had taken the coward's way out by refusing to confront her own desolation and sense of abandonment created by her mother's suicide. Obviously she had been afraid of it.

"Thank you, Harry," she said into the night. Then she went back indoors and called him and left the same message on his answering machine.

She smiled, thinking about Harry getting her little message when he returned from work in the early hours. She wandered into the guest room and switched on the lamp. She looked at the bed Harry had slept in last week. The room had been cleaned and the bed linen changed, but her pillow was still there — the same pillow his head had rested on.

She lay on the bed, clasping the pillow to her breasts, her knees curled up, her eyes closed, thinking about Harry, wishing she were back in his arms, making love to him. Because when Harry Jordan made love to her, she had felt loved. And that was pretty special.

32

The homicide squad room was still buzzing with activity at dawn when Harry finally called it quits. He had gone through the transcripts of the interviews and the evidence found at the scene, and he had played Terry Walker's answering machine tape endlessly. Each time he heard Suzie's last words, it was like a blow to the heart.

After the first time Rossetti couldn't bear to listen to it again, but Harry was searching for background sounds, anything extra that might have filtered onto the tape. He had finally sent it over to the lab to see what they could do electronically to amplify it.

He hardly needed Dr. Blake's autopsy report. It seemed a terrible pity that Suzie had had to be defiled a second time in order to discover what her last meal had been, and whether she had taken any drugs or poisons, and which of the terrible slashes had been the one that actually caused her death.

Both he and Rossetti had begun referring to Suzie as "the victim," putting a distance between the girl they knew and the body in the morgue.

"We'll get this son of a bitch, though,

Prof," Rossetti said soberly.

He looked like a different man from his usual soigné, Casanova persona; now he was somber-eyed and angry. Harry felt exactly the way he did.

"We're homicide cops, Rossetti," he said, trying to jolt them both back into the reality of their position.

"Yeah, but we're still human," Rossetti retorted.

They walked out to the parking lot together, stood around, hands shoved in their pockets, saying nothing. Rossetti kicked a stone; it struck the Jag, and he said moodily, "Sorry."

Harry shrugged; it didn't seem to matter. He slapped him sympathetically on the shoulder and said good night.

They walked to their cars, turned, looked back at each other.

"Where you headin' now, Prof?" Rossetti asked.

"I thought I'd go by the club, see what's doing." Harry knew he wouldn't be able to sleep. He would work out in the gym and burn off the false energy. "What about you?"

"I thought I'd try the church, put in a little prayin' time. Give it a chance anyhow."

Harry hoped God could do better than they were. He climbed into the Jag and drove very slowly through the cool gray dawn to the Moonlightin' Club.

★ ★ ★

The club was quiet. Just a few young guys hanging around, sipping Cokes and talking. Even the music was muted — instead of rap, they were playing a Whitney Houston album.

He said hi in passing, went to the locker room, and carefully stowed his handgun away. Not that it meant much, he thought as he shut the locker door securely. Any one of the kids here tonight more than likely possessed a firearm, most of them more sophisticated than a police officer's handgun.

He took a quick shower, changed, then hit the gym. He did a half hour on the treadmill, then he lifted free weights instead of using the machines. He needed the sheer physical feel of being in charge of himself tonight.

Another half hour later, sweating and exhausted, he went back to the locker room, took another shower, and got dressed. He was reaching for his holster in his locker when he saw a slip of paper tucked underneath.

He slid the note carefully from beneath the weapon. The message was scrawled in black ballpoint.

"The shooter at the 7-Eleven is Isaiah Tulane aka Gregory Tallman aka Ike the Man. Right this moment he is keepin outta sight at 9 West Street. The dead guy was a friend."

It was unsigned, of course. But Harry had no doubt it was accurate. He took ten seconds out to wonder how they'd gotten into his

372

locker, then reminded himself severely that this wasn't day camp. Most of the guys who frequented the club had criminal records, and most had been involved in drugs. Lockers were easy meat for them. He felt lucky that the only time they had abused the trust between them was to inform on a murderer who had shot one of their own.

Nevertheless, he was guilty of the sin of complacency — he hadn't expected this to happen. He had been careless and was just lucky it hadn't all gone bad. It wouldn't happen again.

Nobody looked his way as he walked back out to the car — they just went right on doing what they were doing. Harry grinned as he got on the radio phone and summoned up the squad cars. Sometimes life offered up a little bonus after all.

He got Rossetti on the phone too. "How'd your praying go?" he asked, still smiling.

"You know better than to expect an immediate response," Rossetti retorted. "Still, I guess I feel better."

"Then this will make you feel even better and increase your faith in the Almighty." Harry told him about the note. "I'm on my way to pick up the arrest warrant as we speak," he said, elated. "See you on West Street, old buddy."

Arresting the killer was an anticlimax. He was in bed, sleeping off a heroin hit and he offered no resistance. Later he became truculent and told them the name of his accomplice.

"It was him shot the guy, not me," he muttered as Harry paced around him in the interview room.

Rossetti sipped his coffee, aware that Tulane was dying for a cup. And a cigarette. He took out a pack of Camels, ostentatiously shook one out, rolled it around in his fingers, then stuck it between his lips. He tossed the Zippo from hand to hand, drawing out the tension.

Tulane's eyes were fixed on the cigarette. He licked his lips. His face was ashen gray, his mouth parched, and as the drug left him, he began to shake.

"I need a smoke, man," he said, still angry. "Ain't you guys supposed to offer suspects that? And coffee?"

"Sure." Rossetti lit the cigarette and wafted the smoke away with his hand. Tulane sniffed it up like it was cocaine.

"Oh, man," he moaned, "you are one mean shit."

"Detective Jordan, will you make that two demerit points against Mr. Tulane?" Rossetti grinned.

"There's all the coffee and cigarettes you want just waiting for you, Isaiah," Harry said mildly.

He knew it was just a matter of time. Rossetti had the guy wound up, and his accomplice was going through the same motions in the next room. They had the weapon and the rusting white Ford transit van. They had these guys nailed, and in the next hour or so, they would confess. Meanwhile, their lawyer had arrived, disgruntled at being hauled out of bed. Harry yawned. It seemed as though this night had gone on forever.

It was ten in the morning when they had their confession, and when Harry finally drove back home, he was worried about Squeeze. He needn't have been — the dog was used to a cop's erratic hours. He greeted him with a lazy wag of the tail and lumbered cheerfully to his feet.

Harry slipped on the leash and took him for a brisk walk up and down Beacon Hill and around the Common. He stopped at a Starbucks and had a decent cup of coffee for a change and shared a cinnamon twist with the dog before they walked home again.

There were two calls recorded on his machine. The first was his mother.

"Harry, thank you for coming to my birthday," she said gaily.

Harry groaned. She was so up, and he was exhausted. Besides, the party seemed like a decade ago.

"Wasn't it just lovely? Sometimes I think I outdo even myself. And thank you for bringing Mallory. She was certainly an extra treat. Such a lovely woman. Your uncle Jack says you're crazy if you let this one go just because you're wedded to your job. And I must say I agree with him." She laughed again. "Let's have lunch soon, dear boy."

There was a pause, and then she added as though she had just thought of it, "Don't you think there's something faintly ridiculous about having to make an appointment to lunch with you, when you live right around the corner? You could just drop in any old time. Oh, except I forgot to tell you, I'm off to Prague next week with Julia. I know you'll ask yourself why on earth I am going to Prague, so I may as well answer you now. It's because I've never been there. *Au revoir*," she added, then put the phone down with a firm click.

Harry grinned. Miffy was nothing if not predictable. He waited for the second message.

It was Mal. She said in that soft purring voice, "I was just thinking about you. I want to say thank you, again. For everything. Good night, Harry."

He wanted to hold her, hug her to him. Instead, he smiled and patted the answering machine affectionately. He hoped he would dream of her when he finally got to sleep. But in fact he did not. He did not dream at all.

33

Mal was on his mind when he woke up, though. He edged Squeeze's head off his chest, sat up, ran his hands through his hair, then dialed her home number. He got the answering machine and sighed. Of course, it was two thirty. She would be at the office. He called there, but she was still at lunch, not expected back until around three.

At three he was sitting at Ruby's counter having breakfast, with Squeeze tucked underneath, as always.

"Good thing he's a police dog," Doris said loudly at him. "Otherwise the patrons might object on hygienic grounds."

Harry glanced at the other customers, gulping Bud, coughing over their Marlboros, and mopping up gravy with their bread. "Not these patrons, Doris," he called over his shoulder, as he went to the pay phone near the door.

Squeeze had his head on his paws. He lifted his eyes, watching him, but he did not move. He knew when Harry meant action.

"Ms. Malone is in a meeting at the studio," Harry was informed.

"Okay," he said resignedly. "Tell her I called again. I'll get back to her later."

He went back to the counter and picked, disgruntled, at his usual ham and eggs.

"You know what, Prof? You don't eat right," Doris said, leaning her elbow on the counter opposite him. "You ever eat anything 'cept this crap?"

He glanced moodily at her. "Sure I do. I eat cinnamon buns, pepperoni pizza, and Matisse sandwiches."

"I ain't never heard of a Matisse sandwich, but what you need, Prof, is a good woman who cooks for you. Proper food, y'know, like they tell you to eat in magazines."

"The women I meet don't cook," he said sadly. Then he remembered Mal's refrigerator with the quail and stuffed zucchini blossoms. "Well, maybe some."

"Then go for it, Prof, because if you don't snap her up soon, you'll be the one in Mass General. In the cardiac intensive care, wishing you'd never heard of Ruby's famous home fries."

It wasn't Doris; somehow the food just didn't taste so good today. He drank a Coke, paid the check, waved good-bye, and walked to the door. This time Squeeze followed him.

Back in the squad room, it was as though he had never left. He sat in front of the computer going over the facts about Suzie's death. Something about it didn't quite add up. For one, nothing had been stolen: the stereo and TV were still there. Still, the odds were she had interrupted him before he had a chance to remove the goods and stash them in his car.

He examined the photographs of the body. Suzie's battered face was covered in dried blood. He peered closer at it, took a magnifier from the drawer, and looked again. He picked up the phone and called the crime lab, asked them to blow up the detail of Suzie's forehead. He couldn't quite believe what he had just seen, but he was pretty sure he was right.

He looked at the photograph of the black lace panties lying on her bed. Yet there had been no rape. The crime lab had them, along with her sheets and the other articles present at the crime scene — the bag and the peas, the knife, samples of blood, and the fingernail scrapings. The detritus of a wasted human life.

He looked at the pictures of the knife. It was small, with a thin narrow blade. It was the same type that had been used on Summer Young. He pulled up Alec Klosowski's statement on the computer. The description of the suspect and the type of vehicle also tallied.

He shook his head, disbelieving. Suzie had been randomly butchered in what he guessed was an impulsive crime. The deaths of the three young women students had been premeditated. They had been stalked, abducted, and raped, then killed cleanly in an act of planned sexual violence.

He called forensics again and asked when they would have something for him, anything.

He just needed to get on with it.

"Give us another couple of hours," the head of the crime lab told him.

So he took Squeeze for a walk alongside the Charles River. Mooching along with his hands in his pockets, he gazed at the sidewalk instead of at the scenery. The dog walked soberly at heel, sensing this was not a playful catch-the-ball-type day. Then, lured by a cackling group of gulls on the embankment, he flattened himself to the ground and squeezed under the fence.

"Get back here, you idiot," Harry yelled as the dog chased after the gulls, sending them shrieking angrily into the air. Squeeze barked joyfully, Harry laughed, and the dog trotted triumphantly back. This time he leaped the fence, then resumed his position just slightly behind Harry, as though nothing had occurred.

"Mutt." Harry cuffed him affectionately, then he returned to his thoughts.

What if there was a connection between the student killings and Suzie Walker's? The killer had obviously known Suzie's movements, the way a stalker would. He had known she was on night duty and that the apartment would be empty. She had surprised him by coming home early. He ran his hand through his hair. The similarities worried him.

Technically, his shift didn't start until eight that night, but he had already put in a day's work by then, when the blowup of Suzie's face came back from the lab.

"What do you make of that, Rossetti?" he asked, pointing to the dried blood mark on her forehead.

Rossetti peered more closely. "Looks like an imprint of something. Like something was stamped on her forehead."

"Exactly. Only it wasn't stamped. She fell forward onto it. Look at it again, Rossetti. See that — the two loops linked by a straight piece, the little bump in the middle. Doesn't that bring to mind the famous curb-bit Gucci uses on their shoes? Rossetti, our man has expensive taste."

"Just like the serial killer." Rossetti's astonished eyes met his. "But it's a different type of crime. Unpremeditated, no abduction, no rape, repeated stabbings."

"Think of this scenario, Rossetti. He had her marked out as his next victim. He was stalking her. He knew she was on night duty. Remember, she *lost* her keys. He didn't have to break in to her cottage — he'd already had the goddamned keys copied. She came home unexpectedly, caught him there, and he panicked. He had planned to abduct her and kill her later. But he killed her then because he had no choice. She struggled, fought him, hit him with the heavy bag of frozen peas. He wasn't used to that, and he savaged her because of it. It's the serial killer, Rossetti. I'm certain of it. I feel it in my gut."

Rossetti looked at him. "You think the chief is gonna go for this theory?"

"If you forget the style of the crime and that it wasn't premeditated, everything fits — from the knife to the expensive shoes. What else can the chief think? Our killer has struck again, Rossetti. It was a little earlier than he had planned, that's all. We'll wait until we get the rest of the evidence from forensics before we talk to the chief, but I'm betting on it."

He didn't get around to calling Mal that night, and when he finally got home she had left a message saying she guessed they were just missing each other and she was sorry. Harry thought it was pretty tough conducting a love affair over the telephone. Especially when the parties couldn't reach each other.

Suzie Walker's funeral took place at three o'clock the following day. The plain little Baptist chapel she had attended since she was a child was filled with mourners, including a large contingent from the hospital.

Harry noticed Dr. Waxman and others from the medical faculty, as well as those of the nursing staff who could get the time off, and representatives of the clerical and administrative staff.

The family were at the front of the chapel, dressed in black: the mother and father, the sister, and a younger red-haired brother, as well as grandparents and uncles, aunts, cousins, and childhood friends. The casket before the simple altar was loaded with pretty white flowers — peonies, daisies, roses, and baby's breath — and tall candles burned beside it.

Harry and Rossetti stood at the back, and later, at the graveside, they kept discreetly in the background while Suzie's simple casket was lowered into the earth. A police photographer videotaped the proceedings and the TV crews were also there. Mrs. Walker screamed, her husband grabbed her, and they leaned into each other, desperate with grief.

Harry closed his eyes, unable to watch. He reminded himself that he had a job to do here. It was not unknown for a killer to attend the burial of his victim. Later, he would have to ask the family if they had noticed any strangers among the crowd. He doubted it — the killer would be too shaken up, shocked out of his precise routine into doing something risky, unplanned.

When it was over, he and Rossetti returned to the precinct. More news had come from the lab: pubic hairs had been found on the black lace panties and they were not the victim's. And scalp hair had been found on the sheets: Caucasian, gray tinted black. It might be possible to get a DNA reading from the small particles of cell tissue still adhering to the root, but it would take time.

"Looks like you got it right, Prof," Rossetti

said, elated, as they went to talk to the chief.

Afterward they went to a bar and brooded over a beer, not saying much. Later they met up with the chief of police and the mayor at the local TV studio, while the chief was videoed for the six o'clock news, telling the public that the serial killer had struck again.

Suzie's smiling young face appeared on the screen, followed by film of her funeral that afternoon. Then the mayor said his piece about safety in his city, and that they had evidence and expected to make an arrest soon. Harry and Rossetti stood respectfully in the background looking grim, handguns bulging under their jackets.

Immediately after that, Harry called Myra the dog-walker and asked her to take care of Squeeze. Then he drove to Logan and took the next shuttle to La Guardia.

He called Mal before takeoff and left a message: "It's six thirty and I'm just about to board the shuttle. I'll be at your place around eight fifteen, with a little luck. I know it's short notice, but I hope you're going to be there." He hesitated, then added, "I need you, Mal."

Just as Harry was boarding the shuttle, the man was returning home from work. He waved to a neighbor as he drove slowly down the street, then pulled into the driveway and into the garage. He went through the same routine with the locks and bolts, scanning the rooms as he walked through them for any-thing untoward. There was anxiety in his eyes this time, almost as if he expected to find a couple of police officers taking his house apart, searching for evidence.

It was the knife that bothered him. He remembered distinctly putting it in his pocket before he left. But now he couldn't find it. He wondered where he might have dropped it. He had searched the car and retraced his own trail from the garage through the house. He could have dropped it in her house, on the street, anywhere. And if he had, he knew the police would have it by now.

Worried, he went into the kitchen, opened the refrigerator, and stared at the usual meager contents, as though expecting the knife to be where he usually kept it.

He poured vodka liberally into a tall glass, omitting the ice this time, then went into the sitting room and switched on the TV.

He stood in front of the set as the world events unfolded, gulping the neat vodka. He was hungry since he had been too agitated about the knife to go to his usual bistro for supper. Instead, he had picked up a sandwich. He went back into the kitchen, came out with it, took a bite, and stood in front of the set again.

There she was! Suzie Walker was looking directly into his eyes. He swallowed a piece of cheese that had gotten stuck in his throat.

"Cunt," he groaned, "cheap lousy bitch. Just look what you made me do."

He was still spitting invectives at her when they rolled the video of the funeral. Then the chief of police came on, and the mayor. He listened, mouth agape, when they said they had definitive evidence that the man who had killed Nurse Walker was the same man who had killed the three young students.

"Go carefully in this city," the mayor warned all women. "And do not go alone. Be aware, and when you go out, stay in a group. We do not expect the killer will go free for long. Everything points to an arrest very soon."

His legs buckled, and he sank into a chair. The sandwich dropped unnoticed onto the immaculate carpet, staining it.

He licked his dry lips and told himself they had to be lying. Even if they had the knife, there were no prints — he had washed and dried it carefully afterward. And he had worn rubber gloves, been meticulous about that. He had left nothing else, he felt quite sure.

They were trying to calm the public's fears by saying an arrest was imminent. No one had seen him that night except Suzie. All they had was the knife, and that was clean.

He sighed, relieved. They were bluffing. He was absolutely certain they did not know his identity.

He switched off the news, then noticed the

sandwich and the mustard stain on the carpet. Cursing under his breath, he hurried to the kitchen to get the spot remover. He hated mess.

34

Mal could have danced for joy when she got Harry's message. She canceled her plans to go to the theater with friends and dashed out to pick up some food.

She was in the kitchen preparing salad dressing when Harry arrived. He stepped out of the elevator and into the hall with the Venetian mirrors and soft pale rugs, and she ran to greet him.

He was wearing the black leather jacket, the jeans, and a blue shirt. He was unshaven, his dark hair was rumpled, and there was a tired look in his eyes. She thought he was the sexiest man she had ever been lucky enough to set eyes on.

But what she said was "Glad you made the effort — sartorially, Harry."

He groaned. "Give me a break, Malone, will you? I've come straight from work, traveled hundreds of miles to see you."

"Then I hope you like what you see."

He looked her up and down as she twirled in front of him, giving him her best smile. She was wearing a long silky skirt with a pattern of tiny blue flowers in a color that matched her eyes, and a tight black scoop-necked top.

Her feet were bare, and there was a Band-Aid on every pink-nailed toe. A white cook's apron covered a great deal of her, and she fairly crackled with vitality and joie de vivre.

"I like the apron," he admitted cautiously, "especially if it means you're doing the cooking."

"I am."

He wanted to eat her up, not dinner. She kept on looking at him. He said, "Doris told me I don't eat right. She said I need a good woman to cook for me."

"Doris said that?"

"Yeah. I told her it would be bad for Ruby's business, but she told me it would be good for my cholesterol."

She threw him a mocking look. "Now we've got that out of the way, won't you please come in?" She stepped to one side and waved him inside. "My home is yours, detective."

He walked toward her, then stopped in front of her. "Sartorially and otherwise, you look . . . adorable," he murmured, cupping her face in his hands and kissing her on the nose. "Definitely adorable, even if you do smell of garlic."

"At least it's not Bactine."

"It never was." And then he clutched her to him and kissed her properly.

She had that wonderful sensation again of being lost in his arms, not knowing anything else but the way his lips felt on hers, the pressure of his hard body as he gripped her.

"Oh, Mal," he said, finally taking his lips away and dropping kisses into her hair, her forehead, her closed eyes. "I need you."

Her eyes shot open. She leaned back in his arms, staring at him, thrilled. "It's like *adorable*," she told him. "No one has ever said they *needed* me before."

He shook his head ruefully. "Well, this guy does. It's been a long, hard few days."

She led him into the sitting room, eased off his jacket, maneuvered him into a comfortable chair, and asked if he would like a glass of champagne.

"Got any bourbon?" He looked wrecked, dead-eyed, exhausted.

She nodded. She wondered what could have happened between Sunday evening when she left him and now. She went to the sideboard, put ice in the glass, and topped it up with Jack Daniel's.

"Thanks," he said quietly.

She looked doubtfully at him, her head on one side. "I read somewhere — it must have been *Cosmo*, because they know all that kind of stuff — that when your man comes home tired, the best way to his heart is a good meal. So I seem to have got it right this time. I'll busy myself in the kitchen while you put your feet up and listen to some soothing music."

She changed the CD from Santana to a Mozart concerto, turned down the volume, smiled at him over her shoulder, and disappeared into the kitchen.

Harry wasn't even hungry, although he hadn't eaten. He was just glad to be here with her. He needed her. In more ways than the one she had assumed he meant.

He sipped the bourbon, savoring the sweetish flavor on his tongue. The aroma of something good came from the kitchen, and the soft music crept into his mind, soothingly, as she had intended. A feeling of well-being came over him, and if it were not that she was so close and so on his mind, he might have fallen asleep.

She came back into the room silently on bare feet. He said wearily, "I'm sorry, Mal. I shouldn't have come tonight, I guess, but I just wanted to be with you."

She sat at his feet and rested her head against his knee, happy he was there. "Feel free, any time."

With an effort he shook off the events of the past few days and brought himself back to the present. "What I need," he said with a smile, "is a really good meal. I'm eager to know how the chef at this high-class establishment rates."

"Follow me, sir, please," she said, taking his hand.

The round table in the kitchen was set for two, with Matisse-blue linen placemats and the sunshine yellow and blue plates. A green salad sparkled in a glass dish. There was walnut bread and a slab of sweet French butter, and spinach fettuccini with a fresh tomato sauce topped with tiny vegetables. The candles were lit, and a bottle of white wine was chilling in an ice bucket on the console.

Harry looked at the feast, then at Mal. "You did all this?" he marveled.

She nodded. "You'd better taste it before you give out compliments."

He poured wine into their glasses and held her chair for her. *"Madame la Chef."* He kissed her as she sat down, and her lips clung to his.

"We'll never eat at this rate," she murmured breathlessly.

"Oh, yes we will. This is wonderful, Mal. And you got it just right. I never would have thought of it, but it's exactly what I feel like eating."

She served the salad, offered him bread and butter, and watched anxiously as he tasted the pasta.

"It's good," he said. "In fact, it's more than good. It's terrific. Best thing I've eaten in days."

"Well, I guess almost anything is better than Ruby's," she said, but he could tell she was pleased.

He moved the food around his plate, and she watched him uneasily. He wasn't eating. She wondered what was wrong. What had he meant when he said he needed her? She had thought he meant he cared about her, wanted her. She had even had the tiniest thought that maybe he'd meant he loved her.

"It's no good, Mal," he said, sitting back in his chair. "I'm not exactly here under false pretenses, but I am here for reasons other than just wanting to be with you."

Her heart sank like a stone. She wondered if he had been pretending to care about her all the time and now he was going to get to the truth. And somehow she knew what that truth was.

She got up and cleared the plates busily from the table, avoiding his eyes. She could feel them boring into her back as she went into the sitting room. She sank into a chair, her legs curled under her.

He followed her and sat opposite, in the same place where he had eaten the jolly Matisse sandwich just the other night.

It wasn't so long ago, she told herself protectively. They had only known each other a few weeks. And they obviously did not know each other as well as she had thought, or else why would he have been able to fool her like this?

"Mal," he said, reading her mind, "it's not what you think."

She adjusted her point of vision to somewhere over his head. "Really?" she said coolly.

"What happened between us, what we feel about each other, that's the same, Mal. Nothing has changed."

She shrugged. "Maybe you're right, and we're just back where we started."

"I'm here because I wanted to see you," he insisted. "But I'm also here on business."

She had known it. She got up and began pacing the room. She said angrily, "You made love to me because you want to use me. That's it, isn't it, Detective Harry? Well, I suppose it's not the first time it's happened to a woman. And I guess I'm equally to blame. It takes two to make love, after all."

Harry shook his head. "That's not the way it was, I swear it."

"You mean you enjoyed it? Well, I confess, so did I. Why don't we just leave it at that, Harry. You go your way, and I'll go mine." She turned and glared at him. "I don't *need* you."

He got to his feet and grabbed her arm. "Goddammit, but I *need* you. What's wrong with you, going off half-cocked when you haven't even heard what I have to say? Why must you always assume the worst?" She tugged her arm away, and he let go of her abruptly. "I guess that last question is irrelevant, since I already know the answer. You're so locked into your own insecurities that you can't grow up."

"What do you mean?" Her blue eyes blazed at him.

"Tell me, Mal, what does it matter that the photo-fit brought us together? I met you be-

394

cause of it, and I'm grateful for that."

"You are?" She threw back her head and laughed. "And now I know why."

Harry gritted his teeth. He took a deep breath, then said coldly, "Okay, so it's over between us. But since I'm here, I might as well tell you the other reason I needed you." She glared suspiciously at him, and he said impatiently, "Oh, for God's sake, Mal, sit down, why don't you. You look like an Afghan hound with a bad haircut, about to take a bite out of me."

"Ohhhh!" She subsided into the sofa, punching the pillows furiously with both fists.

"Be quiet, and just listen for once," he barked. "I have another life besides this one of ease and luxury that I lead with you."

"Lead with me? Huh! A couple of parties, a weekend — you call that *a life?*"

He grinned suddenly. "You have to admit it was luxurious."

She picked up a rose-chintz pillow and held it in front of her face. "You're a prick, Harry Jordan," she muttered from behind it. "Why don't you just leave."

"Oh, no, you're not going to get rid of me that quickly. You're going to hear what I have to say, Ms. Malone. And when I've finished, think carefully before you reply. Ask yourself if you can live with the consequences. Because I'm telling you, I cannot."

She took the pillow from her face. "What

can you possibly have to say that's so important?"

"Did you by any chance see the news today?" She looked blankly at him. "I guess not. Then I'd better begin at the beginning. Okay, Malone, when I left you Sunday night I went to work."

She said warily, "I remember, the graveyard shift."

"That's just what it turned out to be. For someone I knew."

"Someone you knew? You mean someone *died?*"

"A young woman was murdered. She was a nurse working in the emergency unit at Massachusetts General. I didn't know her well, I just used to see her whenever I went there on business. We would say hello, pass the time of day. She was a pretty girl, with gorgeous red hair. Rossetti was forever trying to get a date with her. She turned him down every time.

"Sunday night we were called to the cottage where she lived. She had been stabbed repeatedly, her throat cut, her face slashed. She was kneeling facedown in a pool of her own blood. Her little black cat was sitting next to the body."

Mal pressed her face back into the pillow. She could see the scene all too vividly. "Don't," she cried, horrified. "Please don't. I don't want to hear this."

"She had been dead for almost thirty-six hours," Harry continued remorselessly. "She died while you and I were dancing at my mother's birthday party."

"No!" She clapped her hands over her ears.

He stood over her and pulled her hands away. "The same guy killed her, Mal. The one in the photo-fit."

She leaned back against the cushions. Her frightened eyes were fixed on his, and he felt a pang of tenderness. He had an urge to put his arms around her, to forget all this. But this time he could not.

"That's *four* young women he's killed, Mal. *Four lives* taken. Four families devastated by their loss. They were all somebody's daughters. Somebody's friends. Somebody's lovers, maybe. Anyhow, they were precious to those who loved them. And they meant nothing but a perverse moment's satisfaction to the evil man who killed them."

She hung her head, staring at his feet, saying nothing. Her long eyelashes curled so sweetly at the tips. It was ridiculous, he knew it, to be so moved by such a small detail.

Mal thought of Summer Young and pretty Suzie. "What do you want from me?" she whispered.

"I want you to tell me what you know about the man on the photo-fit."

Her head shot up. "I already told you. I don't know him. That's the truth, I swear it."

"Then what was it about him?"

She turned her head away. "I can't tell you."

Harry groaned. He rolled his eyes heavenward in frustration. He grabbed her by the shoulders, hauled her to her feet, and thrust his face into hers. "Goddammit, *why* can't you tell me, Malone?" he roared. "How can it be more important than what happened to Suzie Walker? You're *alive*, for God's sake."

She was staring at him, numb with horror. Harry let go of her and backed away. "It's okay, Mal, it's all right. I'm sorry. I shouldn't have asked you. You have a right to your privacy. Just forget it."

He turned and walked into the hall and picked up his jacket from the chair where he had thrown it when he came in, aeons ago.

"I apologize," he said sincerely, "for taking out my frustration, my own inadequacies, on you. I let those women down. I should have had the killer before he even got to Summer Young. Before he killed Suzie."

"Is that what you meant when you said you needed me?" She knew her voice had a tremor in it, and she swallowed hard, trying to smooth it out.

"I wasn't thinking about your influential show," he said, his eyes linking with hers. "I meant I needed you the way a man *needs* a woman sometimes. As a comfort, a friend, a lover. And that's the other reason I came here tonight, Mal."

The lump in her throat just wouldn't go away. Her long silky blue skirt rustled as she walked toward him. "It was the eyes that shocked me. . . . I knew someone with eyes like that once."

It was the eyes she remembered most about him, though they had been hidden behind heavy glasses. The lenses had magnified them. They were dark, hypnotic, drilling into her very soul.

"Was it the same guy?"

She shook her head. "The man I knew wore glasses. He — he frightened me. That's all it was."

"So badly you couldn't cope with showing our picture on your show? A killer with the same eyes?"

"It was foolish, I know. But that's the truth."

He could see she was upset. "You want to tell me about it?"

"There's really nothing more to tell." She reached up, touched his face lightly. "I'm sorry, Harry. About Suzie. And I'm sorry for what I said." She took a deep shuddering breath. She had made her decision. "It's my duty to feature the photo-fit on the program. I see that now."

He still didn't know what else about the man disturbed her, but he guessed she would never tell him. It was one secret that was too private to be shared with anyone. "Are you sure you want to do this?"

"I'm sure. We'll start working on it tomorrow. We tape Thursday. That doesn't leave us much time."

"All I'm asking is five minutes."

She shook her head. "I'll postpone the show we had scheduled. I want to build the whole program around the case."

"Oh, Mal." He shook his head ruefully.

"I know, I know. Why couldn't I have said this at the beginning and saved the agony trip?" She looked appealingly at him. "I never learn, do I, Harry?"

"You will," he said, drawing her comfortingly into his arms and holding on to her as though he never wanted to let go.

35

Mal woke before Harry did the next morning. It was very early, just five o'clock and still dark. He lay sprawled on his back, one arm outflung, the other wrapped around her as she curved into him, anchoring him with her leg. In the faint glow from the window, she could make out the lines of his lean muscular body and his sleeping face. His mouth was slightly open; his breath came softly, and his firmly closed eyes gave him an innocent boyish look.

She stretched herself along the length of his body and ran her fingers lightly over his chest and along his flat belly. His dark hair was crisp in her fingers. A tremor rippled through him, and she smiled, letting her hand rest there, feeling him harden. She ran her tongue over his lips, then kissed his open mouth, lightly at first, then hungrily as he slid his arms around her, locked her against him.

After a minute she lifted her head; his eyes were still shut. She slithered out of his grasp, all the way down.

His fingers were tangled in her hair as she tasted him, made love to him. He groaned. "Wait, Mal, wait baby, please. . . ."

He rolled away from her before it was too

late, then sat up and drew her to him. He held her face between his hands, looking deep into her eyes.

"I need to make love to you," he whispered. He drew her onto his lap, then he bent to kiss her breasts, circling the nipples with his tongue until she shivered with pleasure. He banded his arms around her as though he would never let her go, and then he made slow and beautiful love to her.

Afterward she could feel his heart thudding against her own, feel their mingled sweat cooling on their hot bodies. The scent of their lovemaking was in her nostrils, and the taste of him still in her mouth. She felt as though she had absorbed him through her very pores and now she was floating in a silvery space that belonged to the two of them alone.

Harry ran his hands down her smooth back, feeling the little bumps in her spine, marveling at the delicacy of her body, the delicious curves and hollows, the sweet scent of her.

"Tell me, are we in heaven, Malone?" he whispered, nibbling at her earlobe.

She hooked her arm around his neck, holding him. She wanted to keep him there forever. "It's the closest I've ever been to it, detective," she murmured happily, still in that space where the very air seemed charged with little electric currents.

The room was just coming into focus, the

dawn light filtering through the cream silk curtains, and Harry murmured wonderingly, "Has the world turned to silver while we slept?"

She opened her eyes, glanced around, then smiled. "And I thought it was just you," she murmured, returning her head to the crook of his neck. "Do you realize that we slept together?" she added. "Properly. In a real bed, and not just on cushions on the floor."

"I realize about the bed, but I don't remember much sleeping."

He lay back, and she shifted in his embrace, still entwined with him. She was silk and velvet and perfume, and all woman. He glanced at his watch. The green digital display glowed with the fateful numbers that told him he had to get moving if he was going to catch the early shuttle. He looked down at her, curled against him.

"I know, I know." She sighed. "You have to go." She rolled away and dangled her long legs over the edge of the bed. "I remembered the bagels."

"How did you know I'd stay?"

"Call it intuition." She slid from the bed, stretching her arms over her head in a smooth feline movement that made him want her all over again.

He watched her walk, naked, to the closet, graceful as a dancer — until she turned to look at him and stubbed her toe on the chair.

She clutched her foot, hopping around and yelling, and he laughed.

"I don't know about you, Malone. Maybe you're just accident prone." He got up from the bed and strode toward her, kissed the top of her head, ruffled her hair, then continued to the bathroom.

She glared after him. "Callous bastard," she called, then she began to laugh. She heard the shower running, and she pulled on a pair of white boxers and a gray sweatshirt and made her way into the kitchen.

Last night's meal was still on the table — except for the bread and butter, which they had eaten between bouts of lovemaking, and the wine, which had fueled them through the night.

She put up the coffee, sliced bagels and slotted them into the toaster. She took out cream cheese and strawberry jam and set them on the counter, along with the pink flowered mugs, the low-fat milk, and a bowl of brown sugar.

She listened. The shower had stopped running. She pushed down the toaster, ran a hand through her hair, and was waiting, smiling, when he walked in the door, fully dressed.

He looked first at her, then at the burned-out candles and the debris on the table, and finally at the toasted bagels waiting on the counter.

"You're a miracle woman," he said, laughing. "I take a shower, and *voilà*, breakfast is served."

"Don't get too used to it, detective. I'm on my best behavior this morning, that's all." She grinned at him. "There always seems to be lots of food, but have you noticed we never actually get around to eating it?"

"I noticed. And I'm starving."

"There's plenty of cold pasta. And salad."

"I'm sorry, Mal," he said. "It was a wonderful meal. The best I can remember in a long time. I guess other things just took priority."

"I haven't forgotten," she said quietly. She took a bagel and spread cream cheese on it. "Strawberry jam?"

His eyes widened. *"On a bagel?"*

She eyed him uneasily. "Why? What do you usually have?"

"Oh, lox, salami, maybe tuna."

"The jam has no fat," she said firmly, handing it to him.

"Yes, ma'am, Ms. Malone." He took a bite and made an enthusiastic face, and she laughed.

"It's eat and run, I'm afraid." He gulped down the coffee — black the way she had remembered he liked it.

She leaned against the counter, her arms folded. "I'll need everything you can give me on the case," she said, suddenly serious.

"As soon as I get back to Boston," he promised.

"The details of each murder, but more than that, details about the women themselves. Who they were and what they were. And their families. I want to focus on them, let the audience out there, watching television after supper in their nice comfortable homes, with their own daughters safely beside them, understand that this might have been their child. Their lives shattered."

She began to pace, absorbed in planning the program. He could see she was really into it, and he was grateful.

He drained the coffee and picked up his jacket. "I'm sorry, Mal. I have to run."

She came back from wherever she had been, looked at him, then sighed. "Okay."

"It's not okay, but I have to do it." He put on his jacket, took her hand, and pulled her gently to him. He touched her cheek, smiling. "Did anyone ever tell you you are adorable?" he said.

She nodded. "Someone just did."

"Even when you're *mean*," he added the stinger, laughing. Then he kissed her on the mouth and walked quickly away.

She heard the ping as the elevator arrived and watched the doors open, then close again, taking him away from her. She put her fingers to her lips, feeling his kiss still on them. He would be back — she knew it.

★ ★ ★

The Boston Serial Killer was getting plenty of publicity. With a fourth murder under his belt, the national media were giving him strong play. The videotape of the chief of police and the mayor was shown on all the national network newscasts, along with Nurse Suzie Walker's funeral, and the tabloids went to work on it with graphic details of the stabbings and gory faked-up pictures of the supposed crime scenes.

"Not since the Boston Strangler put the women of this city into a state of fear and trembling has there been anything like this. And in a city with many colleges and a high proportion of young females in its population, most are again living in fear," they said on the news.

By the time Thursday morning came around and they were ready to tape the show, Mal had all the information she needed. Her researchers and assistants had been working overtime; the Boston police department had been more than cooperative, and the mayor had called her personally to thank her.

"Don't thank me yet, sir," she replied crisply. "Wait until you've seen the show. And then if there's any thanks, they should be given to Detective Harry Jordan, because without his persistence I would never have taken this on."

She refused to think about her own personal

fears and misgivings as she prepared for the taping. She was single-minded, totally focused.

Before the show she sat quietly, lost in thought while Helen did her face. Then she read through her notes while her hair was blow-dried.

When she went back upstairs and out onto the floor, everything was ready. She caught sight of Harry in the shadows behind the cameras, but she was not thinking about him. All her energy, all the force of her personality was channeled into what she was about to say to those waiting families across America.

She took her place on the little upright sofa that was not meant for relaxing and placed her notes on the low table in front of her, next to the bowl of soft pink roses. Unusually, she was wearing black tonight: a simple V-neck long-sleeved dress, black hose, and black suede heels. She wore no jewelry, except for small pearls in her ears. She looked like a woman in mourning.

"Ready, Mal?" the director called. She nodded, and he signaled to the cameras to roll.

They had rehearsed it earlier, but then she had left out the emotion. Now it brimmed from her — you could see it in her eyes, feel the tension in her body, hear it in the soft level tone of her voice.

"Tonight I am asking you to grieve with me, and with four families who have each lost a precious child. I know there are some of you out there who have also suffered that same terrible loss. You are aware of how it feels, what it means. And there are others, watching now, whose young daughters are safe in bed. Or perhaps they are doing their homework, or maybe just acting up and wanting to know why they have to go to bed, anyway.

"You fathers must remember when they were newborn and you first held that tiny infant, your baby girl. And how you felt about her at that moment. I'll bet you vowed to yourself you would always love her, guide her. Protect her.

"Just the way that young Suzie Walker's father did, and Summer Young's, and Rachel Kleinfeld's, and Mary Jane Latimer's.

"Let's look at these families, shall we? We shall begin with Suzie."

The home video of Suzie Walker's first birthday party began to roll. Her three-year old sister, Terry, blew out the candles for her. The infant Suzie looked at her, big-eyed, then her mouth puckered, and she began to cry. "I guess she wanted to blow out the candles herself," Mrs. Walker's laughing voice came over the soundtrack.

There was more: quick flashes of Suzie as a toddler, then walking hand in hand with her father at the zoo. Suzie missing her front teeth. Suzie as a gawky red-headed teenager, pretty and pert in a fluffy blue dress, clutching the hand of her partner on prom night. Suzie curled up asleep on the sofa, an open textbook beside her.

"I want to thank Mr. and Mrs. Walker for so generously sharing their lovely daughter's memories with us," Mal said softly. "And also for allowing us to show the following pictures."

A montage followed of the exterior of Suzie's cottage, with the yellow crime-scene tape; the burly officers guarding the door and the squad cars outside; then the gurney with her body in its black plastic body bag being rolled hurriedly into the waiting ambulance. And finally, the funeral, with the distraught parents, the grieving brother and sister, as Suzie was laid to rest.

"A simple American family, nice as apple pie, you might say. As normal as yours, and not much different from any other family, in whatever state, in whatever town or city you live in. But Mr. and Mrs. Walker no longer have a daughter. And you, Mr. and Mrs. America, do.

"The reason they no longer have their younger daughter and will not see her progress in her chosen career of nursing — and she was a good nurse, dedicated, caring. The reason they will not see their younger daughter marry, will never see her children — their own grandchildren. The reason that the joy has gone out of their lives and left them devastated — is

410

this man. Ladies and gentlemen, parents, take a good long look."

The photo-fit filled the screen, and for a few seconds there was silence. Then, voice-over, she said, "This man — this killer — was seen by three eyewitnesses. Their description was the same. Caucasian, possibly in his early fifties, short, stocky, five foot seven or eight. A shock of thick dark hair that the police now know is naturally gray but tinted black. And dark, intense staring eyes. He was driving a dark utility vehicle, perhaps a Jeep Cherokee or a station wagon."

There was no hint of a tremor in Mal's voice as she spoke of the killer. She looked directly into the camera, thinking only of the victims and the man who had to be caught.

"I ask you. The Walker family asks you. Please, if you think you know this man, if you believe you have seen him, get in touch with the Boston Police Department at this special emergency number. Your call will be free, and the lines are open now."

The camera focused on her face again as she said, "And now I'd like you to meet Gemma and Gareth Young, the parents of Summer Young."

The camera panned to her side and picked up Gemma and Gareth Young sitting on the sofa holding hands. They were pale but composed as she thanked them for agreeing to be on the program. She said that she knew how difficult it was and that she admired their courage. And then she asked them about their daughter.

Standing in the shadows in back of the cameras, Harry wondered how she had gotten the parents to appear. Watching her with them, he realized she must have appealed to them personally, asked for their help, and told them she was willing to do everything she could through her program to catch the man who murdered their daughter.

He admired her skill as she led them through their memories. "An only child, born in the summer of our days," they said, smiling. "And a child meant to gladden our hearts in the winter of our lives."

Mal reached forward and touched their tightly entwined hands. Her eyes glistened with unshed tears as she thanked them.

And then the face of the killer filled the screen again, as she told in a quiet, shocked voice what he had done to Summer Young. And Summer's last words to Detective Harry Jordan.

The man was sitting in front of the television set, drinking neat vodka, his eyes fixed on Mallory Malone's face. He gripped the fine crystal glass tightly, as she followed Summer Young's story with Rachel Kleinfeld's. She spoke with Rachel's twin sister.

And then she showed *his* picture again. And

she talked about *him* again. And she told everybody what *he* had done again.

Then Mary Jane Latimer, the prettiest baby of them all, cavorting in the tiny waves at a holiday beach, blowing out her candles. The parents had not been able to bring themselves to talk about their daughter, but her grandparents were there, gentle, soft-spoken people who talked with dignity about what a treasure she had been, what a joy to them. "But then, we all think that about our own, don't we?" the grandmother said wistfully.

"No!" he yelled suddenly. "No, we don't, you old bitch!" And he hurled the vodka at her face.

But it was *his* face on the screen again, and the vodka was trickling down *his* hair and over *his* eyes. He gripped the crystal glass tighter, not even noticing as it cracked, then shattered.

The details of the killer were repeated and the emergency telephone number given one more time.

Mal said, "Please, if you think you know this man, if you have any information at all, I urge you, *beg* you to call this number. Or simply call your local police department and talk to them."

She thanked the families for their assistance and said it was their urgent desire, their *need* to see this man caught so that he could not kill again, that had made them put aside their own private grieving and expose their souls to their fellow Americans.

"When the time comes," Mal said, "they want their daughters to be remembered as living people and not merely as victims. Because being a victim bonds them to their killer. *He* made them victims, but what they all *were*, were lovely young women on the brink of their lives. And let none of us forget that, when the time comes to convict this terrible man. Remember that they are not victims — they are all our children."

Mal looked through the camera directly into the eyes of her audience. Her soul was in her own eyes as, deeply moved, she said quietly, "Parents, guard your children. Young women out there, please take care, be on your guard. You will not be safe again until this man is behind bars."

And then her face was replaced by the image of the tightly linked hands of Gemma and Gareth Young. Then it too faded into nothing, and the credits rolled.

"*Lying bitch,*" he roared, leaping to his feet. "*You filthy lying little nothing! I decide who lives and dies, not you!*"

He stood, trembling with rage, his face mottled purple. His feet crunched on the broken glass as he stepped forward. He glanced down. There was blood on the carpet. He stepped quickly back again, shocked. He stared at his bleeding hand and then at the remains of the glass. He hadn't even realized what he had

414

done. He stumbled backward with a cry of panic. There was blood on his carpet, his blood. . . .

He ran to the kitchen, turned on the faucet and stuck his bloody hand under the cold water. Trembling, he inspected it. He went to a drawer, took out a pair of tweezers, and picked out the small pieces of glass. Then he examined the wound again. It was not deep — there was no need for stitches. He wrapped gauze around it. He was not worried about infection, he knew the vodka would act as an antiseptic.

He found the spot remover and went back into the den. Kneeling on the floor, he scrubbed at the stain, but the more he scrubbed, the worse it seemed to get. Defeated, he got to his feet. He couldn't live with it; it just wouldn't do. If he couldn't get the stain out, he would have to replace the whole carpet.

He stood, swaying slightly, looking at the television screen. The news was on, and he was looking into his own eyes again. They were talking about him again, about what he had done. *Again.*

Of course the photo-fit did not resemble him in the slightest, except for the vague details, the height and weight.

He had been right when he thought he would make Suzie Walker a star. He had given all his girls their fifteen minutes of fame.

The media would drop it soon enough when no one was arrested and there were no further killings. He was sure of that — they always did.

But Mallory Malone was another matter. She never let a case drop. He knew he would have to do something about her.

He switched off the set, turned out the lights, and walked heavy-footed upstairs. He needed to think this out. He needed advice.

At the top of the stairs, he pulled the key on its silver chain from under his shirt. Then he unlocked the door to the special room and stepped inside.

36

When it was over, the atmosphere in the studio was thick with emotion. Everyone was in tears, even the hard-nosed crew who had seen it all. Everyone except Mal and the stalwart families whose determination to tell their stories and catch the killer had brought them through.

Mal thought she would never forget the linked hands of Summer Young's parents. The image of their intertwined fingers that were gripped tightly together, as though to convince themselves that they still had each other, that there might still be a chance they could go on, even though life would never be the same, was a symbol of courage. The lost look in their eyes had told of their personal devastation, just as the determination in their voices had conveyed their resolve to find the evil rapist and killer who called himself a man.

Mal hoped with all her heart that all the people watching tonight would remember that.

Still shaky from the emotional impact of the program, she banished her fatigue and spent time with the victims' families. She congratulated them again on their courage and their steadfastness and thanked them for their help.

"But it's you we have to thank, Mallory," Mrs. Walker said, her tired face lighting with a smile that made her suddenly look heart-rendingly like her daughter. "Without you, we parents might never have had our say. Now all those people will know how it feels when something like this happens to your daughter. And maybe because of it, when the killer is caught and brought to trial, the victims will not become lost in the legal wrangling. They will still be real people, butchered by a man for his own terrible satisfaction."

"They won't be forgotten," Mal promised grimly. "Believe me, I'll see to that."

She called Harry over. He did not talk to them about the killer. He figured they'd had about as much as they could take, and they were finally thankful to say good-bye and be escorted back to their hotel.

"We thought about forming a kind of club," Summer Young's father told Harry wistfully. "You know, for people who've lost their child like this. We could meet, talk it out. It would be a kind of group therapy, I guess."

His brown eyes were somber, with grayish shadows underneath. He looked as if he hadn't slept in weeks. Harry wished him well as he said good night.

When they were gone, Mal collapsed onto the hard little sofa on the set. The lights had been killed, and she was in semidarkness. She leaned forward and put her head between her knees, suddenly faint. Fatigue washed over her like a heavy blanket, and her limbs felt as though they were stuffed with lead. She could not have gotten up if she had tried.

Harry sat down beside her and rested his hand tenderly on her soft hair. He ran his fingers down her neck and massaged it gently.

"You did it, Mal," he said quietly. "And no one could have done it better. The phones are ringing off the hook at the police number. You were wonderful."

She shook her head wearily. "The parents were wonderful, not me. Could you believe them, Harry? How strong they were, how much courage?" Tears threatened again, and she choked them back. "I'm praying for their sake that you get him."

"We will."

She lay back against his arm, totally depleted. She had gotten through the day on caffeine, Coca-Cola, and Snickers bars — things she never normally consumed — and now she was paying the price. Her blood sugar had plummeted, and her emotions were hovering somewhere between depression and hysteria.

"I don't know how you feel about this," Harry said, "but it's been a long hard day, and you haven't eaten. I booked a table at a discreet little place I know in the Village. The food is simple and good, and no one will bother us."

She turned and looked at him; his clear gray eyes had an expression she was not used to seeing. There was tenderness, compassion, concern. But beyond that was something deeper.

"Whatever would I do without you?" she murmured.

He took her hand, pulled her to her feet, put his strong arm around her as they walked from the darkened set. He said, "I hope I never have to answer that question."

He had called ahead and warned the owner not to mention the program, just to give them his quietest table. The request was honored. The room was low-ceilinged and beamed, French country-style, and the tables were simply set with cloths the color of old terra-cotta frescoes and bunches of white daisies in Mediterranean-blue jugs. There was fresh bread and a dish of *tapenade*, and a good Bordeaux had been opened and decanted.

The owner, Monsieur Michel, quickly took the order from Harry. He poured the wine and brought Evian, then left them alone. Mal thought it all so serene, so normal — the contrast with what they had just gone through was almost shocking.

It was late, and only a few other couples were lingering over their meal. Little table lamps cast intimate pools of light, and it felt as if they were alone. Mal sipped her wine and smiled across the table at him. "The wine is velvet," she said.

He nodded. "Some years it's just plain old velour, but this one's good."

She felt the tension begin to soften at the edges. Her limbs no longer had that leaden feeling and the muscles in her neck started to unlock. She leaned back in the chair. She told herself it was over.

A comfortable silence hung between them; they felt no need to fill in the spaces, and they sipped their wine, passed an occasional comment, and smiled gently at each other.

When Monsieur Michel brought the food, she tasted everything, ate a little, sipped her wine, and gradually was at ease again. Then Harry paid the check and took her home.

Back at her penthouse they walked, arms around each other, into her room. She sank onto the bed. Exhaustion was claiming her, and she could barely keep her eyes open. She lay back as he removed her black suede shoes, then unzipped her black dress. He lifted her, eased the dress up over her hips, and off. He hooked his fingers in the waistband of her black pantyhose and slid them down.

Mal wriggled her bare toes in relief, docile as a doll as he unhooked her bra. Then he rolled her into the bed, laid her limp head on the pillows, and pulled the cool smooth cotton sheet over her.

She felt languorous with sleep, craving it,

sinking into it. The big bed seemed to enfold her. Then Harry was lying next to her, his warm body like an anchor of security in a disturbed world. And she knew no more until morning.

She awoke to the smell of coffee and to sunshine shafting through the windows. The weather had been rainy and cool for so long, she thought it just might be a good omen.

Harry was singing under his breath in the kitchen. It made her solitary apartment feel like a home, having a man there she cared about.

She cleaned last night's studio makeup from her face, took a quick shower, brushed her hair, and put on a long white terry robe.

Harry was in the kitchen, leaning against the counter, arms folded, one leg crossed lazily over the other, waiting for her. His hair was wet from the shower. For once, it was neatly combed. He was wearing last night's smart linen pants and good blue shirt, but without the tie.

She stood in the arched doorway, and they took each other in. He thought she looked clean and pink-cheeked, as scrubbed as a schoolgirl; and she thought he looked tough and handsome and as stalwart as Braveheart.

"Thank you for last night," she said, oddly shy.

"It was my pleasure, Malone."

"I mean for everything. The dinner was just

right. Thanks for bringing me home and putting me to bed. Staying with me."

"Didn't I tell you I was a well-brought-up guy? I always see my women safely home?" He grinned at her, and she smiled back.

"I hope you don't stay with all of them," she said with a pang of jealousy.

"Not all. In fact, right now, only you, Malone."

He unfurled himself from the counter and held out his arms, and she walked into them. Clasped against his chest, she never wanted to move.

He said, "The phone's been ringing off the hook."

She tilted back her head, surprised. "I didn't hear it."

"That's because I turned down the volume. You must have a dozen messages on your machine, and it's only seven thirty."

"What about you?"

"I called in to check. The lines were jammed after the program. Hundreds of callers think they might have seen him. Every one of their statements will be carefully analyzed, and every one that's not a crank will be looked into. The calls to your show are all being taped."

She looked astonished and he added, "There was enough preshow publicity — the killer is pretty sure to have seen it. There's always a chance he will phone in. He might enjoy seeing himself as a media star, might start bragging, showing off. In fact, he might walk right into the trap you set so cleverly, Mal. If he does, we can trace the call in minutes."

"And then you'll have him."

"If good fortune goes with us. Right now it's just a chance, but it's better than nothing." He sighed and took his arms from her.

She said resignedly, "I know. The shuttle."

"I'm afraid so." He put on his smart jacket from the night before. "I wonder what lovers did before they invented planes."

"They stayed home and married the boy next door."

He kissed her. "Just think of all those wonderful love affairs that might have been. Right now I wish very much I lived next door to you."

"But you don't."

He shook his head. "Unfortunately, no. But I'll be back as soon as I can. I'll be working all hours this week though."

"I'll come to you, then," she decided quickly, unable to bear the thought of not seeing him.

He hesitated. "I may not be able to spend time with you."

She locked her arms around his neck — she didn't want to let him go. "I don't care. I'll just be there waiting for you whenever you get back. I can look after Squeeze, take

424

him for walks, cook dinner."

"What if I can't get home for dinner?"

"Then Squeeze and I will dine together, and yours will be reheated in the microwave when you finally decide that home is where the heart is."

He laughed. "It's a deal." He took the housekey from his pocket and handed it to her.

"What about Squeeze?" she said.

"Don't worry — he only attacks strangers and people he doesn't like."

He kissed her properly before he left, and when he finally took his mouth reluctantly from hers, it was harder than ever to let him go.

"Mmm," he murmured, "lilacs. . . ."

"You got it right this time, detective."

He strode into the hall and lifted a hand in good-bye. "Call and leave a message what flight you're taking. I'll be there somehow," he promised.

37

Mal went into the study and checked her calls. They were mostly from friends and colleagues congratulating her on a superb program. There were two hang-ups, which surprised her, but it was early in the morning and perhaps whoever had called had been worried they might wake her.

She packed a bag with a few simple things and added a couple of books she had been meaning to read, as well as some notes about the next two programs. Then she put on a white linen shirt and jeans, a comfortable tweed jacket, and glossily polished loafers. She clipped pearl studs in her ears and wore a man's plain steel Rolex.

She picked up the bag and was just taking a final glance around when the phone rang again. Thinking it was Harry calling from the airport, she picked it up immediately.

She sank onto the bed clutching it to her ear. "Hello," she said with a smile in her voice. She waited expectantly for him to say, "I miss you already," but there was no sound.

"Hello," she called again, sharper this time. There was nothing. She held the phone away from her ear, puzzled. Someone had to be there — why weren't they answering? Or maybe there was a fault on the line. She hung up and took the elevator downstairs, where the car was waiting to take her to the office.

The doorman stopped her on the way out. "I wanna tell you, Miss Malone, I ain't never been so touched by anything I seen." Tears stood in his eyes. "Those poor families, it just ain't right. I sure hope what you did last night helps catch him. I got a coupla daughters, and now grandchildren, and I know where these parents are comin' from. I felt for them, Miss Malone."

She shook his hand and said, "I just did what I could to bring it to the public notice, Vladimir. Now we have to hope for the best."

She got the same sort of reaction the rest of the day: from her driver, the woman at the cleaners, the girl at the pet store where she stopped to pick up a toy for Squeeze, and the guy behind the counter at the grocery, where she bought food for the weekend.

When she finally got to the office, it was in turmoil.

"This place is busier than a beehive with a visiting queen," Beth Hardy greeted her as she came in. "Are you all right?" she asked, still worried. "You looked like hell when you left last night. You went through it all with them. It was as real as if it were your own daughter you were talking about. At least, that's the way it came across."

"I'm okay, Beth. It was worse hell for the families than for me. They still have to wake up this morning and remember they don't have a daughter anymore."

"There's about a million calls — we just can't keep up with them. The list is on your desk." Beth was already on the phone again.

Mal went to her office, dropped her bag onto a chair, then ran her eyes down the long list of calls, thankful that she didn't have to answer them all herself. There were a lot of important names on the list: celebrities, movie stars, rock stars, important people in business and industry. They all had kids, and they all felt the pain and the pressure to do something to help.

She walked to the window and looked down at the surging traffic and the hurrying pedestrians. Somewhere out there, in this city or in Boston or Chicago or wherever he came from, this monster was waiting to strike again. She shivered.

Switching her mind determinedly away, she called the airline and got a seat on the two o'clock, then called Harry at the precinct to tell him. She had expected to leave a message, and when he answered, the surprise made her smile.

"You slacking, detective?" She slid down in her chair and put her feet on the desk, swiveling gently from side to side.

` He chuckled. "It's you again, Malone."

"You expecting someone else maybe?"

"Only about a thousand others — thanks to you. This place is like one big answering service. They've put on extra lines, extra staff, but they're still jammed."

"Anybody who sounds like him yet?"

"Not so far as we can tell. But there's still time." He hoped he was right — he'd been kind of betting on this one happening. "Are you calling to say you've changed your mind, Malone?" he demanded, but she could tell he was smiling.

"You're not shaking me off that easily, Harry Jordan. I'm on the two o'clock."

"Then I won't be able to pick you up. I'm sorry, Mal, but the chief and the mayor have called a press conference. I'm due there right about the time your flight gets in." He sighed. "I warned you it would be hell this weekend."

"No, it won't. I'll just get a taxi."

"I'll order a limo — charge it to me."

She laughed. "Playing the starlet again, huh?"

"No. Just playing safe. I don't want anyone I don't know personally picking you up."

She was startled. "What do you mean?"

Harry didn't want to scare her, but she had to understand she had put herself on the line. They were dealing with a brutal killer, and he might target her for revenge. "You're on his turf, Mal. This is his city, the place where he operates. You need to take care of yourself —

that's all I'm saying. Or at least, let me take care of you."

She said, shaken, "I think I'd like that better."

He grinned. "Aw, come on, is this the Malone I know and love? Malone, the toughie, the rottweiler who sinks her teeth in and doesn't let go? The independent cuss who always has to have the last word?"

"*I* have to have the last word! What about you?"

"I thought it was you."

"Well, *I* thought it was you."

He sighed exaggeratedly. "There you go again, having the last word."

She laughed. "I'll see you later, you oaf."

"You can bet on it. And Mal? Take care."

Her face and those of the victims were all over the front pages in the newsstands at La Guardia and at Logan in Boston. She ducked her head to avoid the TV news cameras, there to greet a politician. They couldn't believe their luck in catching the woman of the moment.

"What are you doing in Boston, Mal?" they called. "Are there any new developments? Are you here to help catch him?"

"It's a private visit," she replied, hurrying past. But she was pleased that Harry finally had the kind of public awareness he needed.

The car was waiting for her. It filtered slowly through the busy Friday afternoon traffic and eventually dropped her off at the beautiful house on Louisburg Square.

She stood outside for a minute, admiring the sloping streets, the gardens in the center of the square, and the perfection of Bulfinch's lovely bow-windowed nineteenth-century architecture. Then she climbed the shallow front steps and let herself into Harry's house.

Squeeze was lying in the center of the spacious hall. She could have sworn his eyes lit up, he was so pleased to see her. He ran to her, his tail wagging, making little whining greeting noises.

She bent to hug him, patting his soft thick silver fur. "Hi, Squeeze, good boy. Ohh, are you good," she murmured affectionately.

The dog followed her to the kitchen, where she put her basket of goodies on the counter.

She stared around with a pleased little smile at being in Harry's home. The kitchen was immaculate — she guessed he hadn't set foot in it all week.

She gave Squeeze his new chew toy, then opened the refrigerator. She laughed at the contents: an ancient box of half-eaten pizza, an out-of-sell-by-date carton of low-fat milk (so he did care after all, despite Ruby's ham and eggs); leftover Chinese takeout; and half a dozen bottles of club soda. Plus two bottles of his favorite champagne. It was exactly what she would have expected.

She threw out the moldy food, then restocked it with the good things she had brought from New York.

Squeeze followed her again as she poked around in Harry's bedroom. She peeked at the book on his night table — an unopened copy of the latest Elmore Leonard. She smiled at the idea of the detective reading crime fiction. Harry probably didn't get much time for bedtime reading, she guessed. He didn't even get much time for sleep — she'd bet he was out the moment his head hit the pillow. She tested the bed. As she had suspected, it was hard.

She unpacked her bag, put her few things next to his on the shelves in the closet, and hung her black leather pants and tweed skirt alongside his collection of ancient 501's and his two pairs of pants. She checked: the labels were Armani and Gap.

In the bathroom she made space on the old marble washstand for her lotions and creams and put her toothbrush in a matching mug to his.

It was like playing house, she thought, satisfied. Harry and Mal, a duo, a pair, a team.

The telephone rang, and Squeeze rushed past her, barking at it. She picked it up.

"He always barks like that," Harry said. "I believe he thinks he's answering it. Sometimes I wish he could."

She laughed. "Hi, detective. I have a confession to make. I've been investigating the investigator. I peeked into your refrigerator, your closet, and your bathroom."

"Then I have no secrets left?"

"None."

"Since you're still there, I guess I must have passed some kind of test."

"All of them. With flying colors." She hugged the receiver to her cheek as though she were holding him. "Where are you?"

"At city hall, wishing I were anywhere else. Are you going to be all right there alone?"

"Of course I'll be all right. Besides, I have Squeeze. He's no substitute for the real thing, but he's still adorable."

"Like you, Malone. By the way, I called Miffy. She's going to invite you to tea."

"*Your mother* is inviting me to tea? Detective, this is sounding serious."

He laughed. "Careful, Malone. Besides, Miffy is rarely serious. Look, I have to go. I'll see you as soon as I can escape from here. I'm not sure when, though. Uh-oh, I'm being paged. I'll call again, Mary Mallory Malone."

She hung up the phone, and it rang again immediately.

"There you are, dear girl," Miffy said. Mal could just imagine her beaming smile, as though she were talking to a person standing next to her and not into the phone.

"Harry told me you were coming for the weekend and that you would be all alone, and I said to myself, well then Miffy, you simply have to have Mallory over for tea."

There was a pause while Miffy drew breath and checked her old Cartier Tank watch. "Goodness, is that the time already? My dear, it's closer to drink time, don't you think? I'll tell you what — we can have both. Why don't you pop right over now? I'm just around the corner you know, on Mount Vernon Street."

She gave Mal the address, then said, "I'm so looking forward to seeing you again."

"Me too," Mal said. She laughed as she realized those were the only words she had been able to get in, except for hello. As she applied fresh lipstick, she thought there would be no problem filling in the gaps in conversation with Miffy Jordan.

Somehow her jeans and loafers did not seem quite the right apparel for tea on Beacon Hill. She changed quickly into a short pleated tweed skirt and beige suede pumps. She brushed her hair, sprayed on a little Nocturnes, and called to Squeeze.

With the dog on the leash, she strolled out of the square, across Charles Street, and along Mount Vernon, enjoying the walk. The whole historic area was filled with charming leafy streets and ivy-covered buildings. Antique shops lured her, and cafés and coffeehouses sent out tempting signals, and she promised herself that tomorrow she would explore properly.

38

Miffy Jordan's old Greek Revival–style house was built of faded-red brick, with a white-pillared portico, long windows with black-louvered shutters, and pretty wrought-iron balconies. It was set back from the street behind a formal garden, a lawn as smooth and green as a billiard table, and a short iron fence. It looked as though it had stood on that spot forever, a part of American history as well as the family history of the Jordans.

Squeeze turned in at the gate without having to be told, and Mal guessed he came here often with Harry. "Home away from home, Squeeze, huh?" she said, walking to the portico and ringing the bell.

Miffy flung open the door so quickly, she must have been standing behind it.

"My dear Mallory." Miffy gave her that beaming smile. "How lovely to see you." She kissed her heartily on either cheek, then handed her a Kleenex.

Miffy was wearing a blue silk shirt, a pleated gray-blue skirt, and flat Ferragamo pumps. Mal felt glad she had changed, though she suspected that, anyway, Miffy was not the sort of woman who would have given a damn.

Two matching beige pugs with black muzzles came bounding toward her, their round eyes bulging with delight at the sight of Squeeze. They wuffed and leaped and cavorted round him, but Squeeze sat on his haunches, looking like visiting royalty, occasionally deigning to give them a glance.

"Will you just look at those silly creatures," Miffy exclaimed, exasperated. "You'd think they'd have learned by now that Squeeze doesn't consort with miniature dogs — they are beneath his notice. But they still grovel, just dying for attention." She laughed. "I know just how they feel sometimes."

She swept Mal through the elegant hall and up the graceful curving staircase to what she called "my own little sitting room."

"It's cozier than the grand one downstairs," she explained, showing Mal into a lovely second-floor room with tall windows and the graceful iron balconies Mal had seen from the outside.

The room was done in shades of Miffy's favorite yellow, with creamy-yellow-sponged walls and elaborate cornices picked out in white, like frosting on a cake. Deep-gold taffeta curtains puddled in rich folds on the floor. The soft green needlepoint carpet was scattered with tiny flowers, and the brocade sofas and chairs were upholstered in teal and green. The antiques were breathtaking, extremely valuable, and perfectly kept. The elaborate frame of the blurred old mirror hanging over the marble mantel had been carved in England in the seventeenth century, and the paintings on the walls were all portraits of women dating back more than a hundred years.

Miffy waved her to a chair. A tea tray was set with a silver pot and pretty flowered Limoges cups, as well as an array of little tartlets and pastries. A second tray, with glasses and ice in a crystal bucket, waited on the graceful eighteenth-century rosewood sideboard.

"Now, Mallory, tea or gin?" Miffy looked at her expectantly.

Mal chose tea with lemon. Squeeze sat next to her, a snuffling little pug pressed affectionately on each side of him.

"Like bookends, aren't they?" Miffy said, shaking her head in amusement.

Mal looked interestedly at the portraits lining the walls. And Miffy looked interestedly at her. She thought Mal was quite lovely, and after seeing her program, she was sure that Jack Jordan was right: Harry would be crazy to let her go. Mal had put her heart into her work, and it could not have been easy to do such a program, to have to know the terrible details of the murders and to have kept the dignity of the families intact, as well as that of the victims. But Harry had warned her not to speak of it, so she would try not to.

"Those are all portraits of Peascott women," she told Mal. "This is a Peascott house, you know, not a Jordan one, like Harry's on Louis-burg Square. My great-great-grandmother was actually born in the bedroom I occupy now, though everyone after that had the good sense to find more hygienic surroundings to give birth in.

"The portrait by Tissot, on your left, is of my great-grandmother, Hannah Letitia Peas-cott, painted on her honeymoon visit to Paris. They did the grand tour, you know, she and my great-grandfather Peascott. She was so very pretty, don't you think? *And* she lived to be a hundred and two years old. Good genes, the Peascotts," she added approvingly.

"Now this one here is of my grandmother, Felicia Alice Peascott. It's a Sargent, of course. Poor woman, she went down with the *Titanic*. She was traveling alone, somewhat mysteri-ously. It was never talked about, but the rumor is that she had run off with a friend of the family who was also on board, also traveling mysteriously alone. So romantic, don't you think?

"And this John Ward portrait is of my own dear mother, looking very Duchess-of-Wind-sor, only of course much more attractive and less sticklike. And with loads more charm. They said Marietta Peascott was the most charming woman you could wish to meet."

Miffy sighed regretfully. "She died too young, you know, when I was just a girl. A hunting accident. She insisted on riding to the hounds. The foolish woman never would admit that she just wasn't good on horseback. My father said that for her, pride really came before the fall. But we loved her then, and I love her still."

Miffy took a breath and a sip of her tea and smiled at Mal. "Well, that's a tiny potted history of the Peascotts, or at least the most recent of them. Except for myself, of course."

Mal said, enraptured, "But how wonderful to really know your family. I never met my grandparents, never even knew I had any. I barely knew my father. And as for my mother . . . well, her family was a kind of mystery too. She never spoke to me about them. I'm afraid the Malones have no grand heritage, the way the Peascotts and the Jordans do," she added regretfully.

"These days heritage counts for very little." Miffy offered her a plate of exquisite fruit tartlets. They were so pretty, they looked like miniature still-life artworks. "What counts is what you have, my dear. Enterprise, talent, hard work, and courage." She hesitated — she knew she shouldn't, but she just had to.

"I so admired what you did last night," she said quietly, "though Harry would hate me for talking about it. He didn't want me to upset you, said you'd been through enough as it was. And I can see he was right."

She leaned forward and patted Mal's hand. "But what you did for those poor families was truly wonderful. Those young women will never become the forgotten victims. And when he's caught, no one will allow this sadist to be a media star. And he will be caught, Mallory, my dear. Thanks to you."

Mal said modestly, "But I was only a conduit, a means to an end. It's all those people working hard behind the scenes who will catch him, the people Harry told me about. All those patient police officers tracking down every gardener and handyman in Boston to see if they use the same rose fertilizer. Forensics examining every tiny bit of evidence. And detectives like Harry and Carlo Rossetti and all the others who think nothing of giving every minute of their time to preventing another murder from happening. They're the ones who are doing the work. I was merely in the fortunate position of being able to present it to the public."

Miffy looked admiringly at her but didn't pursue the point because she had said enough and knew Harry wouldn't want her to.

"More tea, my dear?" she asked. "Now tell me, what do you and Harry have planned for the weekend? You could always pop up to Jordan's Farm, you know. It'll be quite empty. Oh, I forgot to mention that I'm off to Prague tomorrow with my friend Julia Harrod. Just a long weekend. Now there's a fascinating city, or so I'm told at any rate." She laughed merrily. "I can't wait to see it, I've got that old

440

travel urge again. I can never resist. But do go up to the farm if you wish, my dear. I saw how much you liked it. And while you're there, try and pull up a few weeds in my rose garden. Can you tell me how is it they have the ability to spring up overnight?"

She drew a breath. "Now, if you've finished your tea, why not let me show you around. I'll tell you a bit more of the Peascott history as we go. After all, now that you're going —" She stopped herself just in time. "Oh dear," she said, laughing, "Harry would never forgive me for 'running off at the mouth,' as he would so vulgarly put it."

By the time she left an hour later, Mal's head was whirling from Peascott exploits on battlefields and whaling ships, as well as in the casinos at Monte Carlo and in Parisian garrets, where one black sheep had spent several years attempting to become "an artist."

"Without a scrap of talent," Miffy had told her, "but with a great deal of charm." He had married his mistress and model, a girl from Corsica, who Miffy was sure had put a much-needed Latin snap-crackle-and-pop into their stern New England bloodline.

Mal was still smiling as she let herself into Harry's house. She closed the door behind her, thinking how pleasant these old houses were, so filled with history and character. It was as though, in some way, they still retained the personalities and the happiness of the people who had lived there over the past two centuries.

She fed Squeeze some Alpo, flipped through Harry's CD collection, and put on the good Sade album, the first one. She arranged kindling in the empty grate and put a match to it, and when it flared, she threw on a couple of smaller logs. The blaze filled the room with a satisfying glow. And then the telephone rang.

She picked it up, fairly singing his name. "Hello, Harry."

She was smiling as she waited for him to say hello back, but there was no reply. "Hello," she said again, more cautiously. Again there was no answer. Yet she knew someone was on the line.

Her spine crawled as she put the receiver down. She glanced apprehensively over her shoulder, suddenly aware of being alone. Squeeze was standing in the doorway, looking at her. He looked big and solid and wolflike, and so comforting she could have hugged him. Anyhow, it was probably only a wrong number. She was just on edge, that was all.

But when it rang again, a few minutes later, she said in a subdued voice, "Who is it?"

"It's me, of course. Who were you expecting?" Harry asked.

"Ohh, it's you," she sighed, relieved. "Did you call a few minutes ago?"

"No. Why?"

"Well, someone did, only when I answered,

there was no one there. I mean, I'm sure some-one was there, but they didn't say anything. It happened before too. This morning, at home."

"It must just be a coincidence," he said, but he was frowning. "My number is unlisted."

"So is mine."

"Well, there you go. There's no way a person could get either my unlisted number or yours, let alone both. Chalk it up to error, Mal."

"Okay," she said in a small voice.

He sensed she was nervous and said quickly, "Look, I'm on my way home. I'll be with you in half an hour. Don't worry about a thing, okay?"

"Okay." She sounded relieved.

Harry clicked the off button on his mobile phone and said to Rossetti, "I know I'm the ace detective and I'm supposed to know, but how would a regular guy go about getting an unlisted number?"

"Easy," Rossetti said, in between bites of a frosted jelly doughnut. "Get it from a friend."

"What friend is going to give out an unlisted number?"

Rossetti was slumped over his desk. His usual immaculate appearance was shot to hell. His stubble matched Harry's, his pants were wrinkled, his shirt sleeves were rolled, and his silk tie was unknotted and hung like a gaudy ribbon round his neck. He gave Harry a withering glance. "Prof, you want an unlisted number, you flash your badge. What the hell's wrong with you?"

"Not me, Rossetti. The killer."

Rossetti sat up quickly. He had overheard Harry's part of the conversation and what he was getting at suddenly clicked. "He had Mal's number?"

"Someone did. And mine." Harry shrugged. "Of course it could be coincidence — two hang-ups, two different numbers. But the same woman *answered* those numbers, Rossetti, and it gets me nervous."

Worried, he dialed the telephone company and asked under what circumstances they would give out an unlisted number. He was told only for a medical emergency, and even that would have to be verified by a doctor. They had not divulged his number nor Ms. Malone's.

"Then you're right, Rossetti," he said. "The only way would be from a friend."

"Speaking of friends, it's Vanessa's birthday in a couple of weeks. You guys still comin' to the party?"

"Wouldn't miss it." Harry was already on his way out.

"In a hurry, aren't you?" Rossetti yelled after him, but Harry only laughed.

When he stepped through his own front door twenty minutes later, he thought at first it was the wrong house. He was used to being greeted by silence, stillness, the emptiness of a house left for long stretches unused. Now it was filled with the scent of a log fire and food cooking and Sade singing about love. He felt like a husband coming home after a long day at the office.

"Honey, I'm home," he called out mockingly.

Mal poked her head around the kitchen door. "So you are, *sweetheart*," she retorted. The dog was standing next to her. Squeeze stretched luxuriously, first his front legs, then the back, then ambled slowly over to Harry.

"Talk about love me, love my dog," Harry said, amazed. "You're here a couple of hours, and already he's switched allegiance."

"Not true." She retreated into the kitchen. "He's been for a long walk, he's had a good dinner, and he's lazy, that's all. Don't worry, Harry, he still loves you."

She was standing at the stove stirring something in a stainless-steel pan. He came up behind her and slid his arms around her, kissing the back of her neck. "And how about you?"

She said ambiguously, "I haven't had a long walk yet, or a good dinner."

He inspected the soup in the pan. "Mmm, you make that?"

"Nope. Zabar's made it. And the rest of your supper."

He laughed and spun her around in his

arms. "Why didn't you eat already? It's after nine o'clock."

"Without you, I wasn't hungry."

"Did I mention I was glad to see you? And that you look good in jeans."

She laughed. "Yeah, now we're a matched set."

As he headed for the shower, he called over his shoulder, "I've got a surprise for you. Remind me to tell you about it later."

After they ate, they took Squeeze for a walk. Harry sniffed the balmy air eagerly as they walked down the front steps. "It's starting to smell like summer," he said.

"And exactly how does summer smell?"

"Oh, leafy, green . . . humid."

"Fresh-cut grass and new-mown hay?" she reminded him.

He grinned. "You got it. Oh, I almost forgot. The surprise." She slowed, looking expectantly at him. "I've got the weekend off. Rossetti's covering for me, and they're giving me a break."

Mal's face lit up with the radiant smile that sent a shaft of sunshine through his heart. She said, "You mean I'm stuck with you full time?"

He tucked his arm through hers as they strolled down the sloping cobbled street. The dog ran ahead of them in little circles. "I thought we might go out to Jordan's Farm and snatch a couple of days of peace and quiet.

You need it, Mal, and God knows, so do I."

They walked down to the Embankment, then back up Chestnut Street to Louisburg Square, talking about their plans to leave early and make the most of their precious time together. Out of the corner of his eye, Harry vaguely registered a gunmetal Volvo parked on the corner, but the most thought he gave to it was that Boston was surely a Volvo town. Then his mind switched back to Mal and the fact that tonight she would be sleeping in his bed.

"Just like the three bears," she said with a grin. "If you include Squeeze."

39

The Volvo was still there at six the next morning when they piled into the Jaguar and took off for the farm. Harry figured it must belong to a neighbor. It was surely a small world.

Out on the highway heading north though, he noticed a black Infiniti with heavily tinted windows traveling behind him. No matter what speed he went, it was right there in his rearview mirror, keeping pace with him.

He frowned but said nothing to Mal, who was snuggled happily in her seat, eyes closed. He thought apprehensively about the telephone hang-ups and decided that was all they were. His serial killer just wasn't clever enough to obtain unlisted numbers. He was a plodder. Suzie Walker's unexpected return had thrown him into a panic and made him act out of character. He was a man who planned his actions over a period of time; he never acted on impulse. That was the reason they would catch him one day soon.

His exit was coming up, and he signaled right, keeping an eye on the mirror as he swung onto the off-ramp. The Infiniti kept right on going, and he breathed a sigh of relief. He told himself he was getting paranoid and put it out of his mind.

The man in the gunmetal Volvo had kept well back, out of Harry's view. He had seen Mallory Malone on the TV news yesterday, arriving at Logan. And he already knew everything there was to know about Detective Harry Jordan. He made it his business to know and understand his enemies; that way he was the one in control. He knew which exit Harry would take, and he was just half a beat behind him on the road to Jordan's Farm.

Mal thought Harry had been right about summer. The sun was blazing down as they climbed from the Jag. There was real heat this time, and the country air smelled fresh and juicy, like ripening fruit and bursting rosebuds.

Squeeze dashed around the corner of the house while Harry hauled the bags from the car and Mal stood there, absorbing the stillness. A woodpecker rat-tatted on a tree somewhere nearby. "I feel as though I'm a character in a Woody Woodpecker cartoon," she said, laughing.

"Well, you don't look it. You look real and very beautiful. Fresh air suits you."

"How about that," she marveled. "You actually paid me a compliment without adding a nasty little qualifying clause."

"I thought it was you who had the nasty clauses."

"There you go again," she retorted, going

up the steps to the porch.

He rolled his eyes heavenward, exasperated, as he followed her, carrying the bags. "I'm going to take you fishing, calm your nerves."

"I've never been fishing." She wasn't sure it was her style. "It looks so boring."

"It gives a man time to think. And a woman," he added hastily. "There's no discrimination around here."

Jordan's Farm was just as lovely as Mal remembered. The house seemed to wrap itself cozily around her, enfolding her in its peace and serenity. She could feel the continuity of life it offered, the knowledge that no matter what happened, it would always be there for Harry to return to.

Harry watched as she ran a hand reverently over the satin surface of an old table, touched a worn velvet cushion, picked up an old photograph, and bent to smell the flowers in a pottery jug on the window ledge. He knew what she was feeling.

"It's called spirit of place," he said quietly. "It's a feeling, an emotion that some of these old houses seem to retain, like decades of compressed memories."

Mal remembered the bleak soullessness of the "home" she had shared with her mother in the Golden trailer park. She knew you didn't have to be rich for your home to have "spirit of place," but there had to be love.

"I'll fix some coffee," Harry said briskly,

snapping her out of the past, "then we're go-ing for a long walk. After that, I'll feel guilty if I don't pull out a few weeds. Then we can go fishing."

A few hours later they were sitting on the bank of the busy little stream, dangling their feet and child-sized fishing lines into its clear waters. They leaned back against a convenient willow, happily watching the water rippling over smooth stones, wondering if any speckled trout were lurking in the still pools near the opposite bank.

"Did you ever actually catch a trout?" Mal asked suspiciously.

"Sure I did. I was about twelve years old at the time." He grinned at her.

She sighed. "So how are we going to have trout for dinner, if we don't catch any?"

"Easy. Uncle Jack has a trout river running through his place, the real McCoy. Every time he comes by, he brings some for Miffy. She can't bear to tell him that she hates the darned fish, so we happen to have a freezer full of them."

She nodded. "Logical, though not quite what I expected." She relaxed against the tree. "Still, it's a pleasant way to pass the time."

"I told you it was good for thinking." He glanced at her out of the corner of his eye. "Want to tell me more about Golden?"

"It's really not very interesting."

"To me it is."

It seemed easier, somehow, sitting on the bank of a stream on a sparkling early-summer day, light-years away from those hard times when she was young and still innocent because she hadn't yet discovered any different. So she told him about her struggle to survive, to create something from the unloved chaos of her young life, her need to become someone. And she told him about her husband and how she had admired him and looked up to him, but that it couldn't work because he wanted her to give it all up, and that meant giving up Mallory Malone and becoming no one again.

"It's not true, you know," he said when she had finished her story. "You'll always be Mal Malone, the person you grew to be, and you'll always be Mary Mallory, a victim of family circumstances beyond your control. Our parents are responsible only for a part of us, Mal. The rest is up to us. We are who we are because of what we do, the choices we make, the paths we take. Miffy Jordan is the woman she is because of herself, not because of what her mother was. It's the same with me, and with you."

She was still unsure, but she hoped he was right. Then the line jerked in her hand. She grasped it tightly, staring down into the water. "Look, look!" she yelled. "A fish!"

Squeeze leaped to his feet. He hovered excitedly on the edge of the bank, then took a flying leap into the stream, sending a shower of water over them. Shrieking with laughter, Mal fell backward. Harry grabbed the line, but it was too late — the fish was gone.

"I'm glad," she gasped, still laughing. "I could never have let you kill it anyway."

She jumped as his cell phone beeped. Their eyes met apprehensively. "Sorry." He pulled a face and picked it up. He listened, said no and yes, he would be right there, and good-bye. Then he looked at Mal.

"Don't tell me," she said, subdued. "You have to go."

"That was Rossetti. They've had a couple of suspicious calls from the Boston area. They've got surveillance on them. It's doubtful, but there might just be a chance one of them is the killer. I have to go, Mal."

She scrambled to her feet and brushed the grass from her skirt. "I'll get my things."

"No need. I'll be back in a few hours. I'm not letting hoaxers ruin our weekend."

"What if it's not a hoaxer? If it's really him?"

"If I'm that lucky, I'll send a car for you. But somehow I have a hunch it won't be our man."

He changed, then she walked with him to the car. "I'll have dinner ready just in case," she said. "And I promise it won't be trout."

Harry laughed as he waved good-bye. He watched her in his rearview mirror as he drove back down the lane. She was standing on the porch with Squeeze beside her, and he thought she looked as though she belonged there.

"There are two tapes, Prof," Rossetti said.

They were driving through the busy downtown Saturday traffic on their way to Cambridge, home of the first caller.

"Plainclothes have this one staked out. He calls himself the Boston Killer on the tape, but his name is Alfred Trufillo. He's called three times so far, made all the calls from the same pay phone half a block from where he lives. Doesn't sound clever enough to be our man, but it's worth a shot. He also goes by the name of Alfred Rubirosa — smart huh? Must think he's a playboy or somethin'. Anyways, it's long odds, but a couple of things he said about the bodies made the hair rise on the back of my neck. Like he knew more than we did, y'know what I mean?"

Harry listened as Rossetti played the tapes. He knew exactly what he meant. "Either the guy was there," he said. "Or it's a coincidence, a lucky shot. It's Rachel Kleinfeld he's talking about, right? The body in the boathouse?"

Rossetti nodded. "Take a listen to the other one." He put on the tape. This voice was more cultured and had an unctuous quality. "Like a preacherman," Rossetti commented. "We don't know about this guy, except he was making threats to Ms. Malone."

Harry bristled as the man on the tape described exactly what he was going to do to

454

Mallory Malone in graphic and vindictive detail. The voice was as smooth as watered silk, and knowledgeable about the anatomy he was describing in detailed medical terms.

"It's a mobile phone," Rossetti said. "We traced the number. It's in the name of a company, Gray's Anatomical Supplies in South Boston. Trouble is, there's no such company. And the address is a post office box, taken out about a week ago. But we tracked him to an apartment house nearby."

Harry thought about it. "*Gray's Anatomy* is one of the bibles of medical textbooks. You think he's playing with our heads here?"

Rossetti shrugged. "I ran it by the pathologist. He said the medical terms were accurate, but what he was describing about the bodies wasn't. He said he was probably an amateur with a fetish for medical equipment and terminology. Some folks get a buzz that way, he said. Some guys put on white coats and pretend to be doctors. They've even been known to go into hospitals and treat patients, and no one knew the difference — until they were caught."

Rossetti took his hands from the wheel and casually straightened his tie in the mirror. Harry threw him a look, and he laughed. "Not nervous about my driving, are you, Prof?"

"Any reason I shouldn't be?"

"Nah. You're safe with me. And with these

suspects, because I'm not bettin' seriously on either one."

Harry thought regretfully of his interrupted peaceful Saturday afternoon with Mal. He hoped he could make it back in time for dinner. He wondered what she was doing.

As the afternoon drew on, Mal made herself a cup of Earl Grey tea. She sat on a green wicker sofa on the sunset porch and looked out over the lawn to the willow-shaded stream. Squeeze nudged her arm for a biscuit, which she foolishly gave him, because, like his owner, he was just too charming to resist. Then she watched the sun go slowly down in a flare of neon orange, until there was just a faint greenish reminder in the darkening sky that tomorrow it would be around again.

She picked up the tea things, called to Squeeze, and went back into the house. She turned on the lamps and wondered whether to light the fire but decided it was too warm. Anyhow, she didn't want to turn on the air conditioning, because the breeze coming in the open windows was so pleasant.

She went upstairs, took a shower, and changed into a long dark green skirt and a soft cream silk shirt. She put on a little mascara, a touch of lipstick, and dabbed Nocturnes on her throat and wrists.

She sat for a while on a chintz-cushioned window seat, gazing out into the evening. As the twilight deepened into the intense blue-blackness of a country night, the porch lamps switched on automatically.

The night seemed silent compared with the constant growl of the city, but when she listened hard, she heard all kinds of tiny sounds: the rustling of nocturnal creatures, a whirring of wings, the bubbling of the brook.

She was just thinking lazily about going downstairs to see what there was for supper when she heard a different sound.

She shot up, put her head on one side, her ears straining. It was the kind of noise you made when you stepped on a fallen twig. Then she remembered Harry telling her there were deer in the woods, and she shrugged it off.

Squeeze was sitting in the hall staring at the front door when she came down the stairs, his ears pricked. He turned and saw her, gave a little whine, then resumed his listening pose.

She was suddenly aware how alone she was — there wasn't another house for miles. Apprehensive, she went to the front door and locked it. Then she rushed around locking all the other exterior doors — the one leading into the kitchen, the one onto the sunset porch, and the odd little wooden door that she assumed led into the basement.

Squeeze was still sitting in the hall when she returned. He wagged his tail, then ambled toward the kitchen. "It was nothing, was it, boy," she said, convincing herself. "Just the deer."

The kitchen had been the original small farm building, and the rest of the house had simply grown around it. It had white wooden cupboards, old wooden floors, and dark beams. The plaster stretches in between the ceiling beams were painted a cheerful sunshine yellow that Mal thought must light up the whole room, even on the coldest snowy winter nights.

She found some tapes and put on Beethoven's Pastoral Symphony because it seemed to suit the time and place. She turned it up loud, then went and rummaged through Miffy's well-stocked pantry and refrigerator.

She was happily chopping tomatoes for a sauce when she heard a noise again. Only this time it sounded like footsteps. And this time Squeeze leaped for the door, his fangs bared in a snarl.

Her heart jumped into her throat as she remembered Harry saying the dog attacked only strangers. He might have been joking, but right now it didn't feel that way.

The windows were still open to catch the evening breeze, and the light from the porch shone through the screens, but when she looked, no one was there.

Squeeze sank to the floor, whining, still staring at the door. Her mouth went dry as panic hit her. Harry had told her that she was on the killer's turf now, that he might seek revenge. Then she thought of the young women he had already killed, and their families, and sudden rage and adrenaline flooded her veins, lending her courage. If the killer was coming after her, he wasn't going to find her an easy target.

"You bastard!" she yelled, unthinkingly echoing Summer Young's last words. "You fucking bastard, you're not going to get me!" She ran to the windows, slamming them shut, until the house was tight as a fortress.

Still panting with rage and panic, she retreated to the kitchen, looked around wildly, drew the curtains, then grabbed the phone and called Harry's number at the precinct. It rang and rang; finally the machine picked up. Banging down the receiver, she took a deep shaking breath, wondering what to do next.

She thought about dialing 911 — and then thought again. She told herself to be calm, to act rationally. Odds were, it was just some wild creature roaming round. She could just imagine the headlines: "Mallory Malone Calls Cops to Save Her from Deer." They would go to town on the fact that she was at Detective Harry Jordan's farmhouse. She didn't want her personal life splashed all over the tabloids, especially now, when it would upset the impact and dignity of the program that had just aired.

Still, her hands trembled as she opened a

bottle of red wine and poured herself a glass. Sipping it, she told herself not to be so foolish. Then she noticed Squeeze, sitting on his haunches, staring fixedly at the kitchen door.

The hair on the back of her neck prickled. She took another gulp of the wine, watching the dog watching the door. She should have called the cops, but it was too late now. She was in the middle of the countryside, miles from anywhere. "Goddammit, Harry, where the hell are you when I need you," she muttered.

It flashed into her mind that when Harry had taken her on a tour of the house, he had shown her the "mud room." It contained a collection of old boots and jackets, and a glass wall-cupboard with an assortment of guns he had said were used for shooting wild duck.

Calling the dog, she walked quickly through the hall. Her heels clicked as loud as pistol shots on the wooden floors. She thought nervously, it was a dead giveaway. She slipped off the sandals, then opened the mud-room door.

It was little more than a closet, with one tiny window set high in the wall. Faded green Barbour jackets hung on iron pegs, giving off a musty smell from years of rainy weather, and old rubber Wellingtons moldered next to scarred leather riding boots in various sizes and states of decrepitude. A collection of wicker baskets and some vases were stored on shelves next to the deep pot sink, and a vegetable trug with an uncleaned trowel sat on the long wooden table beneath. On the wall immediately before her was a glass-fronted cupboard containing half a dozen shotguns.

Mal tried the door, but it was locked. Apologizing silently to Miffy, she picked up the trowel, smashed a pane, unlatched the door, and took out the nearest gun.

She had never held a gun in her hands before, and this one was a beauty. It was a Purdey with an exquisitely carved silver stock, engraved *Harald Jordan 1903*. She hoped nervously that it still worked. Then she remembered she would need ammunition.

Her hands shook as she hastily searched the cupboard for bullets, or cartridges, or shot, or whatever it used; she didn't even know. Anyhow, there wasn't any. "Oh, God," she whispered, crumpling. What good was a shotgun without ammunition? She stared helplessly at the gun. At least it looked the part.

She ran back to the kitchen, turning out the lights as she went, imagining eyes watching her through the window.

In the kitchen her courage suddenly deserted her. She switched off the light, then her legs turned to jelly, and she sank into a chair facing the door leading to the hall. Squeeze plumped down next to her, and she thought, comforted, that he would defend her. She had no idea where Harry was. All she could do was wait and hope.

★ ★ ★

The man stood in the shadow of the willow tree by the stream. He watched, puzzled, as a shadowy figure walked across the sunset porch and peered into the lit windows. He could see it was a tall, thin man in jeans and sneakers, and there was a second man two paces behind him.

The man's hearing was sharp as a dog's, and he heard the sound of the car long before they did. He slipped deeper into the shadows, running silently across the grass until he came to the lane at the front of the house. In the distance he could see the car's headlights bouncing over the dips, and he guessed it was Harry Jordan coming back.

He ran as fast as he could down the lane, trying to beat the car. When it was almost in sight, he stepped behind the trees and lay facedown on the grass so that the lights would not catch the pale glimmer of his skin. Behind him he heard the black Infiniti starting up, then its engine gunning as it roared, without lights, down the lane toward the oncoming Jaguar. He held his breath, listening for the crash.

Harry didn't see the oncoming car, but he heard it. He spun the wheel hard to the right. The Jag responded brilliantly, but it couldn't cope with the ditch and the tree. There was a terrible scream of hot rubber, a rending of beautiful steel, and a crash of splintering glass.

"Son of a bitch!" he yelled, wiping the blood from his eyes, staring back over his shoulder at the speeding vehicle. He did a double take — it was the black Infiniti from this morning.

"Oh, God," he muttered, panicked. "Oh, God, Mallory."

He got the seatbelt unfastened, but he couldn't open the door. He banged and pushed, but it wouldn't budge. He tried the other side — same thing. He glanced up and saw stars, real ones as well as the ones spinning in his head from where he'd thumped it on the wheel. Then he remembered he had been driving with the sunroof open.

The car was at a forty-five-degree angle, with the two right wheels in the ditch. He hauled himself up and out, then slid to the ground. He started to run.

The man picked himself up from the grass. He saw Harry running toward the farm and gave a bitter laugh. Whoever was driving the Infiniti had saved Mary Mallory's life tonight and almost killed the detective instead. He began to jog steadily back to where he had hidden the Volvo, beneath trees on a side road a couple of hundred yards away.

He climbed into the car, smoothed down his hair, slipped on his nice tweed jacket, and tied the silk cravat. Then, with the lights off, he drove slowly back down the lane toward the road leading to the freeway. He would not take the freeway, though. Instead, he would use the secondary road through the small towns and villages.

He switched on his headlights. It was a slower route, but if the police were out looking for the black Infiniti, nobody would bother about a well-dressed man driving a station wagon. After all, everybody drove a Volvo in the country.

Mal froze as she heard footsteps pounding up the drive. "Oh, no," she gasped, cold with terror, "oh, no . . ."

Someone was trying to open the front door.

Squeeze leaped to his feet and ran into the hall, barking frantically.

Mal clutched the shotgun to her chest. Cold sweat trickled down her spine, and her throat had turned to ashes — she couldn't have screamed if she tried.

The footsteps were outside the kitchen door now.

Scrambling unsteadily to her feet, she aimed the shotgun at the door. Squeeze galloped in from the hall, just as someone tried the handle.

She shut her eyes and counted to ten. It was now or never, and she had no ammunition. . . .

Harry put his shoulder to the door once, then again. It crashed inward. The kitchen was in darkness. He flipped the switch and stared at Mal, clutching the shotgun with her finger on the trigger. Her eyes were squeezed tightly shut, and she said through gritted teeth, "Get out, or I'll kill you."

Harry began to laugh.

"Don't shoot — I beg you, Malone, don't shoot!" he chortled, weak at the knees with relief. "Oh, God, if only you could see yourself." The chuckles just wouldn't stop coming.

Mal opened her eyes and glared furiously at him. "Oh, *great,* Harry," she said icily. "You're just in time for dinner."

40

Blood was dripping into his eyes from a long gash across his forehead. "Oh, my God, he shot you," she said.

Harry put his hand to his head, still grinning with relief. "No, he didn't. But I thought for a minute you were going to."

He took the shotgun from her numb hands, broke it open, and checked the chamber. "It's empty," he said, astonished.

She nodded, feeling like an idiot. "I couldn't find any bullets."

"*Shot*, not bullets," he corrected her, and she glared at him, then charged him, pummeling his chest with her fists. He grabbed her hands and put them around his neck, then got a grip on her, clasping her so close, she could hardly breathe.

He buried his head in her hair, kissing any available part of her: her hair, her neck, her earlobes. "I thought I'd lost you," he muttered, his voice breaking with emotion. "I thought I'd put you in danger, left you alone, and the maniac had found you —"

"I swear he was out there," she whispered, clinging to him.

"Someone was," he said, grimly. "I met

466

them on their way out."

She pulled back, looking up at him. *"You saw him?"* Then the killer really had been out there. A shiver of horror ran down her spine.

He shook his head, the blood from the cut trickled down his face. He wiped it away impatiently, heading for the phone. "I don't know who it was, but I recognized the car. It followed us from Boston this morning. And it just rammed me, driving without lights down the lane."

He dialed the local police, quickly told them what had happened, then called Rossetti. An APB was put out immediately on the black Infiniti, which was sure to show damage from the impact with his Jag.

Mal sat in the same chair she had sat in a few minutes earlier, expecting her end to come. Her legs were shaking, and her heart was racing like the Jag's engine. She suddenly remembered that Harry was the injured one and that, apart from shaken nerves, she was perfectly all right.

"He almost killed you," she said, stunned.

Harry put down the phone; he turned, and grinned at her. "Forget about me — he killed my Jag. Right now it's a heap of screwed-up metal in a ditch."

She inspected his wound tenderly, then fetched a towel and water to clean it. "It needs stitches."

Harry grabbed her hand and held it to his

cheek, then to his lips. "Listen, you're okay and I'm okay," he said. "The only victim this time is the car. But I'm gonna get the bastard who did this."

"You don't think it's him?"

He shook his head. "Somehow it's not his style. He's a stalker, a plotter and planner." He looked her in the eyes and said levelly, "Mal, if he'd wanted to get you, he would have. Believe me, he's that clever." He added with a shrug, "Besides, the car was wrong. A black Infiniti. It doesn't match with our descriptions of his vehicle. There's always the possibility he has two cars, but anyhow the Infiniti doesn't work with his profile."

The wail of police sirens shattered the country silence, and suddenly the house was filled with detectives and uniformed policemen.

A long time later, when the house had been thoroughly inspected inside and out, as well as the wrecked car in the ditch, they were taken to the local hospital. Harry had stitches put in his forehead, while Mal drank weak coffee from a paper cup, waiting anxiously.

She looked up as Harry finally emerged. They had shaved part of his hair for the stitches, which ran from his right eyebrow to the top of his skull. The black stubble made his face look even paler, and there was an exhausted look in his gray eyes.

In the police car taking them home, Harry leaned back, eyes shut. She could see he was in pain, and she held his hand, glancing concernedly at him. A couple of uniformed cops had been left on guard at the farm, and they bade them good night as they went indoors.

Harry poured himself a neat whiskey and drank it quickly down, preferring it to the painkillers they had offered him at the hospital. It had been a long day. His head was throbbing, and the rest of his bruised body was beginning to stake a claim on the pain threshold. But worse was the fact that Mal had been in danger, and that he had put her there by leaving her alone. Somehow it had never occurred to him that Jordan's Farm was not the safe haven it always had been. Still, he was sure the Infiniti driver wasn't the serial killer. But if not, then who the hell was it?

He was still mulling over the question the next morning, when he awoke in the old double bed that had been his since he was a boy. Mal was lying curved around him; he could feel the softness of her breasts against his back and her gentle breath on his skin. One long leg was flung over his, and she was clutching his hand as she slept.

It was almost worth getting his head smacked up just to have her there, acting like a protective mother hen with a damaged chick.

He turned and slid an arm under her, and she opened her eyes. They were so deeply blue, it astonished him all over again, and her long curling lashes gave her an air of innocence. But the smile in her eyes was replaced by a worried frown as she inspected his head.

"I guess this is called role reversal," Harry said, kissing her. "Little Woman looking after Big Strong Man. Better be careful, I might get to enjoy it."

"Surely you know that it's always the women who look after men?" she said firmly. "It's only the male ego that makes you think otherwise. Better not relax and enjoy it too much, Mr. Detective, or you'll lose that macho edge and be forced to admit that women are stronger."

He laughed, but then she kissed him and he forgot all about what she had said. He ran his hands over her smooth body. "Silk and satin," he whispered, nuzzling her neck.

She slid from his arms and stood there naked, stretching lazily. "The wounded are not allowed to make love. They get breakfast in bed instead."

He drank her in. She looked wonderful naked, as tempting as Eve's apple. "That's not a fair exchange," he grumbled. "Whoever told you that?"

"The doctor at the hospital last night." She threw on a robe and walked to the door. "A *woman* doctor," she called over her shoulder as she headed into the bathroom.

"What does pain matter when I can have a woman like you in my arms?" he demanded when she emerged from the shower.

She rolled her eyes, unrelenting, and marched to the door. Just then the phone rang. Suddenly apprehensive, she waited while Harry answered it.

"Morning, Prof," Rossetti said. "How's the head?"

"It's Rossetti," he said to Mal. She nodded, relieved, and went downstairs to make breakfast.

"Not good, Rossetti," Harry replied gloomily.

"Yeah? Sorry to hear that, but what I'm gonna tell you ain't gonna make it feel better. You seen any of the newspapers this morning?"

"No. Why?" Harry suddenly didn't want to know.

"The tabloids have a couple of nice pics of you and Malone. The captions are pretty much the same: 'Mallory Malone in Hot Affair with Cop in Serial-Killer Case.' And the pics are of you with your arm around Malone, walking in the grounds of Jordan's Farm. Which, just so you know it, is described as 'a love nest.'"

Harry groaned. "That's all she needs."

"You too, detective," Rossetti reminded him. "Whoever took those pics might also have been driving the black Infiniti. I twisted a few arms, metaphorically speaking, and got a name and address. You'll be glad to know, Prof, that the guys who wrecked your car are

471

now in custody on charges of dangerous driving and removing themselves from the scene of an accident, plus trespass and anything else I can think of to throw at them."

"Then it wasn't the killer, after all," Harry said, relieved.

"Unh-unh, just your plain old tabloid paparazzi. That's what happens when you date the rich and famous," he added. "You can consider yourself lucky they didn't point their lenses in your bedroom window."

Harry looked at the window they had left innocently open last night with the curtains drawn back. "I'm gonna have to be more careful."

"You got it, Prof. Meanwhile, take care of the head. And Ms. Malone — she did a great job. The phone calls have tapered off. Nothing solid so far, not since the two false alarms yesterday."

Harry hadn't even thought about the two men they had taken into custody for questioning yesterday. He had known as soon as he saw them that neither was the killer. The first was just looking for a moment of glory on television, and the other was a pervert with a mania for gynecological obscenity that would send him to the funny farm. Suzie Walker's killer was still at large.

He told Rossetti he would be with him in a couple of hours, then went downstairs to tell Mal the news.

She was at the stove, slowly stirring scrambled eggs. "You were supposed to stay in bed."

"I've got news."

She put down the wooden spoon, her eyes filled with a mixture of fear and hope. He said quickly, "No, we haven't caught the killer, but we know it wasn't him last night. It was paparazzi."

"The tabloids?"

"I'm afraid so. Rossetti saw the pictures this morning. Nothing too bad. I have my arm around you, and the headlines call Jordan's Farm a 'love nest.' "

Mal realized what it meant. "You mean it was tabloid *photographers* out there last night?"

"You got it, Malone."

"But they almost *killed* you, driving like that. How could they? How *dare* they?" She flung down the spoon and paced, her arms folded, her mouth tight. "Have they sunk so low, they're prepared to *kill* for a cheap picture? My God."

"At least it wasn't the serial killer."

She stopped pacing. "No, it wasn't." Chilled, she remembered last night's terror.

"So you don't have to worry about that. Only about the headlines trumpeting your personal life."

She gave him a dazzling smile, dizzy with relief. "The hell with my personal life. It was worth it, detective."

"I hope you'll still feel that way when I tell

you I have to get back to town."

"You mean now? Right away?"

"Well, after the scrambled eggs."

"Uh-oh, the eggs." She snatched the pan from the stove and stared horrified at the so-lidified mass.

"Good thing I remembered the bagels," he added, "and the muffins. All you've got to do is brew the coffee, Malone."

"And then we're on our way." She sighed gloomily.

"Like I told Squeeze, it's a cop's life," he said. But he kissed her before he went back upstairs to take a shower.

Two hours later, they were at Logan Air-port and he was saying good-bye to her. He glanced around the crowded departure lounge and the staring strangers, then he said what the hell and kissed her anyway.

"They've read it in the papers. Now they'll know it's true," he whispered in her ear. "I'll call you later tonight."

"I'm not going to complain," she said. "I know it's a cop's life."

"Not all the time, it's not."

Mal watched him walk quickly away from her. She knew his mind was already back on the serial killer. Her heart gave a little leap as he turned and met her eyes. Then he lifted his hand in farewell and disappeared around the corner.

She was smiling as she boarded the flight to

La Guardia. And she smiled again, later, back in the safety of her apartment, when she picked up his message on her answering machine.

"It's just the walking wounded, checking in to make sure you arrived home safely, Malone. Sorry about this weekend, and about the tabloids — though the picture of you isn't bad. I'll see they do it better next time. Call you later."

She had just kicked off her shoes when the phone rang. It was Beth Hardy.

"I see you and the Handsome Detective are hitting the headlines," she said. "In a *love nest*, no less."

"It's going to get worse." Mal told her quickly about the previous night. "So you can expect more headlines, and I guess more pictures in the future. But not at the 'love nest,' because the Handsome Detective, as you call him, is back on the job. And you know the old saying."

"Out of sight, out of mind? Somehow I doubt it. The HD was certainly most attentive on Thursday after the show. My advice is to roll with the punches. Anybody who says anything bad about you and Jordan is just jealous. See you tomorrow, sweetheart."

Mal was taking off her socks when the phone rang again.

"I was just wishing you and I were back at the love nest," Harry said.

Mal felt that little quiver in her heart again.

She sank onto the bed, smiling. "Oh, sure," she said. "You can invite the paparazzi, and we can do a few retakes for them."

She heard him sigh. Then he said regretfully, "It might almost be worth it. A few stitches, a wrecked classic Jaguar, shotguns, notoriety — what more can a guy expect from a nice weekend away with his woman?"

"Your *woman*, detective? Aren't we being a little presumptuous? I mean a couple of dinners, a party, a little hugging and kissing here and there?"

"Hardly amounts to much, huh?" he said gloomily. Then he laughed. "Malone, I don't know why I bothered to call. I can tell you're back in form."

"I'm glad you did, though," she said in a voice like a caress.

"Me too," he said gently. "Take care, Malone. I'll call you again tomorrow."

The line went dead, and she lay clutching the receiver to her ear, reluctant to leave him. No matter how they bickered, life seemed emptier when he wasn't there.

She showered and put on a robe. Suddenly exhausted, she remembered she had had only a couple of hours of sleep. Yawning, she fixed herself a cup of tea, then wandered into the study to pick up the rest of her messages. There was another envelope waiting on her desk.

She opened it, sipping wild berry tea as she

read the one-line message. It said: WELCOME HOME, MARY MALLORY.

The hot tea slopped over her trembling hand, scalding her as she sank into the chair, but she hardly felt it. She stared mesmerized at the flimsy piece of paper. A shiver rippled coldly down her spine, and goose bumps sprang up on her skin. The note wasn't from Harry. It wasn't the paparazzi.

There was only one other person besides Harry who knew her real name.

41

The man was out in his garden, tending his roses. Some were already in bloom — tight exquisite blossoms in deep burgundy and crimson. He thought they were as perfect as roses should be, controlled in their beauty, unlike blowsy cabbage roses and unruly climbers, which he hated. He examined each fresh bud carefully, frowning as he saw clusters of greenfly sucking the juices from his carefully nurtured plants.

He hurried into the garage where he stored his gardening supplies and quickly mixed the chemicals. Then he sprayed each leaf, each plant, each bed, meticulously. When he felt sure he had annihilated all the aphids, he went back into the house, locked the doors, and washed his hands carefully.

He glanced at his watch. It was seven P.M. He wondered if Mary Mallory Malone was home yet, and he smiled, imagining her face when she found his welcoming little message. It had been quite a coup, getting hold of her address and her telephone number. In fact, he was astonished at how easy it had been. Sometimes he surprised even himself.

He put on a clean shirt and a good jacket,

combed his hair, and inspected himself in the mirror. Taking a cloth from the drawer, he dusted his black Gucci loafers. Satisfied with his immaculate appearance, he drove into town to the bistro he favored on Sunday nights.

It was quiet. They gave him his favorite table near the window, and he ordered his usual roast chicken and mashed potatoes. This time he asked for a half bottle of wine instead of the single glass he normally drank. After all, he thought, as he unfolded the newspaper and stared at the picture of Mary Mallory Malone with Detective Harry Jordan at their love nest, he had a lot to celebrate tonight. They did not know who he was, and they would never find him. He was on the winning edge again — and this time he meant to enjoy it.

He was going to play a little game of nerves with Ms. Malone, before he declared war on her. Shake her up a bit, like this weekend for instance. Those damn fool photographers had acted like amateurs, shooting out of there with no headlights like Russian spies. All they'd had to do was put on their high beams. Jordan would have been so dazzled, he wouldn't have been able to see the car — or anything else — for a minute, and by then they would have been past him and gone.

He sipped the wine appreciatively. It tasted particularly good tonight. Then he went to the pay phone in the entryway and dialed her number. He smiled when she answered immediately. He could recognize fear in a woman's voice — after all, he had heard it many times before.

He replaced the receiver and returned to his table, made pleasant small talk with the waiter for a couple of minutes, then ate his meal in a leisurely fashion. Afterward he ordered the apple pie with vanilla ice cream and enjoyed every mouthful. Then he paid his bill and drove sedately through the city to the pied-à-terre he kept in Cambridge. It suited him to have two addresses. He often used this apartment when he had to get an early start on a work day. Besides, you never knew when it might come in handy for other reasons.

Harry was sitting in his office playing the tape of Suzie Walker's last words over and over again. He knew the tape by heart. Each time he played it, he asked himself why she had said "What are you doing here?"

He played it again, listening intently for the inflection on *you*. The emphasis was so minimal, it was almost imperceptible, and her voice was choked up, so it was difficult to be certain. It might be nothing, as they had all at first assumed. But Harry couldn't be sure. There was just a chance that Suzie had recognized her killer.

He thought about what her sister Terry had said: that the boyfriend had done it. They had questioned the young intern. He almost looked the part — short, stocky, and dark. But he was too young to have gray hair, and he had an unshakable alibi. He had been on duty at Beth Israel Hospital and both his colleagues could vouch for his whereabouts that entire night. So the intern was definitely out as a suspect.

Besides, there was too much evidence for it to be merely coincidence; Harry knew in his gut this was the serial killer. But if Suzie had known the killer, that narrowed the field considerably: her family, her friends, her colleagues at work. It could be a guy at the gas station where she filled up, or someone at the coffeehouse, or at the café where she ate, or at a bar she frequented, or a club or shop.

He sighed, thinking of the amount of work it would take. Then he talked with Rossetti, called the chief at home, and got permission to get extra help in tracking down every friend, acquaintance, and passing casual encounter in Suzie Walker's life.

He looked at the photo-fit again. He took a couple of pieces of paper and covered the lower and upper parts, leaving only the eyes. The artist had done a good job in capturing the menacing stare. He could only imagine the terror of the poor young women who had confronted it.

He glanced at his watch, wondering if he should call Mal again, but it was eleven thirty and she would probably be sleeping. Instead he brought up her file on the computer.

He reread her résumé with its simple listings of birth, home, school, and jobs. Mentally, he filled in the spaces with the tragic events he knew about. He stared at the screen, puzzled.

Mal had told him she had attended Washington State in Seattle, and that's what it said on the résumé that records had obtained for him. But the dates didn't tally. He made a mental note to check with the college the next day and find out why Mal had taken five years instead of four to complete her studies. And then he wondered exactly where she had disappeared to, in that missing year.

Mal was not sleeping. She was pacing the floor trying to understand what was happening. She told herself she was being foolish. Someone obviously was playing a trick on her.

But still she couldn't sleep.

The next morning, New York was hot and humid. She was too weary to tackle the gym, so she dressed and walked to the office. Waiting impatiently for the traffic light to change, she shifted from foot to foot, skimming a hand over her hair, already feeling sticky and wishing she hadn't decided to walk. Suddenly she had the uneasy feeling she was being watched. The hairs at the back of her neck stood up. She swung around angrily. Half a dozen innocuous-looking people were behind her.

Their eyes were glued on the light, willing it to turn green and willing the traffic not to overshoot it so they could dash across.

Fool, she reprimanded herself angrily. This wasn't Jordan's Farm, she wasn't alone, and nobody was following her. Nevertheless, she glanced uneasily over her shoulder several times as she hurried along Madison, and she felt relieved when she finally swung through her office door to safety.

"Seen the morning papers?" Beth greeted her with a grin. "The Handsome Detective and Mallory Malone are all over the place. Those paparazzi are onto a gold mine. It's a good thing the IID returned to Boston before the pictures got even more revealing."

Mal snatched the newspaper from her, scanning the caption over a photo of the two of them sitting by the stream, fishing. "Country Idyll For Mallory Malone and Boston Heart-throb Cop." She flung it down, disgusted, imagining the paparazzi with their long-range lenses. Stealing their privacy, their intimacy.

"At least they ended up in jail," she said angrily. "But Harry ended up with nineteen stitches in his head."

"Spoiled his beauty, huh?" Beth said, sighing. "Nah, nothing could do that. So how are things between you and the HD, anyway?" She twisted a strand of dark hair round her finger, looking expectantly at Mallory.

Mal thought moodily. "Combative, I would

say," she decided. "And — well, kind of fun."

"And sexy," Beth added.

Mal threw her a startled look, and Beth laughed. "It's written all over you, sweetheart. You are positively glowing. Besides, you look exhausted."

"I look exhausted because I didn't sleep last night," Mal confessed. Then she told her about the Welcome Home note.

"It has to be some joker," Beth said calmly. "I mean, those tabloids are even better than we are at getting addresses and telephone numbers. They're probably delving into your past even as we speak, looking for dirt."

Mal stared apprehensively at her. "You really think they're delving into the past?"

"Yours *and* Harry Jordan's," Beth said firmly. "The two sleuths are being sleuthed, is my guess. And what you got was just a warning shot."

Mal hoped Beth wasn't right. She went to her office and closed the door, then called Harry at the precinct. He wasn't there, of course, but she left a message for him to call her. Then she tried to switch her mind back to work and this week's show.

Harry parked the Jeep outside Mass General. He ran up the steps and through the swing doors.

Dr. Waxman was on his way out. He threw

484

Harry a startled glance, then retraced his steps.

"What the hell happened to you, detective?" He leaned closer, inspecting Harry's head. "You here on police business? Or do you need my services in the emergency room?"

"Not this time, doc, thanks. It was just a minor fracas with an automobile. No bones were broken, and my brain seems intact."

"Don't worry about the hair — it'll soon grow back in," Waxman said with a grin, unconsciously smoothing back his own thick dark locks. "By the way, I saw your picture in the paper this morning."

"I'll bet you did," Harry replied gloomily, and Waxman laughed.

Harry glanced down at Waxman's feet — he was wearing black Gucci loafers. A warning tremor fizzed up his spine. "Nice shoes, doc," he commented casually.

"Expensive but comfortable," Waxman said. "When you're on your feet as many hours a day as I am, you appreciate every bit of comfort you can get."

"Dr. Waxman, you're just the man I came to see." Harry grabbed his arm before he could walk away. "It's about Suzie Walker. I need to know who she worked with. Who her colleagues were, her friends. Anyone who knew her."

Waxman's eyebrows rose. "Don't tell me you think it's one of us? Here at the hospital?" he asked.

"Let's just say we're looking at everyone she came in contact with. It's just procedure, doc, nothing to be alarmed about."

Waxman's eyes clouded as he thought uneasily about it. "Jesus, Harry, you'll have us all looking over our shoulders if you go around questioning everyone."

"That's why I'm asking you first. She worked with you. You knew her better than the other doctors here."

"Yes, well, I suppose I did. Though Dr. Andrews knew her too — she did a stint in obstetrics. And Starewski, in neuro. In fact, Harry, most everybody must have known her. You're asking me a damned difficult question. I'll bet if you asked anyone here, they'd have the same problem. A hospital is a small world, you know, even one as big as this."

Harry heaved a sigh; he knew Waxman was right. "Well, if you can think of anyone in particular, anybody you get a feeling about . . ."

Dr. Waxman nodded. "I'll do that," he said, already walking away.

There was no sassy chat from the nurses at the duty desk this morning. They were subdued, still caught up in the horror of Suzie's murder, still worried about safety. He asked them the same questions he'd asked Dr. Waxman and got pretty much the same response.

"I hope whatever happened to your head

has nothing to do with this," the duty nurse said.

"Nope, just a personal problem," Harry replied, uncomfortably aware that with a line of stitches bisecting his partially shaven head, he looked like something from Frankenstein's laboratory.

"That must be some 'personal problem,' " the nurse murmured.

He met Rossetti coming back down the hallway. "Sometimes I think I live here," Rossetti said gloomily. "But you surely look as though you belong, Prof."

Dr. Blake came hurrying around the corner. "Morning, gentlemen," he called, lifting his hand in acknowledgment as he hurried past. Then he stopped, turned around, adjusted his horn-rimmed glasses, and stared hard at Harry. "What the hell happened to you, detective?" he asked mildly.

"Oh, just a run-in with the paparazzi. You can read all about it in the tabloids this morning."

Blake came toward him, inspecting the wound. "I never read the tabloids," he said. "I don't know any of the people who appear in them. At least not until today I didn't. Not a bad sewing job, though. Get that done here?"

"Upstate, doc, at the local hospital."

"Couldn't have done it better myself. You look as though you could use a vacation, though. If I were your doctor, with a wound like that, I'd recommend a few days off."

"No chance. They've got me tied to the stake at the precinct until we solve this case. Taking the dog for a walk is about as far as I'll get for the next few weeks."

"Too bad," Blake said, smiling as he hurried on his way.

"Prof," Rossetti said, "did you notice that Blake was wearing Guccis?"

"Yes. So was Waxman, and more than likely a dozen of the other doctors. I guess that eliminates interns and anyone else who can't afford them from suspicion."

"Unless it's someone with a status symbol thing," Rossetti said thoughtfully. "Y'know, like an intern who really wants a Ferrari but will settle for a pair of pricey Italian shoes. Makes him feel classy."

"You may be right," Harry admitted. "Meanwhile, put a check on every doctor in this hospital. I want to know who they are, where they come from, where they worked previously, whether they are married, and what their home lives are like."

Back in the squad room, he picked up Mal's message about the Welcome Home note. He figured it was the tabloids; they were experts at accessing information. It might also have been some nosy reporter who had been calling the unlisted numbers and hanging up. It made sense.

He called Mal at the office. She answered right away and sounded as though she had been waiting for his call.

"Hi, Scarface," she said cockily, but he detected an undertone of nerves.

"I could always claim I earned it in a duel."

"Like Errol Flynn?"

He sighed. "First it was Bogart and Scarface, and now it's Flynn. Right now, with half my hair missing, I look more like Bruce Willis."

"That's not bad," she said.

"Squeeze barely recognizes me."

"*I* barely recognize you. But that's because every time I see you, you do a disappearing act."

"My mother warned me my job would be my downfall."

"Your mother was right. Besides," she added wistfully, "I think I'm missing you."

"*You* are missing *me*, Malone? *Missing* my strong manly presence?"

"Yup."

He waited for her to say something else, but there was silence.

"About the Welcome Home note," he said. "It has to be the tabloids."

"After what happened, do you really think they'd do a thing like that?"

Harry wasn't convinced, but he wanted to reassure her, take that little wobble of nerves from her voice. "They know how to get things like unlisted numbers, addresses, where to find the dirt on people —"

Suddenly she made up her mind. It couldn't go on — she had to tell him. "Harry," she interrupted him, "I need to see you."

He knew she wasn't joking. He didn't ask questions, he just said, "Okay. I'll be there as soon as I can."

"My knight in shining armor," she said softly.

"I hope I can live up to that. I'll be there around seven, okay?"

"I'll be waiting," she said quietly.

She sat on her pretty garden terrace, waiting for him, looking out over Manhattan's skyline — the turrets and towers that she had conquered as Mallory Malone. But her past as Mary Mallory was not over and done with yet. And because of what she now believed in her heart, she had, finally, to tell Harry the truth.

He was right on time. He walked into her apartment and into her heart precisely on the stroke of seven. They stood looking at each other across the room.

He glanced ruefully at his old leather jacket and jeans. "One knight in slightly tarnished armor, reporting for duty, ma'am."

"Oh, Harry," she said, still looking into his eyes. She loved him when he was silly, and she wanted to laugh, but it got stuck in her throat.

He saw she was nervous and slung an affectionate arm around her shoulders. "What's up, Mal? Come on, you know you can tell me anything."

She gulped back the panic and got a grip on herself. "It's important, Harry. You see, now I think I know who he is."

Harry took a deep breath. He had always suspected that Mal knew more than she was telling, but not this much. He saw the panic in her face and tightened his arm reassuringly around her.

"Okay," he said quietly. "Just take a deep breath, Malone, and begin at the beginning."

"I didn't want to tell you," she said. "It's in the past, I didn't think it related to the murders. To us. But now I know it does, I *feel* it."

"Okay, Mal, I'm listening." He sat next to her and held her hand.

42

Mary Mallory was eighteen when she met him. She had never had a boyfriend, never dated, flirted, necked, or petted. She was a virgin.

The café where she worked six nights a week as a waitress was a simple place, patronized by office workers and staff at the nearby hospital who wanted an inexpensive meal, and he was one of the regulars. He always sat at one of her tables, if he could, and after a few visits they got to smiling at each other and saying how are you tonight, that sort of thing. She liked him because at least he looked straight at her instead of through her, and he treated her as a person, not just a plain, overworked waitress.

She thought at first he must be in the military, his hair was cropped so short. But then she decided he couldn't because he also had a neat little beard. Besides, he was nearsighted, as she was, and always wore glasses with heavy black frames to read whatever book or journal he brought with him.

Chicken with mashed potatoes, gravy and biscuits was his favorite meal, and he always cleaned his plate. She smiled. She'd bet when he was a kid, his mother had told him he wouldn't get ice cream unless he finished his broccoli. Somehow that made her feel a tenderness for him.

One night, after he had been coming to the café for several weeks, she went to take his order as usual. He put a marker in his book and smiled at her, then asked her name. He had nice white even teeth and a friendly expression, but she was so surprised, she blurted out, "Mary Mallory Malone," without even thinking. Then she added, embarrassed at the way it sounded, "But now I'm always called Mary."

"I like Mary Mallory," he said. "It's different." He asked if she worked at the café full time.

"Oh no, I'm really a student," she replied, with a shy smile.

"You work such long hours," he said, surprised. "When do you find time to study?"

"At nights, mostly," she confessed. "I like it then, it's quiet, no one bothers me." And then she blushed. No one ever bothered her anyway, yet here she was, talking like a regular person.

"I know how it is," he said seriously. "I put in a lot of hard years as a med student. Now I'm an intern at the hospital, and I'll tell you, the workload doesn't get any easier." He showed her the medical textbook he had brought along. "I can't afford to let up," he said. "Just got to keep on studying until I get where I want to be."

She wondered where that was but was too shy to ask, so she took his order, and he returned to his textbook.

He waved good night to her when he left and she found he'd given her a good tip. Mary smiled as she cleared his table. She realized, surprised, that she had actually had a conversation. With a man.

The next night she washed her long limp hair and tied it back with a ribbon. She wore a new blue T-shirt and a sixties kind of multicolored Indian-looking skirt that she had bought for a couple of dollars from the secondhand shop. She looked up expectantly every time the bell over the door jingled, but he did not show up that night. Nor the next. When he did not come for a whole week, she resigned herself to the fact that he had probably found a new place whose food and waitresses he preferred.

Then, unexpectedly, on a busy Saturday night, he was back again. The café was crowded, but she promised him the little corner table he favored as soon as it was free, and while he waited, he drank a glass of red wine.

"So how're you doing, Mary Mallory?" he asked when she finally got him seated.

She stood waiting with her order pad poised. "Just fine, thanks," she said, smiling at him. "We haven't seen you in a while, though."

"Family problems." He shrugged. "I had to

go home for a few days."

He didn't tell her where home was, and she didn't ask. He ordered the chicken and said, "I can't stand the food in the hospital canteen. I miss my mother's cooking, and the chicken and biscuits here are a kind of nostalgia trip."

"It must have been nice to go home then," she said, but he looked at her, puzzled. "For your mother's cooking," she explained.

He nodded. "Oh, sure. I guess you already know what I want to order."

She wrote chicken and biscuits on the order pad and showed him. He laughed. "You got it," he said.

When he had finished his meal, he asked her what she was studying. "Media communications and journalism," she said. "So I can ask the questions instead of having to answer them."

"Good answer, Mary Mallory," he said approvingly.

She found herself waiting for him, ready with a smile, when he next came in, eager to take his order. Chatting a little, making real conversation, wasn't so hard after all, she told herself happily.

One night he came in late. He was the last customer to leave the café, and when he paid his check, he said to her, "I'm not in a hurry tonight. I'll drive you home, if you like."

She rushed into the ladies' room to check her appearance, suddenly nervous. She combed her hair and smoothed her skirt and applied a touch of lipstick. She wished she had some perfume, hoping the aromas of the steamy little kitchen didn't still linger on her clothes. Then she took a deep breath and walked out onto the street where he was waiting for her.

The car was a brand-new BMW convertible. He held open the door, and she stepped in, feeling like a princess. He pressed a button and the top slid smoothly down. Then he switched on the radio. It was a bit chilly, but she enjoyed the way the wind tugged at her hair as they drove toward the dank little house she shared with several other students. The soft music on the radio created an intimate little world, enclosing the two of them, and she leaned her head back dreamily against the fine leather cushion. She wished the drive would never end.

"This must be it," he said, peering at the ramshackle building she called home. A street lamp shed an unfriendly yellow light on the brimming garbage cans and rusty bicycles, and a prowling dog stopped and sniffed, then lifted its leg on the BMW's tires.

"Goddammit!" he yelled viciously. "Get the hell out of here!" He glanced angrily at her. "They should exterminate animals like that. All they do is spread disease."

She was surprised by his anger, especially since she was acquainted with the dog. It belonged to a neighbor and was a friendly creature who sometimes came and sat on their porch. Still, it was unfortunate that the dog had chosen to lift his leg on his smart new car.

"I'm sorry," she said. "That's just the way it is in this neighborhood."

He shrugged. "I'll go by the car wash on the way back." Then he slid his arm along her shoulders.

Mary Mallory looked at him, big-eyed with surprise. She was holding her breath with the shock of it when he pulled her toward him and kissed her on the mouth.

It was her first kiss, and she quivered with the unexpectedness of it. Her emotions had been locked inside her for so many years, she was like a volcano ready to erupt.

He let go of her, then leaned across and opened the passenger door. "See you next week," he said.

She slid out of the car, said a hurried good night, and stood on the sidewalk in front of the house, waving as he drove off. She put her hand to her lips, still feeling the imprint of his kiss, half relieved and half disappointed that he hadn't done it longer.

Still, a man had finally kissed her, and she was elated. Now she was like the other girls — she knew what it was like. It was only later, as she lay awake, analyzing every millisecond of what had happened, that she realized he had not asked her for a date. It must have been just a friendly kiss after all and not a real "boyfriend" kiss.

When he came to the café a few days later, she peered hopefully at him through her thick glasses, brightening when he gave her a big smile and said hello and how are you, Mary Mallory?

It was the *Mary Mallory* at the end that gave his greeting a special personal little meaning. With a little thrill of excitement, she hurried to get his usual order. He lingered over a glass of wine until it got quite late and she was ready to leave, and then he looked at her and said, "Like a lift home?"

She nodded, beaming, and ran to put on some lipstick and comb her hair. It was raining this time, so they couldn't put the top down. But he turned up the radio, and symphonic music swelled and echoed in her ears as they glided smoothly through the wet night. She thought happily that this must be what it felt like when you were rich. And happy.

When he kissed her good night again, his lips were hard, but he did not put his tongue in her mouth, the way she had heard girls say boys did. She clung to him. No one had ever held her close before, not her mother, not her father. She was starved for affection, for approval, for identity, and suddenly this man was giving her all those things. By holding her, kissing her, he was saying you are *someone*, Mary Mallory, you're a pretty girl, you're sweet and intelligent, and I really like you. In her mind, his arms around her meant she was loved.

She waved good-bye again as he drove off, but he didn't wave back. She supposed he hadn't seen her, standing in the dark and the rain. But the next night he was back at the café again. And again he waited to drive her home.

It was a cold, misty night. Mary Mallory shivered in her flimsy Indian skirt as she hurried to the parking lot across the street where he was waiting. But inside, the car was warm and the music was already playing.

"Get in," he said, a touch impatiently.

"Sorry." She slid quickly into the seat next to him.

He glanced around the lot. There were three or four other cars, but no one was around. He swung the BMW quickly out and drove too fast down the street.

They had been driving for about fifteen minutes when Mary Mallory realized they were not on the road leading to her house. She had been so content just being with him, co-cooned together in the warm car with the soft music swirling around her. She had closed her eyes and imagined she was his wife and they were returning home together from a party.

She smiled at him. "Where are we going?"

He shrugged. "I thought we'd go somewhere quiet where we could talk. Where we don't have to look at the garbage cans and smell the dog pee."

She said, ashamed, "It's not very nice, I know."

He shrugged again, concentrating on the driving.

They were on a quiet road with woods on either side. The ground-mist rose like thin gray smoke, fluttering through the leafless branches. She thought with a shudder that it looked haunted by witches.

He drove onto the soft verge and stopped the car. Then he put on the hand brake and leaned back in his seat, staring straight ahead. There was nothing in front of them but a deserted road: no houses, no lights, no other cars.

He turned and looked at her, and Mary Mallory smiled at him. He leaned across and removed her glasses, then he put his arms around her. She sighed, leaning into him, turning her face willingly up to his, ready for his kiss.

Her eyes were closed, and she could feel his hands on her long hair. He pulled it viciously. Her head snapped back, and every taut hair sent shooting stars of pain through her scalp. She thought her neck must be broken. She stared at him, bug-eyed with fear. A knife gleamed in his left hand.

"Don't scream," he said coldly, holding the knife against her throat.

Mary Mallory felt the panic shooting up her spine, she was hot from it, trembling with it. "Don't," she whispered. "Don't —"

He put the knife on the dashboard, and she sagged with relief. Her head snapped back again as he smacked her across the face with the flat of his hand, then a second time.

"No!" she screamed. He looked in her eyes, she was gasping from the pain, wild-eyed with terror. He began to punch her, over and over until she was submerged in a sea of pain.

Mary Mallory knew she was going to die, that was why he had brought her here. Now his hands were under her skirt. She kicked out wildly, he grabbed her by the hair again, and she screamed.

He picked up the knife and held it to her throat. "Shut up," he said in a strange expressionless voice, as cold and brittle as ice chips.

She was sagging into a black hole from which there was no escape. It was fogging the sides of her eyes, clouding her brain . . . she had to pull herself together, she had to fight. She brought her knee up and jabbed it at his groin, but he was too quick for her. He gave her a menacing glare, then a quick chop to her neck, and she fell into that black bottomless pit.

He was still lying on top of her when she came flailing back up from the depths. Stickiness oozed between her legs, and she thought he must have cut her with the knife. Then she looked at him, half naked, and she knew what he had done.

She thought, it's over. Now he will kill me. She watched him pick up the knife again and knew she was right. He bent his face closer, staring intently at her, as though he were memorizing her face. In the faint light from the dashboard, his eyes were dark evil orbs, drilling into hers until she thought they penetrated her very soul, the way he had penetrated her body. He ran the knife lightly across her throat, as though testing its sharpness.

The scream wouldn't come; it was locked inside her, stuck in her throat. Distantly, she thought she heard the wail of a siren, but she knew that even if it were the police, they would be too late.

"Son of a bitch," he snarled, pulling himself off her. The blue lights were flashing in the distance. He quickly turned on the ignition, gunned the car, and shot down the road, leaving the flashing lights in the distance.

And Mary Mallory knew she was on her own again — with a madman. She pulled herself into a sitting position, clutching her blouse across her breasts, pulling down her skirt, not daring to look at him. She stared out of the window, planning on jumping, but they were speeding. Her hand was on the door handle. She knew she would be killed if she did it, but she didn't care anymore.

Suddenly they were back in familiar territory, turning into her street. Hope flickered in her leaden heart.

He stopped the car at the corner. He leaned across, took her hair in his fist again, pulled her head back, and stared into her eyes. *"If you breathe one word of this, I'll kill you,"* he said in a voice as icy as chilled steel.

He let go of her, opened her door, and pushed her out. *"Remember, I'll kill you,"* he warned again as he slammed the door. He spun the car around and shot back down the street, away into the night.

She stared numbly after him. Her legs were trembling, and blood was trickling down the insides of her thighs. Clutching her shirt closed, she stumbled down the sidewalk, praying she wouldn't meet anyone. She was lucky — it was Friday night and the house was dark. Everyone was out partying.

Mary Mallory slunk inside like a beaten dog seeking a hole to hide in. She looked at herself in the mirror. Her eye was blackening, and there were red welts across her face. She took off the shirt and stared horrified at her breasts, already purple with bruises, the nipples ringed with bite marks. Then she took off her tattered Indian skirt and her torn underpants and saw blood seeping from her vagina and the stickiness that was his semen. She lifted her head and howled with the pain and shame and agony of it. She wished he had killed her.

Hours passed while she simply lay on the floor, crying. Her legs would not move — she was paralyzed with shock and pain. Dawn was breaking when she finally dragged herself upright. She went to the bathroom and turned on the faucets, waiting until the tub was almost full. Then she took the razor and stepped in, wincing as the hot water stung her wounds, gradually submerging herself, until only her head was clear.

It would be easy, she thought dully. He had almost done it for her. A few more minutes, and she would have been dead anyway. They said it was not painful. Not that pain mattered anymore, but the thought of just drifting into sleepy oblivion lured her gently, like a moth to a flame.

She jolted upright, as a car pulled up outside. Had he come back to get her after all? Then she heard the laughter and voices and realized it was the other students returning from their party. She pulled out the stopper, climbed from the tub, wrapped herself in her old terrycloth robe, and slid, like a shadow, down the hall to her own little room.

She did not emerge for two days. Finally, weak from shock and hunger, she put on a long-sleeved sweater and jeans. She pulled a baseball cap low over her eyes, and even though it was raining, she wore sunglasses.

She got her bike and cycled down the street to the pay phone to call the café and tell them she was sorry, but she had had bad news from home and would not be back. Then she went to the convenience store on the same block and bought milk and corn-flakes and Snickers bars and retreated to her room again.

As she ate the cornflakes, she considered what to do. She had no girlfriends to confide in, and she couldn't tell the college counselors. They might think that it was her fault. Maybe they would even call the police. She could never talk about it, never tell what he had done. . . . Remembering the knife and his threat, a wave of terror washed over her. Her hands shook so badly, she had to put down the spoon — the cornflakes were choking her. She decided she would try to ignore what had happened, lock it away in her mind with the other horrors, the lifetime of rejections. It was all she could do.

A couple of weeks later, when the bruises had faded sufficiently and she was able to face life again, she went back to class. A short while after that, she bumped into one of the wait-resses from the café on the street.

"Hey, Mary," she said cheerily. "Hope everything is okay again at home."

Mary nodded and said yes it was, thanks.

"By the way," the waitress said, "the young guy you used to chat with has left too. He said he'd been transferred to a hospital in another state."

Mary Mallory's heart lifted with hope. "Too bad," she said. But what she meant was *Thank you, God.*

43

Harry lifted her hand to his lips and kissed it. He took each finger and kissed each one. He admired her for telling him, for her rigid control and the matter-of-fact way she had spoken. But he knew the hurt and the fear went deep. "I'm sorry, Mal," he said gently. "I would do anything to erase that terrible memory from your mind."

She leveled her gaze at him. "There's more," she said quietly.

Their eyes locked, his shocked, hers filled with shame. Harry got up, poured himself a bourbon, and took a gulp. "You don't have to go through with this," he said. "You can't be sure it was the same man. I don't want you hurt anymore. Just forget about it — it's in the past."

She shook her head, determined. "It's my duty. I have to tell you."

He sat beside her again and took her hand in his, gripping it tightly as he listened.

Mary Mallory was alone in the trailer, waiting for the Coast Guard to tell her what she already knew in her heart: they had given up hope of recovering her mother's body. She sat on the orange vinyl sofa and looked at the dingy room. In some strange way she could feel her mother there more positively now than when she had been alive. The sharp odor of her cigarettes still lingered, and the bitter aroma of stale coffee, and the sullen smell of poverty.

She went into the bedroom and stared at her mother's clothes hanging on the metal rail. There were so few, and they were so old and tired. They looked infinitely pathetic. She wanted to cry.

On the shelf was her mother's purse, red patent with a jaunty gilt buckle, pitted from age and the salt wind. She remembered going to the store with her to buy it, when she was just a child. And she remembered how thrilled she had been to see her walking down the street swinging her new red bag. But that was long ago, and the red bag had remained on the shelf since the day they arrived in Golden.

Her mother's shoes were tossed on the floor: a pair of shabby sneakers, the cheap black pumps bought a decade ago on sale and never worn, and her old strappy white sandals. Mary Mallory picked up a sandal and put her hand inside it, feeling the place where her mother's foot had rested. She had never realized before what tiny feet she had, only size four.

Her mother's fuzzy blue mohair sweater lay on the unmade bed where she had tossed it before venturing out into the great storm.

Mary Mallory held it to her face, breathing in the mingled scents that meant "mother." Tears spurted from her eyes. They rolled down her cheeks like fat raindrops, merging into a torrent as grief overcame her. She flung herself onto the bed, clutching the sweater to her chest as though she were holding her mother.

"Oh, Mom, I need you, I need you," she wailed. "Mom, I wanted you to need me. I wanted to say I love you, but you didn't wait for me, and now it's too late. And it's all gone wrong. I wanted you to help me, you were all I had." And she sobbed her grief into the soft blue sweater.

The next day the man from the Coast Guard came by to tell her it was unlikely her mother's body would ever be recovered. Mary Mallory nodded in acknowledgment and said thank you for all your help. They said no problem, then she closed the door and she was alone.

She went back into the bedroom and brushed the dust from the slab of unframed mirror propped against the wall. She took a step back and studied her reflection. She put her hands on the slight curve of her belly, then turned sideways and looked again. She groaned with despair. A baby was growing inside her from the seed of the rapist, from the madman who had wanted to kill her. She groaned again, overwhelmed by self-loathing.

She was sure the child would be a monster.

How could it not, with a madman for a father and a mother who hated it with every inch of her being? Surely it could sense that loathing, even in the womb?

Afraid she would end up as crazy as her mother, she pulled herself together, put on the blue mohair sweater, and went for a long walk, asking herself every step of the way what to do.

She sat on the cliff, staring out at the gray ocean. It heaved sullenly under a low steely sky. She imagined her mother down there and thought sadly that in death, her mother's surroundings were as gray and drab as in life.

She sat for a long time, trying to work out a plan. She wanted the alien embryo removed from her belly. She wished and wished for it to happen, and she prayed to God to expel it, but it was a long shot, she knew it. She would have aborted it if she had known where to go, who to ask — but she had no one. In the end there was only one thing to do.

She would drop out of college, have the baby, then give it up for adoption. But seven long months stretched ahead of her. How would she live? What would she do?

Mary Mallory scrambled to her feet. She gave one last long look at the sullen gray ocean. She stretched herself tall, breathing in the sharp cold salty air, willing herself to have courage, to be strong. "You *will* win," she told herself grimly. Then she blew a sad farewell kiss to her mother, turned on her heel, and walked back along the cliff road to the trailer.

She quickly collected all her mother's things, her clothes and small personal belongings, and put them in plastic bags. She collected their few dishes and pots and pans, remembering the last time they had packed them so joyously for their new life. She added the half-smoked pack of cigarettes on the kitchen table and the almost-empty can of coffee and the remnants of food from the refrigerator.

She stood looking at the half-dozen plastic bags on the floor; they contained all that was left of her mother's life. Overwhelmed by its pathos, she began to cry. After a while anger took the place of sadness. What had happened to her mother was not going to happen to her. Somehow she would get through. She would become "someone" if it killed her.

She piled the plastic bags into the trunk and climbed into the driver's seat. She turned for one last look at the place she had called home. Then she drove to the town dump and hurled the plastic bags, filled with the pathetic remnants of her mother's life and memories, into oblivion.

She climbed back into the turquoise Chevy and headed out of Golden. She would never go back.

She drove north and east, as if drawn back

by a magnet. She had only a little money — certainly not enough to pay for motel rooms — so she slept in the car and dined at cheap roadside burger stands until her squeamish stomach heaved in revolt. Then she bought Wonder Bread and Kraft cheese slices, and somehow the familiar childhood diet stayed down and she began to feel stronger.

Golden was a long way behind her, and the outskirts of a city were in front of her. She glanced at the sign: TACOMA 10 MILES. She looked at the gas gauge. There was less than a quarter of a tank left, and just like before, when the gas ran out, that was where she stayed.

She found herself in a suburb in the poorer end of town, but she couldn't complain because she knew where she belonged. There were plenty of rooms for rent in the area, and she walked around looking at the signs until she found a house that looked cleaner than the rest. She knocked on the door.

A youngish man answered. He had a long face and large teeth like a horse, but a pleasant expression.

He smiled at her. "I guess you've come about the room?"

Mary Mallory nodded. "Can you tell me how much it is? Because if it's too expensive, I don't want to waste your time."

He looked her speculatively up and down, then beyond her at the old car by the curb.

"You have a job?" he asked mildly.

She lifted her chin and looked him in the eye. "Not yet," she said in a steely voice, "but I sure as hell will."

Their eyes met, and he laughed. "You betcha, woman," he said, still grinning. "Okay, there are two rooms. One's kind of small, up in the attic, but it's real cheap. The other is on the first floor. It has the big bay window you see above you and is more spacious and more expensive." He told her the prices, then said, "Care to take a look?"

"I'll take the cheaper one," she said, already heading back to the car to collect her things.

"But you haven't even looked at it yet," he protested.

"I don't need to. Your house is clean, and the price is right. Beggars can't be choosers," she added, lugging her duffel from the trunk.

He ran down the steps after her. "Here, let me help you." He lifted the bag easily and said, "By the way, my name's Jim Fiddler."

"Mary Malone," she said, shaking his hand.

"This is all you have?" He peered into the cavernous empty trunk.

"That's it." She slammed it shut and followed him up the steps. "About that job," she said hopefully, "you wouldn't happen to know of any around here, would you?"

"Try the supermarket," he said over his shoulder, leading the way up four flights of stairs. "They're always looking for help. You can't miss it — it's two blocks away. And if you strike out there, try the drugstore, or Burger King."

As she panted up the final steep flight of stairs, she told herself sarcastically that she had really come a long way — from one supermarket to another. Then she stepped inside the small attic room that was to be her new home, and her decision to do better than this, to get out and move on and become someone, hardened into rocklike resolve.

The room was small, all right. There was just about enough space for a single bed with a scratched wooden headboard, and a chest of drawers that doubled as a nightstand with a wobbly, pink-shaded lamp. Metal pegs were screwed into the wall for clothes, with a sagging pink curtain that pulled across to hide them. There was a pink rug on the wooden floor, and a pink armchair in front of the dormer window that didn't let in much light. Even though the chair was old, it looked comfortable, and there was a wooden standard lamp on one side of it and a small table on the other.

"Not much, but at least it's color-coordinated," Jim said with a cheerful grin. "This do for you, Miss Malone?"

"It's perfect," she said, and she meant it. All she wanted was to kick off her shoes and sit in that old chair and not have to drive or even think.

He said, "The rent is payable one week in

advance." She looked around for her purse, and he added, "That's okay, whenever." He peered closely at her. There were shadows under her eyes, and she gave off nervous vibes. She looked very young and absolutely exhausted.

"Care to join me in a cup of coffee?" he asked casually. "It was just brewing when you arrived."

She looked suspiciously at him through her big glasses, then decided he was only being kind. It was just that she wasn't used to kindness.

She beamed gratefully at him. He thought, surprised, that when she did that, she lit up like the Fourth of July.

Mal followed him back downstairs. She worried that they might prove a problem in the coming months, but she pushed that out of her mind and settled for thinking only about the immediate future. That was the way she intended to get through the next months: day by day, hour by hour, even minute by goddamn minute if she had to.

Jim's apartment took up the entire basement. Another young man was standing in the kitchen, slicing a cake, and he glanced up as they came in.

"This is Alfie Burns, my partner," Jim introduced him casually. "Mary Malone, our new tenant in the attic."

"Welcome, Mary," Alfie said, taking out an

extra mug and pouring coffee.

He was very tall and very thin and *very* handsome, Mary thought, studying him over the top of her mug. The hot coffee steamed her glasses, and she took them off and rubbed her eyes.

Alfie said, "Hey, anybody ever tell you, you've got beautiful eyes? I've never seen such a deep blue." He heaved a dramatic sigh. "Wouldn't you just die for them, Jim? You should think about contact lenses," he advised. "Shame to hide such beauty behind those big bottle-tops." He laughed, but it was a good-hearted kind of laugh, and Mary knew he wasn't making fun of her.

They asked where she was from, and she told them Oregon, and that her mother had just died and she was dropping out of college for a year because she had no money and couldn't cope.

"Poor kid," Jim said sympathetically. "Listen, about that job at the supermarket — the manager's a friend of mine. You tell him you know me and that you're living here, okay? He'll do his best for you, I'm certain of it."

Jim was right. Mentioning his name to the manager worked like a charm, and the next day Mary had herself a job as a check-out girl. Everything seemed to be going smoothly — even the morning sickness had subsided, though she was careful to eat as little as possible in the hope that the baby would not grow and the bulge would not get much bigger. Sometimes she worked the morning shift, sometimes the evening, but either way by the end of the day, her legs had swollen and her feet ached.

She walked slowly back home and trailed up the endless flights of stairs to her room, where she sat with her feet in a bowl of cool water until the ache eased. Then she went to the kitchen downstairs, heated a cup of soup or made a sandwich, and went back to her room to read one of the books she borrowed from Jim. Occasionally he would pop his head out as she passed his door and say, "Hey, how about a cup of coffee and some gossip, Mary?"

But it was Alfie who would do all the gossiping, about their friends and the parties they went to, and who was going out with whom. She liked hearing about it, even though she didn't know their friends; it made her feel a part of their lives.

"Do you have a boyfriend, Mary?" Alfie asked casually one evening a few months later. He was drinking beer, and she and Jim were drinking coffee. She took a sip and said, "Oh, no. Definitely no."

"But you're not gay," he continued.

She looked shocked. "Of course not."

He smiled at her. "Mary Malone, you are the most unworldly innocent I have ever met."

She stared at him, suddenly realizing what he meant. "I — that's all right. . . ." she stammered. "I — it's just that I never met anyone before. . . ."

They laughed, and Jim said mockingly, "Of course *I'm* not prejudiced. Some of my best friends are gay."

"The thing is, Mary, how did such an innocent like you get yourself pregnant?" Alfie asked gently.

The heat of embarrassment flushed from her toes to the top of her head. She was nauseated with shame as she realized they knew. She hung her head, fighting back the tears, saying nothing.

"Have you seen a doctor?" he asked. His voice was kind and without a hint of criticism.

She shook her head. "No."

They looked at each other, eyebrows raised, sighing with exasperation. "Sweetheart, this is not going to go away like a cold in the head," Alfie warned. "You've got to take care of yourself, make arrangements, decide what you're going to do."

Mary lifted her head. They were sitting at the kitchen table opposite her, staring at her with concerned eyes. "Arrangements?" she asked nervously.

Jim sighed again — she was from another planet. "For the birth, Mary. You can't have it here."

She hadn't thought about that, hadn't been able to face up to the fact that one day the child would be born. That it would live, and she would be its mother.

"Maybe you want to tell us about it," Alfie suggested, but when she looked at him, horrified, he said quickly, "Okay, okay, you don't have to. But we're concerned about you, Mary, and we want to help you before we go."

"Before you go?" she repeated, her jaw dropping.

"Jim and I have decided to put the house up for sale. We're off to live in paradise, on a tropical island in the South Pacific. We can't just leave you here, like unfinished business, and not know you're going to be okay. We'd be lying on the beach wondering what the hell happened to you. So we want to help. But in order to do that, you have to fill us in on a few details."

"Like when is it due?" Jim prompted. He reached out and took her hand. "Come on, Mary, get it over with. 'Fess up."

He held her hand while she told him. The baby was due in three months, and she didn't know what she was going to do because she couldn't bear to think about it. But she did know she wanted to give it up for adoption. "I never *ever* want to see it," she cried passionately. She looked apprehensively at them, but they didn't seem shocked.

"I did a little research," Jim said. "There's a place out in the suburbs that takes care of young women in your delicate condition. I hear it's very pleasant, a big old house set in some gardens. It's not luxurious, but it's well equipped and peaceful. And it's free."

"A home for unwed mothers," Mary said dully.

"They don't call it that anymore," he said briskly, not allowing her to indulge in despair. "Be practical, Mary. They take you in and look after you. Your baby will be born there, and they will take care of the adoption procedures. In other words, sweetheart, they take a load off your shoulders. Just look at it this way — in three or four months you'll be able to go back to college. They won't even have to rehabilitate you and get you a job."

"I still have my scholarship," she said, as a ray of hope penetrated the gloom of the future.

"Sure you do. So here's the number, and there's the phone. Why don't you give them a call? Alfie and I will take a walk around the block. Perhaps we'll go pick up a bottle of wine. We'll drink to our tropical island and your future at college. Okay?"

Mary could have kissed him, but she was too shy. She waited until they left, then took a deep breath and made the phone call.

A pleasant-sounding woman answered, and she explained nervously who she was and what her circumstances were.

"Come and see us tomorrow, if you can make it," Mrs. Rhodes said briskly. "Places go fast here."

Ranier House was a long drive away in a

leafy suburb that petered out into real countryside a mile farther down the road. It was raining, a fine Irish-mist sort of rain that soaked her hair as she walked the short distance from the parking area to the glass front door, and the garden smelled fresh, of rich loamy earth.

The house had been built as a country estate by a wealthy logging baron at the turn of the century and was a mix of English Tudor-style gables and Washington State red brick. It was big and square and forbidding, with bare wooden floors and white walls, like a school. It had plain pull-down shades at the windows and worn-looking furnishings, and the smell of institutional cooking lingered in the hallways.

A couple of heavily pregnant young women came by, arms linked, as she waited in the hall. They eyed her up and down as they walked past. She thought, horrified, that in a couple of months she would look like that.

Mrs. Rhodes hurried into the hall. She was small, thin, and brisk. Mary told her the details: her age, where she was living, her job. She explained about college and the scholarship. And she told her about her mother. Mrs. Rhodes wrote it all down, then asked who the baby's father was.

Mary shook her head, her mouth set in a firm line. "There is no father," she said grimly.

"But my dear, if the child is to be adopted,

the natural father should be informed." Mrs. Rhodes looked at her with irritation. They were all the same — they never wanted to tell.

"I'd rather kill it," Mary said in a calm, dead voice.

Mrs. Rhodes glanced sharply at her. She could see from her face, hear in her tone that she was dealing with a severely traumatized young woman. The mother recently dead . . . the girl just eighteen . . . they had better do something to help her.

"Very well, my dear," she said, trying not to sound patronizing. "I think it would be best if you came to us at the end of the month. You can work out your notice at the supermarket and contribute whatever small amount you can toward your upkeep here. If there's nothing, well, so be it. Ranier House is run as a charity. We'll see you through, and that's the important thing."

44

Mary had been locked in a safe little time warp — she had not thought beyond the next day. All she had wanted was to continue living in her own attic room, occasionally sharing a cup of coffee and a sandwich with Jim and Alfie, and picking up her paycheck regularly every Friday. Now it was over. Jim and Alfie had made up their minds, the house had been sold quickly, and they couldn't wait to be off. The hardest part was saying good-bye to them.

They shared a final celebration dinner the night before they left. There was a smile on her face, but she was dying inside. They had been kind and treated her as an equal. They had been her friends.

When the taxi came to take them to the airport the next morning, Jim hugged her. He ruffled her hair and said, "Chin up, Mary Malone. You'll get through it. I'll be thinking of you." And Alfie kissed her hand and said, "Go for it, Mary. We'll drop you a postcard."

She stood on the steps, waving good-bye until the taxi turned the corner, then trailed heavily back upstairs and packed her own bag. The next day she took up residence in the home for unwed mothers.

There was a nursery wing at Ranier House, and she often heard the sound of babies crying, but she never wanted to see them. Eventually the matron insisted that she look around, and she walked her through, pointing out the facilities: the labor ward, and the delivery room where she would give birth, with curtained-off beds where two young women lay sleeping. "Being a new mother can be exhausting," Matron warned her.

"Not for me," she said quickly. "Mine is being adopted right away."

Matron frowned. "I'm afraid it will take a few days," she said. "We have to know the baby is healthy and feeding properly, and then we'll wean him. We'll have to expel your breast milk, make sure he's thriving before he can go."

Mary stared at her, horrified. "I can't do that," she said, panicked. "I can't breast-feed it, I can't —"

Matron had heard it all before. "We'll see," she said calmly.

As usual, Mary kept to herself as much as she could in those last few weeks of waiting. She didn't want to talk to the other girls because when she left, she wanted to put this behind her, as though it had never happened. It was the only way.

The days dragged by, though they kept the expectant mothers busy all the time, and even those who were giving up their children were taught how to look after an infant, how to bathe and diaper it, and about sterilizing bottles — all the things Mary did not want to know.

She learned what would happen when she went into labor, that it would probably take a long time — ten, twelve hours, maybe longer — because first births always did. She told herself she didn't care, she just wanted it over and done with.

The morning she went into labor, she received a postcard from Jim and Alfie. It was a blurred, brightly colored picture of a palm-fringed island, and they had headed it, "From Paradise."

"Good luck, Mary," they had written. "And remember, Paradise is where the heart is."

Her water broke right after that, and the contractions came not much later. They surprised her with their intensity, but she told herself bravely that they were bearable. Matron came to inspect her. She said the doctor would be along shortly and that she was doing fine, but she had a long way to go yet. Mary glanced at the clock on the wall: it was eleven A.M.

At eleven P.M. she was lying in a metal hospital bed in the labor ward with the sides up to keep her from falling out when she thrashed around, crazy with pain. She gritted her teeth and told herself to take it one minute at a time, one second — just get through it, and tomorrow it would be all over, and she would be free. The pain ripped through her, and she gasped, clenching her jaw, not making a sound.

"Scream, for God's sake girl, why don't you," the nurse said, astonished. "If ever a woman was entitled to a good scream, it's now."

But Mary just clenched her jaw tighter. The face of the man who had raped her floated in front of her closed lids. His staring dark eyes were drilling into hers as she wavered between the agonizing contractions. She would rather die than give him the satisfaction of screaming.

Eventually, when she thought she could bear it no longer, at around five in the morning, they gave her an epidural, and suddenly the pain was no longer there. She floated in a pleasant haze somewhere above the bed, and then they dragged her back to reality. "Push, Mary, come on, girl, get on with it. Push more, harder, harder. . . ."

She didn't feel the baby sliding out of her, but she heard its cry. She wanted to put her hands to her ears and shut it out, but she couldn't move — her feet were in the stirrups, and the nurses were holding her hands, and she was trapped. All she could do was lie there and think horrified, *That's his baby. The monster has been born."*

"It's a girl," the doctor said, handing the infant to the nurse to clean.

"I don't want to know," she muttered, lost in a muzzy nightmare. She began to cry, and the nurse wiped her tears. "It's all right," she said kindly. "You were brave, Mary. You can cry now."

A short while later she was safe in bed in a curtained-off cubicle in the ward. The window was wide open, and the sun had just come up, and its warmth touched her face. She felt peaceful and very calm; it was all over now.

"Mary," Matron said.

Her eyes flew open, and she stared near-sightedly at her.

"Here's your baby," Matron said, holding out a pink-wrapped bundle. "It's feeding time." And she laid the baby down in the crook of Mary's arm.

Her whole body went rigid with shock. Her throat was as dry as cinders, and she was unable to speak. She could feel the small weight resting against her arm, but she could not look at it.

"Unbutton your nightdress, dear," Matron said.

"I can't," she croaked, unwilling to look. "I can't."

"She's a beautiful baby," Matron coaxed. "She needs you to feed her. Come on now, Mary. Accept your responsibility."

Mary dragged her eyes away from Matron and looked unwillingly at the creature who was about to draw nourishment from her. She stared at her daughter for a long moment, then she lay back on the pillow again and closed her eyes.

The sweet scent of lilacs drifted on the breeze from the tree outside her window, and their fragrance filled her with sudden blissful happiness. She looked at the child again. The baby's eyes were exactly like hers, big and blue and slightly unfocused. She had a round pink face and a sweet rosebud mouth and a delicate fuzz of blond hair. The baby was not a monster at all — she was beautiful, perfect. And she was hers.

Mary leaned back against the pillows, her arm around her baby. She ran a finger wonderingly across the blond down on her head. The scent of lilacs surrounded her, and the sunshine warmed her. And she knew that what she felt for the small, helpless infant, was pure love.

The next day she told them she had changed her mind and could not give the child up for adoption after all. Matron tried to reason with her, pointing out all the difficulties that lay ahead. She would miss her college education, men did not marry single mothers, and she would have to work hard and be both parents at once. Besides, they had a well-to-do couple waiting to take the child, ready and eager, with a nursery all prepared. The baby would have a wonderful life as their daughter. She would have a proper home and a real family; she would go to good schools and college.

Mary dug her heels in and stubbornly refused to listen. Finally they recognized defeat and helped her find a small studio apartment and a job in a drugstore.

The day Mary took her little girl "home" was the second happiest of her life. She had a week before she started work, and she had to find someone to look after the baby. The tiny apartment was hot in the June sunshine, and it smelled damp, but it was soon homey, awash under a sea of blankets and bottles, with tiny baby clothes hanging over the shower rail to dry.

She called her baby Angela because she was such a perfect little angel. She pushed her around the streets to the local park in a third-hand stroller given to her by Ranier House, and she fed her and bathed her and dressed her up in the free hand-out clothes, as if she were a little doll. The baby gazed at her with those huge blue eyes, and Mary cooed loving words to her, *"Precious,"* she said, and *"baby,"* and *"darling,"* and *"I love you."* The words were like a foreign language, but they came easily to her, now that she knew what love was.

In order to go to work, she had to wean the baby onto a bottle, and she exhausted herself pumping out her milk and sterilizing bottles and doing all the other hundred-and-one little tasks that are necessary with an infant. When the day came for her to start work, she wheeled the baby three blocks to the baby-sitter's house and handed over the bottles of milk and the diaper bag and all the other infant paraphernalia. She kissed the baby good-bye, then hurried off to the drugstore and work before she broke down and cried.

She worried all day, and at lunchtime she called to see how she was. "She's doing okay," the woman told her laconically. "At this age they just sleep a lot anyway."

Maybe the baby did sleep all day, but she certainly didn't sleep nights, and neither did Mary. Just when she would climb wearily into bed and close her eyes, Angela would cry again. She tried feeding her, tried putting her in bed with her, tried holding her and walking around and around the small room. But Angela was a night person, and the baby-sitter reaped the benefit of a sleepy infant all day, while the exhausted Mary crawled around the store trying to keep her eyes open and her wits about her, then walked the floor all night.

A couple of months passed. She had made several mistakes at work, and the manager warned her, but when she goofed again and gave a woman change for fifty instead of five and her cash didn't tally, he hit the roof.

"That's it, Miss Malone," he said. "I'm sorry, but you can't go on like this. You sure as hell can't hold down a job the state you're in."

"You mean I'm fired?" she asked, close to tears.

He sighed and gave her another chance. "Just think what you're going to do about it," he warned. "You can't be a mother and work full time."

But Mary couldn't be a mother if she didn't work full time because there wouldn't be enough money.

It was December, and Christmas was looming when she finally realized she couldn't go on. The baby cried all the time, and she thought guiltily that it was because she was unhappy — she didn't have a proper home, a full-time mother, the right care and attention. All Mary had to give her was love, and that was cheap. Anyone would love her.

Her pay disappeared on rent, the baby-sitter, and food. There was nothing left over, not an extra cent. She didn't even have enough to buy her baby a Christmas gift. She sat limply in a chair at the side of the crib, watching the baby toss her head from side to side, wailing. She didn't have the strength to pick her up. Total despair overwhelmed her. She was at the end of her rope.

The baby slept that night, but Mary paced the apartment, asking herself what to do. The next morning she dropped the child off and dragged herself unwillingly to the drugstore. Somehow she got through another day and picked up the pay packet, which had mostly been spent even before she received it. She bought a newspaper and a Snickers bar for a treat and walked wearily back to pick up Angela. This time when she saw her, the baby smiled.

Mary's heart turned over, and she smiled back, hardly believing it. It was like a shaft of sunlight on the gloomy cold December day.

Later, when the baby had been fed and was lying content for a few minutes on a blanket on the floor, Mary opened her pay packet and counted out the money. She stared at it, surprised. He had given her two weeks' pay instead of one. Then she saw the pink slip still in the envelope, and her heart sank. He had not even had the guts to tell her she was fired.

The baby lying peacefully on the fleecy blanket was so sweet and pretty in the pink baby clothes that were already too small. Her heart plummeted as she finally faced the truth.

At about eleven o'clock Angela began to cry. Mary walked around and around with her in her arms, patting her back, shushing her, telling her she loved her, until at last she dozed off again. She put her in the crib and went to the little cupboard she called a kitchen and fixed a cup of tea. Then she sat down and began to scan the newspaper for jobs.

It was two weeks before Christmas, the column was short, and nobody was hiring. Her pay and the week's severance were still on the table where she had flung it. She calculated quickly that by the time she had paid her rent and the baby-sitter and bought a few other necessities, she would have about twenty-three dollars. And she would have to buy baby food and new baby clothes.

She thought of welfare and shuddered, burning with remembered humiliation. Her mother had inflicted that on her, and now she was repeating the pattern and inflicting it on her own daughter. She was trapped in the same old downward spiral — and so was her daughter. They would never get out, never survive. She was looking into the bottomless pit of their future.

Glancing at the newspaper again, her eye was caught by a picture of a small child, a pretty little girl. Mary read the article quickly, then she read it again. Slowly this time.

The child was the daughter of a wealthy Seattle couple, and she had been born with a heart defect. They had fought desperately to save her, flying in expert doctors from Texas and London to try to help. Time and time again, their hopes had been raised that she would be miraculously made well. But a few days ago the child had died. The mother said she would never get over it, that every time she went into the empty nursery, it broke her heart all over again.

Mary didn't give herself any time to think about what she was doing. She put the rent she owed in an envelope for the landlord and said she was sorry, but she could not afford to stay on. Then she packed up her few things and her baby, put them in the ancient Chevy, and drove through the cold night to Seattle.

She knew where they lived from the newspaper article and found their house easily — a beautiful place overlooking Lake Washington. She sat in the car in the dark, holding her baby, waiting.

When the sky began to turn gray, she gave the baby a bottle, changed her diaper, and wrapped her in her fleecy blankets. She folded a quilt around her for extra warmth, then held her tightly, watching the house for signs of life. The sky was turning pink when a light went on upstairs, and she knew that the family was waking up.

She wrote a note and pinned it to the baby's blanket. She looked lovingly at her little daughter, she kissed her tenderly and held her close for the last time. Then she walked silently up the drive and laid her on the wide stone steps.

She hesitated, thinking about the note. It said, "I know you need her and can take good care of her. Please love her." She was sure she was doing the right thing; it was the only thing left.

Still, she hesitated. Her heart was in the pit of her stomach as she looked down at her baby. She loved her so much, but if she kept her, they would both go under, in Golden or its equivalent. Her beautiful daughter deserved better than that.

Mary raced back down the drive, into the car, and away.

They never traced her, though she was sure they tried. She left the state and got herself a new job many hundreds of miles away. It was a year before she dared to return to Seattle and take up her studies at the university again. She did not cry for her baby. The hurt was too deep for that, and she buried the memory in her mind, the way she had buried all the other bad things that had happened.

45

"I kept my vow," Mal said wistfully to Harry. "I never went back to that house. I never saw her. The first years were the worst. I can't explain what it means to lose a child like that, to know she is alive and so close, I could almost touch her.

"But she is their daughter. They needed her as much as she needed them. They gave her their hearts and their love and shared their lives with her. And no one ever knew the truth about her real father." She looked beseechingly at Harry, as if seeking his approval. "I had no choice. It was the only way she could be free."

Her eyes were dark with anguish. Harry understood the struggle she had gone through, dealing with the guilt and the despair, always wondering if she had done the right thing. Mal had endured all those years alone and unloved, and she had paid a terrible price.

He drew her into his arms and held her close, rocking her. She clutched him, trembling. She could not cry; her tears had been shed long ago, torrents of them, until there were none left. She felt his fingers touch her closed lids, then his lips, barely stirring her long lashes in a gentle kiss. He traced the contours of her face, the cheekbones, her soft trembling mouth. Her eyes were still closed. She couldn't look at him, couldn't bear to see his pity.

He unfastened her shirt and slipped it over her shoulders, then her skirt. His fingers followed the curve of her neck, the swell of her breast under the pale satin chemise, in the subtlest of touches, light as a breeze. Slipping the chemise over her head, he ran his hand down the length of her body.

He inclined his head. "Beautiful," he whispered in her ear. "You're a beautiful woman, Mal." His mouth sought hers, caught her soft lower lip, tasting it, then covered her in little butterfly kisses, infinitely tender.

In the bedroom, he stripped quickly, then sat next to her on the bed. He took her hands, pulled her to him. "Open your eyes, Mal darling," he said urgently. "I want you to look at me. Look at me."

She didn't want to, couldn't bear to know what she would see.

"Look at me, Mal," he commanded. "I need you to look."

He was holding both her hands. There was no escape. Slowly, she lifted her lids. His lean handsome face swam into nearsighted focus: his rumpled dark hair and strong stubbled jaw. His gaze was fierce, commanding her.

"Look into my eyes, Mal," he said, gripping

her hands tightly, because he did not want to lose her now.

She lifted her head, stretched her neck proudly, and set her mouth in a grim line, ready to tell him she did not need pity. All she wanted was justice. Then she looked into his beautiful gray eyes and could not look away. They held her just as close as his arms did, when he made love to her.

She was aware that his body was hard and beautiful, that his eyes were telling her something. His energy flowed into her fingertips, filled her senses, yet he had not moved, had not kissed her, did not attempt to make love to her. His eyes commanded her, drew her into him and her limbs seemed to soften until she was weightless, floating in a silvery opaque space: All she knew, all she saw was his eyes, and the tenderness in them.

He leaned toward her then and whispered in her ear. "This is love, Mal. It's touching each other's minds as well as bodies. I'm taking you into my head, into my heart, and I want you to do the same."

The breath came out of her in a little gasp, and the pulse in her throat jumped as he angled his head to kiss her again — light and soft and infinitely tender. "Do you feel it, Mal? Now do you feel it?"

He was kissing her neck, letting his lips drift down the smooth curve of her shoulder, across the swell of her breast, circling the nipples, down the gentle slope of her belly. He kissed the soft inner side of her thighs, the tender female parts of her, and then he inched his way up her body again until she cried out from wanting him.

He was hard and ready, but he took her slowly, wanting her to know that he loved her, that this was what lovemaking should be: a man and a woman in total harmony with each other, in mind as well as body.

When he finally entered her, she cried out and wrapped her legs and arms around him, moving with him, feeling the fire in him, the pleasure and the power of it as they reached the peak of ecstasy together.

But when it was over, it was not finished. He was still inside her, still clasping her. He ran his hands over her sweat-slick body, dropped kisses on her face and neck, sucked the little gasps of air from her open mouth. "Now do you feel it? Now do you know what love is?" he murmured.

"Oh, Harry." She was breathless with the sudden joyous feel of it. "I love you, Harry," she said.

They lay entwined together in their own private rarefied silvery space. She had no secrets anymore. After a while he disentangled himself, went to the kitchen, and fixed her a cup of the tea she liked.

Carrying it carefully, he placed it on the night table, and she smiled her thanks.

"I should be thanking you," he said, humbly. "No one should have to go through what you did. No one should ever have to live through those experiences, or relive them in the telling. But there's one important question I have to ask you. Are you sure in your heart — and your gut — that it's the same man as the one we're looking for?"

"Yes," she said quietly. "His name is Wil Ethan." She breathed a sigh of relief. Finally it was out.

"We're going to need your help, Mal, if we're to catch him before he kills again."

This time she did not hesitate. She knew she could trust him. "I'll help," she agreed. Her sigh when she said it was soft, but Harry knew now exactly what those words had cost her.

46

The publicity machine went into overdrive. Mallory Malone had sensational news to divulge on her program that week. They could not say what it was, except that it was deeply personal. And in a departure from her usual taped format, it would be live, and there would be no studio audience.

The staff and crew of Malmar Productions were not told what the news was, either. Even Beth was in the dark.

"Are you sure you want to go through with this? Whatever it is?" she asked Mal with a worried frown when Thursday finally crawled around. She thought Mal looked like hell — shadowy-eyed from lack of sleep, wired from too much caffeine and tense as a coiled spring.

Mal prowled the empty sound stage like a cat in a cage seeking a way out. She glanced up at Beth and saw concern in her eyes. "I have to. It'll be okay."

Alarmed, Beth caught her arm. "Don't do it, Mal. Cancel — there's still time. We have enough shows taped, we can run another one instead."

"I have to do it."

Mal wandered around the studio without

seeing it. All she saw were the private pictures in her head.

Harry strode into the studio half an hour before the show would begin. He spotted her sitting alone in the semidarkness while the last-minute action whirled around her. Her eyes were closed and her head was tilted back as though she were resting. But he knew from the tensely clasped hands that she was not.

He walked over to her, put his hands on her shoulders, and bent and kissed her cheek. Her eyes flew open, and she said gratefully, "Oh, Harry, you're here."

He sat next to her. "Everything's set. All the incoming phone lines are tapped, including your home line, and there's a police guard on your apartment." After tonight, the killer was going to know that she knew. They expected him to make a move, but he didn't tell her that.

He looked apprehensively at her; he hoped she would make it through. He kissed her lightly on the lips. "Fingers crossed, Mal," he said, holding up his hands. "This could be the end of it."

"Fingers crossed," she replied.

It was time. The hot lights illuminated the simple set with its hard little sofa and the low table with the bowl of lilacs and peonies that Mal had requested. She was wearing a simple blue sweater and skirt; her blond hair was brushed back from her forehead, and she wore not a scrap of jewelry. She did not look like the famous TV personality, the forceful interrogator, the tough investigator. She looked tired, almost plain, as though a light had been turned out inside her.

She took a seat, picked up her notes, rifled nervously through them, then put them down again. In the darkness beyond the lights, she saw Harry with Beth. He lifted his hand and showed her his crossed fingers. Then the director counted off the seconds, and they were rolling.

Mal said good evening in a calm voice, looking directly into the camera. "Tonight our program is different. You will remember a few weeks ago that the families of the young women who had fallen victim to the Boston Serial Killer were generous enough to share their grief and their deepest feelings with all of us. Their steadfastness in wanting the killer brought to justice prompted many different emotions in many of you and in myself.

"I have never spoken about what happened to me until this past week, when I could no longer live with it. I began to despise myself for keeping my own ugly little secret, when those other young women had not even been given the chance to speak out. Now I must try and do it for them.

"A friend said to me, 'You are alive, and

they are dead. What can you be hiding that is so important?' "

She took a deep shaky breath. "I was hiding the fact that I was a rape victim — and very nearly a murder victim.

"I want to tell you about it, to impress on you how it feels to be that person. The one who has been brutally violated and is about to die. I want to tell you about the pain and the humiliation and the shame that kept me from speaking about it until now. And about the fear. Because this man threatened me. He said that if I ever told anyone, he would find me and kill me."

She lifted her chin proudly. "Well, William Ethan — for that was the name you told me, though now we know it was a lie. Here I am, and I'm telling America about you."

The camera moved closer, looking deep into her eyes. "I'm telling about *the rapist and murderer you still are.* Because I believe that you are the same man who raped, mutilated, and killed Mary Ann Latimer. And Rachel Kleinfeld. And Summer Young. And Suzie Walker."

Beth looked at Harry, her eyes wide with horror. "Is this true?" she whispered. He nodded. "Oh, my God," she gasped. "Oh, my poor Mal, my poor, poor Mal."

"I'm going to tell you what he did and how it happened," Mal said, "so you will know how it feels to be at his mercy."

Beth grabbed Harry's hand and clutched it tightly. Tears slid down her cheeks as her friend told the terrible story of that long-ago night.

When Mal had finished, she was silent for a moment. Her shoulders drooped with fatigue and strain; she was almost at the end of her tether. She gripped her hands tightly together, drew herself up, and willed herself to be strong, to go on.

It was as if the light went on inside her again, and she was Mallory Malone, the clever TV investigator, the beautiful woman, the celebrity. She was no longer the victim. She was a strong woman, homing in on the killer like a heat-seeking missile.

"I was able to provide the information for this new Identikit picture," she said, clearly in control of herself now. "This is exactly the way the killer looked when he was younger, when I met him."

The picture of a crop-headed, bearded man with piercing dark eyes filled the screen.

"And this is the way he may possibly look now." A picture of the same man, aged, took its place. "I'm asking you please, if you know him or anyone who might resemble him, to call us.

"And now I have a message for William Ethan — though I am certain he no longer uses that name. I know you are out there, listening and watching. And I want you to know that from now on, America and its people will be out there, watching and looking out — for you.

"There is no escape for you now. And when you are caught, which will be soon, you will no longer awaken to enjoy the freedom of a pleasant summer day or a crisp winter morning. You will no longer participate in our society. You will be taken like the beast that you are and locked away in a prison with bars to hold you. You will never again breathe the fresh clean air of freedom that is the prerogative of normal, decent Americans."

She looked straight into the camera and said to her audience, "I had to forget about myself, about my own fears. I had to come clean and tell you, because we have to try to stop these killings. Digging up my ugly memories is nothing. We want to stop digging more graves.

"Thank you for listening to my story. I hope you understand and that you will help. Remember those parents, remember those young women. Please, don't let any of us forget them.

"Good night. And thank you again."

There was total silence in the studio.

Mal stared down at the notes she had not used. She had spoken freely, without prompting, straight from the heart.

She got up and walked out of the circle of light, then spread her arms wide as if to embrace them all — the production team, the crew, the cameramen. "Thank you for putting up with all the secrecy, and for everything else I put you through this week."

They stared back at her, then broke into spontaneous applause. As though unlocked from a spell, Beth ran and flung her arms around her. "Oh, Mal, I'm so so sorry," she said tearfully.

"Don't be, Beth," she said gently. "It's over now." But it was Harry she was looking at as she said it. He took her hand and said quietly, "Thank you, ma'am."

She leveled her eyes at him. "Thank *you*, detective," she said, meaning it.

All the telephone lines were jammed before she and Harry even reached the door. They drove straight home. His hand still gripped hers and she felt comforted, as though his strength were flowing into her. He slid his arm protectively around her shoulders as they walked into her apartment building and took the elevator upstairs.

Inside all was peaceful; the fire was burning in the grate, the lamps were lit, and the apartment was fragrant with the smell of flowers.

Every surface was covered with roses: Mal knew Harry must have ransacked the florists of Manhattan for them. They were glorious, fat full pale pink buds about to burst into bloom.

"They're Vivaldis," Harry said. "I couldn't find any called Enigma, but I thought that was kind of passé now anyway, if you see what I mean."

He thought with relief that it was worth every rose in town just to see her smile again. He took her hand and kissed it. "You did good, Mary Mallory Malone, ma'am. You're the best, you're the top."

"I'm the Eiffel Tower," she finished. "Or did the song say the British Museum."

"You're better than both." She moved into his arms, and they hugged as though they never wanted to let go. "Thank you, thank you, thank you," he murmured into her ear. "I know how hard it was. No, it's not true, I don't really know. I can never know. All I can do is thank you, along with a great many other Americans. I don't know how you did it."

"How could I not?" she asked simply.

"I don't know how you feel about this," he said, changing the subject, "but you've been living on coffee and Snickers bars for the past few days. I took the liberty of ordering in a little food. Just in case," he added.

They walked hand in hand into the kitchen and he showed her the treats arranged on a pretty tray. "Miffy just got home. She called Le Cirque," he said. "She's been going there for years, and Sergio will do anything for her."

He opened a bottle of merlot, poured a glass, and told her it would put the roses back in her cheeks again.

"As if I didn't have enough roses," she said, smiling.

"That's my girl," he grinned, pleased.

"Woman." She put him straight. He raised an eyebrow, and they both laughed.

Mal felt as though life had suddenly switched back to normal mode again. It was just her and Harry, alone in their own little world. She wished it would never change. But even as they nibbled at their exquisite supper and sipped red wine, she knew he was waiting for action.

She could see it in the restless way he glanced around the room, deliberately not looking at the telephone. She knew he was waiting for the killer to call.

At first the man had been amused by her program, titillated by the idea that everyone was talking about him. He had laughed at the ludicrous representation of him as he was supposed to be today. He had aged far better than they had depicted and looked a good ten years younger. They had got the hair wrong, and because he had worn a beard when he was young, they couldn't get the jaw right. Lucky for him. But the early picture still had him worried. True, it had been many years ago, but somebody might remember him.

He went to the kitchen, poured himself some vodka, then wandered over to the window and stared angrily out at his roses. The greenfly were sucking the life out of his carefully nurtured plants. Anger at the aphids, over which he had so little control, spilled into violent anger at Mary Mallory. He shut his eyes, and a turmoil of red floated in front of his closed lids. He wished it were her blood. He wondered how much time he had left.

Grabbing the keys to the Volvo, he ran to the garage. He was out of there in a second, driving quickly. They were closing in on him, but he would get her first, the cheap overconfident bitch. He wanted her dead, and he knew the perfect way to do it.

As he drove, he congratulated himself again on having had the foresight to keep tabs on Mary Mallory. She had been his first. He had botched the killing, and he had always been afraid of her.

He had not left the state as he had told the waitress at the café. All the time Mary Mallory was in Tacoma, he had been just a short drive away in Seattle. He had rented a cheap car, so as not to be recognized, and followed her. He saw she was pregnant and knew it could only be his. He had kept track of her, knew when she had disappeared and when the baby was found in Seattle, knew whose it was. In fact, he knew more about her daughter than she did.

He was searching for a pay phone on a quiet street corner. Her phone must be tapped, but he knew how the police worked. If he was quick, he would be safe.

The hours slid by. It was one in the morning and still not a peep from Mal's phone.

"You should go to bed," Harry said, but she shook her head, drooping against him.

"Not without you," she murmured sleepily.

And then the phone rang.

47

They shot apart. She looked at Harry, wide-eyed with fear.

It shrilled again; shattering the silence into sharp little fragments.

"It's now or never, Mal," Harry said, letting go of her.

She stared apprehensively at the shrilling phone. She licked her suddenly dry lips, then picked it up.

"Hello," she whispered.

"Well, Mary Mallory," the man said. "That was a very creditable acting performance you gave tonight."

The sound of his voice sent a tremor through her. It was like an earthquake, shaking her foundations. She couldn't breathe, couldn't speak, didn't want to listen. But she had to keep him on the line. . . .

"I've been thinking," he said. "Isn't it about time I met my daughter?"

Mal gave a terrified little gasp. Harry was listening on the other phone. The man's voice sounded muffled, as though he were holding something in front of his mouth.

"She must be about the same age you were when I met you," the man went on. "Now isn't that an interesting thought?

"And you know what, Mary Mallory?" he continued. "I'm on my way to visit her right now. But don't you worry, she won't know who I am. I'm too clever for you, Mal. Too clever for all of you. You'll never catch me."

He was timing the call on his fancy sports watch. He switched off seconds before they could complete the trace. He was home free. Again.

It had been a brilliant idea, he thought, killing two birds with one stone. He would light up those tabloids like never before.

The line went dead. Harry was on the mobile phone to the squad room, where they were monitoring the call. He said, defeated, "He was too quick. All we know is that the call was made from Boston."

She had crumpled into her corner of the sofa, looking like a woman who had just had a bad encounter with a steam roller.

He said, "The girl is in danger, Mal. You have to tell us her family's name, so we can trace her."

"I don't want her to know about him," she cried, panicked.

"I promise you, she never will. Please, Mal, before it's too late."

She gave him the name he wanted, then sat on the sofa, a tight ball of agony while Harry called the Seattle Police Department. It was easy. The family was a prominent one, well known in the city for its charitable contributions and its humanitarian work. They had a daughter and two sons. The girl was now a sophomore at Boston University.

Harry looked at Mal. They stared, horrified, at each other. "Oh my God," she wailed. "Oh my God, Harry —" but he was already talking to the chief of police in Boston.

Two minutes later, Harry slammed down the phone. "Get your coat," he said.

She pulled herself together, ran to the bedroom, and grabbed a jacket and her purse. He had the elevator waiting. "Where are we going?"

"Boston. We can just make the next shuttle if we step on it."

An NYPD patrol car was waiting outside. Harry thrust her into the backseat and got in next to her. With sirens wailing, they sped through the traffic to La Guardia.

He was right, they did just make the flight. He held her hand all the way to Boston. They hardly spoke, and she thought sadly that there was nothing to say. All she could do was pray for the girl who was her daughter.

Rossetti was waiting at Logan. "You're not gonna believe this, Prof," he said, "but the kid wasn't in her dorm. She was supposed to go to a concert tonight with her friends, but she complained of not feeling well. She went to the clinic, and they admitted her to Mass General with a suspected kidney infection. I've got uniforms posted outside her room and in the halls."

They were hurrying, half-running through the terminal. The squad car was parked outside, and they piled in.

Rossetti said, "Like you said, Prof, we kept it low key. The girl doesn't know the killer has targeted her. She knows nothin' except she's sick."

Harry was thankful that at least she was safe. Then he remembered uneasily the imprint of the Gucci shoe on Suzie's forehead and that several of the doctors at Mass General wore them.

He said to Mal, "I'm going to drop you off at my place. You'll be okay there with Squeeze to look after you. I have to get back to the precinct."

They were at the Louisburg Square house in minutes. He let her in, and the dog came running. Harry looked around and checked the windows and doors. Their eyes met for a long minute before he left. "Chin up, Malone," he said with a grin. "It's all going to be okay." And before she could reply, he was gone.

Back in the squad room, he reran the computer list of male doctors in Boston and the surrounding area. The FBI had delved into their past lives as well as the present, and every cv was on the list. He knew where they were born and when; he knew the details of their educations, from grade school to university, and all the marriages, births, and deaths. He knew their medical qualifications and what towns or cities they had lived in prior to Boston. He knew their home addresses and what schools their children attended, and who their wives were.

An image of Suzie Walker came into his mind. He could hear her saying over and over again, "What are *you* doing here."

Suzie had worked closely with Dr. Waxman. He pulled up Waxman's curriculum vitae and read his life history again.

It was simple enough. Aaron Waxman was fifty-six years old and married to his college sweetheart. He lived in the suburbs and had three children, one of whom was in med school. He came from a blue-collar family in Chicago, had never been involved in any medical disputes, and was known as a good doctor. He drove a black Mercedes, and his wife drove a white Suburban.

Harry frowned: he couldn't find a gap in Waxman's life that suggested aberrant behavior. The doctor scarcely had time; his hours were long, plus he was a busy family man, deeply involved in the affairs of the local Jewish community.

Frustrated, he drummed up the names of the other doctors Waxman had said Suzie had worked with. He worked patiently down the list. All were longtime married and all were family men — except for Dr. Bill Blake.

He studied Blake's credentials again. He was forty-eight years old, and for such a comparatively young doctor, he had held a lot of different positions, moving around the country from San Francisco, to Los Angeles, to Chicago, to St. Louis, to Boston. He had impeccable credentials from good medical schools, and he had been employed by the City of Boston as a medical examiner for the past three years. On the personal side, he had been a widower for seven years, lived alone in an apartment in Cambridge, and drove a gray Volvo.

Something clicked in Harry's mind. He remembered the Volvo in the hospital parking lot and Squeeze frantically trying to get in there, barking and snarling. He even remembered the number. Did it belong to Blake? But it couldn't be him — he worked with the cops, they all knew him.

He said uneasily to Rossetti, "What do you know about Dr. Blake?"

"Bill Blake?" Rossetti looked surprised. "He's okay, I guess. Kinda odd, you know, but that's just a personal feeling. Any guy who does what he does for a living seems odd to me."

Harry pictured the chilly white-tile autopsy room with the air conditioning blasting and Blake humming with the knife poised over

Suzie Walker's naked body.

Something wasn't right. He felt it in his bones.

Acting on a hunch, he called the Seattle hospital where Mal had told him Wil Ethan had worked as an intern. He asked them to double-check on a William or Bill Blake. An hour later, they got back to him. A Dr. William E. Blake had been an intern there many years ago.

"William *Ethan* Blake," Harry said triumphantly to Rossetti. *"He's our man."*

Dr. Blake parked the gunmetal Volvo in his usual spot. He strode into the hospital and walked straight into a uniformed cop.

"Sorry, sir." The uniform stepped back respectfully, and Blake breathed again.

"What's happening?" he asked, looking nervously over his shoulder.

The cop knew Dr. Blake was the medical examiner — he had seen him at several homicides and had no reason not to trust him. "The chief placed guards on all the entrances, Dr. Blake," he replied. "There's a young patient he wants protected."

"A student?" Blake knew the answer before he even replied.

"That's right, doctor."

"I guess Detective Jordan must be in charge," Blake said coolly. "We've done a lot of work together. I hope it's not going to be another disaster for him."

"We hope not, sir."

"Jordan's not here, is he?" he asked, perfectly at ease.

"No, sir, he's back at the precinct. But we're expecting him."

"I wonder, is Miss Malone with him?"

"She flew in from New York, sir, a couple of hours ago."

He walked as calmly as he could down the hall, then exited by the fire door and sprinted back to the parking lot. He sat in the Volvo thinking about what to do. He knew it was over and he wondered how long he had before they got on to him. He didn't care — all he cared about was the bitch who had ruined him.

48

Dr. Blake cruised slowly down Charles Street, keeping an eye out for patrol cars. He swung right on Pinkney, pulled into a no-parking zone on the corner of Louisburg Square, and slapped an "Emergency Doctor" sign on his dashboard.

From where he was parked, he could see the house. Only one light was showing, and it came from Harry's garden-level apartment. If Harry was on his way to the hospital, she must be in there alone.

He pulled off his nice tweed jacket and threw it onto the passenger seat.

Rage welled inside him, as he thought of what Mary Mallory had done. She had exposed him, spoiled his master plan, ruined his meticulous life. His hands were trembling. He thrust them into his pockets, and his fingers closed around the knife in its plastic sheath.

He watched the house for a few minutes until he was sure no cops were lurking in the shadows. No one came in or out; nobody was around. He strolled across the street. Light shone from the big bow window on the left; the curtains were drawn, and the sound of Sade singing "Cool Operator" filtered into the night. He smiled grimly — it was an appropriate choice.

At the top of the shallow front steps, he rang the bell, glancing uneasily over his shoulder into the lamp-lit street. Inside, a dog barked.

"Quiet, Squeeze," Mal said, clutching his collar. She stared nervously at the door, wondering who it could be. It rang a second time. Squeeze was on his hind legs, barking his head off. "Who is it?" she called out shakily.

"Police, ma'am. Officer Ford. The Prof called the chief, asked him to put a guard on you. If you don't mind, Miss Malone, I'd like to come inside for a few minutes, check the rear entrance, make sure you're secure."

Mal breathed a sigh of relief. He must be all right because he had called Harry the Prof.

She shut Squeeze in the bedroom. She could hear him whining as she hurried back across the hall and opened the front door.

His foot was inside. He thrust the door into her chest, pushed her backward, slammed the door shut. He had her in an armlock, her back pressed to him, his hand over her mouth. From the bedroom, the dog barked loudly.

She struggled, and he smiled, enjoying her helplessness. It was one of the parts he always liked best.

"You opened your big mouth, Mary Mallory," he whispered into her ear. "I warned you what would happen if you told. Everything was fine. I left you alone, you left me

561

alone. Now you've gone and spoiled it all."
He was scowling like a petulant schoolboy
whose treat had been taken away from him.
"Don't say I didn't warn you," he murmured,
sliding the knife from his pocket.

His grip relaxed for a split second, and she
jammed her elbows back as hard as she could.
They sank into something soft, and he gasped
for air.

She had got him in the solar plexus, the area
just below his sternum, with a vulnerable network of nerves. He doubled over in pain, letting go of her as the air whooshed out of him.

She was screaming, making for the door,
and the dog was barking loudly. He panicked.
Someone was sure to hear, to come running. . . .

He threw himself after her in a rugby tackle,
grabbing her by the ankles. She crashed to the
floor, twisting, pulling herself away. He
gripped his fingers into her short crop of hair,
jerked her head back, and thrust his knee into
the base of her spine. "Be quiet," he snarled.

The knife was at her throat, but she was
still screaming. He was sweating with the effort. The others had not been like this — she
was stronger than he had expected. He ran
the knife across the soft flesh along her col-
larbone.

Mal felt blood oozing and the cold steel
against her throat. She was catapulted back in
time to that long-ago night, on the deserted

road with the mist wreathing through the leafless trees. The ugly image of him, half naked after he had violated her, flashed through her mind. She remembered the press of cold steel against her flesh then, and his calmness as he had run the blade across her throat, testing it. . . .

Now she could feel his eyes burning into her, willing her to see, to look at him, before he killed her. . . . They drew hers like a magnet. *She had to look at him.* He stared into her eyes.

He knew he finally had her. He was in control again.

"So, Mary Mallory," he said, relaxing and beginning to enjoy himself. "I see you've learned a thing or two since we last met." He gave a sneering little bark of a laugh. "What a pathetic little nobody you were. The surprise of it was that you actually thought a man like myself would be interested in you." He laughed again. "Cheap feminine vanity was what brought your downfall, not me, Mary Mallory."

Mal stared into the eyes that had haunted her dreams for almost two decades. They were drilling into hers as he told her what a poor imitation of a woman she had been when he met her, how he had known she would be easy, how he had despised her.

Hatred bloomed like a giant flower inside her. The knife was at her throat, but she was no longer afraid. She felt immune from his taunts, immune from his evil.

Closing her eyes, she prayed for strength, telling herself to remember what this man had done to her, how he almost ruined her life, the anguish he had caused her. She thought of Rachel and of Mary Ann, of Summer Young and Suzie. And then of her own unknown daughter, who had so nearly been his next victim. And she knew somehow she had to kill him.

He was enjoying himself, telling her what he was going to do to her. He wanted her to hear every detail of what was about to happen to her, the pain she would suffer, the hell she was about to enter.

"Remember, I'm a pathologist," he whispered. "I'm an expert. Except I usually dissect people *after* they are dead." He laughed at his own joke as he told her graphically exactly which parts of her he was planning to cut out and what he would do with her.

Mal shut out his obscenities and concentrated on gathering her strength. Somewhere in the background, she could hear Squeeze barking and his claws on the bedroom door, but this was no time to tell herself what a fool she had been to shut him in. *She was going to die. . . . Oh Harry, Harry,* she thought. I want so badly to see you again.

He looked up, frowning. The dog was becoming a problem. The neighbors would be sure to hear him and come over to complain or call the police. He had to get her out of here. He was on his knees, bending over her. "Get up, bitch," he said, grasping her arm and pulling at her.

It was her only chance. She twisted round and stabbed her fingers in his eyes. He cried out in pain, let go of her. She kicked out at him — he grabbed her foot, and she fell to the floor. She screamed, fighting with her elbows, knees, fists. The rug twisted under his feet, and he came crashing down next to her. Lashing out with the knife, he caught her on the cheek, but she didn't even feel it. She was engulfed by rage.

She was no longer fighting for her life. She was fighting for his death.

Squeeze made a final leap at the door handle. He zapped it with his paw the way he did the snooze button on the alarm clock, and at last it swung open. He hurled himself down the hall, fangs bared in a snarl.

Too late, Blake saw him coming. Squeeze launched himself through the air and sank his teeth into Blake's shoulder.

Mal scrambled to her feet. Harry had told her the dog was like Houdini — he could squeeze out of anywhere, including his bedroom. But she wasn't finished yet — she was crazy to kill him, to kill. . . . She ran to the kitchen to get a knife.

The dog sank his teeth into Blake's throat,

and he screamed. His fingers scrabbled on the carpet, he found the knife. He told himself he was cleverer than the dog, he was cleverer than all of them. And he drove the knife into the dog's chest.

Mal came running from the kitchen with Harry's butcher's knife. She heard Squeeze whimper and saw him stagger backward. His legs trembled, his head drooped, and with a whimper he sank to the floor.

"Oh, God," she screamed, horrified. Tremors ran through the dog's body, rippling his thick silver coat. Blake was hauling himself to his feet. He was covered in blood, and she could see where the dog had ripped his neck open.

They stared at each other for what seemed an endless moment.

Mal stood, the knife lifted, ready to strike. She could kill him now, while he was weak. He turned and staggered to the door. His eyes were full of hatred as they met hers again. Then he was gone.

The knife dropped to the floor with a clatter. She put her head in her hands, moaning. She couldn't do it — *she just could not do it. If she did, then she would be evil like him.* She ran to the door, slammed it, and locked it.

Tears pricked her eyes as she looked at Squeeze. Blood was seeping into the rug all around him. Dropping to her knees, she touched his soft fur. His beautiful pale blue eyes looked at her. He was panting, in quick short breaths, his tongue lolling from his mouth.

She ran to the phone, dialed the emergency police number, and said that Dr. Blake had just been there. He had tried to kill her but had almost killed the dog instead. They should tell Detective Harry Jordan the killer was on the loose again. And she was going to need a vet right away.

Dr. Bill Blake knew he did not have much time if he was to complete what he had to do, but he had promised his mother, and he always kept his promises to her.

He got in the Volvo, wrapped the expensive silk scarf over the wound in his neck, put on his jacket, and smoothed back his hair. It was imperative that he look normal and calm, a regular citizen on his way home. They had his license number, but it would lead them to his Cambridge pied-à-terre, because that was the only address listed on his records. Still, the concierge there would be sure to tell them where his home was, so he had to get there first.

Traffic was minimal, the green lights were with him, and he did not encounter a single patrol car. It was as though his mother were helping him, he thought with a little smile. Blood was seeping through his sweater, and he pulled the jacket tighter. He tried not to think about the pain, concentrating on his driving.

It seemed no time before he was turning into his manicured suburban street. There were no patrol cars with flashing lights, and he felt invincible again as he drove into the garage. He was home. He had beaten them after all.

He locked the garage and let himself into the house, bolting the door after him. Staggering into the kitchen, he opened the refrigerator and took out the vodka, filled a tumbler with it, and took a long drink. He felt lethargic and weak, and his hand shook. He had lost a lot of blood. He was a doctor, he knew what was happening to him, and he knew he had to hurry. He downed the rest of the vodka, then he walked, step by slow step, up the stairs.

At the door to the special room, he sank to his knees. He was breathing heavily. Blood flowed freely from the wound in his neck, spattering the carpet, but he no longer cared. He fumbled in his shirt for the key and scrabbled at the lock trying to fit it in. It took all his effort to turn it.

The room was in darkness, except for the dim greenish glow from the big aquarium along one wall. He was on his hands and knees now, crawling painfully toward the shining sea-green tank. The liquid gurgled gently, soothingly, and the light in the tank had a strange underwater radiance.

At last he was there. He rose up on his knees and lifted his hands in supplication. "I'm home, Mother," he said. "I've come home, just the way I promised you."

The woman revolving slowly in the limpid ocean-green liquid could not answer him because her mouth was stitched shut. She could not see him because her eyelids were stitched. She could no longer suckle him because her nipples had been cut off. And she had been dead for many years.

Her fleshy body was in as perfect condition as the day he had embalmed her, and her stitched-up mouth seemed to smile in a way it never had when she was alive.

He had always known he would stop her evil talk, once and for all, one day. It was one of the reasons he had decided to become a doctor. Doctors could get away with things other people could not. They had access to poisons and drugs; they could decide the cause of death and sign the certificate with no questions asked. When he learned about forensic pathology, it was like being handed a gift. As a pathologist, he knew exactly what to do with a dead body.

He had killed her on a sunny summer afternoon by the side of a dreary little lake in Washington State. She had not been feeling well and he had told her he would take her for a drive. He had been feeding her small amounts of arsenic in her orange juice — not enough to kill her but just enough to make her complain to the neighbors that she was sick.

They sat on the bank overlooking the lake and he listened to her bitching about him as usual. "Heaven knows, you're the doctor," she ranted on irritably. "And you can't even cure your own mother. You never were good for much as a boy, and now you're even worse. You're not even a man."

He hadn't thought twice about it. His glance was as chilly as his heart as he turned and chopped her across the neck. Her eyes went big, and she stared at him, surprised, as she sank into unconsciousness. He dragged her from the car, ripped open her dress, and began to punch her, his head down like a boxer. Punch after solid angry punch. He sat back to catch his breath, then he fell on her, biting her, clawing her. And then he raped her. He thrust into her again and again but couldn't climax. She was right. He was a failure.

Crazed with anger and humiliation, he took the scalpel and slit her wrist. Her bright red blood spurted out and he felt the excitement mounting inside him. He grabbed her other wrist and ran the knife across it, and as she was dying, his own juices spurted along with her blood.

He was shaking with the thrill of it, the sheer exhilaration of what had happened. He was the one in control now. He thanked her every night of his life, after that, for finally showing him the way.

He wrapped her in the body bag he had brought with him, zipped it up, and lifted her into the trunk of her own white Lincoln Continental. He turned on the radio, humming happily along with the Brahms violin concerto as he drove slowly back home.

When he was safely back in the garage and the door had clicked shut, he opened the trunk, lifted her out, and carried her into the kitchen. There was no blood, no mess — everything was in the body bag. He had his equipment stored in the garage — the instruments, the embalming fluids, the containers. He covered the floor with plastic cloths, put on his rubber gloves, and began.

A couple of days later he informed his mother's few friends and neighbors that she had suffered a stroke and died in her sleep. He said it had always been her wish that she be cremated and that there would be no service. Those who wished to remember her could send a donation to the charity of their choice.

A few weeks later he told them he had been offered a job out of state. He put the house up for sale and said good-bye. Then he packed her embalmed body into the trunk, along with the rest of his baggage, and drove to Chicago.

With the proceeds from the sale of her house, he was able to buy a nice home in

Bloomington Hills. When he moved in, he gave her her own room just like before, and built an aquarium for her so he could see her whenever he needed to.

It gave him great pleasure to watch her spinning gently in the eddying preserving fluid, smiling soundlessly at him as he told her about "his girls."

Later, he moved to San Francisco, then to L.A. for a while, then on to various other big cities with colleges where there were plenty of girls. And finally, he moved to Boston.

He knelt before her, his hands clasped meekly. The blood was still seeping from the wound in his neck.

"I've finished now, Mother," he said.

He lay down in front of the aquarium. He took the bloodstained knife from his pocket, and wiped it fastidiously. He turned his hands palm up and stared at them for a long moment. Then he drew the scalpel cleanly across first one wrist then the other, the perfect pathologist to the end. He held up his bloody hands to show her. "I did it, Mother," he screamed. "I did it."

His knees crumpled, and he sank to the ground. He lay on his back, watching his blood and his life gush away, as he had with others so many times before. He turned his head slowly, so he could see her. Hatred bubbled from him like the blood.

"Bitch," he said.

★ ★ ★

Harry wished he were driving the Jag — the Ford's sirens were screaming as he cut through the straggling traffic, shooting the red lights, but it still wasn't fast enough for him. He was trying to keep all thoughts of Mal in the back of his brain, concentrating the force of his energy on Blake. Mal was okay. He didn't want to let himself think what he would have done to Blake if he had killed her, but it would not have been nice.

The Ford's tires screeched as he swung sharp left into the nice suburban street, the squad cars following noisily behind. Lights flashed on in upstairs windows as startled neighbors leaped from their beds to see what was happening. But the house of Dr. Bill Blake was dark and silent.

"This is it, Rossetti." Harry flung open the car door and reached into his shoulder holster. The Glock fit his palm like a glove, smooth and lethal. Keeping to the shadows, he walked to the house, Rossetti behind him. The SWAT team spilled from the patrol cars, went down on one knee, and shouldered their rifles, aiming at the doors and windows. Lights were set up and focused on Blake's neat, well-kept house, and down the street officers were keeping back the swelling group of neighbors. Clutching their bathrobes around them, they gawked in astonishment at the drama taking place on their quiet, respectable street.

Roadblocks had been flung hastily up around Boston, and patrol cars were on the lookout. Harry didn't know if Blake was in there, but they could take no chances.

He took the microphone and said, "Dr. Blake, you are surrounded. I'm asking you to open the front door and come out with your hands over your head. It's in your own best interests to comply."

The silence from the house was palpable. A plane droned high overhead, and the stars glittered in the clear sky.

"Blake, this is your last chance," Harry said into the mike.

The marksmen shifted their positions, creeping closer. Some were stationed on the roof of the house opposite; more had gone over the wall to the back of the house.

The silence stung his ears. Harry glanced at Rossetti. He shrugged. "I'll bet a hundred he's in there."

"Let's go for it," Rossetti said.

Harry gave the signal, and shots rang out, shattering the upstairs windows. Still nothing happened. Harry shot the lock off the door, but it still wouldn't open.

"There's enough goddamned bolts for a fortress," Rossetti muttered, struggling.

Keeping close to the house, they ran around the side. Rossetti smashed a window, then flattened himself against the wall, listening. The silence was so total, Harry could hear his own blood pounding in his ears. He quickly punched out the rest of the glass, and they were over the sill and inside.

Searchlights lit the kitchen with a surreal glow. The refrigerator door was open, and an almost-empty bottle of vodka stood on the counter. Even from that distance Harry could see blood smeared across the white tiles. He looked down, following the trail through the open doorway, into the hall. He looked at Rossetti and nodded.

The SWAT team filtered silently after them, flattening themselves against the wall. Three of them dropped to their knees, their rifles trained on the dark area at the top of the stairs.

Harry's mouth was set in a grim line as he remembered Summer Young's last words. He thought, sickened, of the way pretty Suzie Walker had looked when they found her, and of Dr. Blake carving her up, again, on the autopsy table, his knife poised over her as he hummed a happy little tune. He thought about the terrible things Blake had done to Mal, and that she had never gotten over them. He wanted to get Blake so bad he was trembling.

He took the stairs two at a time, Rossetti after him. At the top, they swung around, checking. The upper hall was empty, all the doors were shut, and everything was in darkness. Rossetti nudged Harry, indicating with his eyes a faint greenish glow under one door.

Harry heard something. He leancd forward,

listening, to the faint gurgling sound. Like a swimming pool, he thought, puzzled.

He gave the thumbs up to the hit squad; they raced up the stairs. He flung open the door, and he and Rossetti charged in, guns ready.

Harry held out his arm to stop the men. Blake was lying in a pool of his own blood. His eyes were open, and it didn't take a genius to know he was dead.

"What the fuck . . ." Rossetti exclaimed, stunned.

Harry lifted his eyes from the body on the floor to the mutilated dead woman spinning slowly, around and around, in the aquarium, and he knew he was looking at the sickness that had lain in the soul of William Ethan Blake.

"Christ," Rossetti said, shaken, "it's like a fuckin' horror movie."

Officers crowded in the doorway, staring stunned at the grisly scene. "Okay, guys," Harry said. "Show's over."

He was suddenly drained of all emotion. It was beyond him how any man could do such a thing, how he could live with it all these years, the desolation and evil of it.

"Let the ME in," he ordered as a doctor shouldered his way past the officers. "Business as usual," he said grimly to Rossetti, as the familiar routine began all over again: the police photographer, the medical examiner, the guys from the crime lab. It was a cop's life.

"You'll have to excuse me," he said to Rossetti, suddenly formal. "I have to go and see Mal. If he asks, tell the chief I'm off on personal business." At that moment he didn't give a damn what the chief thought. After observing what Blake was capable of, he needed to see for himself that Mal was okay.

Rossetti thought Harry looked as sickened as he felt. "Summer Young was right," he called after him. "He was the biggest bastard of them all. But she can rest easy now, Prof. And so can Suzie and the others." He crossed himself as he said their names, praying that what he had said was true.

49

Mal was sitting on the yellow brocade sofa in Miffy's pretty little drawing room. The family portraits gazed down at her, and the black-nosed pugs were pressed against her like a pair of cushions. Miffy sat anxiously opposite, wearing a gold satin Chinese robe with a cloud pattern on it. She was pouring tea.

"Cucumber on the white, smoked salmon on the brown," Miffy explained, passing her a plate of neat little finger sandwiches.

Mal took a cucumber and smiled her thanks. "Are you sure you wouldn't like to lie down?" Miffy asked worriedly. "After all you've been through . . ." She didn't finish her sentence because she was afraid to put into words exactly what Mal had been through. It was too terrible, too terrifying. Too close for comfort.

"I'm waiting for Harry," Mal explained. "I have to tell him about the dog."

Miffy understood. "Well, at least we know they found that terrible man, Blake," she said. "He can't harm anyone now." Harry had called and told her that Blake had killed himself.

Mal took a bite of the cucumber sandwich. It tasted fresh, simple, and delicious. She took another bite, suddenly ravenous. She smiled. "I could eat the whole plate."

By the time Harry arrived, she had finished half the sandwiches. He strode through the door, then stopped and stared at her. Everything he felt about her was in his eyes. Concern, fear, relief. Love.

She was wearing one of his mother's white cotton nighties with a yellow bathrobe thrown over it. A gauze pad covered a cut that ran from just below her left eye to her jawbone.

He went to her and put his hand on her shoulder. "Are you all right?" he asked quietly.

She looked up at him. His hair was wild, as though he had run his hands through it a million times, and she liked what she read in his eyes. "Now I am," she said.

"It's all over, Mal. He's dead as a doornail. He killed himself, the same way he killed all the others. It's the best thing he could have done."

She sighed. "The bastard," she said softly.

"We know how he got the phone numbers," he said. "He came to the precinct and brought a report over. Rossetti said he left him in the office alone for ten minutes, and when he came back, he was fiddling with the computer. He made some excuse about being fascinated by it. Rossetti thought no more about it."

She nodded. He had been clever — almost clever enough to get away with it. She hesitated, but she had to ask. "What about my . . . the girl?"

"She's okay. She doesn't know anything, isn't even aware she was involved." He knew what she was thinking. "She'll never know about him, Mal. No one knows."

Mal understood that the girl was no longer *her* daughter. She belonged to the family who had taken her into their lives and their hearts, who had sheltered her, guided her, loved her. The girl would never know about her connection with Dr. William Blake, would never have to carry that horrifying burden. She was bright, young, and lovely. She was happy, and that was the way it was going to stay.

"She's free. Finally," she said with a sigh.

Harry took her hand and kissed it. "So are you," he said, and she smiled at him. "I almost blew it," he added. "I thought you would be safe at my place. I didn't know Blake knew where I lived. I should have realized when I saw the Volvo — I'd seen it parked in the square."

"Squeeze did his Houdini act — he squeezed out of your bedroom just in time. Blake stabbed him. The knife just missed his heart. He's lost a lot of blood, but they operated, and he's going to be okay."

Harry sank onto the sofa next to her. He put his head in his hands. "Jesus," he said, thinking how nearly he had lost everything that night.

She took his hand, and they looked searchingly at each other, hardly believing it was finally over.

Miffy thought what a handsome couple they would make. She surely hoped he wasn't going to let her slip through his fingers.

"Another sandwich?" she asked, smiling.

50

It was a couple of weeks later. The light summer rain fell soft on Harry's face as he rounded the corner to Ruby's. Squeeze tugged on the leash, stopping to lap up a puddle here and there. The vet had shaved his chest fur, and the scar gleamed a livid red. "Take your time, old fella," Harry said indulgently. Squeeze had earned all the time in the world. He thought they looked like a matched set — his scarred head and the dog's scarred chest — like a couple of tough street scrappers. "Ain't nobody gonna mess with us, old fella," he added, grinning.

The bell over Ruby's door jangled as he walked in. Shrugging the rain off his black leather jacket, he looked around, taking in the scene. It was much as usual. The windows were steamed, shutting out the dark wet evening, smoke curled blue to the nicotine-yellow ceiling, and the smell of decades of hash browns and fried chicken, of draft beer, coffee, and cigarettes, lingered in a comforting haze.

As usual, it was packed. Every table was taken. He caught Doris's eye over the counter, where she was busy assembling huge slabs of chocolate fudge cake and vanilla ice cream on thick white plates. "Be with ya in a sec," she mouthed.

She served her customers, then came over, wiping her hands on her apron. "Yeah?" she said.

"Yeah what, Doris?" He grinned at her.

"Whaddya want?"

"I want a table, goddammit."

"Don't ya always come at my busiest time," she grumbled. "If it weren't that your brave dog needs a good meal and a rest, I'd tell ya to wait your turn, detective." She patted Squeeze's head, and he wagged his tail, gazing hopefully at her. She sighed, "He sure knows a soft touch when he sees one. Just like his master."

"Mal Malone will be joining me" — Harry checked his watch — "in about fifteen minutes."

"Well, why the hell didn't you say so?" She scanned her tables, then marched to the corner booth, raking the customers and the half-empty cups of coffee with narrowed eyes. "Youse guys finished?" she demanded, hands on hips. "Can't ya see there's a line waiting?"

Harry grinned — Ruby's never changed and, thank God, neither did Doris. She had them out of there in five minutes. The table was cleared and wiped with a damp cloth, and red-checkered paper placemats were laid down. Cutlery and napkins appeared in a flash, and a water glass containing a yellow daisy. "It's all I could find. Think yourself lucky," she muttered, slamming it on the table.

"Thanks, Doris. You're terrific," Harry said.

Squeeze whined, still looking hopefully at her, and she said, "Thought I'd forgotten you, huh?" She went behind the counter and returned a few minutes later with a bowl of steak. "Nothin' but the best for you, brave boy," she added, watching him wolf it down. "He's the most famous dog in Boston," she said proudly to Harry.

"I know." He grinned at her. "And I'm the most famous cop."

"And big-headed with it," she sniffed. "You wanna beer? Or did you invest in a bottle of champagne for Miss Malone?"

"Beer will do just fine," Harry said mildly.

He glanced at the door and remembered the last time he had waited for Mal, in this same booth, on a rainy night just like this, not so many weeks ago. It was miraculous how a guy's life could change, just like that, from a chance encounter. He ran his hands through his rumpled hair. Maybe he should have dressed up for her, put on a proper jacket and shirt. No tie, though. He drew the line at that.

The doorbell jangled, and she was standing there, looking around, eyebrows raised slightly as though wondering what the hell she was doing there. He grinned as he loped toward her. Mal never changed.

"Hi," he said, holding out his hand.

"Hi to you." She shook it.

He looked her up and down. She was wearing a blue work shirt, jeans, and a black leather jacket. "Snap," he said, grinning.

"If you can't beat 'em, join 'em, is what I figured," she said.

Their eyes linked, shutting out the smoky little café and the other patrons. "You okay?" he asked. She nodded, sending her blond chrysanthemum crop bouncing, the raindrops sparkling like sequins under the lights.

"This way, ma'am." Still holding her hand, he led her to the corner booth at the back.

"*Our* table," she said, remembering.

"Doris brought you a flower." He showed her the yellow daisy, and she smiled.

"Doris is okay."

"Salt of the earth," he agreed.

"I know, you have a soft spot for waitresses." She remembered Jilly.

"And TV detectives." He watched her as she slid into the booth with that nice little movement that brought to mind the way she had looked in that minimal flutter of a dress she had worn to his mother's party.

Squeeze emerged from under the table. He sat on his haunches, gazing devotedly at Mal. "Hi, Squeeze," she said, taking his paw. "How's my boy?"

"Love me, love my dog." Harry sighed.

"You wish!" She smiled mockingly at him, and he sighed again.

"You know something? You don't change, Malone."

Doris bustled toward them. She wiped her hand on the front of her apron, then stuck it out. "Hi, Mal, how're ya doing?" she asked, beaming. "Is the cheapskate buyin' you champagne tonight, or just the usual?"

"Just the usual, I guess," Mal said. "How are you doing, Doris?"

"Can't grumble." Doris straightened her cap and looked earnestly at her. "I wanna tell you, you're one brave woman, doin' what you did. Gettin' out there and sayin' what you said. It's because of you the Boston Serial Killer got caught. Us women gotta stick up for each other, like I said before."

"Thanks, Doris." Mal turned pink at the praise, and Harry stared at her, astonished that she still was so shy she blushed. "I just had to do it," Mal admitted, and Doris patted her shoulder approvingly.

"Beers are on me," she called over her shoulder as she walked away.

They looked at each other across the table. "You up for Vanessa's party tonight?" he asked.

She nodded. "Of course. I wouldn't miss it. I'll get to dance with you again."

He grinned and ran his hand through his hair. "A little hot salsa, huh?"

He wriggled his shoulders, looking sexy, and she laughed. "I can't wait."

"You seen Squeeze's medal?" Doris asked, back with the beers, as proud as if he were her own dog.

"A medal?" Mal looked astonished at Harry.

"The chief gave him the Dog Medal of Honor. He didn't really qualify because he's not technically a police dog, but everybody figured he'd earned it."

Squeeze slid from under the booth again. He lifted his paw and gazed adoringly at Doris.

"You gotta teach him a new trick," she sighed. "This is gettin' kinda monotonous."

She hurried back to her counter. Harry whispered to Mal, "Wait."

She was back again in a flash with another helping of steak. Harry heaved an exaggerated sigh, and Doris said defensively, "So he'll get fat? So what?"

"He's earned it," Mal agreed. "And besides, it's more fun than the medal. Thanks, Doris."

"Want me to order for you?" Harry lifted a questioning dark brow at her.

"Sure, I like a surprise." She folded her arms, ready for a challenge.

"Two ham steaks, home fries, and all the trimmings, Doris please." He looked at Mal, grinning. "Like the lady said, if you can't beat 'em, join 'em."

Doris went off to place the order, and Mal took a sip of beer. She gazed at Harry across the table. His rumpled dark hair was growing in over the scar, and there was a fuzz of blue-black stubble across his jaw. He was so close, she could see the tiny dark flecks in his clear gray eyes. He was the best thing she'd ever seen in her life.

"So? Now that it's all over, what happens to us?" he asked coolly.

She lifted her eyebrows in surprise. "Is this a *new* Detective Jordan I'm hearing?"

"It's just the old one, come to his senses." She looked hesitant, and he added, "You think we're going to fight, Mallory, Malone, ma'am?"

"I'd prefer it if you'd just call me Mal," she said.

He rolled his eyes, exasperated. "Okay, Mal. Are we fighting now?"

"*You are* fighting." She glared at him.

"I thought it was you."

"Well, you would, wouldn't you!"

They stared at each other, then he grinned. "Just think of the making up."

A smile lurked at the corners of her mouth. "You were saying? About us?"

He shrugged. "It's tough. What with a cop's hours and a TV personality's hours. And you being in New York and me in Boston."

Mal took a deep breath. She knew it was now or never. "Think maybe they need a weather girl at WNET Boston?" she asked him with a smile.

Squeeze sank down, laid his head on her feet, and heaved a happy dog sigh.

Harry glanced at Mal. Their eyes locked. "Seems we've both lost our hearts," he said. And he leaned across the table and kissed her.

We hope you have enjoyed this Large Print book. Other Thorndike Press or Chivers Press Large Print books are available at your library or directly from the publishers.

For more information about current and upcoming titles, please call or write, without obligation, to:

Thorndike Press
P.O. Box 159
Thorndike, Maine 04986 USA
Tel. (800) 223-2336

OR

Chivers Press Limited
Windsor Bridge Road
Bath BA2 3AX
England
Tel. (0225) 335336

All our Large Print titles are designed for easy reading, and all our books are made to last.